THE ARYABHATA CLAN

THE ARYABHATA CLAN

SUDIPTO DAS

olive turtle

NIYOGI BOOKS

Published by
NIYOGI BOOKS
Block D, Building No. 77,
Okhla Industrial Area, Phase-I,
New Delhi-110 020, INDIA
Tel: 91-11-26816301, 26818960
Email: niyogibooks@gmail.com
Website: www.niyogibooksindia.com

Editor: Manali Das
Cover design: Misha Oberoi
Layout: Shashi Bhushan Prasad
Illustrator: Kamalika Dutta and Sudipto Das

ISBN: 978-93-86906-13-7
Publication: 2018

Printed at: Niyogi Offset Pvt. Ltd., New Delhi, India

To Baba

Kubha's family tree

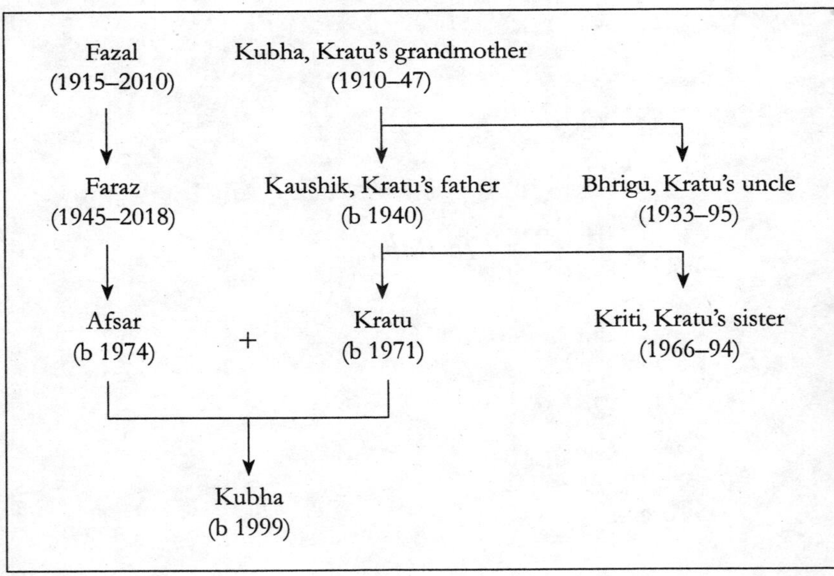

Contents

PART-I

Hasht Bihisht

(4 January 2019. Somewhere not far from Delhi)

They pushed Kubha inside the claustrophobic room and closed the door from outside. Her naked body shivered in the extreme cold. She tried to recall if it was only a day since she had been kidnapped from the JNU campus and brought here. Hadn't it been one degree in Delhi? She pondered. But it wouldn't be any warmer here, she knew for sure.

How far had she been brought from Delhi? And for how long had she been sedated?

The piercing pain that was fast spreading, from down there, to her whole body, left very little to her imagination. For a moment, she felt as though she had suddenly stared at the sun with her bare eyes—the surroundings sinking into a fading darkness.

She wished the sedative had been stronger.

The two young men, very unassuming and meek, the type, Kubha felt, she would barely notice even if they had been in her own class, hovered in her thoughts. They had held her hands tight, the grip tightening as soon as she had opened her eyes. She had seen their tensed faces, looming over. With her head hung from the edge of a wooden takhtposh, she could get the inverted view of a portion of the octagonal room and the people around.

When she had tried to raise her head, someone had pushed it down, brutally. A drop of saliva, which had accumulated in her open mouth, dropped from the side of her lips and fell onto the dirty floor. As the effect of the sedative was subsiding, she could feel the pain engulfing every part of her writhing body. She felt as though someone had inserted a burning piece of charcoal inside her, incinerating whatever she possessed, her body and her soul too.

As her head dangled from the takhtposh, her wavering eyes had met a few times with those of a middle-aged man standing by the wall, calmly. From the few upturned glimpses of his that passed by her sight, and the few times their eyes met, she knew his eyes had been turned down, away from her.

'To avoid further damage,' the words of her psychology teacher at the Cupertino High School had flashed through her mind, 'the best thing to do is to go slack, or to even feign enjoyment … *Struggle turns them on …*'

She walked slowly towards a corner of the claustrophobic room and let herself slither down the wall and fall on the floor. Lying on her back on the freezing stones which made up the floor, she remembered her great grandmother, her namesake, the other Kubha. 'I've to live,' she mumbled to herself. 'I can't die … *I've to do something …*'

She tried to organize her thoughts, analyzing each and everything she could gather since she had been abducted.

☼

Kubha must have fallen asleep. She was woken up by a loud noise. Shivering badly in the bitter cold, she looked up at one of the four doors of the room, the one that was bigger than the others, the one that connected the square room she was in to the octagonal one, through a short dalan. The noise, she knew, came from the big octagonal room, the very thought of which froze her more than the cold.

'Yes,' said someone, 'that's what we've to achieve—an Islamic State. We all are volunteers of the Majlis-e Muqaddis-e Hind, the Council of the Purifiers of Hindustan. For centuries, India has been the most prosperous Dar al-Islam, the grandest house of Islam. In the seventeenth century, the Mughal India alone accounted for one-fourth of the world's GDP. Even the entire British Empire was never as rich. Neither was the Caliphate or the Ottoman Empire. It's sad that India later slipped into the hands of the kafirs, the infidels, the non-believers—first, the Christians and then, the Hindus ...'

Kubha listened carefully as the person tried to explain why it was the need of the hour to do something drastic, something unthinkable, something which would shatter the world, something which could finally snatch Hindustan away from the hands of her kafir rulers ...

Though the person spoke Urdu, his accent sounded familiar to Kubha. It was, she felt, a typical Bengali accent, the sort of which is made fun of in the movies and on the internet. Her grandfather, her father's father, she was sure, would speak Hindi in the same way. This person, she said to herself, had to be a Bengali.

'*Wa-uq tuluhum, haythu thaqif tumuhum*,' he thundered, 'kill them wherever you find them. *Wa-akhrijuhum, min haythu akhrajukum*, drive them out from wherever they drove you out. There's no ambiguity. It's the 191st verse of Surat Al-Baqarah, the 2nd chapter of the Quran. A later verse says: fight them until everything becomes al-Din-ul Illahi, the Religion of Allah ...'

'But professor,' someone interrupted, 'doesn't Din-ul Illahi mean universal religion? Didn't Akbar too use a similar expression, Din-i Illahi, to mean exactly the same? I don't think this verse should be misinterpreted as a clarion call to establish an Islamic State everywhere ...'

Kubha's attention was interrupted by a knock on one of the side doors of the room. She crawled towards the door, following the direction of the knock. She heard the knock again. 'Beti,' she heard a male voice say from behind the closed door, 'you don't have much time. Fast. Listen to me carefully.'

'Who are you?' Kubha asked.

Something in the voice of this person on the other side of the door aroused some hope within her.

'That doesn't matter. Listen to me carefully,' he sounded impatient. 'You've to escape. I'll tell you how …'

'Who are you?' she asked again.

'Beti,' the person on the other side pleaded, 'you can't escape without my help. They will kill you. Do you understand?'

'I can't escape,' she broke down for the first time since she had been brought here. 'I'll die …'

Her voice trembled. She collapsed on the floor, hitting her head hard on the wall. Everything around her appeared dark, like when a train suddenly enters into a long tunnel with all the lights switched off and when the repetitive sound of the rolling of the metallic wheels reverberates in the darkness, in a hypnotic spell.

☼

Shamsur Ali was seated on the takhtposh, presently pushed to a side of the octagonal room, which is at the centre of the naqb khana, an underground dwelling. This central hall is encircled by eight interconnected smaller rooms. This design, Shamsur had learned, was called hasht bihisht, the eight heavens, by the Mughals.

Shamsur's presence in this underground hasht bihisht was not a very obvious thing.

'No one would expect a former president of the Bangladesh Academy of Science and a professor of physics at the Dhaka

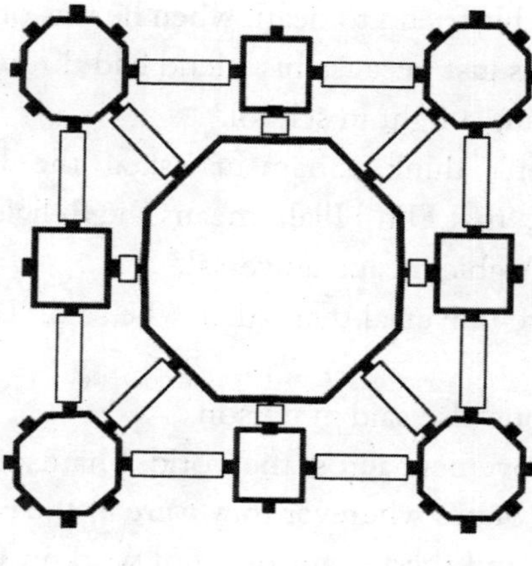

The central hall is encircled by eight interconnected smaller rooms.

University to be here,' he himself had said at the beginning of his introduction.

The small group of carefully chosen volunteers, who had assembled here for a specific purpose, listened to him keenly. His task, for now, was to just familiarize the young men to his thoughts. It was not that he himself espoused everything he said. But then, he had his own agenda and anything that served his purpose was perfectly acceptable to him. 'Isn't that what your Gita says too?' he had once said to a Hindu politician. 'Do your duties. Don't think about what's right and what's not.' No doubt, the politician had been left confused at the end of the discussion.

There was something in the way he spoke, always exuding confidence and appearing authentic. He would have a mesmerizing effect on his listeners most of the times. People would seldom contradict or argue with him. But to his great annoyance, one of the boys had been asking him too many questions of late. Presently, he controlled himself. He believed this boy could be of great use in the future. 'Professor,' he remembered being told, 'this boy choked his friend to death when he was only 12. Do you know why? It was just because his friend had thrown his skullcap on the floor during a fight in school.'

'So you don't think,' Shamsur asked the boy who had interrupted him, 'that Din-i Illahi means the Religion of Allah?'

'"Illahi" in Arabic means universal.'

'What's more universal than Allah?' he said. 'Boys, don't you all agree?'

'Yes,' everyone else said in unison.

'There's a movement across the world,' Shamsur continued, 'to recreate Islamic States wherever they were in the past. But what's working in Iraq and the Levant may not work in India. We need different strokes for different folks. And we've to take lessons from history. In the past, violence was the way in creating the grand Islamic States such as the Caliphate and the Ottoman and the Persian empires, stretching from Saudi Arabia to Afghanistan. The entire population had to be brought under control with force and then converted to Islam. But see what happened in India. The Mughals never had to apply as much force. They didn't have to convert the whole of Hindustan to Islam either. Yet, they had the richest-ever Islamic State in the world. Even now, we don't want to use much violence. It's not needed. Rather, we will do something really intelligent. *We will make the Indians kick the ball into their own goal.*'

☼

When Kubha opened her eyes she felt comfortable. She found herself lying on a thick mattress laid on the floor. There was a warm blanket too, wrapped around her naked body. Something flashed through her mind, suddenly. She pushed off the blanket immediately. The cold, stuffy air hit her like a whip, cutting through her skin. The warmth of the blanket and the comfort of the mattress had made her more vulnerable. She wanted to pull herself together and sit up. She exerted all the strength she had. But she couldn't. She turned her head in despair, to locate the door, from behind which the man had knocked. How long back had that been? She couldn't remember. She breathed heavily. She felt very thirsty. Her lips were dry as was her tongue. She struggled to keep her eyes open. Glimpses of images of her close ones ran through her mind, like a movie reel winding fast in the spool. A dazzling light seemed to have suddenly blinded her. She felt as though she was falling into a deep pit of darkness …

'Are you fine?' a feeble voice appeared from some distant faraway place. Did she hear it again? 'Are you fine?' Presently, it was a little louder, and closer too. She tried to open her eyes again and this time she could. She saw a familiar face hanging over her eyes.

Instantly, she could recognize the face. She had seen it many times, but from a different position, in an altogether different situation. Then, she remembered, her head would be hanging down, and this face would always appear before her oscillating gaze, like how anything on the ground appears to someone on a roller coaster, randomly, in snippets. Her eyes would oddly meet with his, a few times. He would always stand by her head, leaning on the wall of the octagonal room; his eyes lowered, his face calm. She could only get a partial view of him, from his waist up. The most notable aspect of the roundish face with rough skin was the pair of old-fashioned black specs with big rectangular frames. Even the thick lens wouldn't blur his deep, dark piercing eyes, the looks of which would give her some hope. Seeing the face again, she regained that hope.

'Take some water,' he said in English, helping her get up. She knew instantly that it had been him, whom she had overheard talking in a Bengali accent. The hope, which had kindled in her just a few moments back, doused immediately.

Kubha held the glass tightly with her trembling hands and emptied it in one go, a lot of the freezing water spilling out and dripping over her body. He gave her a dirty piece of cloth and she wiped the water off her body. She was naked, shivering in cold, yet she didn't feel unusual or awkward, as though being naked had become an acceptable norm to her by now. Neither did the person, who she knew was the one whom the others addressed as "professor", evoke any reaction of shock or surprise. He passed on to her an aluminum can with a round handle, the type of which she had never seen earlier. She drank the cold milk from the can—her first meal, so to say, in a very long time, perhaps a day, or even more. He got up from her side and sat on a chair, which she remembered hadn't been there earlier.

'I'm sorry for all that is happening to you,' he spoke in English tinged with a heavy Bengali accent. 'But you know, our prayer, our sacrifice, our living, our dying, all is for Allah. This is the nusq, the sacrifice, you're doing for Allah.'

'Who are you and why am I here?' Kubha asked firmly. She wondered where from she had suddenly got a brash daredevilry, an audacity to ignore everything. Perhaps, she felt, she had nothing more to lose, nothing more to fear.

He smiled. He turned back towards the closed door, the main one, the bigger one of the four in the small room.

'They will take you soon,' he said calmly, pointing towards the door.

Kubha knew very well what he was referring to.

'There's not much time,' he continued. 'If you cooperate with me, I'll give you a chance to escape from here.'

'What do you want?'

He pulled out a piece of paper and a pen from his pocket and handed them over to Kubha. 'Write a letter to your parents pleading them not to attend tomorrow's conference and also to hand over everything to my person. Otherwise …'

There was a knock at the main door.

He smiled. 'Wait for a few more minutes,' he shouted, turning towards the door.

'Okay, professor,' someone reciprocated from behind the door.

'You'll be taken again,' he said firmly. 'As I told, there's not much time.'

'That's why you've kidnapped me? To blackmail my parents?'

'Not exactly,' he got up. 'For that I should have kidnaped them, not you.'

He paused for a few moments, perhaps pondering whether he should say anything further. He sat down again on the chair and fixed his specs which had slid down a bit his big nose.

'You're an intelligent girl. I know everything about you. I know that you're half Muslim, that your mother is an American born to Pakistani and Iranian parents, that she still calls herself a Muslim, even though she has been married to a Hindu for more than 20 years. And, I'm told that you know the entire Quran by heart.'

'And that's why you got me here?' Kubha interrupted, 'to have me raped again and again by a bunch of frustrated Muslims who would help you create an Islamic State?'

She started trembling in the sudden excitement which made her exhausted. She leaned against the wall.

Shamsur smiled. 'So, you've eavesdropped on our conversation. That's good. I don't have to say much. You already know why I've got you.'

'No, I don't know,' Kubha rebutted. 'I just don't understand why you're doing this to me.' She broke down.

Shamsur allowed her to cry for a while. When she stopped, she heaved a sigh, took a long breath and looked at him, the firmness of her look made Shamsur remove his gaze from hers. He got up.

'It's easier to recruit Arab Muslims,' he said, lifting the chair. 'Their education is extremely regressive, their governance is horrible, there's rampant injustice everywhere, there's not much employment either and finally, there's the excesses of the Western countries since the Second World War. It's easy to use the radical concepts of Islam and prey on the recruit's sense of identity, give them a purpose in life.'

He paused, perhaps to check Kubha's reaction. She was presently unperturbed, expressionless. Was she confused? Was she feeling more helpless?

'In India it's different,' Shamsur continued. 'Muslims here are much more civilized and intelligent. Besides, the state of affairs in this country is not as bad as it is in the Arab and the rest of the Middle East. But there's still one thing. There's the same crisis of masculinity. Many Muslims here are as sexually repressed and religiously indoctrinated as are their brothers in the West. Rape can work like a dope for depraved young people wishing to exert their manhood, that too in a way approved by Islam. You're a part of their orientation.'

He started walking towards the door, carrying the chair with him. Kubha remained stunned, unable to react. Before opening the door, he turned back. 'I'll let you escape from here soon,' he said.

'Why?' Kubha was unyielding. 'I know a lot about you now. I can expose you.'

'I said, I'll let you escape,' he said with a sly smile. 'I didn't mean, you would actually do it. *No one has done it till now.* ' He left the room, shutting the door.

The moment the main door closed behind him, Kubha heard the knock on the other door. She pushed herself towards it. 'Listen to me carefully,' Kubha heard the hushed voice from behind the door. 'I'll tell you how to escape from this hasht bihisht. Just listen to me.'

The main door opened with a thump. Someone had kicked it open and it banged against the wall, making a loud noise. Kubha already knew what would happen next. The voice behind the closed door fell silent, again. While being dragged out of the room, she stared at the door.

The term "hasht bihisht" reverberated in her mind. She understood enough Arabic and Persian to know what it meant. She wondered at the irony that the place where she was being raped, again and again, was known as the Eight Heavens.

Kucha-i Salamat

(Later that day, 4 January 2019. Inside Hasht Bihisht)

Shamsur Ali had created a very hectic schedule for his team. The day of action was approaching fast. He was still not satisfied with the progress. He was still to see the same level of aggression, ruthlessness and conviction as he had seen in Iraq and the Levant. There, he recalled, each one was a real fighter, a ferocious lion that would see even the most beautiful deer in the jungle as a mere prey. Not a single Yazidi girl would be spared. They would behead the old ones in front of their children and then rape the young ones brutally. When many of them died, they would feed them to the dogs. The ones who survived became sex slaves.

Shamsur himself never supported such inhuman acts. But then, he knew, savageries were integral parts of the movement. The more barbaric the fighters, more would be the success. He enjoyed the power and the importance he presently had. Nothing mattered more to him. He would never become the king, he knew, but he was happy being the king-maker, the mastermind. Even the people in the top echelons of the Islamic State listened to him, consulted him, trusted him. Not many in their rungs were as intelligent and intellectual as him.

Shamsur stared at the almost-lifeless body of Kubha, lying on the takhtposh. The barbarity and the sadism of his men satisfied him. But ironically, the most barbaric of them, the one who had been asking uncomfortable questions to him, was the one who didn't cause any harm to Kubha. That was, Shamsur knew, not a good sign. He would have to eliminate him. And he already had the plan in place.

'Professor, the repeaters are all functioning,' informed the one who was an engineer, specially trained in setting up and handling telecommunication systems. 'We can now operate the satellite phone from here.'

'Wouldn't our position be traceable if the call is intercepted?' Shamsur enquired.

'I've included an encryption software which would make the deciphering very tough. I don't think it would be easy to extract the GPS data from the garbage. And we'll keep the video call as short as possible. Any call less than a minute is even harder to decrypt.'

'Good. Plan for the video call tomorrow morning, just a few hours before the conference begins.'

'It's a great plan, professor, much better than sending a scanned letter to her parents or even making her talk to them. Seeing their daughter in that condition, they would do anything for us.'

'We're running out of time. The General Election in India is just a few months away. A lot of ground work is still pending. *It's not just a Babri Masjid*.'

As Shamsur was talking to the engineer, Kubha tried to get up. The last part of the conversation the professor was having with someone had jerked her into life. It couldn't be anything else. She was sure of it. '*It's not just a Babri Masjid*,' Shamsur's words resounded in her head, perhaps a million times. Presently, she didn't have even an iota of doubt about what they were planning. What perplexed her though was why a group of fanatic Muslims would indulge in such a thing. Rather, she had had the belief, till now, that it would be the handiwork of some really crazy Hindu radicals. Whoever could be behind this, she reminded herself, she had to do everything in her might to prevent it, *at any cost.*

Kubha very well understood the significance of preventing her parents from attending the conference the following morning. Handing over everything to Shamsur's people would mean an end to all the efforts made by so many people to unearth one of the biggest frauds of the recent times and prevent a catastrophe of unthinkable proportion. All the brutal killings would go in vain if not the disaster was averted. Kubha remembered the scene of the ghastly murder of her grandfather and his aide at their ancestral home in Khushawar—their esophagus and stomach totally burnt, their throat badly swollen, their skin perforated with innumerable holes.

The thought of a video call with her parents suddenly brought some strength inside her. Was she excited that she would get to see her parents? She was excited indeed, but not with the prospect of seeing her parents, but rather with the hope that she could perhaps somehow let them know, come what may, that they shouldn't hand over anything to anyone and that they shouldn't stop from going to the conference. But how would she convey the message? Shouting it out over the phone was surely not an option, she realized. These people would kill her if she did anything like that.

Someone pulled her up and dragged her to her room, closing the door from outside.

'I've to live,' she mumbled to herself. 'I can't die. *I've to do something* …'

She remembered her great grandmother, her namesake, who had always been an invisible strength that would make everyone in her family feel secure and protected, even at times of distress. Over the years, she had realized though, that the other Kubha was more of a mythical entity created by her own people, to serve their own purpose. Perhaps, it gave an extra sense of security and confidence, she felt, to believe that someone extraordinary, out there, would steer them out of a storm. Presently, she knew whatever she had to do, she had to do it alone. But still, perhaps like a legacy of her family, she took solace in the other Kubha.

☼

Kubha heard the knock again on one of the side doors. She ran towards the door. '*I've to be alive*,' she said impatiently. 'I've to escape out of here.'

'You'll be alive,' the unknown person on the other side of the door assured her. 'Don't worry. Listen to me carefully. This place is a hasht bihisht. A central big gah-i musammani is surrounded by eight gah-i mukhtasari.'

'Gah-i musammani?' Kubha asked.

'It's the big room in the centre with eight sides. It's surrounded by eight smaller rooms, gah-i mukhtasari. Four of these smaller rooms are square and the other four musammani, with eight sides. You're in one of the square rooms and me in the octagonal. You have one more octagonal room on your other side too and I've two square rooms on both my sides. All these eight rooms are arranged in a circle around the gah-i musammani …' He paused.

'Are you listening?' he asked.

'Yes,' Kubha responded, 'I am.'

'Your room has four doors,' he continued.'The one at the front opens into the big central musammani hall through a short dalan, a passage. Two doors open into the two smaller musammani rooms on your either side. The door at the back is something that makes the hasht bihisht a bhulbhulaiya, a labyrinth, where you can be lost forever.'

'I've seen the big central hall has eight doors. Each of these doors opens into one of the side rooms, isn't it?'

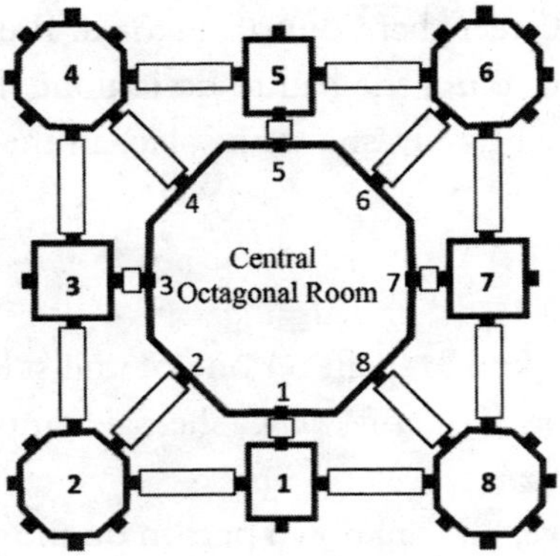

Eight smaller rooms are arranged in a circle around the big octagonal hall.

'That's correct. All the square rooms have four doors. But my room has eight, one on each of its eight sides. The front door opens into the big hall through a dalan. A side one is connected to your room through another dalan. A similar one on the other side is connected to another square room like yours …'

'And what about the remaining five doors?' Kubha interrupted impenitently.

'They lead you nowhere.'

'I can't understand anything,' the restlessness in her voice was apparent. 'Why are you telling me all these?'

'Beti,' the man pleaded, 'it's no time to be impatient. Just listen very carefully. So, you now know that each of the octagonal side rooms has five doors which will take you nowhere. There are four such side rooms.'

'And,' Kubha completed, 'there are 20 such doors which create a bhulbhulaiya.'

'And each of the four square rooms too has one such door. So, there's a total of 24 such doors in each hasht bihisht. Now imagine what happens when there are a number of hasht bihishts connected to each other? You will keep on searching for the way out for the rest of your life.'

Kubha realized why the professor had said no one had ever escaped from here.

'There's a divine number you've to remember if you want your way out. It's 313. It's the number of Muslims who fought the Battle of Badr along with the Prophet.'

Kubha was aware of the significance of the Battle of Badr in the history of Islam. It was the first decisive battle the Muslims fought against their enemies, the Quraishis of Mecca, whose army was thrice as big as theirs.

'It doesn't matter how little you are,' Kubha listened to the voice coming from behind the door, 'or how big your enemy is. If you're on the right path, you'll always find a way out. So, 313 is the key to the right path.'

Kubha learned that once she would be out of this hasht bihisht, she would enter into a long underground tunnel running

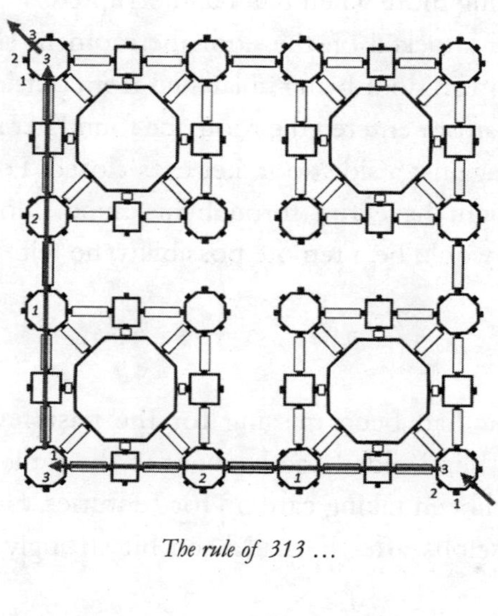

The rule of 313 ...

for miles and passing through two bhulbhulaiyas on the way. The moment she would encounter an octagonal room with eight doors, she had to strictly follow the rule of 313 to get her way out of the bhulbhulaiya.

'Exit through the *third* door to your left,' the person said slowly, stressing on the word "third". 'Then go straight, never taking any left or right till you enter into the *third* octagonal room. You've to always go straight. Remember, it's again the number "3", *the third octagonal room*. Next, you leave *one* door to your right and exit through the next. Remember, it's the number "1" now—*leave one door to your right*. Thereafter, you again keep going straight till you enter into the *third* octagonal room, from where you exit through the *third* door to your left. It's again the number "3" and you're out of the bhulbhulaiya, back to the tunnel.'

He repeated the same thing twice and made Kubha explain it once.

'We call this tunnel kucha-i salamat, the safety street. We've been using this for centuries for the safety and upkeep of our place, our buildings, and I'll do so till I'm alive … ' He was going to say something more when Kubha interrupted.

'Stop,' she knocked on the door the moment she heard the sound of the main door being unlatched from outside.

When Shamsur entered the room, he found her sitting on the floor leaning against a side door, her eyes closed. For a moment, something might have run through his mind. No, he assured himself. That would be a remote possibility, he felt.

☼

Daulat Parwar had been missing for the past few days. One night, he was blindfolded and brought to the same place which his family had been taking care of for centuries. He might have fallen unconscious after he had been hit strongly on his head from behind. When he came back to his senses, one side of his head still paining severely, he found his hands and legs tied with ropes so strongly that he could barely move himself. He found himself lying on a cold floor of a dark room. Once he acclimatized with the darkness, he knew exactly where he was. He knew this room as gah-i mukhtasar-i musammani, the small octagonal room. As the eldest son, he had inherited an unusual trove of knowledge, along with a responsibility which his family had been bestowed with hundreds of years ago. Even his other siblings didn't have any air of it and that was how it had been since the very beginning.

Some light trickled into his dark room from under two doors. He knew there were eight of them in the room. He made some futile effort to make some sense out of the faint sounds that oozed through the thick wooden door and the massive solid walls made of ajir bricks. He knew the sounds were coming from the badi gah-i musammani, the big central hall.

When his back ached, he tried to turn and lie on his side; and while doing so, he suddenly heard the sounds of heavy breaths, just for a moment, so distinct that he felt as if someone was just beside him. With both his hands and legs tied, his mobility was very limited. He moved his head as much as he could till he was able to hear the sounds of the breaths, continuously. Someone was writhing in pain, panting heavily and breathing with much difficulty. He felt restless.

He moved his head to another position and he could hear everything from the central hall, each and every sound, each and every conversation, even the whispers, so clearly that he felt as though he was present there in person.

He felt relieved that he hadn't shared this particular tidbit about the hasht bihisht to Shamsur. One of its octagonal side rooms had been constructed such that, from eight different positions within it, one could distinctly hear each and every sound from the other eight rooms—the central hall and the seven side rooms. Any sound made from these eight positions would also be audible clearly in the corresponding eight rooms. Daulat had experienced this particular thing only once in the past, many years ago. Standing in a particular position in this room, he had distinctly heard the flicking sound of the lighting of a match when his father had struck the match in another room. He was told that a similar, but much simpler technique had been used in the construction of the whispering galleries of the Gol Gumbaz in the southern city of Bijapur.

For the next few hours, he changed his positions and listened carefully to whatever sound originated from the central hall and the small square side room to his left. To his utter shock and horror, he almost *saw* everything unfolding before him. The beastly roar of Shamsur's people, all the clamour, all the brouhaha, as though it was a celebration of triumph. Everything stunned him. How badly he wished the girl would shout, shriek, and let the pain and agony inside her come out every time she was being violated. She would soon turn into a huge dark cloud, he thought, accumulating the karor ansu, the million tears, within her. He prayed to the ever-protecting Almighty to give the girl more strength, to make her more resolute. He prayed to the Almighty to pierce the cloud that the girl was holding within her, with a lightning, and unleash a deluge on the earth, killing Shamsur and his men. He asked the Almighty to shower on him the severest of the punishments because he had sinned in trusting an animal like Shamsur and breaking the vow his family had taken centuries ago. Apart from the eldest son of his family, no one else had ever heard of this underground tunnel.

Daulat tracked when someone entered into or left the square room next door. Every minute sound, or the absence of it, would tell him of something. He knew how long and how much the girl cried silently in her room; how much she shivered in the extreme cold, perhaps lying on the freezing floor; how much she struggled to endure everything and still keep herself alive; how many times she lost her consciousness and how many times she pulled herself up.

Daulat knew she had to escape from here because otherwise there was no way to stop the disaster. He had to do everything possible under the sun to protect this imarat-i muqaddas, the holy building, which his family had been entrusted to protect till the end of the world.

Daulat agreed totally with Shamsur Ali that it was no Babri Masjid. In fact, it was, he believed, thousands of that put together.

Making sure that the girl next door was alone, he banged his head twice on the floor at the right position, making a very feeble sound. He knew that when the same sound would reach next door, it would be much louder and appear as knocks on the door. He also knew that when he would talk from the right position in this room, it would appear, from the other room, as though someone was talking from the other side of the door.

For the next few hours, whenever he found her alone, he tried to give her as much information as she would need to escape successfully. He knew very well how difficult it would be to get out of the two bhulbhulaiyas the underground tunnel passed through. He remembered how many times he himself would have been lost in them when his father would leave him inside in order to familiarize him with every nook and corner of the kucha-i salamat, the name by which he would call the long tunnel. But the girl, he wished, should make her way out in the very first attempt. She wouldn't have anyone to take her out of the complicated mesh of doors and rooms and dalans if she got stuck inside. But when she was able to confidently explain back to him the 313 trick to get out of the mesh, he too felt confident. He was amazed at the level of mental strength the girl still possessed after all she had been going through.

He was going to tell her from where she should finally exit the tunnel, when she interrupted him. 'Stop,' she knocked on the door. He too had heard the sound of the opening of the main front door of her room. He fell silent. Soon he heard Shamsur's voice.

'I'll let you go tomorrow morning. But before that, we need to show something to your parents. You've to lie down on the takhtposh for one last time.'

Daulat wanted to tear off the rope with which he was tied up, break the walls and hack Shamsur to death, brutally, chopping his hands and legs into pieces and feeding them to the dogs. The girl remained silent. Shamsur left the room. He heard the sound of the door shutting.

☼

Kubha didn't sleep. After the professor had left, she sat on the mattress, leaning behind. The cold wall failed to evoke any sensation in her, even when she rested her bare back on it. Perhaps, she wondered how fast she had got adjusted to her new circumstances. She didn't want anything else to clutter her mind. She knew she had only this night to do whatever she could. Seeing their daughter in that state, she knew for sure, her parents would become the professor's slave. The professor's plan, she asserted to herself, had to be foiled, at any cost. And doing something stupid wouldn't serve any purpose, she knew.

She got up from the mattress and started walking restlessly in the small room. She banged her head a few times on the wall, knelt down on the floor and stared at the CFL bulb hanging from the domed ceiling till she saw only darkness …

Suddenly, as if a million volts had passed through her body, she jerked herself up. She frantically looked around for something. She lifted the mattress to see if it had gone under it. She shook the blanket. That was when the paper and the pen, which Shamsur had given her sometime back for writing a letter to her parents, fell onto the floor. She jumped on to the paper. Panting heavily, she sat on the mattress, leaning down on the paper kept on the floor. She tried to recall the lines …

"*Awalam yara alladhin kafaru,*" she scribbled the beginning of a verse from the 21st chapter of the Quran on the paper.

"*Jahadaka litush'rika bi ma laysa laka bihi ilmun, fala tuti huma,*"she scribbled portions of another verse from the 29th chapter. "*Fala tuti huma,*" the words played in her thoughts like a hypnotizing hymn, going on and on.

She read the two lines again and again. Then she lay on the mattress for some time, staring at the ceiling.

'*Awalam yara alladhin kafaru,*' she uttered each syllable slowly, distinctly. Then she repeated the same line a few times, in a different way, '*Abalama jala aladana kapala,*' replacing the "wa" with "ba", "ya" with "ja", "ra" with "la", among others, and all vowels with "a".

Since her childhood, Kubha could seamlessly reduce any sentence in Urdu and Farsi, and sometimes in Arabic too, to one that could be represented with only 14 letters. The logic behind such a reduction, she had already learned, was obviously to map each of the 14 letters to one of the seven notes of music in two octaves, so that, she could actually *sing out the sentence.*

Presently, she was a little surprised that she could transform the sentence to its reduced form as fast as she would do in the past. She tried to remember the last time she would have done this—not any time in the recent past, she knew for sure.

'Sa Pa Ni Dha,' she hummed the four notes "Do So Ti La" in the upper octave. She made a fast calculation in her mind to assure herself that those four notes indeed stood for "a-ba-la-ma".

'It's very much like reading a staff notation and singing a song,' her mother would insist. When as a kid she and her mother would regularly play with each other, singing out whatever they wanted to speak, she could instantaneously figure out the notes and sing them. Presently, she did it carefully, taking some time to ensure that she was not making any mistake. It was after all not a game. It hadn't been always a game either, she knew. Her grandfather would often say how this traditional tactic of the natives of their ancestral village of Khushawar was effectively used by the members of Khudai Khidmadgar, the Servants of Gods, during the British era to communicate secretively among themselves in public places. The police would always wonder why few insane people sang to each other in public.

Kubha learned the tune by heart and let herself loose on the mattress, exhausted. She hadn't eaten anything in more than a day—a day, no trace of which she would like to preserve in her life, if at all she lived beyond the next morning. She had already become so weak that last time she had almost passed out on the takhtposh, during the barbaric ritual which was being observed with the regularity and fervour of a namaz. She was not sure if she could take it again. Several thoughts jammed her mind. She might lose all her strength seeing her mother in the morning. How would her mother react seeing her daughter's ordeal? Would her mother be in the right senses to get the message she had prepared so carefully to pass on to her? Would she really have the strength to disobey the professor's diktat?

Kubha didn't discount the possibility of herself being killed. If her parents fell into the professor's trap, what good reason would he have to keep her alive? Even if he didn't kill her, how long would she survive the ordeal? What chance did she really have to escape out of here, when no one had been able to do so in the past?

This night, she realized, might be very well her last night. Had she ever thought of such a nemesis?

She got up.

Standing in the middle of the room, naked, her legs trembling, her whole body shivering, her eyes burning, she took a few deep breaths.

'No,' she said to herself, 'I won't give up. That wouldn't serve any purpose.'

She had to live. *She shouldn't let the professor and his men have their way.*

What was the name by which the man behind the door had referred to the tunnel? She tried to remember. Wasn't it kucha-i salamat? Why would someone call it a safety street? It was rather ridiculous, she herself knew, but still she clung on to that name and felt safe, and hopeful too. She felt confident, she didn't know why though, that she was not standing at the brink of death, that she would really emerge out of the safety street, safely.

Was she hallucinating? Was she trying to create a utopia?

Was she finally at the threshold of creating the greatest of the stories that would be told by the qissa khawanis, the story tellers, thousands of miles away, thousands of years later?

She returned to the mattress, but didn't fall asleep soon …

'Your qissa would be the greatest of all.' She recalled her great grandfather, Fazal's, assuring words …

Qissa Khawani Bazar

(1930. Peshawar)

Fazal had been all of 15 when his father would leave the rugs with him and go to the sarai to meet his friends, mostly Pashtun traders from the nearby places around Peshawar. Fazal would wait for this day of the week, when he and his father would leave their home at Khushawar in the morning with a bundle of rugs tied with a big jute cloth, and take the only bus to Mardan.

The bus, which plied between Charguli and Mardan, wouldn't have much space, either inside or on its roof, by the time it reached Khushawar. As though everything had been rehearsed many times, Fazal would hold the bundle of rugs up and someone would always bend down from the top of the bus and pull it up. By the time he and his father entered into the crowded bus, sufficient space would have been already created for them.

At Bakhshali, when more people got in, it would then be their turn, along with the others, to extend the same hospitality to the new passengers. Fazal had lately started appreciating this particular aspect of the Pashtun way of life, totally in contrast to their violent and bloody feuds in the name of badal, revenge.

'Melmastia is the most important thing of Pashtunwali,' his father would often remind him. 'It demands that the Pashtuns go to any length to show their hospitality and respect to their guests.'

By the time Fazal and his father reached the Qissa Khawani Bazar in Peshawar, changing buses at Mardan and Charsadda, it was already evening. The narrow lanes and by-lanes of the vibrant market would be bustling with activity. They carefully manoeuvred through the crowd. The big bundle Fazal's father was carrying on his back bumped against the people, camels, horses and mules, all that had come from places near and far to this market, which Fazal knew, was two millennia old. Making their way through the horde of men and animals and somehow managing not to get run over by the carts of various shapes and sizes spilling with bazar paraphernalia and also vying for space in the packed streets, he trailed his father.

Fazal threw a passing glance at the dried skins of the Himalayan animals, crowding the counter of a small corner shop run by a short man with a wrinkled face. He waved at the shopkeeper and the latter waved back at him. Fazal always wondered how old or young the shopkeeper could be.

Fazal's father stopped by a crowded shop selling qahwa, the refreshing and light green Chinese tea with a dash of cardamom, and exchanged pleasantries with people Fazal only knew by their faces. By now, he could identify the Persians, the Afghans, the Turkoman, the Hazaras, the Uzbeks and the Hindustanis.

'You can manage today without me?' his father threw the words behind him.

'Don't worry,' Fazal assured his father. 'I'll do it better than you.' He smiled. His father turned back and waited for him to catch up.

'There's an important meeting of the Khudai Khidmadgars at the sarai,' his father said, once he had come by his side.

'I too want to join you,' he pleaded.

His father smiled. 'Sell them fast and join us at the sarai …' he started walking.

On reaching a particular street, his father opened the bundle and laid the jute cloth on the ground. He carefully arranged the rugs in a collage, filling a small gap in the colourful sea of hundreds of rugs displayed by the others.

☼

Fazal had enough knowledge to distinguish between the different types of rugs. The Khushawari rug, the one the people wove in his village under his father's supervision, was a kilim, where the horizontal yarns go over and under the vertical yarns, creating a plane woven surface, not much different from that of a thick jute cloth.

Many years ago, when Fazal's father had brought him here for the first time, he had immediately run away to see the rugs someone was selling nearby. He gaped at the riot of colours and the wonderful patterns of flowers, leaves, creepers, peacocks and many other birds and animals on it. It didn't elude the seven-year-

He gaped at the riot of colours and the wonderful patterns of flowers, leaves, creepers, peacocks and many other birds and animals on it.

old Fazal how bright and colourful those carpets were in contrast to the ones he had seen till then, in Khushawar.

The seller laid the biggest rug for him on the ground. He sat on it and touched the floral patterns with his fingers. 'These are piles of small knots,' his father had said, pointing to the patterns he was staring at with eyes wide open. 'This is a Persian carpet. You tie thousands and thousands of tiny knots to the vertical yarns and create these patterns. We don't tie knots in our rugs.'

Over the years, he learned more about the rugs, hopping from one makeshift shop to another, all set up together side by side on the same crowded street of the bazar. Not many children would be around in the busy market and very soon, he became a much adorable distraction to the carpet sellers.

'Which one do you think is the best?' someone would ask him one day, while opening his bundle of rugs. As though he was an expert, he would raise the corners of the rugs stacked one above the other, touch each of them with his fingers, inspect the knots carefully, check the colours and then give his verdict. 'This one,' he would say, pulling one from below, and the seller would spread the same on the ground for the onlookers to have a better look.

Fazal's father would affectionately stare at his child from a distance, feeling reassured that he would surely take interest in the centuries-old family profession.

'Do you understand how different our rugs are from anything else you see here?' his father asked him one day.

'We don't use so many colours,' Fazal replied.

'Yes, that's true. The Persian carpets use the most colours. The Bokhara rugs use mainly dark colours such as deep brown and red. And we use only few contrasting colours—mostly patterns of red, blue or black against a white, cream or grey surface.'

'Our patterns are also very different,' Fazal pointed out.

'You will very soon relieve me of all the work,' his father patted him fondly. 'Yes, you're absolutely correct. The Persian has

'The Persian has roundish floral patterns. The Bokhara has nakhshah with daireh and likunah.'

'... the Bokhara from Afghanistan has octagons.'

roundish floral patterns. The Bokhara has nakhshah with daireh and likunah. You will soon read about these circles and lines in geometry. When there are four sides in a pattern, it's a rectangle or a square; when there are eight, it's an octagon. The Bokhara from Afghanistan has octagons.'

His father went on explaining how their rugs from Khushawar have an intriguing combination of the floral patterns of the

Rugs from Khushawar have an intriguing combination of the floral patterns of the Persian and the geometrical shapes of the Bokhara.

Persian and the geometrical shapes of the Bokhara, along with innumerable symbols and signs, the kind of which he didn't see in any other rugs.

'Each of these symbols and signs,' his father would often say, 'tell us of some stories we've long forgotten. Someday, may be you or your children will discover these stories. For many hundreds of years, we've carefully preserved these stories in our rugs, only for you ...'

That day, when Fazal's father arranged the rugs on the ground and hastily left for the sarai, leaving him alone for the first time to sell the carpets, he remembered his father's words. He stared at the peculiar patterns on the rugs in front of him. What stories would they have in them? He pondered. '*Your children will discover the stories* ... ' His father's words played in his mind.

Little did he know that his father's prophecy would one day come true, that his children would actually discover the stories behind those cryptic patterns on the Khushawari rugs. But whether his father had any premonition about the ghastly repercussions of the discovery is a matter of conjecture. If he had known that Fazal's son would have to pay the price of it with his life and a lively young girl of the family with her izzat, honour, some hundred years later, would he be equally excited about the stories his family had painstakingly preserved for generations in the mysterious signs and letters of their rugs? Going by the tradition of Pashtunwali, would he vouch for the deadliest-ever badal to avenge the catastrophe and dishonour that would befall his family?

☼

Fazal didn't take much time to sell the rugs they had brought from their village. Today his mind had been somewhere else, from the very beginning. As he sat behind the rugs, abstracted, he forgot to reciprocate to the pleasantries of the people around with the same cordiality so characteristic of him.

The old man who sold the best Persian carpets always took out some time to chat with him. 'I wish my son were like you,' he sighed. 'Even at this age, I've to travel so far every week.'

A small kid dashed against the counter of the shop on the other side of the road and the colourful pyramids of figs, apricots and pomegranates came crumbling down, scattering the fruits onto the ground. The kid ran away in scare and collided with a man with an end of a pole on his shoulder, carrying wooden cages of squawking chickens. The pole dislodged from his shoulder, throwing the cages onto the ground. The cackling chickens, freed from the broken cages, ran helter-skelter all over the street. A commotion ensued, overwhelming everyone with the series of comical acts. In the melee, a baffled camel pulling an overloaded cart started racing, running the cart over the feet of some people and throwing many others off the street.

Fazal was oblivious to all the happenings around him. Since he had met Badshah Khan a few days ago at the Azad School in Utmanzai, nothing else had crossed his mind. Fazal had been totally engrossed in his mesmerizing words. With his affable but stupefying personality, as towering as his height, and the earnestness in his speech, Badshah Khan had hypnotized not only Fazal, but all the young minds present there. Fazal felt as though he had been ushered out of his adolescence and transported into a sudden adulthood, with a big thrust. Sitting behind the heap of rugs amidst so many people in the cramped market, he recalled each of the words he had heard the other day at Utmanzai:

> *I'm going to give you such a weapon that the police and the army will not be able to stand against it. It is the weapon of the Prophet, but you're not aware of it. That weapon is sabr, patience, renunciation of all violent retaliation and righteousness. No power on earth can stand against it. When you go back to your villages, tell your brethren that there is an army of God, and its weapon is sabr. Ask your brethren to join the army of God. Endure all hardships. If you exercise sabr, victory will be yours ...*

Fazal's thoughts were disrupted when someone fell hard on him. That was when he noticed the brouhaha around him. Once the commotion subsided, he sold the last few rugs and walked fast to the sarai to listen to what his father was talking about.

☼

'It's not for nothing that the qafilas have been bringing the Afghans, the Persians, the Turkomans, the Uzbeks, the Russians and many others from round the world to this place, for thousands of years, since the time of the Koshan Shahanshah, the great Kanishki Namworr,' Fazal heard the thundering voice of his father from inside the sarai. He stood at the entrance and listened to his father addressing a fairly good gathering in the central courtyard of the sarai.

'Everyone who came here had a story to share and that's how this market came to be known as the Qissa Khawani Bazar, the Story Tellers' Market. For many many years, we've listened to these stories from around the world. Now it's our turn to create a story that will be worth telling for the next thousands of years—the Story of the Story Tellers' Market. It's the story of our honesty and truthfulness; the story of sacrificing our wealth, life and comfort for the liberty of our country and its people; the story of our lives in accordance with the principles of adam tashaddud, nonviolence.'

It was not the first time Fazal was hearing his father say all these. Since the creation of the Khudai Khidmadgar, the Servant of God, the previous year, by Abdul Gaffar Khan, his father had been actively involved in getting more and more people into its folds. Such was the popularity of Abdul Gaffar Khan, anointed as Badshah Khan, the King of Khans, that even his reference would augur a feeling of reverence among his people. Fazal, having outgrown the age of incomprehension, realized that such a level of acceptance among the Pashtuns was perhaps because Badshah Khan had instilled new vigour and honour into Pashtunwali, the Pashtun way of life, giving the violent people a new meaning to their lives, which had been earlier relegated to bad blood and savage killings.

'Badshah Khan has decided to support the Peshawar Congress and participate in the Civil Disobedience Movement. Gandhiji has appealed to each Hindustani to join this nonviolent revolution and throw the infidels, the tyrant Angrez, out of Hindustan,' Fazal's father continued with his roaring voice, dissolving the cacophony of the surroundings. 'As Khudai Khidmadgars, as real Muslims, we should remember that the nonviolence Badshah

Khan believes in and preaches to his brethren affects all our lives. Only that has permanent value.'

Fazal identified in the audience the Hazaras, with their distinct eye-folds; the dark-skinned Uzbeks; the Angrez-looking Tajiks, tall and lithe with pale skin and eyes. Not all of them were truly people of Hindustan, like the Pasthuns and the Chitralis. He felt proud that so many people were listening to his father.

Fazal recalled Badshah Khan's words, as his father presently reiterated the same:

> *There is nothing surprising in a Muslim or a Pathan like me subscribing to the creed of nonviolence. It is not a new creed. It was followed 1,400 years ago by the Prophet all the time he was in Mecca and it has since been followed by all those who wanted to throw off an oppressor's yoke. A Muslim never hurts anyone by word or deed. Islam is amal, yakeen, muhabat, work, faith and love ...*

A loud noise disrupted his thoughts. 'Inqilab Zindabad,' a rumble of a hundred voices reverberated in the sarai. 'Victory to the revolution,' resounded the crowd a few more times.

'The picketing starts on 23rd April,' Fazal's father announced. 'But remember, there shouldn't be any violent retaliation, come what may. Remember what has been said in the Quran. *Rabbana, afrigh alayna sabran*, Lord, pour sabr on us. *Wa-thabbit aqdamana*, and make firm our qadm, the steps we take. *Wa-unsurna ala al-qawami al-kafirana*, and help us against the people who are kafir, infidels, the Angrez.'

☼

Fazal accompanied his father and a group of some 20 people from their village and reached the Qissa Khawani Bazar on the night of 22nd April. Lot of people had already gathered there to participate in the picketing that was scheduled the following day.

'The Congress leaders have been sensitive enough to us,' Fazal had heard his father saying to the other traders. 'They have pushed the date of picketing to tomorrow and allowed us to exhaust our stock.'

Seeing the high turnout of the traders, Fazal realized how smartly his father had invoked the Quran to motivate them to participate in the Civil Disobedience Movement.

The next day would be a big day in Peshawar, Fazal knew. 'It would be our Dandi March,' Fazal's father had told many a time. Fazal was aware that little more than a month ago, Gandhiji had launched the nonviolent Satyagraha Movement with the Dandi March, a symbol of defiance of the rule of the kafirs, the Angrez.

Fazal saw excitement in the eyes of everyone. At night, when everyone had retired to the sarai, his father called him to his side.

'I'm proud of you, my son,' he said affectionately, hugging him tightly, for a long time.

Fazal was a little taken aback by the sudden display of emotion. It was not that his father didn't have any such feeling, but Fazal had seldom seen him expressing it in a way that, perhaps, wouldn't suit the personality of a valiant and intrepid Pashtun that he was.

'Let us go for a walk,' Fazal's father said abruptly.

They walked through the narrow streets of the bazar which was caught in an unusual stillness. There were signs of a sudden repose scattered everywhere, as though, it would wake up and get back to the unfinished business just in a while. A cart puller was asleep on the slant floor of his cart, one end of which rested on the ground. A shoe-maker was lying behind a half-stitched shoe, pieces of leather and cloth scattered around him. A few pieces of precious stones from Agra lay strewed around boxes partially inlaid with the colourful stones, a tired and sleepy artisan struggling to complete his work. A richly embroidered wall-cover fluttered on the wall of a shop as a sudden cool breeze gushed through the street.

'It's so calm now,' Fazal's father spoke after a long silence. '*But tomorrow will be so different …*'

'Are you worried, Aba?' Fazal asked his father directly.

'No, not for myself, my son. But I'm worried for you.'

'Why, Aba?'

'Because … ' his father paused and stared at him. He touched Fazal's cheek and then held him tight, by his shoulders. 'Nothing is going to happen to you, my son,' he asserted.

Later that night, when his father had long been asleep on the floor of a small room in the sarai, Fazal was still awake. His father's reaction had suddenly made him feel weary and anxious. He had heard horrid stories of the barbarism at Jallianwala Bagh, a place in the nearby Punjab province, where an unarmed group of protesters had been fired at by the ruthless Angrez, killing more than a thousand people. Would something similar happen the next day, in Peshawar? Fazal couldn't totally ignore such a possibility. Knowing his father very well, Fazal knew, he would be at the forefront of everything, leading the people. If there would be any firing, he would be among the first to be killed. 'A true Pashtun never fears for his life,' he would often say, Fazal remembered. 'And the life of a Khudai Khidmadgar has already been dedicated to others.'

Fazal felt restless. He stared at his father, sleeping so peacefully, as though it was just any other day in Khushawar.

☼

Fazal was suddenly woken up by an unusual cacophony. He took a few moments to realize where he was. He rubbed his eyes and looked at the empty floor where his father had slept at night. Fazal could hear his father's voice rising above the clamour of the crowd outside the sarai—the noise of the footsteps on the staircase and the buzz of the Qissa Khawani Bazar already teeming with the activities of the day. He felt good. The very thought that his father was nearby gave him a sense of security and assurance. He got up from the thick mattress and went out.

'The police has arrested most of the leaders of the Congress and the Khudai Khidmadgar all throughout the night,' he heard his father speaking to a small crowd assembled outside the sarai. 'That means we've our own responsibilities today. We shouldn't forget the 10-point pledge we all have taken as Khudai Khidmadgars. We'll give our lives, but we'll not take any.'

Fazal learned that the sudden arrest of most of the leaders was a big setback to the people. Someone brought the information that few of the leaders would be brought to the Kabuli Thana, the police station adjoining the bazar. It was decided that everyone would assemble at the thana and wait for the leaders to be brought there. By nine in the morning, there was already a big gathering in front of the police station, crowd spilling into the narrow streets of the market.

Fazal was with his father, at the front.

'What do you all want?' asked Isa Monger, an officer Fazal had seen many a time making rounds of the bazar. He hated his long face with a sharp nose and cold eyes, whenever he would pass by.

'We want to meet our leaders,' Fazal's father replied, curtly.

'You can't create ruckus here,' the officer shot back.

'Sir, we're not breaking any law,' Fazal's father said as calmly as possible. 'We'll just stay here till we see our leaders. I assure you there wouldn't be any nuisance.'

'You bastards,' another officer in uniform hasted out from inside the police station and shouted at the crowd, 'who do you think you all are?'

'He is H.A. Metcalf,' someone whispered from behind. 'He's the deputy commissioner of Peshawar. He's a ruthless animal.'

'Just get lost from here before I fire on you,' Metcalf howled.

'We're not going to leave,' Fazal's father said firmly, holding Fazal's hand tightly. He turned towards the crowd and said loudly, 'Brethren, we're not going to just cower in the corner because these people are trying to frighten us.'

He was interrupted by a sudden loud noise. No sooner had everyone realized that the noise was actually a chorus of shrill cries of people than an armoured vehicle screeched to a halt in front of the thana. A troop of army men, all geared with rifles, bayonets and shields, got down from the vehicle. They took positions at the front of the crowd. They pointed their rifles towards the shocked people, who by then had figured the reason of the shrill cries. Many rushed towards the ones lying on the ground. They were writhing in pain. Their shrieks pierced the ensuing hullabaloo. The army men and the police remained unfazed. The dumbfounded people lifted the almost-lifeless bodies crushed under the heavy wheels of the armoured car.

In the chaos, people started running in panic. They fled towards the narrow streets of the bazar. Many ran over the people tending to the ones grievously injured. The others fell on each other. It created a stampede. Fazal bent down over a profusely bleeding old man, lying on the ground. He tried hard to shield him from being smashed under the footsteps of the terrified people. Few of them stumbled over Fazal. They fell hard on the ground, hurting themselves badly.

When the crowd thinned down a bit, Fazal heard his father's voice.

'Don't run away. These are your brothers. Take care of them,' he pleaded to everyone. Many were still around, perhaps thinking if they too would run away. Some better sense prevailed. They stayed back. They dragged the seven dead bodies to the side and lifted the five severely injured ones, blood oozing from their bodies.

'Take them to the sarai,' someone shouted.

Fazal sat in front of the terribly smashed dead body of one of his neighbours in Khushawar. The wheels of the car had run over his stomach, bringing the insides out. The entire place was strewn with body parts, torn clothes, chappals, skullcaps, pieces of turbans and broken sticks.

Fazal saw his father closing the eyes of one more neighbour, lying dead on the ground. His father got up and walked slowly towards the thana. He stopped just short of a few yards from the army men, still standing in upright positions, pointing their rifles at him.

Many more people got up and joined him, standing in rows, silently, their heads held high, their steadfast gazes piercing the police and the army men. That was when a police brought Allah Bakhsh Barqi and Ghulam Rabbani Sethi, the two Congress leaders, to the thana, their hands tied.

The crowd shouted, 'Inqilab Zindabad.'

The two leaders addressed the crowd separately, requesting them to keep calm. 'I'll die before there's a single incident of violence,' Fazal's father assured them. 'Adam tashaddud is our principle. We'll follow that till the last breath.'

As Fazal's father was speaking to the leaders, someone overheard the police officer Isa Monger instructing the armed force to get ready for firing. 'They will fire at us,' he came running to Fazal's father. 'Please ask everyone to leave.'

'No, no one will run away,' Fazal's father thundered. 'They wouldn't stoop down to such level as to kill a group of peaceful people.'

Deputy Commissioner Metcalf pushed back a few army men and came to the front, standing face to face with Fazal's father. 'You're going to instruct your men to leave. And if you dare to disobey me, I'll kill each one of you.'

A few people stepped back. 'Let's leave,' someone said from behind.

Fazal's father turned back and shouted, 'Don't behave in a way that will bring dishonour to Pashtunwali.' There was something in his voice that instilled strength in his people. No one left. 'Behave like a true Muslim. Behave like a Pashtun. Don't run away like cowards. Remember what has been said in the Quran: *Awalam yara alladhin kafaru.* The kafirs don't see the right thing. You're not kafirs. See what's happening around you. Take the side of righteousness, and if need be, lay your lives to protect the honour of your country, your brethren. *Fala tuti huma.* Don't listen to them,' he pointed back towards the police and the army men.

'Stop,' shouted Metcalf. 'Stop, I say, you bastards … '

He was going to say something more when a group of people pushed the crowd and ran towards the front. 'You killed my brother,' shouted one of them. 'We'll not leave you.' He threw a brickbat at Metcalf. The deputy commissioner somehow managed to dodge. He was taken inside the police station, while the army men moved forward, holding the shields to protect themselves from the shower of brickbats that ensued.

Fazal's father tried hard to push the people back. 'Stop it,' he pleaded. 'Don't throw bricks. Be calm.'

'Brick for brick,' shouted someone. 'They killed our brethren. We will kill them.'

In the scuffle, the angry mob overturned the armoured vehicle and set it on fire, all in a matter of seconds. The others couldn't even react.

'Fire,' shouted Metcalf, running out of the thana. The army men pulled the trigger of their rifles. Fazal's father was the first to be hit by the bullet, directly on his chest. He collapsed on the ground. Fazal ran towards him. 'Aba,' he fell on him, holding his father's head on his lap. More people fell onto the ground, being fired at from point blank range. Many more came forward, showing their broad chests. Fazal tried to pull his father out from the heap of bodies, crumbling to the ground, one after the other. By the time he could drag his father to a side, an army man appeared in front of him. He looked up. Before he could do anything, another bullet pierced his father's chest. His body quivered and then fell silent. Fazal tumbled on the lifeless body of his father. Hard boots trampled on him. Someone dragged Fazal and pushed him inside a shop, hiding him behind the wooden counter. That was when he saw his bloody foot. Suddenly, he felt a severe pain. He knew that he had been hit by a bullet too.

Through the slits between the wooden planks that made up the counter of the shop, Fazal watched the carnage that continued for hours. A few bullets crashed against the wall of the small shop and a few pierced through the wooden counter, missing him just by inches. Someone made him put his head down. Through the gaping holes of the counter, he saw three more armoured vehicles screeching to a halt in front of the thana. Many more army men emerged from the cars and fired incessantly at the unarmed people, who kept on coming forward one by one and taking the bullets on their chest.

'Kill all of them,' shouted the deputy commissioner. 'Kill till there's no one left.'

'*Fala tuti huma*,' shouted someone, running towards an army man with the rifle pointed at him. 'Don't listen to them. They are kafirs. They are our enemies. Come forward and lay your lives. They will be soon left with no bullets.'

He couldn't complete. He fell on the ground. '*Fala tuti huma* …' he said a few more times before he fell silent.

☼

For many years later, Fazal would wake up in his sleep, in the middle of the night. The bloody scenes of that day of Santis April, the April of 1930, would haunt him for a very long time.

Zaka likaley de Santis April harcha pa wino;
Che pa de wradz bande werhia we da khwarano winey.

"Santis April"—all have written in letters bloody red;
The day saw easy blood as the poor died and bled ...

Not many could grasp the real meaning of these lines as Fazal did. Whenever he heard such poignant poems written about that day, each word would echo in his head, again and again, bringing back memories of Santis April, memories of his father. He would close his eyes and see his father dying in his lap, with eyes still open, staring at him, as though for eternity.

The words "*Fala tuti huma*", would reverberate in Fazal's mind. His father would often quote those words from the Quran. It had become a slogan of defiance. "*Don't listen to them*".

Little did he know then that the same slogan would be used again, many years later, by a young girl of his family. Surprisingly, then too, it would be used as a slogan of defiance, a rallying cry to rise against the crushing force of the kafirs, and to protect the honour of the country. But, would anyone bring that story back to the Story Teller's Market?

Years later, shortly before Fazal's death, his entire family had come to Khushawar to celebrate his 95th birthday. Among the huge troupe of his children, grandchildren and great grandchildren was the little girl Kubha. Fazal had a special fondness for her, not because she was the youngest of all, but because she would always ask him to tell her new stories of the Qissa Khawani Bazar.

'Why am I not there in any story?' she asked Fazal.

Fazal smiled and pulled her close to him. '*Your qissa would be the greatest of all ...* '

The Khushawari Soundex

(Morning, 5 January 2019. Calcutta)

Kratu and Afsar both stood dumbfounded, overwhelmed by the extremity of the situation. The phone slipped from Kratu's hand. For a moment, he felt as though he had just alighted from a roller coaster ride, feeling giddy, his head spinning. Afsar plunged into the bed, her eyes wide open, her lips trembling, as though a million words, vying to come out, had been suddenly silenced by a stroke.

Afsar suddenly got up and pounced upon Kratu so abruptly that he fell on the bed, unable to keep his balance. She pulled him up by his collar, her heavy breaths falling on him, her eyes red in rage, her whole body shivering.

'I never wanted her to come to India,' she howled. 'This is all because of you.'

She ran away towards the door. Kratu got up swiftly and pulled her back. 'Where are you going?'

'I've to do something. I can't sit here idle in Calcutta. I can no longer trust anyone …' She couldn't say anything more. She thawed like a melted candle, falling on her husband. Her hastened heartbeats travelled into Kratu's body, like the sound of a train reaching someone's ears laid on the track, its vibrations increasing with every passing moment. Kratu helped her to the bed and got her a glass of water.

A collage of many unrelated and random incidents ran fast through Afsar's mind, as she sat on the bed, inanimately.

She remembered how she would stay awake the whole night inside the mosquito net, during their trips to India from the US, lest a mosquito sneaked inside and bit her little girl Kubha, everyone laughing at her overprotectiveness. The same girl, she had seen just a few moments ago, in the blurry images of the video call, was presently being bitten by venomous snakes, all over her body.

She remembered how she had panicked one day when the little Kubha had returned from school with some bruises on her hand. 'Ammi,' Kubha had assured, jumping into her lap, 'I'm fine. I slapped the boy who did this. He started crying.' How many bruises would she have now on her body? Afsar felt as though she was drowning, but still didn't have any energy to move her limbs.

She remembered how much Kubha had been scared the first time she had had her periods. How much she would be bleeding now …

The blurry images played again and again in Afsar's mind, in bits and pieces. Kubha was lying on a takhtposh, naked … Her hands were held tightly … Her head was hanging from the edge of the narrow wooden bed … Her mouth was tied with a cloth …

Afsar couldn't but see the images she struggled so hard to cut off. Suddenly, she gathered all the energy within her and tried to get up. Kratu, walking up and down the room, ran to her. She held his hand.

'Krotu,' she mumbled, between her fast breaths, 'she was trying to say something. I'm sure she was trying to say something … '

'I'm not getting you. Her mouth was tied,' Kratu sat beside her.

'She was trying to sing … '

Kratu didn't wait for her to complete. He jumped up on his feet and looked around for something.

'Where's the damn phone?' he shouted.

He ran around the room hastily. He threw everything off the side-table. He hurled the pillows off the bed. He pulled the bed sheet by its corner and shook it, scattering a few things onto the floor.

'Where's the phone?' he kept on shouting.

Suddenly, he stepped on something and almost slipped.

'You've stepped on it,' Afsar screamed.

Kratu picked the phone from the floor. 'I think the entire call has been recorded. Parush had asked me to keep the auto recorder on.'

He checked the different apps in the phone hastily, taking more time than usual.

'Yes, here it is,' he said excitedly, pressing the "play" button of the recorder. 'It recorded only the audio …'

"*Am I speaking to Mr Kratu Sen?*"

"*Yes, yes, this is Kratu. We've been waiting for your call. We're ready to do anything. Please don't harm our daughter. We'll hand over everything to you.*"

"*What's the hurry? We still have some time before the conference starts.*"

"*No, we'll not attend the conference.*"

"*Good. By the way, isn't your wife around?*"

Kratu fast forwarded the recording till Afsar's shrieks drowned all other sound.

'That's it,' shouted Afsar. 'Can't you hear Kubha's voice?'

'Yes, I do. But there's too much noise.'

'Listen to it properly.'

Kratu did hear Kubha's voice. He had turned his eyes away from the screen during the call. Was there anything more punishing for a father, he thought, than seeing his daughter in that condition? But this was not the time, he knew, to ponder over such thoughts.

'Yes,' he said hurriedly, 'you're correct.'

'She has been always very good at this. I'm sure she's trying to sing out something. Find out the notes she's singing.'

'Wait, let me extract her voice.'

He thanked Parush for the limited access to the cloud he had given him, for testing the beta versions of a lot of advanced vigilance and spying applications that Parush was working on. Immediately, he connected to the cloud through the retinal password and looked for the sound extractor application which, he remembered Parush had said, could segregate even the sound of a particular instrument from a hundred-piece orchestra. All it needed was a sample of the sound. He thought for a while. He needed a sample of Kubha's voice in order to extract it from the recorded audio of the call.

'Do you have any of the voice memos she sends you every day?' Kratu asked.

Afsar ran towards the side-table and searched for her phone. It was lying on the floor. She lifted the phone, but it slid through her fingers and fell again. Kratu came running and picked it up. He emailed the last voice memo saved in the phone to his email id. He threw it on the bed and downloaded the voice memo in his mobile. The cloud had already logged him out. He logged in again with the retinal password and uploaded the voice memo, which would work as a sample for Kubha's voice. He clicked on the "extract" button of the application. The best-in-class Performance Cloud Servers sieved through the millions of bytes of audio data and culled out Kubha's voice in no time.

As the extracted voice played in the phone, the timbre and pitch of each note barely concealed Kubha's agony and despondency. Kratu broke down.

'I wish she had shouted at the top of her voice,' he cried, holding a speechless and petrified Afsar tightly with his hands. He had seen only snippets of the shaky images on the screen of his phone when the caller had turned the camera on Kubha. The moment Afsar had seen Kubha's face—her eyes hovering, her head dangling, her mouth tied—she became hysteric. She shrieked frantically. Kratu had run to the corner of the room. With his fists clenched, he fumed like a fierce lion, held up in a cage.

Kratu shook off his helplessness. He knew he didn't have much time in hand. The conference would start in a few hours.

He played the extracted audio in his phone. 'Now it's much better. Yes, she's actually humming as good as she can with her mouth tied.'

'Let me get the notes?' Afsar shovelled off the thick layers of ice that had frozen her thoughts. 'Play it from the very beginning.'

'I don't know if we've the extracted audio from the beginning.' He dragged the position bar of the audio player to the start and resumed the clip.

Afsar listened to the audio for a few times. It was 45-seconds long and one particular pattern repeated many times.

'Krotu, get me a piece of paper,' Afsar said in haste, playing the repetitive pattern many times. By the time Kratu got a blank sheet and a pen, Afsar had started humming the tune.

'Yes, it's G major.' She took the paper and started scribbling on it. 'That's her scale.'

"<u>Pa</u> Ni Ma Ma Sa Dha," she jotted down, writing the first note "Pa" in the lower octave with an underline.

Each of the 14 musical notes—seven in each octave—of a major scale represents one of 14 letters of Devanagari, two vowels and 12 consonants. In the scheme of things, any text, when represented only with these 14 letters, could be actually sung, rather than spoken.

This technique had been in vogue forever in Khushawar, the ancestral home of Afsar's family. When Kratu had learned of it for the first time, he was awestruck, wondering at the ingenuity of such a simple way of codifying a spoken language. He even came up with a name for the technique. He called it the Khushawari Soundex, in line with the American Soundex, a phonetic algorithm developed in the early twentieth century, for simplifying names in English. The American Soundex used a simple technique of representing similar sounding letters with a single symbol. Accordingly, it gave the numeric symbol "1" to the labial letters "b", "f", "p" and "v", all of which needed the lips to pronounce, hence sounding similar.

'The note "Pa" in the lower octave stood for the letter "pa"…' Afsar started decoding the sequence.

'There's a pause after every two notes,' Kratu pointed out.

'Yes, that's true. So, if you replace each note with one of the 14 letters it represents, we get "pala tata ama" for "P̲a Ni Ma Ma Sa Dha".' Afsar repeated the words "pala tata ama" a few times to herself. 'It doesn't sound like anything we say commonly,' she observed, leaning against the wall. 'Krotu, we don't have time to do it manually. When I was Kubha's age, I could instantly decode anything like this. Now I'm out of touch. I can't do it fast. Do you have the programme handy?'

'Wait a minute … ' Kratu had already started working on his phone. 'It's in the cloud. I haven't used the programme in a long time.'

As Kratu accessed the latest version of the eponymous programme, Khushawari Soundex, from the cloud, Afsar tried to decode the text. The letter "pa", she said to herself, stood for both "pa" and "fa", and "la" could be both "la" and "ra". Often intermediate vowels and "h" sounds are removed. So "pala" could be the Hindi "pahali", meaning first, and also the Urdu "falak", meaning heaven or sky.

'Yes, I've got the programme,' Kratu said excitedly. 'Let me feed "pala tata ama" to the programme and ask it to decode the text in pure Hindi and Urdu.'

Kratu's excitement was short lived. 'It's not making any sense,' he said apprehensively.

'What are the sentences you're getting with "pahali" and "falak"?' Afsar asked. She was getting impatient.

'*Pahali tuti umeed*, the first broken hope.'

'That's nonsense. What's next?'

'*Pahala tuta am*.'

'What sort of programme have you made?' Afsar rebuked. 'The first fallen mango? What's with "falak"?'

'*Falak tuta ummat*. What does that mean?'

'Heaven fallen tribe. This too doesn't make any sense. What else can "pala" be?' Afsar dragged Kratu close and started banging him on his chest with her closed fist. That was what she did whenever she was tense. Kratu pulled his wife towards him and hugged her, struggling to be calm. Nesting Afsar's head on his shoulder and playing his fingers through her hair, he took a few long breaths. Had there ever been a morning as bad as this? He wondered.

'Krotu,' Afsar pushed him. 'Try Arabic.'

'What?'

'Yes, Arabic. She used to often use Arabic to confuse me. I was not that comfortable coding Arabic texts. We never did that when I was young. My father used to play with us with Urdu ghazals and we could code and decode that very fast. But Kubha was very fast with Arabic. "Pala" can be "fala" in Arabic. It means "don't".'

Kratu was already at work. But, before he could change the context of the Information Retrieval sub-programme to Arabic, Afsar pushed him.

'Hell!' she shouted. 'How could I be so dumb?'

'What happened?'

'It's *fala tuti huma.* "Pala tata ama" can't be anything else. These are the concluding words of a verse from the 29th chapter of the Quran. My grandfather used these words as a slogan during the Independence struggle. During the last few years of his life, he had become very close to Kubha. You know how she would eagerly wait for our annual trips to Khushawar during the Christmas holidays and stick to him the whole day, listening to his stories. It can't be anything else.'

'Let me play the entire audio again. Get all the notes.'

Kratu played the entire audio recording a few more times in his phone. Afsar jotted down the musical notes and the corresponding letters they denoted.

'Here is the full text: *Abalamajala aladana kapala. Jada laushala bamalasha ba-amana. Pala tata ama. Pala tata ama. Pala tata ama.*' She passed on the piece of paper to Kratu.

'Many words may be joined. The first word "abalamajala" is very likely "abalama jala" and "abalama" may be "awalam" in Arabic, meaning "don't". And I've a feeling that all these are Quranic verses. Kubha has an uncanny knack in playing around with various lines from the Quran.'

'Let me change the context to Quranic texts. Give me a moment. I have never tried that. But the programme should take it. I just need to feed a good site that has the transliterated texts in English.'

'Use quran.com.'

Kratu didn't take much time. In just a few moments he turned the screen of his phone to Afsar.

'*Awalam yara alladhin kafaru. Jahadaka litush'rika bi ma lasya bihi il'mun. Fala tuti huma,*' Afsar read out the texts. 'The first sentence is from the 30th verse of the 21st chapter and the last two from the eighth verse of the 29th chapter.'

'What do they mean?'

'*People, who disbelieve, can't see. They fight to make you associate with me, that of which you have no knowledge. Don't believe them.*' Afsar looked at Kratu. 'What do you think she's trying to say?'

'*People, who disbelieve, can't see …* ' Kratu repeated the words. 'What's the second line?'

'*They fight to make you associate with me, that of which you have no knowledge.*'

'They fight to make you associate with me, that of which you have no knowledge,' Kratu muttered the line a few times. 'Is she trying to say that we shouldn't disbelieve her? That we've no idea of what's going on? That we shouldn't be blind in not seeing the reality? That we shouldn't listen to the ones trying to blackmail us?'

'What do you mean?' Afsar asked with a sudden firmness in her voice. It was not that she didn't know what Kratu was trying to say. She herself had realized the same. But somehow she was not ready to come to terms with it. How could she not do anything to save her daughter? She herself had seen what Kubha was undergoing. If they could do so much, would they think even a bit before killing her? But then, Afsar deliberated, why would Kubha take so much pain to convey the message? It couldn't be that she had done that in the nick of time, without any planning. She would have had to prepare herself enough to garner the vigour and resolve to do such a thing. Afsar tried to fathom what all she would have gone through, withstanding the trauma and still having the mental strength to hum the right notes. It shattered Afsar to have realized that Kubha had known that her parents would see her in that wretched state.

While a lot of jumbled thoughts were strutting through her mind, Kartu too didn't have any answer.

'What do you mean?' Afsar asked again.

'Afsar,' Kratu said hesitantly, 'I'm not sure what we should do.'

'Okay,' she suddenly seemed to have made up her mind. 'There's no good reason to go to the conference. Let us give away everything they are asking for. I don't care for what truth we're going to share with the world. I give a damn to what a few lunatics are going to do with that monument. I just don't care if there are riots everywhere in India.' She left the room.

In a few minutes she returned with a plastic folder and threw it on the bed. The cover of the folder was open. A few leaves of the delicate birch bark manuscript, her father had recovered from Khushawar and handed over to her in person just a week before his gruesome death, spilled out of the folder.

'Give it to them.'

'Are you sure we should do this?'

'Why not?' Afsar's voice rose a few decibels up. 'I know my daughter. She's very adamant. Just because she's asking us not to listen to them, it doesn't mean she would be safe.'

Kratu didn't say anything. That infuriated her. 'What the hell are you thinking?' she shouted. 'Have you lost all sensibilities? It's our daughter … '

'She wouldn't be safe even if we listen to them.' Kratu interrupted.

Afsar pounced on him. He was dashed against the wall. The phone fell from his hand. He was more surprised than rattled at Afsar's sudden outburst.

The moment Afsar had seen Kubha in that condition, a few minutes ago, she had instantly become hysteric. He himself had become so much mentally disoriented and maladjusted that for a moment his thought process stopped totally. The video call lasted for less than a minute. The reason why the call had been made, and why they had been shown their only daughter of 20 years in that state was very clear in no time. The message couldn't have been crisper.

It was only a short while since the video call had come, and in this short period of time, Kratu felt, he had, perhaps for the first time in his life, realized how long each second could be— really a billion times longer than a nano second that they all talk about so commonly in electronics.

Afsar had calmed down soon, after the initial frenzy. Her present outburst was so sudden that Kratu was dumbfounded. She fumed in anger, pushing him against the wall, trembling.

Kratu's phone rang. Afsar left him immediately and almost like a reflex action picked the phone up from the floor. Her eyes glowed when she stared at the phone. Kratu too had seen the name flashing on the screen.

'Parush,' she stammered, 'where are you?'

'Listen to me carefully,' Parush spoke over the phone, with no hint of excitement or fear. Over the years, Afsar had got well acquainted to the ways of Parush. Presently, his coldness assured her. She knew that in this particular avatar, cold and ruthless, Parush could be as dreadful as possible. And this was the time she needed someone dreadful, inhuman, to save her daughter.

'*Save your Kubha.*' Afsar herself might not have noticed how naturally the words "your Kubha" had come out of her. She knew doubtless that, when it came to Kubha, Parush could do things no one else could even fathom. It didn't matter to her what people had already started saying, of course not openly, about the unusual relationship between Kubha and him.

'I'm already in Agra,' Parush said calmly. 'Trust me. And trust your daughter too. *Don't listen to them.*'

'Do you know of the call?' Afsar couldn't hide her shock.

'Afsar, I don't have any time now. Get ready for the conference. Do exactly as I say. I'll call you again. Nothing is going to happen to Kubha.' He disconnected the call.

'Agra?' Afsar muttered to herself.

'What?' asked Kratu.

The Beginning

(Morning, 5 January 2019. Hasht Bihisht)

How much Kubha had wanted to see her mother. She had tried to lift her head when she heard her mother's shrieks, but someone thwarted her effort. She was hit on her head, hard, so hard that she felt a severe pain in her neck. She gulped some saliva, mixed with the particles of dust and sand that fell into her mouth from the dirty cloth with which her mouth was tied.

She closed her eyes and tried to see her mother. The piercing sound of her mother's wails was presently the only go-between that connected the two of them. The sound gave her the assurance, or rather a feeling of it, that she no longer had to bear all the affliction alone and that there were people to cry for her. The sound made her feel as though her mother had come out of the phone, like a genie that emerges out of a lamp and showers boons.

Ever since she had been brought here, the greatest fear that had inflicted her was that of dying here, all alone. She was intelligent enough to understand that in reality she had to get out of here, all alone, that she had to find a way out of the myriad mesh of the kucha-i salamat, all alone. But even then, the feeling of assurance and hope brought in a great force within her. She started humming the tune she had learned the previous night. She wished her mother would stop crying and listen carefully to her. She knew her mother needed to listen to the tune only once to get the notes correctly. She raised her voice, as much as she could, with the only hope that it would reach her mother's ears. She repeated the last part of the tune many times. Even if her mother missed the whole tune, she tried to convince herself, the last part itself should be explicit enough to convey the message.

Suddenly, the phone went silent. And in no time Kubha was hurled into the side room. The professor entered the room, behind her.

☼

Daulat Parwar had had an inkling of what could happen that day. Positioning himself correctly in the small octagonal side room of the hasht bihisht, he had been carefully listening to everything that happened in the big central hall. That Shamsur would call the girl's mother, and make her witness everything, was comprehensible. But he never could have envisaged what actually would have happened there, in the room, during the call.

The previous night, Daulat had heard the girl humming a tune, before she might have fallen asleep. She, too, would have known what could happen the next morning, he felt. Otherwise, how could she have behaved in that way? It was not that every time she would shatter the room with her shrieks and cries. It had bewildered him how she always maintained such a stoic silence amidst such brutality. Even if her mouth would be tied every time, he would still expect a moan, or some physical signs of protest. The girl had an unbelievable level of physical endurance, he knew. But even having known that, he was astounded when the girl started humming the same tune she had been practicing the previous night, while her mother cried hysterically over the phone.

Lying there on the cold floor of the dark room, his hands and legs tied tightly, Daulat wondered why someone would try to sing in that condition. The girl had anyway amazed him in many a way over the past one day.

The heavy wood of the front door of the neighbouring square room scratched against the hard floor, making a screeching sound. Daulat knew that the girl's ordeal was over, for now. After the door closed, Daulat heard the voice of Shamsur.

'I think this will be enough. The conference starts in four hours from now. Without your mother, the entire thing would be a flop. Your mother will lose all her credibility. No one is going to believe her next time. And she will anyway not have anything to show, as she is going to hand over everything to my person. I don't think we need you any more.'

'She may still go ahead and attend the conference,' the girl said. The calmness in her voice stunned Daulat, once again.

Shamsur laughed. 'No, she wouldn't do that. That's what I think and I'm rarely wrong in any such judgement. Anyway, I came here to let you know that you can leave in the next half an hour, through that door.'

Daulat knew Shamsur would have pointed to the back door of the room, opposite to the main one that led to the central hall.

'If you really manage to escape,' Shamsur continued, 'that would mean the Almighty is mehrban on you and if He bestows His kindness, who am I to stop you? Inshallah, if He wills, you will be out of here.'

Daulat knew Shamsur would have smiled slyly at having said that.

'Thanks,' said the girl, not an iota of fear or helplessness in her voice. 'Can I get my dress back now?'

Daulat realized she had been naked all the time, in this extreme cold.

'Your dress has been burned, lest someone, out of sympathy, gave it back to you.'

Daulat closed his eyes and let out a silent sigh.

'I'll get you a torch. You'll need it. It's totally dark out there. The battery wouldn't last more than two hours.'

Soon, Daulat heard the sound of the front door of the room, closing loudly.

☼

Once the professor had shut the door from outside, Kubha ran towards the side door of the room. She knocked on it, softly, expecting the person behind the door to speak.

'Are you there?' she whispered.

'Yes,' she heard the voice.

'Can you please explain the 313 technique once more? I'll note it down.' She picked up the paper and pen which the professor had brought with him the previous day.

As the person spoke from behind the door, Kubha tried to draw a probable plan of a section of the bhulbhulaiya, with its series of octagonal rooms with eight doors, marking the rooms and doors with numbers.

'Entering into an octagonal room with eight doors,' she repeated, 'I've to exit through the door number "3" to the left. Then, going straight, once I'm in the room number "3", I'll leave

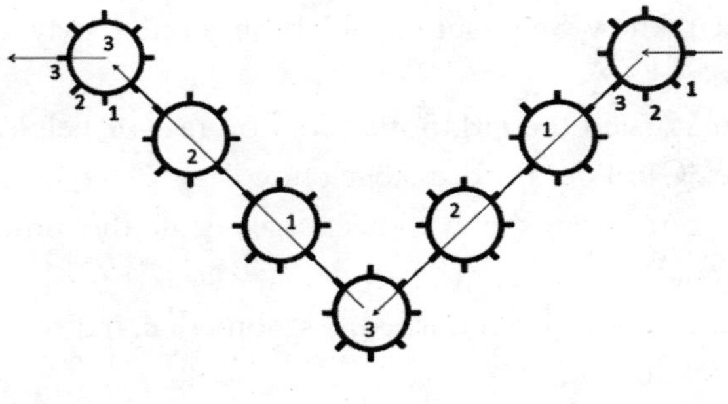

Kubha tried to draw a probable plan of a section of the bhulbhulaiya.

"1" door to the right and exit from the next. Finally, when I once again get into the room number "3", I exit again through the door number "3", to the left. So, it's rather a 33-1-33 rule, not 313.'

'Whatever you say. I was taught like that by my father. *As long as you understand it, it doesn't matter what you call it by.*'

It sounded philosophical to Kubha. She wondered how much a professor could be different from someone she knew was barely literate.

'Why're you not escaping too?' she asked. 'You know everything.'

'I can't leave this place to them. They will destroy everything. I'll fight to death to save har ajir, har sang. Every brick and stone you see here is a part of me. I live with it. I die with it. I belong to the family of the Parwars, the protectors. I've to protect this. I hope the saruj is strong enough. It has held tight the buland foundation for centuries. If it crumbles down now, it must be after my eyes have been shut for ever. I'm committed to its safe keep, in life, in death.'

'I don't know who you are. I don't know if I'll ever see you. Shukriya. Thanks for helping me. If ever I get my turn to help you, I'll do it with my life.' She couldn't control her tears.

She returned to the mattress and lay on her back. She felt a severe pain around her groin. That was when she realized she was bleeding, badly. She felt dizzy. She got up and leaned against the cold wall. She started shivering frantically, breathing heavily. She struggled to remain awake. *She had to be alive*, she reminded herself repeatedly. She remembered her namesake, the other Kubha, her great grandmother, who, she had heard from her father many a time, would always say, '*Don't stop flowing. A river never stops flowing, come what may.*'

She too, like all other in her family, had grown up with inspiring stories of this enigmatic "other" Kubha. Presently, just the fact that the both of them shared the same name gave her a fanciful sense of courage and fortitude. What a bitter coincidence, she realized, that the both of them had to go through the same sort of ordeal. The elder one had endured everything to save her children. But, what for, she wondered, had she been made to endure all these? Did the belief, that all her present sufferings might save her country from a huge catastrophe in the near future, make her stronger, more resilient?

☼

Kubha was alerted by the clicking sound. She had in her hand the piece of paper on which she had made the drawing. She knew it was just a matter of few seconds before the main door would be opened. She tore off a part of the paper, which had the drawing. She crumbled the remaining part and threw it off to the corner of the room. By the time the door opened, she had already managed to crush the drawing into a small lump and hide it under her tongue. Initially, she had thought of hiding it under the mattress. But then, she realized at the nick of time, taking it out might not be easy if there was anyone else in the room.

The professor sat on the chair he had brought with him. He took out a torch from a side bag hung from his shoulder and kept it on the floor. He also took out a vintage table clock and placed it beside the torch. Kubha stared at the clock. It showed 7:45. Was it morning or evening? Kubha had no way of finding out. She was disoriented, both in time and space, she realized.

'It's time for the beginning of the end of all of it.'

The professor's cold words pierced through Kubha's ears, like pointed snowflakes. His deep eyes appeared fearsome under the thick glasses of his heavy specs.

'Thanks for your cooperation. You're an intelligent girl. That's why you'll survive a little longer, as long as you can sustain yourself.'

He got up. He searched for something in his bag. He took out a bunch of keys and went towards the back door. He opened the old, big lock of the heavy door and stood near it, as though waiting for something.

In a few moments, Kubha heard a loud voice, coming from the central room. Someone read a line from the Quran. A louder chorus followed: '*Fa-idha laqitumu alladhina kafaru, fadarba al-riqabi*. So when you meet those who disbelieve, strike their necks.'

The professor pushed the door open, the unusual chorale submerging the creaking sound of the old door.

'*If Allah had willed, He could have taken vengeance Himself. But He ordered armed struggle …* '

The professor waited for the pause to whisper to Kubha. 'Let the prayers come to an end. Wait for 15 more minutes,' he pointed to the clock, 'and then leave.'

'*Those who are killed in the cause of Allah, never will He waste their deeds …* '

Kubha stared at the professor as he walked away, carrying the chair he had brought with him, leaving her alone in the room, for one last time. Kubha closed her eyes and tried to free herself of the surge of thoughts that whirled through her mind. If only she had had a lens, she thought, she would convert the dazzling thoughts into fire. All she needed presently was the fire—the fire to thrive, the fire to drive, the fire to survive.

The sound of knocks shook Kubha. She opened her eyes and stared at the side door, which had become a symbol of hope for her. An eerie calmness made her feel awkward, as if it was a bad omen, the silence before a big storm. That was when she realized to her horror that the prayer had stopped outside.

'When did it stop?' she got up from the mattress.

'May be a minute back. Get ready,' said the unknown person behind the wall.

She felt the severe pain in her groin, again. She could barely walk. As she dragged herself towards the torch, drops of blood trickled down her legs. She felt thirsty. She ran towards the empty mug. She tried to bend down to pick it up, but fell on the hard floor. She grabbed the mug and licked its inside. It was all dry. She swallowed a few gulps of saliva.

Kubha leaned against the wall and struggled to keep her eyes open. She felt as though she had been awake for a hundred nights and finally, a slumber had been engulfing her, slowly, like a mist. She could hear the feeble sound of knocks, as if someone was calling her, from far away. The knocks grew louder.

'Leave now,' she could hear a voice.

Suddenly, as though someone had shaken her up, she jerked into life. The knocks on the door were loud enough, so loud that she feared they could be heard from outside, from the central big room.

'Yes, I'm leaving.'

She got up again, biting her lips hard. She stared at the clock. It was close to eight. It should be 15 minutes since the prayer ended, she guessed.

'Thank you,' she said, turning towards the door, lifting the torch from the floor.

It was not that all her pains had subsided. But somehow, she realized, an unknown force was pushing her.

'Don't run,' she heard the person speak. 'Though there are air pipes all along the way, still, you'll find it difficult to breathe. Don't get exhausted. You've to travel some four and a half thousand guz.'

'What's that?' she asked, getting close to the back door, through which she had to leave, soon.

'It's something like four kilometres, I think. That's the distance you've to cover before you get the first way out of the tunnel. You can't miss that. Suddenly you'll be able to breathe very comfortably. Now go!'

Kubha stared at the side door, for the last time, took a long breath, and stepped out of the room. It was pitch dark outside. She switched the torch on. A dark, narrow, blind alley was all she had for herself. Was she standing at the threshold of death? She thought. Was it the beginning or the end?

She switched off the torch to save the battery and moved forward, slowly, carefully, step by step, not turning back even for once.

'*You have to flow, like a river. Never look back* ...' She felt as though the other Kubha was talking to her.

☼

Shamsur called for an emergency meeting in the central room. Without any introduction, he started speaking.

'Someone among you has helped her escape. Someone has opened the lock of the back door of the room.'

He stared at everyone standing in front of him. He turned towards the one that stood farthest from him. When it came to discipline, he could be as ruthless as possible. And for him, discipline meant obeying him, blindly, not asking any question, ever. This young boy could have been a great asset to him. But he had been asking too many uncomfortable questions to Shamsur. There was no other way to get rid of him, he knew.

'You were the one,' Shamsur talked directly to him, 'who would take the girl to the room from here. And you are also the one who never touched her. Sympathy is not a trait in our world.'

'What do you mean?' the boy protested.

Shamsur kept quiet for a few seconds.

'There can't be anyone else who would help her.'

'You could have also done it.' His calm response shocked not only Shamsur, but also the rest.

Not much later, Daulat Parwar heard the sound of a gunshot.

Yamuna Expressway

(Night, 3 January 2019. Delhi)

The red Swift moved slowly on the Nelson Mandela Marg, skirting the western boundary of the Jawaharlal Nehru University campus. When the car approached the west gate of the campus, in the Paschimabad area of the university premise, the driver stared at his clumsy co-passenger, seated beside him on the front seat. It was a few minutes past nine on a foggy wintry night in the month of January. The neighbourhood was sparse and the surroundings not visible beyond a few metres. The hazy headlights of the few cars that passed by created a misty glow in the dense fog.

The sleepy guard opened the gate, as he would do, perhaps, on any other day. But the driver didn't fail to notice the silhouette of an armed guard scanning everything from inside the small security room. He exchanged glances with his co-passenger. As the guard closed the gate behind him, he knew the smart sticker fixed to the number plate would have already registered the return of the car to the campus. Every car in the campus had to mandatorily get the sticker with the university hologram permanently affixed to the number plate. Without the sticker, the driver knew, the car would have been put through a very strict security check, which would doubtless jeopardize their entire plan.

Entering into the campus, the driver turned left towards the Paschimabad Towers, the multistoried faculty residence, and drove slowly. Upon reaching the basement parking of one of the towers, he brought the car to a stop in front of an identical red Swift with the same registration number, sans the sticker. His co-passenger got down immediately and unscrewed the number plate of their car. He promptly replaced the number plate of the other car with that of theirs. They left the parking lot as smoothly as they had come just a few minutes ago.

'*In records, our car would be here, in the parking, all the while we would be doing our task*,' the driver smiled as he approached the gate.

He took a sharp left turn towards the Paschimabad Water Tank and arrived on the JNU Ring Road. A little ahead, where a narrow road forked to the right towards the Special Centre for Sanskrit Studies, he parked the car on the curb and waited patiently. Not much later could they see the contour of a girl, walking slowly towards the Ring Road, from the Special Centre for Sanskrit Studies.

The driver pressed the gas pedal of the car softly as his co-passenger covered his face with a mask. As the car approached the fork, the girl too had come quite close to it. The co-passenger silently opened the door and alighted from the car. In the next few seconds, he stealthily walked towards the girl, took out a small cylinder from the deep pocket of his overcoat, sprayed a heavy dose of nitrous oxide on her and dragged her towards the boot of the car as she gradually collapsed, having inhaled a good amount of the strong sedative. The driver had already opened the boot. In no time, they secured the heavily sedated girl inside and reached the basement parking of the Paschimabad Towers, where the number plates were again swapped.

Ten minutes later, a red Swift left the JNU campus through the main gate. The smart tracker at the main gate didn't raise any alarm. It recorded the exit of a professor's registered car, which had returned to the campus sometime ago and had been at the designated parking space for some time.

☼

The live-in senior warden of the Yamuna Hostel didn't find Kubha in her room during her night rounds. She tried calling her on her mobile, but it was switched off. She enquired about Kubha among her friends but no one seemed to have seen her after the dinner.

The warden was perhaps the first one to realize that Kubha was missing from the hostel. She immediately informed the security, the provost and the dean of students. A frantic search ensued within the JNU campus. The nearby police stations at Vasant Vihar, Hauz Khas and Mehrauli alerted all the beat constables on patrol.

After half an hour, the warden called Kubha's parents in Calcutta. Afsar, Kubha's mother, called Parush immediately, and in a short while, Parush was zipping through the Yamuna Expressway.

☼

The special SWAT team that Parush had returned from the US to head, on a special request from the PMO, Prime Minister's Office, had suddenly intercepted a communication originating from an unregistered iridium satellite phone. Enough efforts had been made to heavily encrypt the communication data. But, the satellite phone tracking system that Parush had put in place was able to decrypt most of it in real time. The call originated from the iridium device at 9:45 in the night, from within the JNU campus. Lasting just a few seconds, it was too short to be deciphered for its entire content.

'Sir, isn't it a very unusual place for such a thing?' asked the person who called Parush to inform about the interception.

'Yes, very unusual,' Parush agreed. 'Track the movement of the device. Where is it now?'

'The phone was switched off immediately after the call. We don't have any further GPS data. But we'll get to know the moment the phone is switched on again. Sir, these people seem to be very smart. The encryption was very good. I just needed a few more seconds of communication data to decipher the entire call …'

'Where is the phone registered?' Parush interrupted.

'This time, it's the Principality of Sealand,' the person laughed.

'What's that?'

'It's a self-declared principality on sea, some six kilometre away from the coast line of south eastern UK. No country in the world has officially recognized it though. It's claimed to be the smallest state in the world by its owner, the Bates family.'

'Is it possible to find out the previous locations of the device?'

'It will take some time.'

Parush knew Kubha's phone might be switched off as well. He had talked to her around the same time, and she had mentioned her battery was running low. Still, he called her, perhaps like a reflex action, as though she would know something about that mysterious call made from JNU. Her phone was, indeed, switched off.

Parush called someone else. 'Is everything fine?' he asked.

'Yes, sir,' came the prompt reply. 'The entire boundary wall is secured. Nothing can cross over it.'

'Are you also keeping a tab on the vehicles entering and leaving the campus?'

'Each car is being checked,' assured the person on the other side. 'It's impossible for anyone to sneak in or out.'

A few hours later, around two in the morning, Parush got a call from Afsar, Kubha's mother. He was surprised to see her name flashing on the screen, at that time.

'Parush, Kubha is missing from the JNU campus,' Afsar howled. 'Her phone is switched off. Do whatever you can. I want my daughter back. Nothing should happen to her,' she said in a frenzy, in a single breath.

☼

Parush's car zoomed by on the Akbar Road. In the middle of the night, it took him just a few minutes to reach the Bombay Fruits & Vegetables at Connaught Place, the camouflage for the office of the hi-tech SWAT team. The car screeched to a stop in front of the shop. He slid into the shop through a small opening between the shutters of the door. Rakesh, his assistant, was waiting behind the door. Parush had been talking to him continuously on his way to Connaught Place. Closing the door from inside, they rushed to the claustrophobic room at the back side, originally meant to be a space for stocking the shop's provisions.

'The phone is switched off,' Rakesh informed, as Parush sat in front of a big screen with a number of small windows flashing varying waveforms, scrolling texts, beeping dots on maps and live images from various parts of the country.

'It's more than four hours since the call,' Parush said, staring at the screen. 'If we assume that the call and Kubha's going missing are connected, the duration of four hours is enough to travel more than 200 kilometres away from Delhi, even if anyone drove quite slow.'

'Are you sure she was kidnapped?'

'The coincidences are many. I found out from Airtel that her mobile phone was switched off exactly at 9:45 pm and the last location of the phone was the JNU campus. My gut feeling is that the kidnappers took her at 9:45 pm from the campus. Either her phone had already been dead by then, or they would have switched it off immediately and made that short 10-second call from the iridium phone, perhaps to inform that the "work" had been done.'

'Till we intercept the next phone call, we can't say which way the kidnappers have gone. The distance of 200 kilometres from Delhi could mean many places ...'

Parush checked each application thoroughly to ensure that there was no scope for error. Any normal decryption application needed at least one minute of transmission data to decipher an intercepted satellite call. But Parush had put in place a system which could decipher very short calls, lasting just a few seconds. He was not happy that the system had failed to decipher the previous call fully, apart from extracting only the GPS information.

'Initially I hadn't thought they would do anything to Kubha,' Parush said, checking a few things on the big screen in front of him. 'Rather I was concerned about Afsar, her mother.'

'Why?' Rakesh asked, taking his stare off the pad he had been working on.

'In the recent past, three people had similar deaths, all very gruesome, in three different countries. All of them were connected to a particular thing Afsar has been researching on lately.'

'What's the research about?' Rakesh kept the pad aside and sat erect on the chair.

'It's about Khushawari carpets.'

Suddenly, the big window at the centre beeped. Parush and Rakesh became alert.

'The phone has been switched on,' Rakesh was excited, as he tracked another small window in the corner. 'The device is near Mathura, on the Yamuna Expressway, a few kilometres before the Mathura Toll Plaza. It's travelling at a speed of 135 kilometre per hour ...'

'Silence,' Parush interrupted, as the main window displayed a series of sliding horizontal waveforms. Soon the waveforms became static. 'This call lasted 20 seconds.'

Rakesh clicked on an on-screen button on a miniature display on the table which mimicked the huge screen on the wall. The electro magnet woofers of the Focal Grande Utopia speakers vibrated with the sounds of the different audio waves generated out of the various decryption algorithms. A total of 20 algorithms had processed the intercepted audio from the call and created as many audible sound waves. Parush and Rakesh listened carefully to each of the audios, till Parush asked Rakesh to replay a particular one again and again.

'This seems to be the most accurate. Get rid of the noise totally and try to segregate the human voice,' Parush instructed, hanging his head behind.

Rakesh fed the audio to the latest speech recognition software and played the processed audio. This time the voice was quite clear. Parush noted down the few words he could identify correctly.

'*Hasht Bihisht at Bagh-i Filhal*?' he stared at Rakesh, puzzled.

'What's that?'

Parush had already got up from the chair.

'Should I stop all vehicles at the toll gate?' Rakesh asked.

'No. That will make the kidnappers alert. Kubha may be there in the car. They can do anything. Fake an accident on the Expressway some 40 kilometres away from Mathura and slow down the traffic. You've only 10 minutes.'

'That's not a problem,' Rakesh was already working on his pad. 'I see a 96 wheel trailer driven by a Volvo FH16, carrying four dump trucks, at a distance of 35 kilometres from the Mathura toll gate. It's under defense contract and under our surveillance.'

'Get the road blocked by it. Make it look as if the trailer has broken down.'

Parush started putting a few things into a bag.

'Get ready. We're leaving. ASAP.'

☼

Very few people at the AIIMS, All India Institute of Medical Sciences, would have noticed that the Mercedes Benz Sprinter, remodelled as an ambulance, rarely left the parking space. From the outside, there was no way to know that the Sprinter was actually a heavily armoured, ballistic-resistant vehicle with puncture-proof tyres. It served as the mobile office of the SWAT team, whenever needed. The highly secured satellite internet access, with a download speed of 100 mbps, was more than what Parush would generally need, when on the move. The entire computer network inside the vehicle was connected, through a dedicated cloud, to the fastest possible servers. In addition, the the vehicle also had bunks for two people to sleep comfortably, a dry kitchenette, a large refrigerator with enough provisions to survive for a week and a water-free Ecoflow composting toilet.

Presently, Parush got on to the driver's seat and pressed the gas pedal. Rakesh, seated behind, amidst the most hi-tech surveillance paraphernalia, was connected to the video feed from the Mathura and Jewar toll plazas for the past two hours. As Parush zoomed through the empty Mathura Road, towards Noida, Rakesh checked the background of each car, accessing the online RTO database.

'Among the cars which went through both the toll gates,' Rakesh said over the intercom, 'two were back to back at both places. One of the cars belongs to Raju Salim.'

'That notorious MLA from the Rashtriya Dalit Party?' Parush asked, paying the toll at the Noida Toll Bridge.

'Yes. And what's interesting is that, the position of his mobile yesterday at around 9:45 in the night was Hauz Khas, not far from the JNU campus, from where the first satellite call was made and …'

'Kubha was kidnapped,' Parush completed. 'That's interesting. What about the other car?'

'The iridium phone is most likely in that car. It's well corroborated by the location and speed we recovered from the GPS data of the intercepted call.'

'How far are the cars from the trailer?'

'It's quite close. They may reach in five minutes. The trailer is blocking the entire road. The patrolling car has already reached the spot. I've talked to the guard. I've asked him to initiate some casual talks with the occupants of both the cars. He will let me know if anything looks suspicious.'

'Are you sure that the kidnappers wouldn't suspect anything?'

'No,' Rakesh assured. 'The guard seems to be very smart.'

Rakesh's phone rang.

'It's the guard.'

He talked for about a minute with the guard and then picked up the intercom.

'It's very strange,' he exclaimed. 'There are four people, including Raju Salim. All of them have come out of their cars. They are now talking to the driver of the trailer. The guard caught a glimpse of the insides of both the cars—a Jaguar XJ L and a Honda CRV—and nothing looked suspicious to him. You can't hide anyone in a CRV. Hiding inside the boot of the Jaguar also seems unlikely.'

'Smart guys,' Parush quipped. 'I should have guessed that they would not take the Yamuna Expressway, the entire stretch of which is under close surveillance … '

He paused, as though he had remembered something.

'Who was at the other end of the last satellite call?' he asked excitedly. 'You need a decoder to even receive the encrypted satellite call.'

'Give me a moment. I should have tracked that too. Really sorry!'

Rakesh turned towards the table with many consoles affixed to it. He retrieved the raw transmission data of the intercepted call and ran a few operations on it. Then, he logged into the live database of CMS, Central Monitoring System, and recovered the relevant call data records.

'The call originated from the satellite phone,' Rakesh spoke over the intercom, 'and ended on a mobile in Bulandshahr. The present location of the same mobile is Aligarh. Both Bulandshahr and Aligarh fall on another route to Agra, parallel to the Yamuna Expressway.'

'Thanks,' Parush said. 'That's what I was expecting too. It's very likely the kidnappers are taking a different route to Agra, while someone, perhaps their mastermind, who's making the satellite calls, is ahead of us on the Yamuna Expressway.'

The mobile phone must be having, Parush thought, an inbuilt hardware-based decoder in order to decode the heavily encrypted satellite calls in real time. Any application-based decoder would be slow and wouldn't be effective for a live communication, unless they made good use of extraordinarily powerful servers, the likes of which were presently accessible only to the defense establishments in India. It hadn't been easy for Parush to put in place a sophisticated system that would do the same for the special SWAT team. The realization that the similar level of sophistication and technology was already available to others as well, worried him.

Parush knew he had a formidable task ahead to accomplish.

☼

Parush pressed the gas pedal harder. As the Sprinter cruised through the straight road at a steady speed of 150 kmph, Rakesh leaned back on his chair, his eyes glued to the central big console in front of him.

'You were saying something about the Khushawari carpets,' Rakesh spoke over the intercom.

'Khushawar is the ancestral place of Afsar's family. It's a small village near Peshawar in Pakistan. A very intriguing thing about the village is that it has been producing some really unique carpets since, I don't know how long. I'm not much knowledgeable about carpets. What Afsar told me is that, the motifs of the Khushawari carpets, the patterns and designs they use, are quite exclusive, though they have many things in common with the Persian and Bokhara carpets.'

As Parush spoke, Rakesh kept a constant eye on the positions of the two mobile phones, which showed as two blinking dots on a map in the central console. The latest information about the location from the CMS fed the GPS system of the Sprinter, showing the positions of the mobiles quite accurately on the map. The one that belonged to MLA Raju Salim was very close to Agra and the other one, on a different route to Agra, was midway between Aligarh and Hathras.

'Afsar's father, Faraz Fareedi, had moved to the US sometime in the '60s,' Parush continued, 'and set up a modest business selling Khushawari carpets. Soon, he sold Persian and Kashmiri carpets too and by the '80s, his company was among the biggest sellers of oriental carpets in the US. Recently, after his wife's death, he moved back to Pakistan, staying in their ancestral house in Khushawar.

'A few months back, someone by the name of Somak Ajai contacted Faraz. You would very well remember him. Yes, it's the same Somak I asked you to find everything about. He was a senior professor of mathematics at the Delhi School of Economics and a linguist by passion. He claimed many Khushawari motifs were exactly same as those of the traditional carpets his folks have been weaving forever in his ancestral village of Kusumpur.'

'Where's Kusumpur?' Rakesh asked.

'It's a nondescript place, some 30 kilometres away from Patna, near the confluence of the Sone and Ganga. Somak told

Faraz that he was researching on the origin of the carpet motifs and that he believed there is a wealth of obscure history hidden in those patterns and designs. Last November, Faraz met Somak in Delhi, when he visited India. The next week both of them were dead, on the same day, in the same manner.'

'You said that there were three deaths.'

'The third person who was also killed on the same day was Sanath Wickramasinghe, a faculty at the Department of Classical Languages at the University of Peradeniya.'

'The name sounds Sri Lankan,' Rakesh sat erect on the chair.

The position of Raju Salim's mobile phone hadn't changed in the past few minutes. Rakesh zoomed into the map to study the Agra neighbourhood where the blinking dot had stopped moving. He noted the name of the hotel in front of which the dot blinked.

'Yes, he was a Sri Lankan. He was from Kandy. He was an expert palaeographer and calligraphist.'

'Palaeographer? What's that?'

'Someone who studies old inscriptions and manuscripts.'

'What's the connection between carpets and old manuscripts?'

'Afsar once said that many carpet motifs have striking similarities with ancient Indian alphabets, now found only in very old inscriptions which are more than 2,000 years old. Somak had known Sanath for a long.'

'Interesting!' Rakesh said, zooming out from the neighbourhood where Raju Salim seemed to have stopped for the night.

Raju had been in the radar of the special SWAT team for quite some time and Rakesh knew Raju didn't have much clout in Agra. It would be logical, he felt, to believe that Raju had checked into a hotel. He checked the location of the other mobile phone. It had just crossed Hathras. Given the average speed, he knew, it would not take more than an hour to reach Agra from there.

The commissioner of police in Agra had already been given the instruction, very precisely. It was very unlikely, he felt, that anyone in the car, which carried the other mobile, would realize it was being trailed, and escorted too.

'But how can you be so sure that all these three murders are connected? After all, the only common thread between them—the carpet thing—seems very harmless.'

'Well, I shouldn't say the carpet is as harmless as you would think it to be,' Parush said. 'I can tell you this much that it's being used maliciously, with a very sinister agenda, which can have very far-reaching repercussions in India and outside. I'll tell you more on that later. We have a lot of work ahead. Coming to your question, as to whether the three murders were connected, consider this: all three were killed on the same day, one in Delhi, one in Kandy and one in Khushawar, and in the exact same way. They all died of severe lye poisoning. They were all made to swallow and inhale large quantities of sodium hydroxide mixed in methanol. Their dead bodies looked grotesque and horrific. Burnt pieces of intestines burst out of their decomposed bodies. Their throats were badly swollen. There were innumerable holes in their skin and the underlying tissue. They would have had very painful and violent deaths, vomiting blood, losing their eye sight, writhing frantically in the unbearable pain in the abdomen, eyes, nose and throat, struggling till their last breaths. It took a month to connect all the three deaths. That too wouldn't have been possible but for a chilling video that surfaced some time back.'

'Video?' Rakesh took his stare off the map and looked at the speaker of the intercom.

'Yes. A video released by the ISIS.'

'The ISIS? The Islamic State of Iraq and Syria?'

'That's right. The video showed the horrific killing of a few Yazidi men by the ISIS. There was a commentary in Arabic saying that the Quran apparently recommends a gruesome death to the kafirs by forcing them to drink boiling water that will burn the intestines …'

'Oh my God!' Rakesh blurted, 'that was how these three people were also killed.' He already had his hand on the tab, searching Quranic texts.

'The coincidences were too straightforward to think of anything else … '

'Here it is,' Rakesh interrupted, 'the 15th verse of the chapter called Surat Muhammad.'

'What's that?'

'A verse from the Quran, which says: "*They will be given to drink boiling water, so that it cuts their intestines into pieces.*"' Rakesh read out from the screen of his pad. '*Wasuqu maan hamiman faqatta'a am'aahum.*'

'Somak was right. There's a lot hidden in the carpets … '

Rakesh got a call. 'Sir, the commissioner of police is on the line,' he interrupted.

'Put him on intercom,' Parush instructed.

'Yes, Mr Bhatnagar,' Parush talked to the commissioner directly.

'Looks like there's no girl in the car we've been following since Hathras. It stopped at a dhaba near Agra. My men checked the car from as close as possible. Apart from the driver, there's no one.'

Rakesh was staring at the zoomed-in picture of the map. The text that appeared beside the blinking dot read Guru Dhaba.

'The entire thing was a deceit?' Rakesh muttered.

Kachhpura

(Morning, 4 January 2019. Agra)

Parush had a sixth sense that Kubha was somewhere in Agra. He was arguing the same with Rakesh, keeping an eye on Raju Salim's Jaguar, from a distance.

'Rakesh, the deceit is what makes me more confident. I would have been suspicious if we nabbed the kidnappers so easily.'

'But, sir,' Rakesh argued, 'what we think is a deceit may be in reality just an unrelated coincidence.'

'An unregistered satellite phone itself is suspicious. The timing and location of the first intercepted call coinciding with that of Kubha's kidnapping can't be a mere coincidence. The mobile that the iridium phone communicated to traced an alternate route to Agra. That's too much of a coincidence, if we assume it's not related to the kidnapping. Given that mobile phones are easily trackable, it doesn't take much intelligence to keep the kidnappers out of the mobile footprint. They very well could have been in a different car. Don't you think it's quite a simple ploy to mislead us?'

'In that case,' Rakesh argued, 'we could have checked all the cars following the one with the mobile?'

'It's risky, Rakesh. I don't want to take any chances. They could have harmed Kubha in panic … '

'The satellite phone,' Parush was cut off by Rakesh's voice. 'They are calling a number in Calcutta.'

Rakesh had already connected the intercepted call to the intercom, having discovered that the call wasn't encrypted. Initially, he had been perplexed, not realizing why the call wasn't encrypted. But soon he understood that, had it been encrypted, the receiver in Calcutta wouldn't be able to get any head or tail out of it, because it was very unlikely they would possess the sophisticated decoder. He looked at his watch. It was 5:30 in the morning.

'Is it Mr Kratu Sen?' someone spoke in English.

Both Parush and Rakesh listened to the conversation in the intercom.

'Yes,' replied someone at the other end.

Parush didn't fail to recognize the anxiety in Kratu's voice.

'Your daughter is in safe hands. Don't worry. We'll take good care of her as long as you agree to listen to us,' said the voice at the other end.

'The satellite phone is in a place called Kachhpura,' Rakesh informed, the moment the call ended.

'Where is that?' Parush asked.

'It's on the other side of the Yamuna river, about two and a half kilometres diagonally opposite to the Taj Mahal.'

'Anything special about this place?'

A text window popped up in Rakesh's pad displaying the output of the ACPS, Advanced Custom Post Search, which culled the most relevant snippets from Google.

'Looks like, Kachhpura is a very old neighbourhood of Agra, older than the Taj Mahal,' said Rakesh. He read out from his pad:

> *Akbar granted this place, on the both sides of the river, in jagir, to Raja Man Singh Kachhwaha of Amer, whereby the village came to be known as Kachhpura. Shah Jehan, Akbar's grandson, procured this site from Man Singh's grandson, Raja Jai Singh, for the construction of the Taj Mahal and Mehtab Bagh on the two sides of the river facing each other…*

'Any connection with Hasht Bihisht and Bagh-i Filhal?' Parush interrupted. 'We deciphered these two words from the second intercepted call. My gut feeling is this is the location where the kidnappers have kept Kubha.'

'I've already fed these words in ACPS. A vanilla Google search didn't return anything. There's nothing called Bagh-i Filhal anywhere in the world. It may be a wrong decipher.' He stopped abruptly. 'No, it's not wrong,' he shouted over the intercom, looking at what had appeared in his tab. 'Sir, you're correct. The kidnappers are in Kachhpura. Babur made many gardens on the other side of Yamuna, opposite to the Taj and the Agra Fort, and one of those was Bagh-i Hasht Bihisht, the Garden of Eight Paradises.'

'Talk to the commissioner,' Parush instructed, pressing the gas pedal. 'Put the entire region under surveillance in stealth mode. No one should suspect anything. By the way, what's there around the place you located the phone at?'

'There's nothing. I zoomed into the exact location in the map and retrieved the entire land record from the Bhulekh database. It's a wasteland very close to the river. But there are houses within a few hundred metres.'

'I want information about each and every house there.'

☼

Parush knew very well what Afsar, Kubha's mother, could be going through presently. After the last intercepted call, it was very clear that her daughter had been indeed kidnapped. Parush expected a call from her after the kidnappers had talked to her. But when she didn't call even after half an hour, he knew she was hesitant to involve Parush and the police, perhaps fearing retaliation from the kidnappers.

Immediately after the position of the iridium satellite phone had been identified, Parush and Rakesh left behind a constable in plain dress in front of the hotel Raju Salim had checked into a few hours ago, and rushed towards the Rambagh Police Station, across the river. Rakesh made several phone calls, making a series of arrangements. Parush zipped the Mercedes Benz Sprinter through the deserted streets of Agra engulfed in a dense morning mist that stretched the cold night longer. Keeping the vehicle at the police station, they took an old white Ambassador. A constable who lived in Kachhpura drove the ramshackle car, while Parush and Rakesh assembled the mobile communication system in the back seat.

As they waited in front of the dilapidated old mosque built by Humayun in Kachhpura, Parush felt signs of fatigue. In the past few hours, there hadn't been a single moment of inactivity. Neither had he got even a moment's reprieve to think about Kubha. He scrolled the call list in his mobile and stopped at Kubha's name. The time stamp showed he had called her at 9:05 pm. They would have talked for half an hour. So it was within minutes after the call, he realized, that she had been kidnapped from somewhere near the Special Centre for Sanskrit Studies, in the southern part of the JNU campus. That was also the location from where the first intercepted call had been made from the iridium phone.

Parush stretched his leg and leaned against the door of the car, closing his eyes. He remembered the last call he had had with Kubha.

'Porus, I'm getting bored,' Kubha had said, taking his call even before the first ring. 'What great work do you have now? Come here. I want to go to the JNU caves now.'

'Don't worry,' Parush said with a smile, 'I'll take you there. Now …'

'How's that possible?'

'Close your eyes and do as I say.'

'Where from do you get such silly ideas?' Kubha couldn't control her laughter. 'No wonder, no girl has tolerated you for long.'

'You've been tolerating me all your life.'

'Ya, that's true. I'm the weirdest of all …' She paused.

'What happened?' Parush asked.

'I'm looking for a stick. I need one if I've to walk with my eyes closed.'

Parush waited on the call till she spoke again. 'Yes, I've got it. Now guide me. I've closed my eyes.'

Parush opened the advanced call tracking application in his tab and checked Kubha's exact location in the map. 'You're now in front of the Special Centre for Sanskrit Studies. Keep walking. Now you've reached the Centre for the Study of Law and Governance. Leave the road and turn left into the forest trail. Be careful. Tap the stick on the ground.'

'I like the smell of the forest. I never knew that I would fall in love with the trees and birds.'

'A friend of mine who went to JNU told me that anyone who stays in JNU becomes a Bishnoi.'

'What's that?'

'A group of people from the Thar Desert region. They have many legends when it comes to loving nature. There's a story that when people came to cut their trees, some Bishnoi women wanted to protect the trees by hugging on to them. They all got killed in the melee, but they never left the trees.'

'Then I'm surely not a Bishnoi,' Kubha chuckled. 'I can't die saving trees …'

'Be careful,' Parush interrupted. 'The trail curves to the right. Use the stick. Don't hit a tree. By the way, do you have a torch?'

'Yes, I always carry a torch when I go around the campus in the night.'

'Why do you roam around alone in these lonely places in the night?'

'Come on,' she said coyly, 'these places are crowded with trees and flowers. I'm alone because you don't have time for me. I think we shouldn't have moved to India. It was better in the US. You were jobless. You had all the time for me.'

Parush didn't say anything. She was not entirely wrong, he knew. When he had finally come out clean after the long legal battle in the US that had run for a few years, he had decided to take a break for some time. It had been a really long time since he had spent any time by himself, pondering about his own life, trying to figure out what he really wanted, where he was headed to, getting a sense of direction in his totally disoriented and deserted life. Kubha was just a young kid, naughty, full of life—the sort of life he lacked.

Kubha's parents, Afsar and Kratu, might have noticed that the reckless Parush would be tame only in the presence of the little Kubha. Having seen the brash and imprudent ways of Parush over the years, they would have been relieved that finally there was someone who could calm him down, control him. As Kubha grew up and went from middle to high school, her control over him increased too. And for Parush, the short break that he had wanted to take after the long and tiring legal battle stretched for years.

Parush already had enough money to sustain him for life and he was left with no passion, no vice either. People around him gradually moved on in their respective lives. For them, he became an exotic island resort in the middle of a turquoise placid sea, something they remembered only when they would have their vacations. His life centered around Kubha, and hers around him. The gap of a generation between them barely seemed an issue. Kubha had always seen him, ever since she had had her senses, as a permanent accompaniment, perhaps like a teddy bear filled with life that changed its behaviour as she grew. He would be exactly what she expected at any age.

'Hello,' Kubha's voice would have snapped his thoughts. 'You've kept a girl stranded in the middle of a forest, with her eyes closed. And our prime minister has got you to India so that people would be safer.'

She was suddenly cut off by the sound of a thud. The phone line fell silent, but didn't disconnect.

'Hello, Kubha, are you there?' Parush shouted a few times, but there was no response. He was getting worried, when he heard Kubha's voice again.

'I hit a tree and the phone fell out of my hand.'

'Oh!' Parush sighed. 'I'm really sorry.'

'Yes, you should be,' Kubha teased. 'You're getting old Porus. *You can't even protect me.*' She started laughing.

Before hanging up, a few minutes later, she told Parush that her phone was running low on battery.

'Don't get unnecessarily worried if I'm not reachable for sometime,' she said jokingly. '*I can take care of myself.*'

☼

Parush might have slept for a while. When he opened his eyes, he found Rakesh standing outside the car, with the driver.

'Is the Maulavi available now?' he asked.

'Yes, sir,' Rakesh replied. 'I didn't want to disturb you.'

'Let us go and meet him.'

Parush got out of the car and walked towards the mosque. They opened their shoes and covered their heads with the white cloth the driver gave them. They entered the domed big central chamber of the mosque through a lofty arch rising so high that it totally concealed the dome. At each side of the central compartment, the building was lower and comprised four smaller chambers, two of which to the left had no roofs. The Maulavi was seated on the floor, facing a small recess on the wall. Parush recalled Afsar had once explained to him that every mosque had a west-facing wall, called the qibla that faced the Kaaba in Mecca, and that the recess in the wall was called mihrab.

Rakesh and Parush sat beside the Maulavi, facing the mihrab.

'You want to know about the old monuments in Kachhpura?' the Maulavi asked Parush.

'Haan ji,' Parush said. 'I'm writing a book on the lost monuments from the Mughal era. My driver told me you have a wealth of information.'

Parush knew the Maulavi would be flattered. 'Nothing like that my son,' he reacted with a benign smile. 'We've been staying here for generations. Lot of knowledge has stayed within our family. You won't read any of these in books … '

'That's why I've come to you,' Parush cut him short. 'Is there anything called Hasht Bihisht or Bagh-i Filhal in Kachhpura?'

'Any building with a central big room surrounded by eight other rooms is called a hasht bihisht, the eight heavens. Bihisht consists of three gardens and the third one is subdivided into eight smaller gardens. In Islam, hasht, the number "eight", is a symbol of paradise.'

Rakesh stared at Parush. He realized the Maulavi would now go about explaining everything under the sun about hasht bihisht. He knew Parush was getting impatient.

'Is there any such building here, in Kachhpura?' Parush asked, interrupting the discourse.

The Maulavi stared at Parush for some time and started an even loftier rhetoric.

'The Taj is the best example of a hasht bihisht,' he began. 'The magnificent hujra is in the centre, below which are laid to rest the Firdaus Ashiyani, His Highness, the One who resides in the heaven, Abul Muzaffar Shahabuddin Muhammad, whom you all know as Shah Jahan, and his beloved wife, Mahd-i Ulya, Bilqis-i Dauran, Mumtaz Mahal … '

'But the Taj is not in Kachhapura,' Parush tried to get the Maulavi in line to say what he wanted to hear. 'Also, I'm not interested in the Taj at this moment. I would be rather keen to know if there's something in Kachhpura which goes by the name Bagh-i Filhal.'

'Once upon a time, there were many gardens in this part of Agra. I've heard of Bagh-i Hasht Bihisht, Mahtab Bagh, Chahar Bagh. But I don't think there was anything called Bagh-i Filhal. And I wonder why anyone would call a garden by that name. Do you know what Bagh-i Filhal means? It means a temporary garden … ' the Maulavi paused and closed his eyes, the fingers of his right hand toying with the tip of his grey beard. 'There's one person though,' he said, after a brief period of contemplation, 'who might have heard of it, if really such a thing ever existed here.'

'Who's he?' Parush sounded impatient.

'Daulat Parwar,' the Maulavi just threw the name, without saying anything more.

Parush was doubtless irritated. He stared at Rakesh who felt he had to do something in order to expedite the pace at which the Maulavi was disseminating information. Data mining, he realized, was far more efficient with machines. Rakesh cleared his throat.

'Inshallah,' he uttered the word so dramatically that even a visibly annoyed Parush couldn't but smile. 'I'm sure you and Daulat Parwar will lead this poor seeker of knowledge in the right direction. It was just the right decision to have come to you. This banda has plunged into the labyrinth with no thread to pull him out. You are his thread now.'

Parush indicated him to calm down. The Maulavi seemed to be cherishing the ovation. 'All Allah's grace,' he attempted at sounding humble, lowering his head. 'If this Allah's servant can be of some good to others, that's his privilege.'

'Can we meet Daulat?' Parush was in no mood for another round of rhetoric.

'That poor fellow didn't deserve this.'

'What?' Parush didn't want to hear what the Maulavi seemed to be hinting at.

'He knew every brick, every stone in this place. He knew everything about each building and monument that ever existed, the loftiest of them and also the most insignificant one, from the Imarat-i Rauza-i Munauwara to the Gumbad-i Mukhtasari that has been shattered into pieces by the savages of time.'

'May we please present ourselves in front of this illuminated personality?' Rakesh asked.

'You're just late by two days.'

'Oh, no!' Rakesh sighed. 'Has he become one of Allah's loved ones?'

'Only Allah can tell if he has showered his blessings on him and taken him away from this zalim duniya. He has mysteriously gone missing two days ago. He would often spend time with me. When he didn't go home for a day, his son came running to me yesterday … He was not with me either.'

☼

Sitting under the morning sun in the small front yard of the constable's modest house in Kachhpura, sipping hot tea, Parush was confused if "hasht bihisht" and "bagh-i filhal", the two words intercepted from the second call made from the iridium phone, really pointed to Kachhpura. Hasht Bihisht, as the Maulavi had pointed out, didn't mean anything specific that could be connected exclusively to Kachhpura. Neither was there anything by the name of Bagh-i Filhal in Kachhpura. But still, he had a gut feeling that Kubha was somewhere here, in Kachhpura. The location of the iridium phone during the last intercepted call was here too.

Parush dialled Afsar's number, at around eight in the morning. She picked the call immediately. Without saying anything, she broke down.

'Afsar, I'm there. Trust me,' Parush spoke with assurance and conviction. '*Kubha is my life too.*'

Parush had never spoken about Kubha, like that, to anyone. There had not been any such situation ever in the past, when he had to admit what Kubha really meant to him. Certain things were never asked or discussed, even though it was not that Parush, or for that matter many others around him, wouldn't ever ponder over what exactly the relationship between him and Kubha was.

'Porus, I know that, and that's my only hope,' Afsar managed to say.

The conversation didn't last long. He asked for Kratu.

'We trust you,' Kartu's voice trembled. 'And we know, no one can do anything more than you.'

Half-lying on the cot made of strings, as Parush tried to figure out what he should do next, his phone rang, after an hour, at around nine. The name "Pradhan Sevak" flashed on his screen. He pressed the green button to take the call.

'What's going on?' Indar Sinha, the prime minister of India, asked him directly.

'Indar,' Parush spoke calmly, 'I know what I'm doing.'

'Porus, it's not that I'm not aware of your guts or daredevilry. That was what had fascinated me about you. I myself got in touch with you, in one of my visits to the Bay Area. I know what you're doing and what you can do. And that's what makes me jittery at times.'

'*Nothing is going to happen to her.*'

'Porus, very few people call me by my first name. No one dares to do that. And I've given you that privilege from the day one. I've given you privileges I may find difficult to explain to the world, if I ever have to. I've given you so much power because I need you. I'm not saying you're misusing the power or privilege. I know what you're doing. And I know how you're doing too.'

'Indar, I told you, nothing is going to happen to her.'

'Don't repeat the same thing again and again. Even an idiot knows anything can happen to her. I need girls like Kubha, for my country. I need her safe and sound. Do you understand that?'

'Why do you think I wouldn't understand that? You know how much … '

'Yes, I know how much,' Indar interrupted. 'And that's my fear. You just see the outcome and often forget the path. Porus, the path also matters. I don't believe you didn't know there was a threat on her too. Still you didn't do anything. And, by the way, does she go to that remote part of the JNU campus every night?'

Parush kept quiet. Indar never talked much. But he was always as blunt as possible—something that Parush admired the most about him.

Parush had an answer though, but still, he didn't say anything. He had indeed done everything to ensure no one could sneak anyone out of the campus. Every inch of the entire boundary wall of the campus had been under surveillance. Each and every vehicle entering and leaving the campus through any of the entry and exit points were being thoroughly checked and tracked round the clock. It had to be someone really smart, smarter than him, to have dodged the entire security system and kidnapped Kubha from the campus.

'I know you don't have an answer,' Indar said at the end. 'I called you to tell you that I'll wait for one more day and by that time if you can't make any headway, I'm going to unleash all my force. *I don't want to achieve anything big by pawning her.*'

Parush got up from the cot and walked into the house. Indar's last words echoed in his head. Had he really pawned Kubha? He sat on the cheap sofa made of cane and accessoried with small colourful pillows. The constable's wife brought him a plateful of food and kept it in front of him on a low stool. Her young daughter held a glass of water in her hand and stood silently. Parush took the glass from her and asked her to sit beside him.

'Which class do you go to?' he tried to initiate a conversation with her.

The little girl gestured "two" with her fingers and smiled.

'You don't want to talk to me?' Parush asked, fondling her hair.

She shook her head in disapproval.

'She's very naughty,' her mother apologized.

The little girl ran away inside the house. Her mother left too, requesting him to eat the paratha before it gets cold.

Left alone in the room, a deluge of thoughts washed away on his mind. Indar's curt message threw him into a turmoil. He got up from the sofa and went towards the open door of the house, staring at the lazy village getting ready for the day. He returned to the sofa, tore a small portion of the paratha, dipped it into the curd kept in a small bowl and put it inside his mouth. The mashed potato stuffing of the paratha melted in his mouth. Suddenly, he felt very hungry and devoured the rest of the food in no time. Having gulped all the food so fast in an empty stomach, he felt dizzy. He drank a glass full of cold water and stretched on the sofa, leaning his head against the wall behind.

'How exactly would you do this with Bitasta?' Parush remembered Kubha asking him, once he had guided her to the base of the JNU caves, the previous night, just before she was kidnapped. She had sat on a rock, opened her eyes and breathed the cold air.

'Why do you ask?' Parush had said. 'It's almost 25 years … '

'You didn't have mobile and GPS then.'

'I would take her on my bike. She would keep her eyes shut till I asked her to open them. And I would take her to places she hadn't seen earlier.'

'Wasn't she my age when you guys broke up?'

'She was 17, younger than you.'

'Do I remind you of her?'

'Never thought like that. Why are you asking me all these?'

'Trying to make you feel awkward,' she broke into a laughter.

☼

Parush might have dozed off a bit. He wouldn't have noticed when Rakesh and the constable had returned. When Parush looked up, rubbing his eyes, he found them conversing animatedly in soft voices.

'Any news about Daulat?'

'Quite a bit, sir,' replied Rakesh. 'The eldest sons of his family have been working for the ASI, Archaeological Survey of India, for the past three generations. Daulat has been working as a contract worker with the ASI for the past 20 years. I talked to the superintending archaeologist of the Agra circle of the ASI. He personally knows Daulat very well.'

'What did he say about Daulat?'

'Daulat is officially attached to the maintenance work of the Taj Mahal. But he literally looks after each and every listed and unlisted monument in Agra.'

'Why does he do that?'

'May be, he does it out of love.'

'Out of love?' Parush was surprised. 'Had he been an archaeologist or historian, I would have accepted that. But a poor guy, barely literate, and such love for monuments?'

'There's something more intriguing about him.'

'What's that? Don't tell me he's a direct descendant of Shah Jahan,' Parush joked, 'and that he thinks all these buildings are his personal property.'

'Nothing like that, sir,' Rakesh laughed. 'It's something even weirder.'

'Wouldn't it be better,' Parush said with a grin, 'if you just told it, without the breaks?'

'Daulat seems to know a lot of myths about the Mughals, especially their monuments in Agra. Given the fact that many Muslims in Agra make similar claims from time to time, everyone at the ASI would take Daulat's stories lightly. But then, something happened and the entire ASI started taking him seriously.'

'No breaks, please!'

'Sometime in the January of 2003, Daulat came running to the main office of the ASI. He directly went to the superintending archaeologist and told him that the Taj was in danger. He claimed that the wooden foundation of the monument was drying up and that the entire structure would crumble down soon.'

'The Taj has a wooden foundation?' Parush sat erect on the sofa.

'That's what many people believe. It's acknowledged by the ASI too. But, looks like, there's no unanimous view among the historians and the archaeologists about what exactly the wooden structure could be like. Initially, no one took Daulat seriously, as usual. But at the same time, a joint team from the UNESCO and the International Council on Monuments and Sites visited Agra.'

Rakesh paused and scrolled a page on his tab. He read out:

> *The recently started Taj Corridor Project has already increased the embankment of the Yamuna River near Taj to such an extent that it could alter the natural flow of the river and alter the gradient of humidity in soil forming the shores of the river. This could have a long term negative impact on the wooden structural foundations.*

'How did Daulat come to know of it?'

'That's the mystery. He said he had got a dream.'

'That's interesting! A timber pile foundation always needs good humidity to keep the wood moist. Dry timber is structurally weak. But that's not common sense knowledge. I got to know of it when I met someone researching on the conservation of the Venetian buildings, which predominantly have timber pile foundations.'

'It can't be true that Daulat got to know of the UNESCO report in his dreams.'

'He knew it from some other source, some very credible source not known to anyone else. Anyway, did you see the place the last satellite call was made from?'

'Yes, sir, I thoroughly checked the place. It's on the bank of the Yamuna river. It's a very dirty place where people have dumped a lot of plastic waste. There's a remnant of an old dilapidated building, almost in ruins. There's also a dargah and a small mound behind it. I talked to the family that stays at the dargah. No one has noticed anything suspicious. Neither has anyone in the neighbourhood.'

'Who would notice anything outside in a freezing wintry night, when the temperature is close to zero?'

Rakesh was going to say something when his phone rang. Parush listened to the one side of the conversation.

'Raju Salim has met a student from JNU thrice in the past one week?'

'What's the name of the student?'

'Vishnu Godse?'

Hiranyagarbha

(Later the day, 4 January 2019. Agra)

Parush stared at Rakesh, frowning, the tip of his index finger tapping his teeth. Rakesh was familiar with certain mannerism of Parush, certain nuances and gestures which often expressed much more than words. Rakesh had started enjoying his stint with this mysterious person not many people knew much about. At personal get-togethers and parties, people talked in hushed tones about the influence he yielded at the highest levels in the government machinery. The dearth of credible information about his past added to the enigma around him. That he was not married and lived alone was all people knew about his personal life, and that he rarely socialized with anyone beyond a level of official decorum left them with very little option to even extrapolate and cook up stories about him. Rakesh had a special status among his folks, as the one closest to Parush. Often he was asked small tidbits about the person who had the privilege to call the prime minister by his first name.

Before joining the special SWAT team, Rakesh had had a very successful tenure with the Directorate of Signals Intelligence and the DIPAC, Defence Image Processing and Analysis Centre, both under the DIA, Defence Intelligence Agency, the nodal agency for all defence-related intelligence in India. Rakesh was one of the few Parush selected for the SWAT team he was given charge of by none other than the PMO.

'Remember,' Parush had told his new team, 'SWAT doesn't have to always do with *Special Weapons and Tactics*, as has been made to believe by the famous LAPD, the Los Angeles Police Department. Yes, it's true that we have plagiarized the name from them, but our weapons and tactics are different.'

It didn't take long for Rakesh to realize that they could carry all their weapons in a small bag and, when it came to tactics, not many could beat Parush.

☼

Having set up the mobile surveillance system in the small store room, which also doubled as the guest room in case someone *really important* visited the constable's modest home, Rakesh had allowed Parush to take a nap. Keeping a hawk's eye on each of the small windows in the nine-inch monitor with virtual retinal display, he gathered all information about Vishnu Godse. Doubtless to say, he was getting more bewildered as he kept on stumbling upon one fact after another about Vishnu. He wanted to wake Parush up immediately. That was when Parush himself appeared behind him.

'This Vishnu is a dangerous person,' Rakesh blurted. 'He is no less than a terrorist.'

'Don't get excited,' Parush calmed him down. 'Tell me what all you've come to know.'

'Read this,' Rakesh passed on the tab to Parush. 'It's one of the articles written by Vishnu.'

Parush scrolled the screen and glanced through the article filled with historical tidbits about the persecution of the Hindus and the demolition of sacred temples by the Muslims, over the centuries of Muslim rule in India.

'There are a hundred articles like this in the internet,' Parush remarked, not taking his eyes off the screen. 'What's unique about this one?'

'Most of these articles are generally nonsense and full of wrong facts. But this is not.'

'How can you say so?'

'I've cross-checked most of the facts he mentioned and they are all correct.'

'Really?' Parush exclaimed. 'Did Shah Jahan demolish 76 temples in Banaras?' he asked, staring at a highlighted text on the screen of the tab.

Rakesh clicked on an iconized window on the monitor in front of him.

'This particular fact,' he revealed, 'is taken from Abdul Hamid Lahori's *Badshahnama*.'

Rakesh retrieved the relevant page of an English translation of the *Badshahnama* from the online database of the Cornell University Library and transferred it to the tab. Parush read out from the window that popped up on the screen:

> *His Majesty, the defender of the faith, gave orders that at Benares, and throughout all his dominions in every place, all temples that had been begun should be cast down. It was now reported from the province of Allahabad that seventy-six temples had been destroyed in the district of Benares.*

'So what are you trying to say?' Parush asked, staring at Rakesh, tapping his teeth with the tip of his index finger.

'Sir,' Rakesh explained, sitting erect on the short stool, 'his views are very radical. He justifies the demolition of the Babri Masjid. He minces no word in asking the Hindus worldwide to unite and demolish all such Islamic monuments built with the bricks and stones of Hindu temples.'

'I'm surprised he's not yet in my radar.'

'That's because he and his network seem to be active only outside India. He maintains a very low profile here. He rarely talks to anyone in JNU. No one would have ever heard of him if he hadn't got into a tussle with Kubha recently in the campus.'

'Vishnu had a tussle with Kubha?' Parush stopped tapping his teeth.

'Last month, Kubha had written an article in a magazine called *Maitree*. It's published by the JNU Women's Association. There, she ridiculed a group of people who are spearheading an awareness campaign that claims the Taj Mahal was actually a Shiva temple.'

'I remember you told me the fringe group doing this is not connected to any of the right wing Hindu groups we generally track.'

'I had checked the backgrounds of each of them—all are rich Americans of Indian origin. All of them have spent lifetimes earning loads of money. Now they want to do something for the society, for their next generations, for their country.'

'As if,' Parush laughed, 'their poor country of birth has been waiting impatiently for them to pull her out of the ignominy and disgrace she has been through all these years. Kratu, Kubha's father, calls it "Identity Crisis Induced Indomania Syndrome", ICIIS. He pronounces it like the ISIS, the Islamic State of Iraq and Syria. Anyway, carry on.'

'One of the persons Kubha talked very harshly about in her article happens to be Vishnu's father. Kubha posted the article on her FB wall. Vishnu accused her of being a Pakistani agent, referring to her mother's Pakistani origin. A war of words ensued on FB between Vishnu and Kubha's friends. Soon, Vishnu was given a kambal dhulai. The matter went to the dean of students.'

'It's heartening to know the *blanket assault* is still in vogue in this age,' Parush quipped, pulling out a wooden box.

Rakesh got up immediately, as though in a reflex, and bent down to pass on the stool he was sitting on to Parush. Parush gestured him to sit down and himself sat on the wooden box. The uneven bottom wobbled a bit under his pressure.

'We would dirty the blanket with soil and grease before wrapping anyone with it. There were folks specialized in the art of kambal dhulai.'

Rakesh explained that Vishnu's writings had a common theme of resurrecting the lost glory of India's battered past. His target was mainly the 700 years of Muslim rule which, he went on and on bawling, had converted the hiranyagarbha, the golden embryo that the illustrious Bharata Varsha had been for thousands of years, into a stinking hell.

'Did you say hiranyagarbha?' Parush interrupted Rakesh, abruptly.

Being well familiar with Parush's body language, Rakesh knew Parush was excited, but he couldn't realize what could have caused the sudden excitement.

'Yes,' he said hesitantly, 'he repeatedly refers to India as Hiranyagarbha Bharat ... ' Rakesh paused. From his looks, Parush knew that Rakesh was trying to remember something.

Parush smiled. 'I know what you're thinking. The term "hiranyagarbha" sounds familiar, isn't it?'

'I think I've heard the term recently ... '

'I'll tell you where you have heard it. It was there in the pamphlets distributed in Agra last week.'

'Exactly,' Rakesh said.

Parush's sharp memory had impressed him quite a few times in the past. He recalled the context in which the term had been used in the pamphlets that the residents of Agra were stunned to see one foggy wintry morning. Referring to India, the sacred land of the Hindus, as hiranyagarbha, the golden embryo that had given birth to the richest of the peoples, the grandest of the civilizations and the most profound of wisdom, the pamphlets had summoned the Hindus, in very scathing language, to cleanse the Tejo Mahalaya, the ancient temple of Lord Shiva that had been defecated by the Muslims and converted into the Taj Mahal.

'Hiranyagarbha Bharat is one of the deadliest Hindu fanatic groups,' Parush explained. 'It has a legacy of more than a hundred years of blood bath. When it comes to cultural fanaticism, they can be as ferocious and ruthless as possible.'

'But I'm sure,' Rakesh observed, 'we can't put them and the ISIS on the same platform.'

'Oh, no way,' Parush gesticulated. 'Putting both on the same platform would be as ridiculous as likening google to the Indian web portal sulekha.com. But it's doubtless the Hiranyagarbha Bharat is, indeed, very radical by Indian standards. They almost killed Kratu, Kubha's father. He escaped miraculously. But Kratu's sister and uncle couldn't escape. Find out everything you can about Vishnu Godse. I want to know about each and every one he has been in touch with lately.'

'Hiranyagarbha Bharat wanted to kill Kubha's father?' Rakesh couldn't hide his surprise.

'It's a long story … '

☼

Tucked deep into the three picturesque valleys, in the high altitudes of the Hindukush mountains in Pakistan, the Kalash people have preserved one of the oldest cultures of the world uninterruptedly for four millennia. How a few of them reached what is now Bangladesh, in the late nineteenth century, may be a matter of conjecture. But the reality is, a few members of a particular Kalash family fused so well into a Bengali household in a small neighbourhood, amid a captivating labyrinth of rivers—it can very well be called a rural Venice in Bangladesh—that over the years, not many remembered their origin. The only glimmer of their original homeland that lingered was a collection of really intriguing stories that had remained in their family for generations. No one knew how old those stories were or where they had originated from. Eventually, their stories entered into the Bengali brood as bedtime tales, as did a few of them too, through marriages. The fascinating stories of the unknown land of Kalash became a favourite folklore in the faraway village of Gaila in the riverine district of Barishal in Bangladesh and the children of the extended Gupta family wouldn't sleep without listening to those.

One fine morning in the early twentieth century, almost all the members of the Kalash family were found dead in Gaila. The only survivor was a little girl Kubha, barely 10 years old. This unprecedented and unfortunate event shocked everyone. No one could find any good reason why such a dastardly act could befall a neighbourhood which had never seen any crime in the remembered past. The little girl, who survived the slaying, eventually grew up to be an exceptional woman of rare fortitude and grit, who eventually died in the communal riots immediately after the partition of India, protecting her children.

A wonderful legacy that Kubha had passed on to her children was that of her family lore, which would have been lost forever had she not survived the massacre of the rest of her family. Her orphaned children, uprooted from their ancestral home in Bangladesh, grew up in Calcutta. Over the years, Kubha was kept alive only through her stories, which survived, perhaps, as the only souvenir of hers. The saga of her life and death alike, along with the legacy of her fascinating stories, created around her an enigmatic and mystic aura that exalted her to the rank of a supernatural persona in her family. She remained as an inspiration to her successive generations. Over the years, the saga of her mental strength, her sacrifice, her wit, her intelligence, attained a level that surely would have had some elements of myth.

Many years later, during their early days of courtship at Stanford sometime in the '90s, Kratu, a grandson of Kubha, and his girlfriend Afsar, a linguistic paleontologist, discovered that Kubha's stories were not mere bedtime tales. In an exciting turn of events, over the next few months, it was revealed that the stories were actually real anecdotes and near-historical accounts of a heroic Aryan race, the progenitor of most of the ancient civilizations and the cultures of the world. The stories, they realized, were 4,000 years old, older than the *Rig Veda*, the first-ever book written by mankind, and had been preserved for four millennia in the Kalash valleys of the Hindukush, by generations of Kubha's ancestors, through oral transmission.

In the meantime, Kratu's uncle had a mysterious death in a freak car accident in Calcutta. Coincidentally, Kratu's elder sister had also died the previous year in another car accident in the US.

While Kratu was visiting Calcutta, a totally different aspect of Kubha's stories came to light. It became quite clear that the stories, when analyzed properly, revealed a scenario which went totally against the popular theory vociferously propounded by the right wing Hindu reformists about the origin of Indian culture and civilization. The stories seemed to attack the very foundation on which stood the entire Hindu reformist movement. Connecting a few dots, a startling discovery was made about something that had been shrouded in mystery for almost seven decades. It seemed very likely that, in an attempt to erase any trace of these stories, Kubha's entire family had been actually murdered by the members of a fanatic group called the Hiranyagarbha Bharat. It was just by sheer luck that Kubha survived.

Seven decades later, members of the same group murdered Kratu's sister and then his uncle. Soon, Kratu too narrowly escaped a bid on his life. In the melee, Kratu's perpetrator was killed accidentally. There was no more death in the family. It was assumed that the Hiranyagarbha Bharat had ceased to exist.

Kratu and Afsar got married and had a girl. Kratu named her after his grandmother—Kubha.

☼

Parush realized from the contractions of Rakesh's facial muscles that he wouldn't have ever heard anything more weird and unbelievable. The sun was lingering on the western horizon, suddenly sucking the warmth of the day. Parush had wanted to visit the spot from where the last satellite call had been made in the morning. They preferred walking to the place, not very far from the constable's house they were staying at. On the way, Parush talked about the other Kubha and the legacy of her stories, which had led to a trail of murders by a fanatic group.

'I've never heard of the Hiranyagarbha Bharat,' Rakesh conceded.

'I don't think many people would know either,' Parush said, walking ahead of him.

'Did they do anything else, other than trying to eliminate Kratu's family from time to time?'

'I don't think I know anything about that. What I've heard from Kratu is that they never ceased to exist completely. After the mass murder of Kratu's grandmother's family, sometime around 1920, there has been no record of any of their actions for almost seven decades, till the '90s.'

'Do you think they have again struck back now?'

'The stories have been already published. There's no point in killing the family now. That wouldn't serve any purpose. I don't think the stories are a matter of concern any more. Now, it's doubtless, the carpets are. Afsar has been very tightlipped about it. Perhaps, she has been waiting to present her findings first to an academic forum rather than disclosing it to anyone else. Peer review is an important aspect of any discovery in the academic circles.'

'You've said something about the carpet motifs … '

'All I know is that the carpet motifs seem to have preserved a lot of histories, many of which are extremely controversial and can be manipulated. You know how Indian politicians have a tradition of invoking history and stirring a hornets' nest of fear and loathing. A 2,000-year-old Sanskrit text known as the *Manu Smriti* was at the centre of a lot of violence in the '90s, during the hey days of reservation. The mystery behind the origin of the Aryan and Dravidian race hasn't yet been solved conclusively. But, it has been churned well by a wide range of people, from the fanatic Hindu revisionists and reformists in the north to the Dravidian political parties in the south, with an even wider range of interests.'

'So you're saying,' Rakesh tried to organize his thoughts, 'the carpet motifs may expose some weird facts about Indian history, which could be so explosive that a fanatic group like the Hiranyagarbha Bharat would go to any extent to stop it from being publicized. Doesn't it sound unrealistic?'

'It's indeed unrealistic, when you apply logic to it. But remember, fanaticism doesn't follow logic. The execution of the Jews was based on a misinterpreted historical notion that the Germans are the true Aryans, the supreme race of the world, and that the Jews are an inferior race that doesn't deserve to live. What would happen, say, if someone really proved very conclusively that Ram was just a fictional character created by Valmiki? What do you think would happen to that poor researcher? Would she be allowed to publish her works? Wendy Doniger wasn't … Salman Rushdie wasn't too … But what's more intriguing here is not the involvement of the Hiranyagarbha Bharat. It's something else altogether that makes everything much more complicated.'

☼

The monitor flashed out of hibernation precisely at six in the morning, the next day. Both Rakesh and Parush hadn't slept the whole night, staying awake in front of the monitor, awaiting the next call from the satellite phone. When Kratu's mobile number appeared on the screen, indicating that the satellite call was again being made to Kratu, Rakesh directly fed the intercepted signal to the Beats Pill 2.0 Bluetooth speaker, sans the decoding. The encrypted signal would be garbage at the receiver's end. The moment the call was received by Kratu, the speaker made a loud buzzing noise.

'It's a video call, not audio,' Parush yelled. 'Put the video on.'

Rakesh took just a few seconds to display the video on the monitor. First it appeared in a small window. But the moment he filled the full screen with it, he froze. It didn't take even a moment for either him or Parush to realize what Kubha was presently going through. Rakesh, in a reflex action, got up from the stool and left the claustrophobic store room, leaving Parush alone in front of the monitor, stunned. Parush removed his eyes from the screen, almost choking his breath, a lump blocking his throat. He got back his senses a few seconds after the short video call had ended.

Afsar's loud wails were still reverberating in his ears. He had barely looked at Kubha. Suddenly, something flickered in his mind. Wasn't Kubha trying to say something? He tried to recall. He called out for Rakesh, who appeared silently in the room, his head down, trying to avoid direct eye contact with Parush.

'Extract the audio,' Parush said curtly, his dead voice indicative of what could be going on in his mind.

Rakesh quietly acted like a robot, expressionless. 'I can extract each voice independently,' he said, his fingers already playing hurriedly on the keyboard.

Parush just nodded. As Rakesh worked on the sophisticated voice extractor software, which was capable of sieving out each individual voice even from an incomprehensible cacophony, Afsar's wails sounded loudly in his ears. He shut his ears with his hands and banged his head on the wall. Rakesh left the keyboard and stood behind him, helping him sit down on the wooden box.

'I'll take a few minutes. I'll call you, sir. Please take some rest.'

'I'm fine. Get the voices,' Parush replied sternly.

Rakesh took less than a minute to extract the voices. He played each voice independently on the speaker, while Parush listened to each of them intently.

'This one sounds like Arabic,' he said, asking Rakesh to repeat an extract once more.

'Yes, sir, it's Arabic. We've added the speech recognition feature recently. It figures out the language and displays the text. "*Wa-alladhina hum lifurujihim hafizuna*",' he fumbled reading the text. 'Just wait a moment. I'm getting it translated.'

'And do a search on the text too,' Parush added.

'Here it is, the output of the translator,' Rakesh read from the screen of his tab. '"*And those who of their modesty are guardians except from their spouses or what possess their right hands, then indeed, they are not blameworthy.*"'

'What the hell does it mean?' Parush asked.

'The search has returned a lot of things. The text matches roughly with a Quranic verse, specifically the fifth one from the 23rd chapter. It means, "*And they who abstain from sex, except with their spouses or captives whom their right hands possess, are not to be blamed.*" The text also matches with an ISIS manual: "*You should rape the female captive. Allah, the almighty said: Successful are the believers who guard their chastity, except from their wives or the captives that their right hands possess, for they are free from blame.*"'

Parush took the tab from Rakesh's hands and read the content returned by the search engine.

'I can't believe it. The ISIS claims that the Quran justifies rape of female captives?'

Rakesh's bewildered looks told of his similar state of mind. They listened to the other extracts too.

The last of the extracts was that of Kubha's quavering voice, which appeared as a hum of some musical notes. As if it was blasphemous for Rakesh to hear the voice of a girl being raped, he left the room, leaving Parush alone, again. As Parush listened to the 40-second extract, he felt as though he was being whipped every time the voice wobbled. It was doubtless Kubha's mouth was tied and that she was trying hard to produce the humming sounds, which trembled whenever her pain became unbearable.

If Kubha had wanted her parents to obey the diktats of her captors, Parush argued with himself, she would have cried out loud, done anything which would have left her parents without any second thought about what they should do. But instead, she was trying to say something through the musical language she and Afsar often used, as a game. Kubha had tried many a time to teach the language to Parush, but he could never learn it. There was no way he could decipher it now. But his gut feeling told him that Kubha was trying to say that her parents shouldn't listen to her captors, that they should go ahead and attend the conference which would commence in a few hours from now.

Parush sat quietly in the dark room for some more time and then called Kratu, half an hour later.

'Listen to me carefully,' Parush spoke over the phone to Afsar, with no hint of excitement or fear. 'I'm already in Agra. Trust me. And trust your daughter too. *Don't listen to them.* I'll call you again very soon. Do exactly as I say. *You're going to the conference.*'

☼

Parush realized he had totally forgotten to enquire about the location of the iridium phone. It was only when Rakesh entered the store room again and started talking, he tried to orient himself, array his thoughts.

'How can it be?' he asked. 'Is it possible that we've got the wrong location?'

'No, sir,' Rakesh assured, 'we had tested it many times. The GPS data can't be wrong. The call was indeed made from the exact same location. I had placed four people around that place. They were alert all along. They saw no one there.'

'I want to go there now.'

Parush got up and walked fast. It didn't take him much time to reach the same place he had visited the previous evening. Standing before the dilapidated vestige of what could have been a portion of a thick wall of a building in better times, Parush looked around. The cold wind from the Yamuna pierced through his body, still not acclimatized to the near-zero temperature of a shivering wintry morning.

'The GPS shows the location exactly where the broken wall is,' Rakesh said.

'How's that possible?' Parush seemed irritated. 'If the call was made from here why couldn't anyone see the caller? Is it a ghost who's calling?'

Parush walked towards the water, trampling on the plastic waste scattered all around. Rakesh followed him. A dim light glowed like a flicker in the mist. He walked in the direction of the light and appeared in front of the dargah. He heard the sound of a baby crying.

'A family stays here,' Rakesh informed. 'The wife takes care of the dargah. The husband does some odd jobs nearby.'

'Call the husband,' Parush instructed.

Rakesh went inside and returned shortly with a thin, short and dark person, too young to be a father, and too frail to do even the simplest of odd job. He was wrapped in an old, coarse blanket, torn and stitched at many places. Shivering in the cold, he requested Parush to get inside. Lowering their heads, they entered into the ramshackle hut through a low entrance, in front of which burnt meekly a few lean pieces of tree trunks.

'No one comes here,' the man said, requesting them to sit on a junk sofa, 'though the village is just round the corner. You've seen how much plastic is all around. The trucks come and dump once in a few days. It spills everywhere. We don't have anywhere else to go. Otherwise who would stay here?'

'Have you seen anyone new lately?' Parush directly came to the point.

'I told the sir,' the man said, pointing towards Rakesh, 'only the trucks come this close to the river. Even Daulat chacha hasn't come here for some time.'

'Daulat?' Parush stared at Rakesh.

'Do you mean Daulat Parwar?' Rakesh asked, 'the one that works in the archaeological department?'

'Yes,' the man replied, a little surprised that Rakesh knew Daulat. 'Where ever there are purani imaratein, haveliyan, he knows them all ...'

'But here there is no old building or monument,' Parush interrupted.

'Chacha told many a time, "*Don't leave this place. You don't know where you stay. Everything started from here ...* "'

☼

'I want a list of all the monuments and buildings in Agra,' Parush told Rakesh, while walking back to the constable's house. 'There's a mound of bricks behind the dargah. It's doubtless there was something there. Find out about it. Talk again to that person from the ASI you contacted in the morning.'

'*Everything started from here.*' The words of the man at the dargah rung in his mind for some time ... A few scattered thoughts collided against each other and cluttered his thinking.

The way the three identical murders had been carried out and the way Kubha had been dealt with had the conspicuous signature of the ISIS and their activities in Iraq and Syria. It would be logical, Parush felt, to assume that a fanatic Islamic group, with or without direct affiliation to the ISIS, was behind all this. But then, what confused him was the connection to Vishnu Godse and the Hiranyagarbha Bharat that would never join hands with an Islamic group.

'*Everything started from here.*' Parush pondered over the words which, he understood, would not startle him when considered in isolation. But the same words, he felt, when considered alongside Vishnu's writings about resurrecting Hindutva, the neo-radical idea of Indianness, and India's glory lost to the 700 years of Muslim rule could bring in a totally different perspective. Vishnu very strongly espoused the idea of reclaiming, or rather reconstructing the Hindu temples allegedly demolished by the Muslim rulers. Was it that, Parush couldn't but think, the place the last two satellite calls had been made from had some connection to the resurrection of Hindutva?

Symbolism, Parush knew, played a big role in the activities of any fanatic group. The destruction of the ancient Roman city of Palmyra by the ISIS or the Bamiyan Buddha by the Taliban were symbolic actions, aimed at striking off the symbolic identity of anything non-Islamic and resurrecting the glory of the Caliphate era. Couldn't a fanatic group like the Hiranyagarbha Bharat, to which Vishnu's affiliation was doubtless, very well think of something similar? Then, wouldn't it be logical to believe that they too could strike at the symbol of the Islamic past of India, the symbol of the beginning of a new era of alleged demolition and massacre? The words "*Everything started from here*" appeared prophetic to Parush in that reference. But still, he couldn't fathom how something could have the signature of both Hindu and Islamic fanatic groups.

Soon, Parush would himself find the answers to his own questions.

☼

'I'll go for a walk,' Parush said, when they reached the constable's house. 'You can call me.'

Parush had started walking when he turned back.

'I've a plan,' he said to Rakesh, who came running towards him. 'I need you to be on top of everything. We don't have much time. A lot of things have to be arranged for at the venue of the conference, which starts in Calcutta, a few hours from now.'

After explaining the plan in details to Rakesh, Parush called Afsar, at around seven thirty in the morning. 'Do exactly as I say. Trust me,' he assured her repeatedly. 'You know, *I'll save Kubha, at any cost*, come what may … '

☼

Kubha switched on the torch. The narrow, dark tunnel illuminated in front of her for a while, but seemed dark again. She rubbed her eyes, shook her head, but still the darkness didn't seem to wane completely. She felt as though she was suddenly feeling relaxed, far removed from any anxiety or agony, totally oblivious of the situation she was in. The torch fell from her hand and rolled onto the floor before hitting the wall, stabilizing the shaking beam of light that appeared like a calm and enchanting glow created by a thousand glow-worms.

Kubha slowly sat on the cold floor, no more feeling numb, the cold no more biting her. She felt sleepy. She remembered how her mother would turn off the night lamp when she would feel Kubha had fallen asleep. But in reality Kubha would be half-asleep and half-awake in a state where she couldn't see anything, but could still feel a few things, like her mother leaving the bed, waiting a few moments at the door, staring at her and then leaving the room after switching off the night lamp. Kubha never remembered anything after that. Presently, she wanted to switch off the torch. She was feeling sleepy …

PART-II

The Khushawar Manuscript

(1 November 2018. Calcutta)

Little did Afsar know, that was the last time she was seeing her father, Faraz Fareedi, when he had come to meet her in Calcutta, Kubha tagging along with him. That was also the last time the three generations of the Fareedis had been together.

Faraz had lately moved to Pakistan, after the death of his wife. Unlike his elder daughter Afsar, his younger twin daughters, Bahnaz and Bahrukh, had taken keen interest in his flourishing business of sourcing exotic oriental carpets from Asia and selling them in the US. Faraz entrusted the business on them and started staying at his ancestral home in Khushawar, a small village near Peshawar that hadn't changed much since he had been a kid. Most of his extended family had by then started staying in Lahore, but he preferred staying close to where he had been born. People close to him knew that the main reason for his return to Pakistan was Kubha, his granddaughter, who had recently joined a school in Delhi for her undergrad. Every few months, he would visit Kubha in Delhi. Those few days he would be in Delhi, Kubha and her friends had a blast with the "Young Boy", the name she called him by.

This time too, Faraz landed first in Delhi. 'Old Lady,' he asked Kubha the same evening in the hotel, 'how many days can you spare for me?'

'Tell me what you want,' Kubha cut him short.

'I was thinking … ' he threw the words at his granddaughter, wondering how fast she was metamorphosing into a grand, young lady.

'Why can't you come to the point?' Kubha came and sat beside him. She saw sparks in Faraz's eyes. She knew he had some plan in his mind. She smiled and took his hands into hers.

'A few years back, there was a movie,' he said nonchalantly, 'where Amitabh Bachchan took a car from Delhi to Calcutta … '

One thing about Kubha that Faraz liked the most was the promptness with which she understood many things without being told much.

'Does Ammi know about it?' she threw the question to Faraz, taking her phone from the table.

'She knows what?' Faraz asked.

'That you want to drive 900 miles to Calcutta?'

'Well, that's your job. Convince your mother.'

'I'll drive,' she said, not taking her eyes from the phone. 'Rent-A-Car has introduced the GL Class in their fleet. It's available tomorrow.'

Early next morning, the duo hit the Yamuna Expressway, cutting through the dense mist.

'It's just November,' Faraz exclaimed, 'and there's already so much mist. Why do you like Delhi so much?'

'Young Boy,' Kubha chuckled, 'grow up … These are tears of the night, shabnam, tears in heaven. Carpet sellers wouldn't understand.' She paused abruptly, as though she had suddenly recalled something. 'Carpet … ' she turned towards Faraz. 'Didn't you say you've got the old manuscript with a lot of signs and symbols, the kind of which we see in some of our carpets?'

'What use does it have for you?' Faraz pretended to be sad. 'You don't like carpets and carpet sellers.'

'Ya, true,' Kubha broke into a laughter. 'I asked for the manuscript, not the carpets.'

☼

Faraz laid out the tattered pieces of fragile birch bark on the dining table at Kratu's house in Calcutta. Afsar stared at the dilapidated manuscript, her reaction barely hiding her feeling of wonderment.

'Young Boy,' Kubha extolled, 'this is just unbelievable. It looks so much like the old Bible I've seen at the Freer Gallery in Smithsonian.'

'The Bible wouldn't be in birch bark,' Afsar said, bending down on the table to get a closer look of the manuscript. 'The Himalayan birch is a typical material of the old Buddhist texts of the Gandhara region and Khushawar is very much within the locus of the ancient Gandhara territory. It looks very authentic.'

Afsar turned towards her father.

'Where exactly was it found, Aba?'

Faraz placed the last piece of the manuscript on the table.

'I've been thinking for a while if I should do a major renovation of our old house in Khushawar,' he started speaking. 'No one had stayed there for a long time before I returned there last year. I don't want to demolish anything. I want to retain as much as possible. Last week, I got an architect from Lahore. I asked him to take a stock of all the structures in our premise and come up with a renovation plan. That was when I got the ramshackle hut at the back side opened. I don't remember if I've ever entered that hut. It has been always locked since my childhood. As kids, we would peep inside, through the cracks of the wooden wall. I believe there were piles of discarded carpets. If I remember correctly, I've heard a lot of carpets were once damaged badly in a fire. This hut was constructed to store the damaged carpets, perhaps with the hope of reusing them later in some way, which in reality never happened.'

'The manuscript was there?' Afsar looked up.

'Yes,' Faraz continued. 'There was a pile of old newspapers, mainly Jang. The manuscript was wrapped in a paper and hidden inside the pile. An old-paper collector was sieving through the pile, when he kept aside a packet he was not interested in taking. By sheer coincidence, I happened to be there when our caretaker, a very stupid fellow, was almost throwing it away. A few yellow sheets slipped from the packet and fell onto the ground. I picked one up and immediately knew it was not an ordinary paper. It was filled with signs and symbols, many of which appeared very familiar to me. Soon, I realized our carpets have many of those signs.'

'When did you realize it was actually an old manuscript?' Afsar asked.

'The architect told me. I called you the same evening.'

'There were only these many sheets?' Afsar pointed to the bark pages laid on the table.

'The rest were so torn that it was not possible to carry them. A few sheets converted into ash the moment I touched them.'

Afsar looked at her husband. 'Krotu, can you scan all these?'

Kubha helped her father carry the delicate pages carefully to the scanner. As they scanned the manuscript, Afsar made a call.

☼

Afsar spent almost the whole day in her home office, studying the scanned images of the manuscript. Kratu had digitally enhanced the images to a great extent so as to make them appear much clearer and more readable than the original. The torn pieces of the birch bark manuscript were not all in the right order. It wouldn't have been possible to manually arrange the frail fragments of the pages properly without digitizing the pieces and trying to put together the jigsaw.

Kubha was lying half-asleep on the couch, somehow fitted into the already cluttered room, which served as Afsar's office-cum-study.

'What all did you find out?' Faraz asked Afsar in the evening. Too tired from the 26-hour road trip from Delhi to Calcutta, he had been sleeping since morning.

'How are you feeling?' Afsar asked her father, not taking her eyes off the big TV screen displaying the contents of her laptop.

'I'll never travel with your daughter,' he fretted, turning his face away from Kubha.

'Come on, Young Boy,' Kubha kept the Kindle aside and got up from the couch. She hugged her grandfather from behind. 'Be adventurous. Did you ever think we would reach Calcutta in a day?'

'That was a harrowing experience. You don't call it an adventure.' Faraz pulled Kubha from behind and made her sit on Afsar's table. 'But I should say,' he turned towards his daughter, 'this Old Lady will go places very few have dared to go to.'

'That's just incredible,' Afsar said loudly, the two other people in the room staring at her in surprise. 'Aba, this is a gold mine. This manuscript is very likely more than a thousand years old and the content may be older by a few more centuries.'

'Why do you say so?' Kubha and Faraz sat on the couch.

Afsar turned towards them.

'When I first saw the manuscript in the morning, I knew the script was some medieval form used in India, a really long time ago. I'm not a trained epigraphist or palaeographer …'

'What's that?' Faraz interrupted. 'In all these years, I've only managed to learn the term "linguistic palaeontologist", which means a mad person like you, who doesn't look for "love" in the words "pyaar" and "mohabbat", but breaks her head thinking who created them.'

The Old Lady giggled with the Young Boy, the one in the middle, poor Afsar, enjoying every bit of it. She stared at the granddaughter–grandfather pair with affection.

'Young Boy,' Kubha explained, 'epigraphist is a person who studies ancient inscriptions and a palaeographer is the one who studies ancient manuscripts and historical handwriting.' She turned towards her mother. 'You were saying something … '

'I've a friend who's an expert in Indian epigraphy. I talked to him in the morning. Later, I sent the scanned images of the manuscript. He confirmed the script is primitive Sharada. An evolved form of the same is still used by a few Kashmiri Pandits to write the Kashmiri language. The Gurumukhi script of the Punjabis too evolved from Sharada. The one in the manuscript is an old form of Sharada. It was in vogue in the ancient Gandhara region, around the present northwest Pakistan, not later than the tenth century.'

'Ammi, can you display some part of the manuscript on the screen?'

'Why not? Let me show you a page which has both numerals and alphabets. Otherwise, most pages have only numerals.'

Afsar displayed the digitally enhanced image of a reconstructed page of the manuscript on the big screen mounted on the wall and zoomed in on a particular line. 'Most of the manuscript is filled with numerals, like this,' she pointed to the screen.

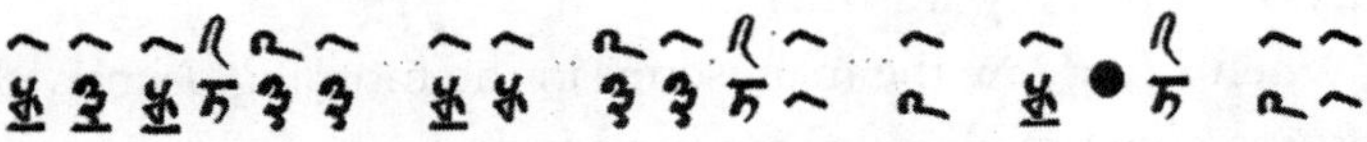

'Most of the manuscript is filled with numerals, like this … '

'One of the symbols looks like the English numeral "3",' Kubha said.

'You're right,' Afsar acknowledged. 'In fact, that's "3" in Sharada script too. You may not know the English numerals have evolved from their Indian counterparts. From India, the numerals first went to Arab and then to Europe. For a long time, people referred to them as Arabic numerals. Now, they are correctly called Hindu-Arabic. Let me show you something … '

Afsar searched through a folder in her laptop and displayed a picture.

'This shows the evolution of the numeral "4",' she said, pointing to the screen. 'The first symbol is what "4" looked like in India in the first century. This was found in some inscriptions and cave writings, where the symbols were etched out in the rocks. Straight lines are easier to engrave on rocks. That explains why the numeral "4" was all straight lines, to start with.'

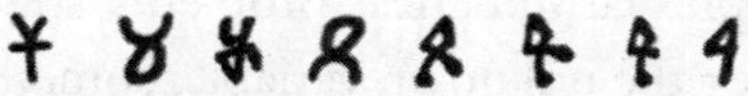

'This shows the evolution of the numeral "4".'

'But the next few symbols are not all straight lines … '

'When you have to write on palm leaves or birch bark with a pen dipped in ink, a continuous stroke handwriting is what comes naturally to you. The upper case "Y" of the first symbol, written in three separate strokes, transforms naturally into the second symbol when written in continuous strokes. That's "4" in the Devanagari script we use for Hindi. The third symbol is "4" in Sharada script, another form in continuous strokes which looks like a lower case "y".'

'I've got it,' Kubha said excitedly, getting up from the table and walking towards the screen. 'The fourth symbol is actually an inverted Hindi "4". The next one is almost the same.'

'And it's how the English "4" looked like in the twelfth century,' Afsar added.

Kubha seemed to be thinking something.

'What?' Afsar asked.

'I'm just wondering,' Kubha replied, 'if the manuscript can really be so old. Isn't it too outlandish to say that such an old manuscript survived more than 1,000 years?'

'It would be outright outlandish, if not for the discovery of a similar manuscript from Bakhshali, a village not very far from Khushawar, more than a hundred years ago.'

Talking about the Bakhshali Manuscript, Afsar mentioned it is perhaps the first-ever document anywhere in the world, known to have used a symbol for "zero".

'Zero is represented by a dot in the Bakhshali Manuscript,' she elaborated. 'It's believed to have been first written anterior to the fifth century and then reproduced many times in the past 1,500 years. Yes, it's that old! It has algebraic equations. It has simple and complex arithmetical problems solved algebraically, using a symbol for the unknown variable, something like how we use "x" and "y" now. And most strikingly, it represents a fraction almost the way we do even today, the numerator placed above the denominator, but not separated by any line.'

The Khushawar Manuscript too, Afsar said, has fractions depicted in the same way. 'Almost all the numerals I found in the manuscript,' she said, 'are fractions: ¼, ½, ⅛, etc. Wait a moment …'

She pulled her chair close to the desk and put her hands on the keypad of the laptop.

'Here it is,' she pointed to the screen on the wall. 'I've typed the fractions in Hindu-Arabic below the Sharada numerals of the manuscript.'

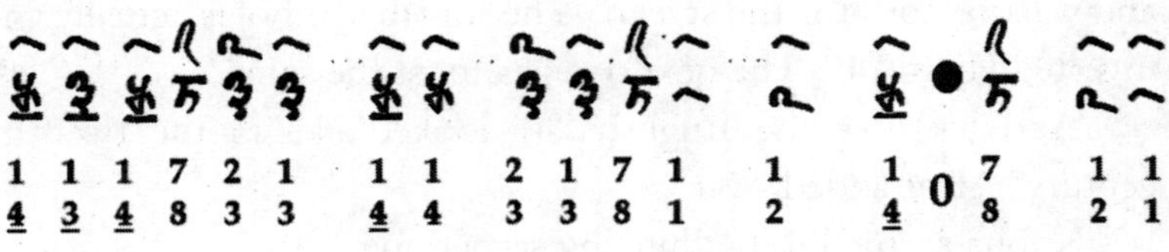

'Here it is … '

☼

The next morning, when Kubha woke up, she found her mother in her office.

'Didn't you sleep last night?' she asked.

'Unless I figure out everything, I can't do anything else … '

'What's that?' Kubha interrupted Afsar, pointing to the screen which displayed some peculiar symbols. 'Is it some other script? I don't think it's Sharada.'

'What's that?' Kubha interrupted Afsar, pointing to the screen which displayed some peculiar symbols.

'I need your father's help to figure that out. These are some of the texts from the manuscript. A few of our carpets too have these symbols. They look like Brahmi, but actually they are not.'

'Brahmi script is very old, isn't it?'

'Yes, it's what Ashoka used in most of his inscriptions in the third century BC.'

'Didn't you ever bother to find out how these Brahmi-like symbols could get into our carpets?'

'That's really strange. I don't even remember noticing these symbols in the carpets. It's ironical that I've been researching on so many things from round the world, but I've missed out something like this right here, in my own house.'

'What's that poem by Tagore you mentioned once? "*I walked for miles for many days …*"'

Afsar smiled. '*I spent much money and visited many lands,*' she recited, '*to see the mountains, to see the oceans. But I forgot to take the two steps from my home and behold with my wide open eyes, the drop of dew swinging from an ear of paddy.'*

Kubha pulled a stool and sat beside Afsar. 'What all have you found out till now?' she asked.

'Apart from the Sharada numerals, which comprise the majority of the manuscript, there are also verses and prose texts in a language, I feel, is close to Magadhi Prakrit. It's a corrupt form of Sanskrit, the colloquial language of the eastern part of India, some 1,500 years ago. The same Sharada script has been used to write the Prakrit texts too.'

'Wait a minute,' Kubha sat straight. 'You told me yesterday that the Sharada script is around 1,000 years old. Now you say that the language of the manuscript is 1,500 years old. How's that possible?'

'This implies the manuscript is a later reproduction of a much older text. Whenever an older work is reproduced later, it's logical to use the script of the time. When Mustafa Kemal Atatürk, the founder of the modern Turkish Republic, introduced the Latin script for the Turkish language, many Turkish classics previously written in the Ottoman Turkish or Arabic script were rewritten in the Latin script. I've seen a copy of the eleventh-century-classic *Kutadgu Bilig*, reproduced in the Latin script of the twentieth century.'

'So, you're implying the original text of the manuscript was composed 1,500 years ago. How sanguine are you about it?'

'I'm no expert in Prakrit, but a cursory look at some of the words does point to that date. It took more than a thousand years for Sanskrit to evolve into the modern languages such as Bengali, Hindi and Marathi. It's not easy to say how exactly the various languages evolved and what exactly the spoken languages in the different parts of India were like during this long period. We don't have much literature in the intermediate colloquial languages, apart from some Buddhist and Jain texts.'

'I would assume,' Kubha said, 'the language of choice for literary and religious works was predominantly Sanskrit for a very long time.'

'That's true,' Afsar agreed, 'even though very few people spoke Sanskrit at home. But, the classical Sanskrit literature of Kalidasa et al had some colloquial and regional flavour in the dialogues. The people from the lower class were usually portrayed as speaking the Magadhi Prakrit. It was the eastern dialect of the old Magadha region, comprising the present-day Bihar and Bengal. The language of the manuscript appears to be quite close to the Magadhi Prakrit of Kalidasa, who is believed to have lived in the fifth century, 1,500 years ago.'

'Interesting!' Kubha commented. 'So, it's something like this: some 1,500 years ago, the people in northwest Pakistan knew the language spoken some 1,500 miles away in Bihar and Bengal.'

'I'm not surprised at that. The present northwest Pakistan was known as Gandhara in the ancient times. It had very good ties with Magadha, though they were at the two frontiers of the India the world knew for millennia. Both were important business and cultural hubs in the Silk Route, the ancient trade link between China, India, Central Asia and the West. Both were important centres for learning and prominent seats of Buddhism.'

'Gandhara had Taxila,' Kubha added, 'one of the earliest international universities of the world, and Magadha had Nalanda. People would have surely moved a lot between Gandhara and Magadha. I do understand what you're trying to say.'

'Moreover,' Afsar stressed, 'Pataliputra, the present-day Patna and the biggest city of Magadha, was the capital of India for more than a thousand years. So, it was not a big deal for someone in Gandhara to know the language of Magadha, especially when the various languages spoken in different parts of India at that time were mutually intelligible.'

'Given the prominence of Magadha,' Kubha said, 'isn't it strange that its language was relegated to one spoken by the lower class?'

'Both Magadha and Gandhara have been referred to as the lands of the despised people, even in the Vedic corpus of literature, as early as 1000 BC, almost 3,000 years ago.'

'Why is it so? Were the Magadhans and Gandharas native people, looked down upon by the Vedic Aryans?'

'A friend of mine has the view that they, though separated by 1,500 miles, were actually akin, ethnically very closely related. Whether they were non-Aryans or natives is a matter of conjecture. From the Mauryas to the Guptas, the Magadhans ruled India for thousands of years from Pataliputra. Buddhism and Jainism both started from Magadha. If the Magadhans were all natives, then that would surely be a remarkable precedence in India where the natives are believed, even though wrongly, to have been relegated to the lower rungs of the social ladder. But, it's doubtless that they, along with the Gandharas, had many non-Aryan, non-Sanskritic aspects. The most striking being their names. Neither the word "gandhara" nor the word "magadha" has a proper Sanskritic etymology. Rather, both seem to be connected to the Munda word "gand" or "gad", as are the names of the rivers Ganga and Gandaki. The Munda languages are believed to be indigenous and older than Sanskrit.'

'Isn't Munda a tribal language?'

'Yes, it's spoken by the various tribes in the central and the eastern India, mainly in Jharkhand and Chhattisgarh … '

'By the way,' Kubha suddenly interrupted, as though she had recalled something important, 'what were we discussing and how did we come to the Munda connection of Magadha and Gandhara?'

'You started it,' Afsar smiled. 'You asked how someone in Gandhara could know the Magadhi Prakrit. In fact, the predominantly Magadhi Prakrit of the manuscript fused seamlessly with what can be called a primitive Pashto language.'

'*The Khushawar Manuscript*,' Kubha said dramatically, as though she was divulging a breaking news item on TV, '*a 1,000-year-old document, discovered recently from the backyard of the ancestral home of the Fareedis in Khushawar, shows a unique fusion of the 1,500-year-old colloquial languages of Gandhara and Magadha, the homelands of a long-forgotten, despised race …* '

It would soon turn out to be a prophetic discourse.

The Long-forgotten Despised Race

(2 November 2018. Calcutta)

This Takkariya manuscript has been written by the Naga Kings,
They have created the nine Varshas of the Naga Island.
The slang-speaking race, the kins of the Banas, they don't pour ashira, heat kettles,
The despised race, the kins of the Banas, they don't pour ashira, heat kettles.
They have created the nine Varshas of the Naga Island,
They rule over the world, from Gada to Gada.

Afsar read out the lines in English from the enhanced image of a page from the manuscript. Kratu had joined the mother–daughter duo after his morning workout, something he had lately started taking a little more seriously. Greatly contrasting to his recent health consciousness though, was his newly found affection for jilipi, which he had once described to his American friend as a concentrated starch batter deep fried in clarified Indian butter and soaked in a sinfully sweet syrup. Afsar's concentration was interrupted when Kratu noisily munched the crispy jilipi, his mouth overflowing with the evil juice. Kubha held a piece of paper below his mouth in the nick of time, saving Afsar's desk from the undesired sweetening. Afsar looked at Kratu in a not-so-sweet concoction of disgust and hopelessness. Kubha wiped her father's chin with a tissue.

'Can I continue,' asked Afsar, 'if you folks are done?'

'Yes,' Kratu answered, settling on the couch. He readied the tab on his lap and lifted one more jilipi from the plate he had kept on the floor, in front of him.

'You think you've heard something like this anywhere else?'

'The slang-speaking race, the kins of the Banas, they don't pour ashira, heat kettles, *maddha-bache bana-bashe nashire duhe tabadi ghamme* … '

Afsar took her stare off the laptop screen and looked at Kratu. 'It's in a modified Arya meter and the text is a perfect Magadhi Prakrit, a corruption of Sanskrit.'

'What would be the correct Sanskrit?' Kratu asked.

'*Mridhra-vachah bana-vamshah nashiram duhe tapanti gharmam*,' Afsar read out the Sanskrit equivalent of the Prakrit text of the manuscript.

'Doesn't the Prakrit sound very much like the Bangla Dadu would sometimes speak at home?' Kubha asked her father, looking at the transliterated English text Afsar had added beside the original text of the manuscript.

'That's indeed a very good observation,' Afsar patted Kubha, scribbling the Sanskrit text with a stylus, alongside the Prakrit text, on her laptop screen. 'Your grandfather would switch to a Bangladeshi dialect of Bengali whenever he was excited or angry.' Her scribble appeared on the big screen mounted on the wall. 'Most of the Bangladeshi dialects,' she continued, 'have preserved many striking aspects of the Magadhi Prakrit, from which has evolved the modern Bengali language. Interestingly though, the formal Bengali you hear in Calcutta or the one used in the books has been highly Sanskritized. Much of the colloquialism has been lost.'

'Dadu would often say, "kammo", in place of "karma", very much like how the manuscript has "ghamma" in place of the Sanskrit "gharma".'

'That's the most noticeable aspect of the Prakrit languages. The conjoined consonants of Sanskrit have been simplified to a great extent in Prakrit. The "r" and "m" in "karma" and "gharma" are of two different types: "r" is a semivowel and "m" a labial consonant, produced through your lips. Pronouncing a conjoined "r" and "m" is not easy. Many kids would find it difficult to pronounce that. But they wouldn't have any problem with "mm".'

'Ya,' Kubha agreed, '"kamma" is indeed much simpler than "karma". It's very much like modern Italian, where the Latin "Circus Maximus" has been simplified to "Circo Massimo", isn't it?'

'Yes, you're right! But, you would never say "kamma" in Hindi. Bengali has preserved the old Prakrit form till this day, that too only in some colloquial dialects of Bangladesh.'

'The Sanskrit "mridhra-vachah" has been simplified to "maddha-bache",' Kubha said.

'But, there's something more in "maddha-bache" than the mere simplification of conjoined consonants.'

'What's that?' Kubha asked.

'Do you remember the concept of case in English grammar?'

Before Kubha could respond, Kratu, who till now had been a little held up with the wiping of the last few drops of the sweet syrup from his chin and neck, jerked into life.

'Sweetheart,' he chuckled, 'are we going to learn about some long-forgotten English grammar now?'

'Not exactly,' Afsar sounded anything but frivolous. 'We'll rather learn a very important aspect of the Magadhi Prakrit.'

'Ammi,' Kubha smiled, 'do you know how funny you look when you talk like this?'

'Like what?' Afsar couldn't hide her surprise in her frowning eyebrows.

'Like a headmistress … '

Kratu supplanted instantaneously, and pretended to be serious, putting his fingers on his lips.

It was not that Afsar was not enjoying the moments, which she knew had become sparser, with time. She stared at her daughter who was no longer the same little one she had been just a few years ago. The Kratu, she had first met more than two decades ago at Stanford, Afsar thought, reappeared only when their daughter would be with them. Over the years, the unpretentious childishness she had fallen for had faded away. But, very surprisingly, she felt, Kubha could bring out the child in Kratu. She smiled.

'Can we get back to work?'

'Yes, please,' Kratu replied, rubbing his tissue-wiped hands on Kubha's tee.

'You were talking about case,' Kubha reminded her mother.

'Yes,' Afsar resumed. 'In grammar, case means the function of a noun or pronoun in a sentence. When I say, "Buddha was born in Nepal", the proper noun "Buddha" is the subject. That's the nominative case, indicating the name of the subject. "In Nepal" indicates the location of the subject. That's the locative case. In English, the locative case is generally indicated with prepositions, such as in, at and on.'

'In Bengali, we often append an "e" to the word to denote the locative case, isn't it?' Kubha remarked. 'We simply say "Nepal-e". We don't use any preposition.'

'Thank God, you took the grammar classes seriously,' Afsar smiled. 'Bengali has taken the "e" in locative case directly from Sanskrit. This "e" is added liberally to most words in Magadhi Prakrit, irrespective of the case.' She paused, and read the Prakrit text from the manuscript once more, '*maddha-bache bana-bashe nashire duhe tabadi ghamme.*'

'That's interesting,' Kubha was intrigued. 'Almost all the words end with an "e", whereas the corresponding Sanskrit forms don't.'

'Yes, you're correct,' Afsar agreed. 'This "e" is the simplest identifying marker for Magadhi Prakrit. No other Prakrit language in India has it.'

Kubha seemed to be thinking something.

'What?' Afsar asked.

'You said Bengali came from Magadhi Prakrit. But we don't add "e" to every word.'

'Modern Bengali has mostly dropped this "e". But one of its sister languages has preserved it till date, especially in the nominative case.'

'Bengali's sister language?' Kratu asked. 'What's that?'

Afsar stared at Kratu for a few moments. 'Can you open up the online edition of any newspaper from Sri Lanka?'

'If you're suddenly bored of deciphering the manuscript,' Kratu couldn't stop laughing, 'you can do something else. Reading a Sri Lankan newspaper may not be the most interesting thing ...'

'Don't worry,' Afsar quipped, 'I'm not yet bored. And you too will realize soon that a Sri Lankan paper wouldn't be that uninteresting.'

'Here it is,' Kratu had already opened up the home page of the *Daily News*. 'It says "Sri Lanka's National Newspaper since 1918".' He passed on the tab to Afsar.

'The first news item is written by someone called Chamikara Weerasinghe,' Afsar said, looking at the tab, 'the second one by Siri Abeyratne, the third one by Ranil Ratnanayake. Weerasinghe is nothing but Veera Singha, Abeyratne is Abhay Ratna and Ratnanayake is Ratna Nayaka. All these, as you can see, are Sanskrit words.'

'And all of them have an "e" appended to them,' Kubha observed, excitedly.

'Yes, you're absolutely correct. Many medieval Jain texts written in a variant of Magadhi Prakrit would always have Mahaveere Vardhamane, not Mahaveera Vardhamana. That's exactly what Sinhalese has preserved in many of its names.'

She went on to explain why Sinhalese and Bengali were sister languages, both having descended from the same e-Prakrit spoken in the ancient Magadha region more than 2,000 years ago.

'In fact,' she asserted, 'the two languages are so similar that in order to translate a Bengali song originally composed by Tagore, a Sri Lankan student at Shantiniketan, Ananda Samarakoon, had to make only minimal changes to it. Later, the same song became the national anthem of Sri Lanka.'

'Wow,' Kubha exclaimed, 'this means, the language of the 1,000-year-old manuscript found in Pakistan and that of the modern-day Sri Lanka are e-connected.'

The small family broke into laughter.

Little did they know that this revelation about the "e" marker and the subsequent turn of events would eventually lead to the unearthing of one of the greatest frauds of the recent times and that it would avert a major catastrophe too.

☼

Later that day, in the evening, the three generations of the Fareedis, along with Kratu, the only link to their Bong connection, went out on a sunset cruise on the Ganges from Outram Ghat. Going by the tradition, they took an un-motorized boat, a few of which, in Afsar's words, have somehow survived the industrial revolution, especially for Calcutta, perhaps to retain an aura of nostalgia and traditional charm.

'This laid-back charm,' Faraz said, climbing onto the boat carefully, 'is something so much a part of Calcutta. Despite everything else that might not have worked in its favour, Calcutta still brings in a feeling of longing and yearning. Delhi is arrogant, Bombay too practical, Madras too traditional. But Calcutta is hung up somewhere in between … '

'It's neither here, nor there … ' Kratu interrupted his father-in-law.

'Baba,' Kubha mock-scolded her father, 'how can you be so unromantic?' She started laughing. 'The Young Boy is at his romantic best.'

'Your father has become old,' Faraz chuckled.

Settling comfortably on the open deck of the small boat, rowed by a sleepy old man, the extended Fareedi family engaged in some childish banter with each other. It was not that the four people hadn't met like this ever in the past, but still, Afsar felt, there was something really special, or rather unique, this time. Later, when she would look back to this day, she would always feel bad that the evening hadn't stretched long enough, that the evening breeze could have been more pleasant, that her father could have pulled Kratu's leg a few more times, that Kubha could have fought like a kid with her grandfather a little longer, that she herself shouldn't have spent a good part of the evening discussing the manuscript. But then, it was not Afsar who brought up the topic.

'I missed a lot of discussion,' Faraz said, leaning against the ramshackle semi-cylindrical cabin of the boat and stretching his legs forward. 'What all have you figured out about the manuscript?'

Like a reflex action, Afsar brought out a small notebook from her bag. Like the un-mechanized boats, her notebook too hadn't changed a bit over a long time. In the age where a notebook no longer meant anything to do with paper and pencil, Afsar's notebook had been always a small physical diary with not as many pages as would be needed to contain everything she scribbled into it. She opened a particular page in her notebook.

'A few things I'm confused about,' she said, staring at the notebook. 'Not only is it written in the Magadhi Prakrit language, but it also talks about the people of Magadha. The references are quite explicit.'

Afsar explained that the people of ancient Magadha had been ethnically quite diverse as early as 1500 BC, when the *Rig*

Veda was perhaps written. It so happened, she believed, that the earlier batches of the Sanskrit-speaking Aryans, who were the first people to have entered into what is now the Punjab in India and Pakistan, mixed freely with the natives, perhaps the ones who spoke some primitive forms of Munda and Dravidian languages. Later, when the newer batches of the Aryans arrived, they despised their older kins, who had been already well settled in their new homeland. Gradually, many of the older ones, along with the natives they had befriended, started moving out of the Punjab, perhaps to avoid the increasing confrontations with their younger kin. A few of them moved to the neighbouring Gandhara region in northwest Pakistan, and the rest came to Magadha.

'Over the next few millennia,' Afsar said, 'the land between Gandhara and Magadha, stretching from the Punjab in the west to Bihar in the east, would become the Hindi heartland. That's roughly where the later Aryans settled. Gandhara and Magadha, the two frontier lands, became the land of the despised people.'

'If I understand correctly,' Kratu pointed out, '"the land of the despised people" doesn't necessarily mean an apartheid regime.'

'You're right,' Afsar conceded. 'On the contrary, I would say, the ethnically diverse people of Magadha and Gandhara were economically, technologically and intellectually ahead of the others, who naturally envied them. It's not by fluke that Magadha was the centre of power, education and spirituality in India for more than a millennium. Chandragupta Maurya, Ashoka, Chanakya, Buddha—all of them ruled the whole country, and virtually the world too, to some extent, from Magadha. Gandhara too had been a centre for learning for a long time. The university at Taxila was one of the earliest of its kind, which attracted people from round the world. It's natural that the rest of the country would speak scornfully about them, out of sheer jealousy. Everything they did—the way they talked, the way they behaved—became a matter of banter to the rest.'

'In Bengali, there's a saying,' Kratu said jokingly, 'when you don't like someone, you say his legs are broken too.'

'Yes, the same happened in this case too,' Afsar smiled. 'Due to the ethnic diversity of the people of Magadha, their colloquial language had many non-Sanskritic features, which were made fun of. They became Mridhra-vachah, the slang-speaking, and Vrishalakah, the despised and contemptible people, the outcasts.'

'If I remember correctly,' Kubha interrupted, 'these epithets—Mridhra-vachah and Vrishalakah—are used in the manuscript for the people who are said to be the rulers of the world. The other people calling the Magadhans outcasts is understandable, but why would someone writing in the Magadhan language and talking about the Magadhans use the derogatory terms?'

'I, too, had the same confusion at the beginning. Then I figured out something. In the Buddhist text *Vasala Sutta*, the Buddha himself is referred to as *vrishalaka*, a contemptible man. Emperor Chandragupta Maurya is also called a *vrishala* in the Sanskrit drama *Mudrarakshasa*.'

'So, are you trying to say,' Kubha said, 'the Magadhans started using the ethnic slur directed at them by the puritans in a non-derogatory sense?'

'It's somewhat similar to the African Americans often using the term "nigga" among themselves, as a term for endearment.'

'That's quite a smart move,' Faraz said. 'The moment the white Americans knew that the blacks themselves were using "nigga" in a non-derogatory sense, they soon lost interest in it.'

'True,' Afsar acknowledged.

'Doesn't the manuscript also talk about the Nagas, the serpents?' Kubha asked.

'The Nagas are said to be the kin of the Banas,' Afsar said, looking at her notebook. 'They have created the nine varshas of the Naga Island and they rule over the world from Gada to Gada. I've no idea what we're dealing with here.'

'Ammi, why are you thinking so much?' Kubha quipped; the naughty smile on her face erased all ambiguities about her intentions. 'I've a friend in JNU. She's from Kohima. She calls herself a Naga. Isn't it possible that the Magadhans were frustrated with the non-stop banters from the Brahmins and that they relocated to the serene hills of Nagaland? My friend often says that they are so much isolated from the rest of India that they feel they are staying in an island. That explains the Naga Island too ...'

'No, I disagree,' Kratu interrupted. 'I think the manuscript talks about us, the Bongs. Nag is a Bong last name. We worship snakes. The Snake Goddess Manasa is considered very powerful in Bengal. I think the "banas" is nothing but the Magadhi Prakrit form of the "bongs".'

All throughout, Kratu tried to keep his face as stern as possible. But finally he couldn't control himself. He broke into a laughter, Kubha joining him too. Afsar, for a while was more stunned than amused and her father, the Young Boy, pretended to be nonchalant, perhaps not to hurt his daughter.

☼

A little later, when the laughter subsided a bit, Afsar was still silent.

'Actually, guys,' she spoke after a few more quiet moments during which everyone else was busy gauging her body language, 'I somehow have a feeling that you both have said something I need to really think about.'

'No, Ammi,' Kubha started laughing again. 'You can't do this.'

'I'm not joking,' Afsar's voice made it clear to everyone that she was indeed not in a mood for jokes or jibes. But she too couldn't remain like that for long. 'Look guys,' she said with a smile, 'most discoveries are made like this. Someone throws some really weird pointer and that becomes the Rosetta Stone.'

'Now, what's a Rosetta Stone?' Kratu butted in, still not able to comprehend the genuineness of Afsar's reactions.

'Forget that,' Afsar said. 'Kubha, didn't you talk yesterday about a long-forgotten, despised race?'

'Yes, I did,' Kubha said hesitantly. 'But I was not serious, Ammi.'

'I know that. But you were not totally wrong. It has been there in my mind too, but I didn't take it seriously. Now, I've a gut feeling you were actually correct. And you were correct today too. The Nagas of Nagaland belong to the same mythical Naga Vamsha, the ancient and forgotten Naga peoples that have left their marks from Kashmir to Nagaland. The Nanga Parbat and the Nanda Devi, two of the highest peaks of the Himalayas, and many places in Kashmir such as Sheeshnag and Anantnag bear their name. "Nagara", the Sanskrit word for city, may be related to them. Magadha was ruled by several mythical and historical Naga dynasties. And Krotu, the Manasa connection of the Bongs is also not irrelevant. There are many missing links though. Let us go home.'

She got up.

☼

'Aba, good that you got the manuscript,' Afsar thanked her father on the way back home.

The next morning, Faraz and Kubha left Calcutta. There was no way for Afsar to know then that she wouldn't see her father again in her life. His last gift to her, the manuscript, would turn out soon to be an invaluable gift, something that would save many lives.

It would almost get Kubha killed though.

Somak Ajai

(4 November 2018. Delhi)

Faraz didn't want Kubha to accompany him to meet Somak Ajai, a professor of mathematics at the Delhi School of Economics. Somak had recently contacted him and told something very fascinating. He was skeptic though, and didn't want to believe Somak. Afsar had been skeptic too, when she had heard about it.

'I've been dealing with carpets for more than 50 years now,' Faraz had told Afsar, 'and I have never come across anything even remotely similar to our Khushawari carpets. If it really existed, I would have come to know of it by now.'

'That's true,' Afsar had agreed. 'But then, why would an old professor play a trick with you?'

'That's why I'm eager to meet him.'

Kubha was equally eager to meet Somak.

'Why are you insisting that I should not accompany you?' she asked Faraz. 'Is the Young Boy planning to do some hanky-panky?'

'Yes, Old Lady,' Faraz giggled. 'Where do I get to do hanky-panky in Khushawar?'

'Okay, enough. I'm coming with you.'

A few hours later, the grandfather–granddaughter duo alighted from a cab at the end of a dead alley on the fringes of the bustling

Malka Ganj, a neighbourhood adjoining the north campus of the Delhi University. They stood in front of the large wooden gate of a cozy colonial bungalow at the centre of a sprawling and thickly wooded land, surrounded by a low boundary wall broken at many places. They felt as though they had been suddenly transported many thousand miles away from Delhi. The bustle and flurry of the city seemed to have ceased abruptly. The unexpected silence morphed very well with the forested Northern Ridge, the lingering dregs of the grand old Aravalli Hills that extended to the backyard of the isolated last house of the lane.

'What an amazing place!' exclaimed Kubha, looking around. 'I can't believe we are in Delhi.'

From nowhere, appeared a stout figure that opened the wooden door. Both of them were woken up from their trance by the creaking sound.

'Aiye janab,' greeted the person, walking towards Faraz. 'Welcome to my little paradise.' He took Faraz's hands and held them tightly. 'I least expected you would be accompanied by such a gorgeous lady,' he said, turning towards Kubha.

'I assume you would be Mr Somak Ajai,' Faraz shook hands with the owner of the house. In a polo-neck, hand-knitted red woolen pullover worn above a pair of crinkled pajamas and a trucker cap fitted loosely on his head, he would have been totally ignored, Kubha felt, had he been in a crowd.

'Yes, I am,' responded Somak, lowering his head a bit. 'Please come in.' He extended his hand and held onto Kubha's, leading them inside. 'May I know your name, young lady?' he asked Kubha.

'She's my Old Lady,' Faraz declared, 'and I'm the only boyfriend she could ever manage to have … '

'We've so much in common,' Somak interrupted. 'I, too, have a girlfriend. If you come next week, you can meet her—my granddaughter.'

'Where's she now?' Kubha asked. There was something about Somak that had already endeared him to her. Somak was so much like her own grandfather, she felt.

'She stays in the Bay Area, in California. She would be visiting me next week. For the past few years, she has been managing to take a break and stay with me for a month and a half. That's when this silent paradise of mine comes alive with the sound of music.'

They had already reached the faded white bungalow.

☼

Faraz was speechless for a while, looking at the carpets Somak had piled up on the floor of the oval living room. 'I just can't believe ...' he mumbled.

'That was my reaction too,' Somak said, standing a little away from Faraz, on the other side of the pile of carpets dumped haphazardly on the floor. 'Did I tell you how I discovered this?'

'Yes. The guy who buys your rugs told you about it.'

'He's not a big guy like you. He's a Ukrainian. He generally sells my rugs in Russia and a few European countries to a closed

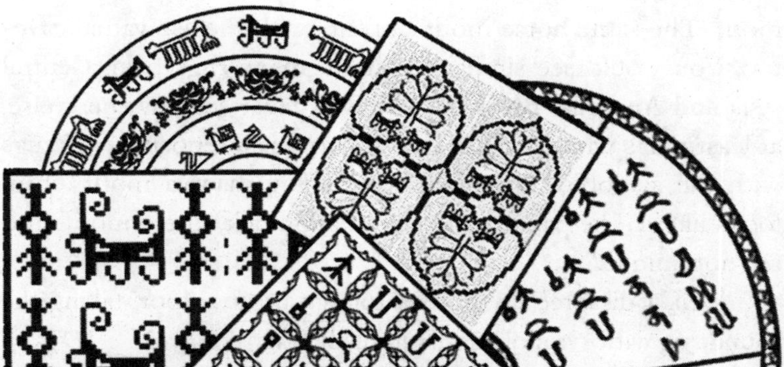

Faraz was speechless for a while, looking at the carpets Somak had piled up on the floor.

group of people. He doesn't even have a website when my milkman too uses a mobile app.'

It had so happened, Somak narrated, that his agent had got a call from a bigger rug dealer in Kiev asking how he could sell a Khushawari rug at a price which was even lower than what he had acquired it for.

'Before that,' Somak said, 'I had never heard of Khushawari rugs. I was told it's a much sought-after rug in the international market and that it's exclusively procured and sold by one dealer in the world. That's when I heard your name. My granddaughter checked your website and sent me the pictures of all the rugs which surreptitiously match with ours.'

Faraz's eyes were still fixed on the floor. 'The figures of the animals and the birds,' he muttered, pointing to the round carpet, a part of which was visible from under the pile on the floor, 'you see in this carpet, are common motifs in many Baluch and Anatolian rugs. I see the same horse motif in three carpets.'

Faraz sat on the floor and pulled out two carpets from the pile—a rectangular one from his left, a corner of which was visible, and a square one from the top with motifs that looked like ashwatha leaves. 'The horse and the tree,' he said, taking the rectangular rug in his hands, 'is a typical Baluch-Anatolian motif. The same horse motif appears with the ashwatha leaves too. You would see similar motifs in many rugs from Central Asia and Anatolia. But what you will never see anywhere else, at least that's what I've believed till now, is a repository of rugs with the symbols. These are typical Khushawari motifs. But, looks like …' he paused and stared at Somak, 'these motifs too are not unique.'

'Well, I disagree …' Somak too sat on the floor, taking the round rug with symbol-motifs in his hands.

Faraz and Kubha both looked at him in a way that elicited a smile in his face. He removed the cap from his head.

'I meant,' he continued, 'I don't agree that these motifs are not unique. They are, indeed, unique, and they are related to our motifs in the same way as Sanskrit is related to Greek and Latin …'

'Are you implicating,' Kubha interrupted, 'that your rugs and ours have both originated from the same source?'

Somak seemed to be satisfied at arousing a sense of suspense among his exclusive audience.

'Would you mind an evening walk?' he asked. 'I had chosen this place to stay, only because there's a jungle behind.'

He tried to get up. Kubha held his hand and pulled him up.

☼

A short while later, walking through a narrow trail cutting across a part of the forested area of the Northern Ridge behind Somak's house, Kubha remembered the many long walks she had taken with Porus in JNU. It was she who had insisted that Porus—that was the name she had always called Parush by all her life—should return to India. Had she not said anything, she knew very well, Porus would still have come with her to India and stayed in Delhi. 'You've made enough money,' she would say, 'and I know you don't want to work any more. Come with me …'

Following Somak and her grandfather in the winding track, already darkened by the thick vegetation that allowed only a little light to sieve through, Kubha thought about Porus. The chill of a November evening was settling inside the forest, slowly, like a drop of ink diffusing into the water. Porus too, she felt, had gradually spread into her, without herself knowing, when and how. Every time, she had tried to analyze her relationship with him, she would always feel dizzy. No one had to tell her that it was perhaps one of the most unusual, or rather weird, relationships anyone could have. She always wondered why her parents, or even her grandfather, had always pretended as though everything was so very natural, usual. Was it convenience, she pondered again, or indulgence?

'Why is the Old Lady so silent?' Somak interrupted Kubha's thoughts. When she looked up, she saw both Somak and Faraz staring at her.

'I'm enjoying the walk,' she managed to say. She knew she was blushing.

As they walked through the wooded ridge, trampling on fallen leaves, bending down under low branches of trees and jumping over meandering streams flowing languidly through the rocky terrain, Somak talked about the history of his family. He was a Maithili Brahmin, belonging to a closely guarded clan of the Brahmins from the ancient Mithila region, comprising parts of the present-day north Bihar and Nepal. But interestingly, he informed them, his ancestors had always lived at Kusumpur, a very small and nondescript village near Patna.

'Kusumpur was never within the boundaries of what we know of the ancient Mithila. We're perhaps the only Maithili Brahmins who never stayed in Mithila.'

'Do your family members weave the rugs?' Faraz asked.

'I don't think we've ever woven any rug. That's what I've gathered from my father. There are still a few families of weavers left in Kusumpur. I heard there were many more in the past. Over time, either they have changed their profession or have left Kusumpur. They are like extensions of our families. For generations, we've trained them, guided them and helped them create the wonderful carpets. In modern parlance, we own the designs. The motifs are our intellectual properties, handed over from one generation to another.'

'The story is similar with us too, in Khushawar,' Faraz said. 'I'm curious to know more.'

According to family legend, Somak narrated, his ancestors had come from Gadal, a mythical place somewhere in the west, whose identity was shrouded in mystery. Accordingly, they called themselves Gadalia, the people from Gadal. It was then not without any basis, he argued, that his folks at Kusumpur referred to the other Maithili Brahmins as Magadia, the people of the ancient Magadha. 'Though Mithila and Magadha are not exactly same,' he explained, 'the term "magadia", I believe, was used loosely to refer to the people of Mithila, which was anyway a part of the Magadha Empire for a long time.'

Kubha could hear the sound of traffic. Suddenly, a wired barricade appeared in front of them, beyond which was a road. Somak guided them to a gap in the barricade. They slipped through the gap and landed on the narrow footpath lining the road. A few cars zoomed past them, slowing down a little ahead, near a roundabout.

'Now, I've a very strong feeling,' Somak continued, as they walked towards the roundabout, 'that Gadal is nothing but the Magadhi vernacular form of Gandhara, and Khushawar, the name of your ancestral village in Gandhara, is just the Pashto form of Kusumpur … '

Kubha had been just behind Somak and Faraz. She took a long stride and caught up with them.

'Are you saying,' she interrupted Somak, 'you guys have migrated from our place? How long back was that? And how can you be so sanguine about that?'

'Sweetheart, you've asked me too many questions. I hope I'll be able to give you all the answers very soon. Lately, I've been working only on this. For the time being, let me show you where it all started.'

'I don't think I'm getting you,' Kubha said impatiently.

'Let's go there,' Somak smiled and pointed towards something ahead, on the other side of the road, which looked like a stone pillar. 'That's one of the many pillars Emperor Ashoka had erected all across India in the third century BC and inscribed his famous edicts on. The inscription on this pillar is in Brahmi script, the progenitor of almost all the scripts in India and Southeast Asia. Many symbol-motifs in our carpets are actually Brahmi letters.'

☼

The sun would go down soon and the twilight was settling in. When Somak led Faraz and Kubha to the Delhi–Meerut pillar at the ruined site of the Kushk-i-Shikar, the Hunting Palace of the Delhi Emperor Firoz Shah Tughlaq, the surroundings were still visible. The pillar, Somak informed, had been transported from Meerut by the emperor with a lot of pain and re-erected on this hill in Delhi in the fourteenth century.

While Kubha was taking a closer look at the inscription on the upper part of the curved surface of the pillar, Somak pulled out a tab from the side bag he had been carrying with him. With a little effort, she could figure out a few alphabets inscribed on the polished surface of the pillar. She had heard of the Brahmi letters, but this was the first time she was seeing them, that too, on a real inscription.

'Look there,' Somak climbed the two big steps of the pedestal on which the pillar stood and pointed up to a particular section of the inscription. Kubha too had to climb in order to see the few lines of the inscription from a close distance. 'Now check this out,' Somak handed over the tab to her. 'I've a facsimile of the lines you're seeing now. I also have an image of the symbol-motifs from one of our rugs. Check it out yourself.'

It didn't take much to figure out what Somak wanted her to see. She could actually correlate a part of the facsimile with a few letters inscribed side by side on the pillar. She had to lean her head back to get a good view of the Brahmi letters, visible a little above her height. A few letters in the facsimile were encircled. A few symbols in the image of the rug were encircled too. She

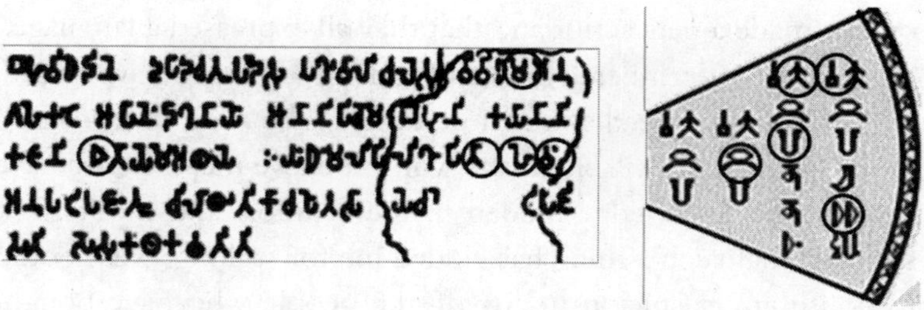

A few letters in the facsimile were encircled. A few symbols in the image of the rug were encircled too.

stared at the tab and the pillar a few times. The sparks in her eyes satisfied Somak.

'I too had the same reaction,' Somak smiled. 'Last year, Maitreyi had pointed out that some of the symbols of our carpets matched very closely with the Brahmi letters of this inscription. We often take long walks in the ridge and every time we stop by this place, resting a bit. Last year, when we had come here, we met an American historian who was studying Ashokan inscriptions.'

'Who's Maitreyi?'

'Oh, how could I forget to tell you that she's my granddaughter? She's visiting me next week. You should meet her.'

☼

On the way back to his home, again through the forested trail—it had already become quite dark by then—Somak talked excitedly about what all he had achieved in the past one year.

'Once I realized that many symbols in our rugs are nothing but Brahmi letters,' he said, pulling out a torch from his side bag, 'I saw a lot of possibilities. There were many other symbols which were not Brahmi. Neither did they match with any known script in India. Even the isolated Brahmi letters were not making any sense. Somehow, I had a feeling that all the symbols, Brahmi and others, made a new script and that they all expressed a language.'

'Have you deciphered the script and the language?' Faraz asked.

'I think so. I need some more time. I'll be soon in a position to talk about it. It will shake the world. Believe me, the rugs have a wealth of knowledge hidden in the symbols and motifs. I'm shocked that such a thing has eluded me for so long. Neither did it arouse any suspicion in any of the people who have bought the rugs from you and me. It's as though the Holy Grail has been lying in front of us for so long and we never knew of it.'

Later that evening, when Faraz and Kubha were taking leave, Kubha stared at the name plate stuck on the gothic stone pillars of the wooden gate of Somak's house. Somak's full name, Somak Ajai, was written on the name plate in gothic style. 'Is Ajai a common last name for Maithili Brahmins?' she asked. 'I've a Maithili Brahmin friend at JNU. He told me that Mishra and Jha are the most common last names.'

'We're Mishras. But we never use that last name. "Ajai" associates us with one of our most glorious ancestors whose real identity has been a mystery. But I've a feeling, our mysterious ancestor is none other than Aryabhata.'

'Aryabhata? Wasn't he a mathematician?' Kubha could barely suppress her amazement.

'Yes, he's one of the greatest mathematicians India ever had. He lived more than 1,500 years ago. It's believed that he was born in a place called Kusumapura, whose exact location hasn't yet been determined conclusively. It may very well be our village, Kusumpur.'

'How did you find that out?'

'That's a long story. Why don't you come to my place next week?'

Faraz and Kubha started walking towards their car, Somak following them. Faraz turned back.

'You should meet my daughter,' he suggested to Somak. 'She will be of great help to you … ' he paused and looked at Kubha with a mischievous smile. 'What's your mother? Langotiya Palwan or something like that, isn't it?'

'She's a linguistic palaeontologist,' she replied, controlling her laughter.

'Oh, really?' Somak exclaimed.

'And I should tell you,' Faraz said proudly, 'she's quite good at it. You may be interested to see the manuscript I gave her.'

'Manuscript?'

'Oh, I should have told you about it. I myself never thought it would be such a precious thing … ' Faraz looked at Kubha. 'Old Lady, why don't you tell him what your mother thinks about the manuscript?'

'It's a 1,000-year-old manuscript, written in some ancient script called Sharada. Young Boy came across it accidentally in Khushawar when he was cleaning an old outhouse.'

She talked briefly about the manuscript and its connection to the rugs.

When Kubha and Faraz left Somak's house, neither of them had any inkling of what all would befall them, just in a matter of a week. And for Kubha, she surely didn't know then, that she wouldn't see Somak again. That long story which he had talked about would remain unheard forever. Neither did Kubha know then that when she would see her grandfather off at the Delhi airport the following day that would be the last time she would see him too.

The Murders

(11 November 2018. Delhi)

Kubha called her mother from the hotel Faraz was staying at. She talked excitedly about the interesting person that Somak was. She talked about the place he had chosen to stay—a 100-year-old colonial bungalow, tucked into the sudden silence under the shades of the Aravallis that faded abruptly into the bustling Delhi. She also told her mother about the aura of mystery he had created around his ancestry, and how everything was in stark contrast to a certain openness and simplicity in his behaviour.

'How many people you know would take you through a jungle trail in the heart of Delhi,' she said passionately, 'but make you feel as though you're walking through any other normal lane or bylane of your neighbourhood?'

'Looks like, someone has really impressed you,' Afsar joked.

'Doubtless,' Kubha replied, 'I've become his fan. In so many ways, he is like my Young Boy. You should surely meet him. He has a natural flair for languages.' She elaborated Somak's theory connecting Gadal with Gandhara and Khushawar with Kusumpur.

'He may be correct,' Afsar said. 'The word "gadal" can really be the Magadhi Prakrit form of the Sanskrit "gandhara".'

The conjoined consonants "n" and "dha" of Gandhara, she explained, were first simplified to "dda", thus arriving at an intermediate form of Gaddara. This further simplified to

Gadara. 'These simplifications are quite common in all the Prakrit languages. Emperor Ashoka would use the epithet Piyadasi for himself in his inscriptions. It's nothing but a simplification of Priyadarshi, via Piyadassi.'

'How does Gadara become Gadal?' Kubha asked.

'That's another identifying feature of the Magadhi Prakrit—all "r" sounds are replaced with "l".'

'What about the Kusumpur–Khushawar connection?'

'That's indeed a very intelligent deduction. The old name of Peshawar was Purusha-pura, the City of Men. It first became Parasha-wara, and was much later persianized by Akbar to Peshawar, meaning the Frontier Town. Very similarly Kusuma-pura, the City of Flowers, would have evolved into Khusha-war. If the "m" sound of the Sanskrit "kusuma" is dropped, you get the Pashto-sounding "khusha". Dropping of consonants is quite common in Prakrit. The Sanskrit "upadhyaya", meaning teacher, became "ojha", a common last name in North India.'

Afsar stopped abruptly.

'What?' asked Kubha.

'If Somak is right, then we've a situation where a group of people migrate from a place called Kusumapura in the ancient Gandhara region to the eastern country of Magadha. They retain the name of their ancestral village in Gandhara and christen their new village Kusumapura.'

She paused for a few seconds.

'The Gadaliyas from Gandhara settle down among the Magadiyas of Magadha ...' She paused again and then repeated the words "gadaliya" and "magadiya" a few times. 'What do you think is common between Gadaliya and Magadiya?' she asked Kubha.

Kubha thought for a few moments and then blurted out, 'It's the word "gad", isn't it?'

'Exactly.'

Afsar was excited.

'*They rule over the world, from Gada to Gada.* Do you remember the line from the manuscript? "Gada to Gada" must be "Gandhara to Magadha". How could I miss this? Gandhara and Magadha both might have come from the Munda word "gad" or "gand". There's no good etymology in Sanskrit for either of the names.'

'Wasn't there something in the manuscript about the Kings of the Nagas too?' Kubha asked. 'Can you decipher the full text now?'

'Bits and pieces are falling in place. I'm close to solving the jigsaw. The manuscript is a sort of ode to a despised Naga race who speaks a slang language, and are also kins of the Banas. *They rule over the world, from Gada to Gada,* which, we know now, most likely, refers to the entire Indian subcontinent, from Gandhara to Magadha. Many dynasties have ruled over major parts of the Indian subcontinent in different ages. We've the Mauryas, the Kushans and the Guptas in the medieval age, when the manuscript was first written. But none was ever known as a Naga race. Also, the identity of the Banas is tricky. But I'll very soon have an answer for all the missing links.'

Sometime later when Kubha was hanging up, Afsar suddenly asked her to hold on. 'You mentioned something about Aryabhata too. What's that?'

'Somak said that his last name, Ajai, has something to do with the mathematician Aryabhata … '

'Interesting!' Afsar interrupted. She repeated "Ajai" a few times and asked, 'Did he say anything else?'

'No,' Kubha replied.

Afsar didn't talk much after that and the call ended soon. Kubha had, by now, become quite acclimatized with such behaviour. Her mother, she had already learned, couldn't multiplex between multiple things. Whenever she was engrossed in something, nothing else would get much space in her brain.

'You should increase your brain-width,' Kratu would often tease Afsar.

☼

The Delhi winters are anyway infamous for its unpredictability. How many flights would be cancelled due to fog is a matter of big concern to the travellers. But, November was not a time when things could go so bad. Suddenly, it had started raining since the previous night. The whole day had been gloomy since morning. Kubha unnecessarily fought with Parush over a very *flimsy* matter when he called her in the evening.

'Why are you so irritated today?' Parush asked.

'I hate this type of weather,' she fretted. 'Why can't you come here once in a while and meet me? You didn't have to return to India and stay in Delhi if we're only talking over the phone. It's a whole week since I came back from Calcutta and you couldn't manage to meet me even for once…'

'Kubha,' Parush interrupted. 'I'll call you back. There's a call from the Ministry of External Affairs.'

He disconnected the line. Kubha was exasperated. She threw her phone on the floor and got out of her room. It was still drizzling and the air had become cold enough for people to pull out their woolens from the closet. The shorts and the old tee with visible signs of wear and tear, in which everyone saw her leaving the hostel in haste, were doubtless not the right kind of clothing for the present weather. The lady security at the entrance of the Yamuna Hostel offered an umbrella to Kubha, but she didn't pay any heed.

The cold drops of rain fell on her bare limbs like pointed snowflakes, piercing her skin like a thousand needles. She shivered for a while, but soon got used to it. She passed by the Convention Centre and the Aravali Guest House. She waited for a few moments in front of Anupam, thinking whether she should enter the restaurant, but then started walking faster along the JNU Ring Road. She would have surely taken a few rounds on the Ring Road, because when Parush caught hold of her from behind, it was more than an hour since he had been trying to reach her.

☼

It had so happened that an hour back, Parush had got a call from someone he knew at the Ministry of External Affairs. Apparently, the Pakistan Embassy had sought immediate help from the Indian Government in investigating the gruesome murder of an American citizen of Pakistani origin, who had been lately staying in Pakistan at his ancestral home near Peshawar. As he had had very strong connections at the highest levels in the government of Pakistan and had been pretty well known in the social circuit, his ghastly death a day back had already created enough ripples there. Given that his elder daughter lived in Calcutta and his granddaughter studied in Delhi, and that he had met both of them in India just a week before his death, they could surely play a big role in solving the mystery behind the murder, which had baffled everyone. The Pakistani Government wanted India to facilitate the engagement of the daughter and the granddaughter of the deceased in all possible ways.

When the urgent request from the embassy reached the Ministry of External Affairs, an acquaintance of Parush recalled instantly that Parush was known to the person who had been killed. It was Parush, who had actually helped him get the Indian visa in a few days, cutting short the customary three-month waiting period for the US citizens with Pakistani origin. Instructing his acquaintance about the various arrangements needed for Afsar and Kubha to travel to Pakistan immediately, Parush first talked to Afsar. He had this exceptional skill of articulating the harshest of things in the simplest of ways, which he used to the best of his abilities to inform Afsar of her father's death.

'The last flight for Delhi leaves Calcutta in less than two hours from now,' Parush said calmly, immediately after giving the news in as few words as possible. 'You've to start ASAP. You can't miss the flight. I'll take care of Kubha. Don't worry. I'm arranging for a chartered flight from Delhi to Peshawar. You will be at Khushawar by tomorrow morning. See you soon at the Delhi airport. I'll be there with Kubha…' He paused, perhaps to allow a little breathing space to Afsar.

'Porus,' Afsar spoke for the first time, with an unusual stillness in her voice, 'you're coming with us too.'

Parush couldn't gauge whether that was a request or an enquiry.

'Don't worry,' he repeated, 'I'm there … Don't forget the passports. Get ready.'

☼

Reaching Kubha was not easy. She was not receiving calls. Parush didn't wait. He immediately took his car out. It was a Monday evening and the traffic was maddening. Still, he managed to cover the 12-kilometre distance between his house on Akbar Road and JNU in less than an hour. The security at the main entrance to the campus recognized Parush's car. He first went to the Yamuna Hostel, where Kubha stayed. Upon knowing that she had left the hostel more than an hour back, he drove to the JNU Ring Road, parked the car near Anupam, and started running along the Ring Road. He was not surprised when he recognized Kubha from a distance.

Kubha's contour from the back, he felt, was so very characteristic of her. He even knew which tee she was wearing. It was not that Kubha didn't have any sense of fashion. But totally contrasting to how extremely gorgeous and attractive she could look, she had a different standard at home.

'How I'm at home,' Parush remembered her saying once, 'is like my nickname, daknam. It's always unfashionable, gross, but comfortable, cozy.'

Parush walked faster and caught up with Kubha. When he held her by her shoulder and pulled her back, she didn't turn back at once, as if she knew it couldn't be anyone else. Had it been some other day, Parush would have reacted in a totally different way. He had always known all the ways to *handle* Kubha, in any situation, since she was a toddler. But presently, it was a situation, he realized, he had never thought of in the past.

'Kubha, your grandfather is dead,' Parush said curtly, pulling her harder and taking her in his arms. The drizzle had already turned into a full-fledged rain, biting both of them hard. He tightened his hug around Kubha and didn't speak for a while. Kubha too, didn't ask anything. That was something Parush liked the most about her. It was, as though, she always knew what he would say or do. She rarely asked.

Parush's car had been parked at the other side of the Ring Road, almost a kilometre away. They walked slowly, side by side, shivering in the cold; Parush's hands wrapped around Kubha's arm, her head leaned a bit on him. He talked in details about everything that had happened over the past one hour.

'When did you last talk to him?' he asked her.

'Yesterday, late afternoon … around four-ish. I talk to him every day.' She was shivering so much that she could barely speak.

'Did he say anything which could be relevant to the investigation?'

Parush pulled her closer and held her tightly, so as to transfer to her the little warmth he might still have left in his body.

'A lot of people come to meet him, but rarely any carpet aficionado. Yesterday, he told he would be meeting a carpet dealer from St. Petersburg. Apparently, he had placed an order for a particular carpet which hadn't been made in a long time.'

'Is that anything unusual?'

'No. But what intrigued the Young Boy ...'

She couldn't complete. For the first time since she had heard of Faraz's death, she broke down, with the mention of "Young Boy". They had already reached Parush's car, a Toyota Fortuner, extensively remodelled from inside. Parush left Kubha, took out the key of the car and pressed a button on it. The blinkers flashed a few times. Parush opened a rear door for Kubha.

'I've set the car in caravan mode. The heater is on. There's a closet in the backside. There are fresh towels and some basic unisex clothing ...'

Kubha had already got inside the car. Parush closed the door.

Once inside the car, Kubha was amazed how altogether different it looked at present. The two rows of back seats were gone. In their place was a plush and cozy little studio, complete with all basic necessities such as a bed, a writing desk, a refrigerator and a closet. The window panes appeared opaque—nothing of the outside was visible. The driver's compartment in the front was completely separated out.

Not wanting to get the clean bed wet, Kubha knelt on the floor. She removed the wet clothes, took a towel out of the closet and dried herself. The warmth inside the car made her feel comfortable. She drank a full bottle of water and lay on the bed, her legs dangling on the floor. Suddenly, she realized that Parush had to change too. She pulled out a pair of off-white pajamas and a light-coloured tee from the closet and wore them fast. She knocked on the door from inside. A phone rang. She located the cordless phone in a holder fixed to a door. She picked the phone.

'Are you ready?' she heard Parush's voice.

'Yes. Now you can change.'

The phone went silent. Parush opened the door.

'Get onto the wheels. Get your passport from your hostel. I'll get ready.'

A minute later, Kubha pressed the gas pedal hard. In less than 10 minutes, she was zooming through the rain-soaked streets of Delhi.

☼

When they reached the Indira Gandhi International Airport, Afsar and Kratu had already boarded the flight from Calcutta. Kubha realized a lot of arrangements had already been made. They were directly taken to the office of the airport duty manager. As they waited for Afsar and Kratu, Parush started the conversation.

'You mentioned your grandfather was supposed to meet a carpet collector …'

'Yes, an agent from St. Petersburg. Young Boy was eager to meet him because he had requested for a particular carpet, the last piece of which had been sold more than 30 years ago.'

'How did the guy know of such a carpet?'

'He claimed that his client had seen it at someone's place and had been interested in possessing one since then.'

'What's special about this carpet?'

'It's a round carpet with a lot of symbols. Since many skilled weavers have been shifting to other jobs, there hasn't been anyone in the past 30 years to work on such a complicated design. Interestingly, we saw a very similar design at Somak's place last week. I told you about him.'

'Was your grandfather sure it was the same carpet?'

'Yes. He had a picture of the design from the dealer. He told me he would direct the person to Somak … '

Kubha couldn't complete. She jumped up from the chair and rushed towards the TV which had been showing all silly news till now. Parush, too, followed her.

'I just can't believe …' Kubha held Parush's hand, as they heard the breaking news:

> *Somak Ajai, an eminent professor of mathematics at the prestigious Delhi School of Economics, was murdered last night. His granddaughter Maitreyi, who arrived in Delhi from the US this morning, discovered Somak's dead body in a badly decomposed state. Detailed forensic report is yet to come. But our internal sources have found the death was caused by severe lye poisoning. It's believed that Somak had swallowed and inhaled large quantities of sodium hydroxide mixed in methanol. Forensic experts told us it was a very painful death …*

Kubha saw the girl, almost her age, talking to the reporters. She knew that would be Maitreyi.

'Both of them died roughly at the same time …' Parush mumbled, 'and almost in the same way …'

A Thousand Severed Heads

(Morning, 13 November 2018. Khushawar)

Parush didn't have much time to watch the news. With a lot of thoughts churning in his head, he left the office of the duty manager at the Indira Gandhi International Airport. Kubha sat behind, stunned, watching the news of Somak's death.

There was enough time, Parush knew. But still he felt impatient. No one had yet arrived from the Pakistan Embassy. Special arrangement had been made by the embassy to stamp his passport at the airport. Otherwise, there was no way to get the visa on time. Afsar, Kratu and Kubha, all American citizens, already had a five-year multiple-entry visa. Parush hadn't surrendered his Indian passport, something that had come in handy when Prime Minister Indar Sinha wanted to induct him in a very special and secretive role reporting directly to the PMO. Not many knew that he had a place in the top echelon of the government hierarchy, at par with a cabinet minister. Arrangements had been made for him to accompany Afsar, Kratu and Kubha to Pakistan on a diplomat visa. Despite all the needful approvals from the highest levels of both the governments, Parush realized, Indar's dream of Smart Governance was still a long way. Very few organizations actually worked as efficiently as he expected. The past two hours had given Parush ample proof of the same.

He called Rakesh, his assistant and his most trusted person.

'Do you have any update on the flight?' he asked him, checking the time on his phone.

'There's an Air Force cargo scheduled for the Ayni Air Base in Tajikistan. We've got all the approvals from Pakistan to land in Peshawar. It wouldn't be a big detour. We've delayed the departure of the flight.'

'Is that the best option?'

'Yes, sir,' Rakesh assured, 'that seems to be the best option, and the earliest too. India controls the Ayni Air Base in Tajikistan. Pakistan doesn't like that too much. But they know very well that this particular cargo is on a friendly mission to supply provisions in the flood-affected areas in the northern Afghanistan. Otherwise, Pakistan wouldn't allow an Indian Air Force plane to land in their territory.'

'Any lead on Somak's murder?' Parush changed the topic abruptly.

The moment he had learned about Somak's death, he had asked Rakesh to be on top of it, though he didn't disclose anything to him about Faraz's death, nor did he inform him who else would be travelling with him to Peshawar. "Only paranoids survive," he always reminded himself of the most famous quote by Andy Grove, Intel's legendary CEO, who had died a few years back.

'Not at all, sir,' Rakesh replied. 'I've talked to his granddaughter. She's clueless. Somak's house is the last in a desolate, blind alley. Even during the day, not many people go there. No one has any idea who came there yesterday.'

'Did Somak talk to someone in Pakistan in the past one week?'

'Many a time. I've the call records. Yesterday afternoon was the last time he talked. The other calls were very short—a minute or two. But yesterday's call was quite long, almost half an hour.'

'You be on top of everything. I want minute-to-minute update ... ' Someone called Parush from behind. He turned back.

A person in khaki uniform said, 'Sir, someone has come from the Pakistan Embassy. He is with the duty manager.'

☼

Parush and Kubha were standing at the aerobridge, waiting for Afsar and Kratu to disembark from their flight from Calcutta. They were accompanied by three people in uniform, one from the BOI, Bureau of Immigration, and the other two from the Air Force. Special arrangements had been made so that they wouldn't have to stand in the normal queue for immigration and customs. The person from the BOI would take care of everything. The two persons from the Air Force would take them directly to the cargo plane, presently waiting for take-off.

Kubha could see her mother, pushing aside other passengers and trying to move forward as fast as possible. A little behind her, Kratu was calm, pulling a luggage. Kubha ran towards her mother and hugged her tight. Afsar broke down, holding Kubha, blocking the narrow aisle of the aerobridge. Parush pulled both of them aside and made space for others to pass by. Kratu didn't stay with them in the aerobridge. He waited outside, at the arrival gate, along with Parush. Kubha brought Afsar with her in a few moments.

Afsar didn't say anything while they all completed the immigration formalities, got out of the terminal building, took an Air Force car and arrived at the loading ramp of a Lockheed Martin C-130J-30 Super Hercules tactical airlifter. It was not a usual thing, at least for Afsar, Kratu and Kubha, to board such an aircraft. But presently, neither of them was in a mental set-up to appreciate it. As they all sat side by side on four seats suspended from the concave wall of the plane, Afsar spoke for the first time.

'It's just a week since I saw Aba off at the Calcutta airport,' she mumbled. 'I can't believe he's no more. It's not that he would live forever, but is this the way to go?'

She turned towards Parush, who was sitting beside her. 'Tell me what exactly happened.'

As the plane accelerated on the tarmac, Afsar's voice sank into the loud noise of the engine and the vibrations of the huge metal boxes that filled most of the hull of the plane.

'We don't yet know the details,' Parush avoided the gory nitty-gritty.

Afsar looked at Kubha, sitting on the other side of Parush.

'Are you guys hiding anything from me? Do you think I'm a kid that you have to do so?'

'Ammi,' Kubha had to raise her voice to be audible to her mother, 'it's not like that. It's just that we don't want to remember those grisly last moments of someone we love. Do you want to hear how ghastly, how ghoulish his death was?'

Parush tried to calm her down. She cut him off, removed the seat belt and went in front of her mother. She lost her balance. Parush held her from the back. She shook him off and sat on the floor in front of her mother, trembling, her eyes red.

'Ammi, he vomited blood … He became blind … He struggled till the last breath, squirming in pain … His dead body looked grotesque and horrific … His intestines had come out … There were a thousand holes in his skin … What more do you want to know, Ammi?' Her voice grew so loud that a few crews rushed towards them.

Parush removed his seat belt and pulled Kubha up.

'Get up,' he said firmly, 'and sit down. Calm down. Do you hear me?'

The crews went back to their seats.

Parush realized that he shouldn't have left Kubha alone at the duty manager's office. The news channel would have shown all the gory details of Somak's murder. He himself had got a similar account of Faraz's death from his acquaintance in the Ministry of External Affairs, but he hadn't wanted either Kubha or Afsar to know of it in so much details. Kubha was still trembling frantically. He put his hands around her. She rested her head on his shoulder and broke down, abruptly, crying loudly. He allowed her to cry. He had heard of a phenomenon called "cloud burst". Perhaps he presently understood what it could be like.

☼

The formalities at the Bacha Khan International Airport at Peshawar were very minimal. Afsar, Kratu, Kubha and Parush were whisked away directly from the tarmac in an army vehicle. They were taken to the VIP lounge, where the paperwork was completed in no time. Pressing her hands into the deep pockets of the long thermal overcoat, Afsar couldn't but appreciate Parush's attention to minute details as she walked behind the others in the near-zero temperature to get into a car that would take them to Khushawar. She shuddered with the thought that had Parush not remembered to pack so much warm clothing amid all the running around in Delhi, they would have collapsed in the cold.

It was not that Afsar was not aware of the biting cold in Peshawar around this time of the year. For the past two decades, they had been flying into Peshawar every year around Christmas, in order to attend the traditional new year celebrations of the Kalash people in the Hindukush mountains, in the ancestral village of Kratu's grandmother, the enigmatic and mysterious Kubha. But the situation under which they had to travel to Peshawar now was so different from all the other times that everything around appeared unknown, alien. Afsar felt the wind was perhaps biting her more, the night was perhaps darker and the air thicker than before.

Escorted and tailgated by more than one heavily armed vehicles, they zipped through the deserted ring road. Seated beside Afsar in the bullet-proof vehicle, Kubha's mind was getting cluttered with scattered thoughts and visuals. She remembered Fazal, Faraz's father, who had outlived many in his generation. She remembered the last time she had seen Fazal at the central courtyard of the ancestral home of the Fareedis in Khushawar, a few months before his death. She might have been 10. Fazal was especially fond of her. Placing her on his lap, he was telling interesting stories from his life, as Faraz, the Young Boy, was going about checking each of the newly woven rugs very closely, and throwing a few additional tidbits as exotic garnishing to Fazal's narratives.

Glancing at a particular rug on Faraz's hands, Fazal had said, 'These rugs have been carrying the *pulse beat* of our family for many many years. I'll die, your grandfather will die, but you will be still alive. *The pulse beat of our family will never stop.* The rugs will keep us alive … We have to keep the rugs alive … '

It was uncanny, Kubha thought, that her grandfather was presently dead. The simple words of Fazal: '*You will be still alive*', suddenly appeared very heavy to her. She felt, as though, the entire responsibility of keeping the rugs alive had been suddenly bestowed upon her. Somehow, she had a gut feeling, the identical deaths of Faraz and Somak had something to do with their rugs, the only connection between the two frontier kins. The *pulse beat* of her family, she apprehended, was perhaps losing the rhythm, getting out of synch. She remembered a popular Bengali folklore, Dadu, her paternal grandfather, would tell when she had been a kid. It was the story of a prince who believed that his life was held captive in a bumble bee and that he would survive as long as the bee lived. It was no doubt that the rugs and her family had an association similar to that between the prince of the story and the bee. Between the rugs and her Young Boy, she pondered though, who could be the prince and what could be the bee.

Not much later would everyone realize, in fact, the bumble bee was Faraz, whose murder had been necessitated in order to *kill* a particular rug. But by then, a lot would have happened, unfathomable to anyone.

☼

Afsar was taken aback by the sight of the huge crowd assembled at Khushawar, her ancestral village. The convoy, she was a part of, cut through the multitude of people, like an oar of a boat cutting through the placid waters of a calm lake. They made way for Afsar and her company. The century-old mansion, which had seen better times, would have been restored to its old glory soon, as had been planned by Faraz. Presently, it stood like an honour guard, at attention, its high-held head partially covered in the morning mist, like a ceremonial head gear. It was as though the old guard of the Fareedis was waiting, with the least eagerness, to give a state funeral to its only all-weather occupant. At its front was the coffin, draped in Pakistan's flag and topped with wreaths and bouquets of white flowers.

As Afsar came close to the coffin, a tall person in police uniform made his way through the crowd. One of the army personnel who had accompanied Afsar and the others in the car from Peshawar introduced the tall man as the DIG, Deputy Inspector General of Mardan.

'Merman,' the DIG greeted her, '*pa khair raghla.* Thank God, you came safe and sound.'

Kubha could grasp the gist of the conversation they were having in Pashto, in bits and pieces. The DIG informed that he had been the first one to know of the murder. Faraz had been scheduled to attend a function at Mardan the previous afternoon, along with the governor of the Khyber Pakhtunkhwa province. The DIG was supposed to send an official vehicle to Faraz at noon. His calls went unanswered when he called Faraz at 11:00 am. When there was no response even after half an hour, he asked the Bakhshali Police Station to send someone to Khushawar and check if everything was fine with Janab Fareedi. Around noon, a hawaldar called him to say Janab's house was locked from inside and that no one had seen him since morning. The hawaldar also informed that the chakar who stayed with Janab hadn't been seen either. That was nothing unusual, the neighbours had said, as Janab would generally stay indoors in the mornings and meet visitors in the evenings. A few of the neighbours, who had been called for, shouted the chakar's name from outside. The baghwan, who had been taking care of the gardens at Janab's haweli for decades, had arrived by then. He went to the back and knocked on the door of the servant's quarter. There was no response. The DIG left for Khushawar immediately and an hour later, when he broke open the main door of the mansion, he found the heavily decomposed dead bodies of Faraz and his servant.

'Janab is a much revered person here,' the DIG said. 'Even the Wazir-e Azam would call for him whenever he came to Peshawar. Given his stature, I immediately informed the governor. It took a while for him to assimilate what I told. People in Khushawar were shocked too. I would say they were more pareshan, perplexed. It was unthinkable that a person like him could be killed in that manner. I checked his phone. The last call was made to Delhi, we figured out, to his granddaughter. People told me he was in India last week. In the evening, we got the postmortem and forensic reports. Janab didn't deserve such an end. We were totally clueless. When the governor called me, I told him to get you here at the earliest. You may help us hack the killer down. *We're not going to spare him.*'

'Der manana,' Afsar thanked the DIG. *'Der kha kar mo wuku,'* she held his hands, totally oblivious that the DIG was feeling uncomfortable. 'You've done a great thing for us,' she repeated many times. *'Khuday pa aman.* May God protect you!'

She walked towards the coffin. The DIG followed her.

'I thought ...' the DIG hesitated to say, 'you wouldn't like to see your father in that state. The Imam was a very close friend of your father. He personally supervised everything, from bathing to enshrouding Janab in the kafan.'

☼

Faraz's extended family had long back settled in Lahore. By the time they all arrived at Khushawar, the mist had become thinner. More and more people assembled around the Fareedi mansion, but there was an eerie silence; even the birds had perhaps stopped chirping. Apart from the hissing sound of the chilly wind blowing from the north, the mild murmur of the leaves and the swaying of the branches of the mute trees, there was no other sound. It was as though the world hadn't woken up yet.

Someone had brought a chair for Afsar and she had been sitting like a statue by the head side of the coffin, placing her joined hands gently on its top. The unprecedentedness of the entire episode had struck her so badly that the sorrow of losing her father had been totally submerged in a sense of utter disarray. Scattered memories of her father flashed in her thoughts, like lightning, and vanished into the darkness that had engulfed her mind. Behind her was Kubha, standing, with her eyes lowered, her hands resting on Afsar's shoulders. A little away from them, on the other side of the coffin, were Parush and Kratu, standing with the police and defence personnel.

Afsar didn't notice when her cousin sister pushed a wheel chair, with Faraz's nonagenarian elder brother on it, and stood beside her. Faraz's brother had too pale a face to educe any feeling on it. Kubha pressed on Afsar's shoulders. She raised her head and saw her relatives. She fell on her uncle's lap and broke down. Kubha raised her and made her sit again on the chair. When the governor of the Khyber Pakhtunkhwa province arrived, the Imam greeted Faraz's brother with a customary adab and took his consent to start the funeral.

'It would have been nice if your sisters had arrived by now from Amrika,' he regretted to Afsar. 'May the Almighty shower his blessings on Bahnaz and Bahrukh!'

The people close to the coffin arranged themselves in an odd number of rows, with the Imam standing in the front, facing the qibla, the direction of the Kaaba mosque in Mecca.

'*Bismi Allahi arrahmani arraheem*,' the Imam began the *Salat al-Janazah*, the Islamic funeral prayer, by quietly reciting Al-Fatiha, the first chapter of the Quran. '*In the name of Allah, the Entirely Merciful, the Especially Merciful …* '

When the recitation was completed, the Imam raised his voice through a megaphone.

'It's customary now to say two duas for Janab Faraz Fareedi, my dear friend. It wouldn't be wrong to do this part of the funeral prayer in a little different way. Instead of praying for my friend, requesting to the God to increase his good deeds, I would rather talk about the wonderful person I got the privilege to know so well. That he had touched the soul of so many of us is apparent from this yazdani anjuman, the divine congregation of thousands of people …

'Let me tell you a story. A long time ago, there was a prophet, a very kind-hearted hazrat. He had severed his head a thousand times. He had plucked out his eyes a thousand times. He had then gifted the thousand heads and the thousand eyes to us, to our ancestors. This is the pak zamin, the divine country of the thousand gifts, mulk-e hazar tuhfazat. Keeping alive this silsilat-e tuhfat started by the Prophet, Janab Faraz Fareedi too has given his life, as a tuhfa, as a priceless gift to us. He will be born here a thousand times. He will enrich our lives with his thousand lives.'

As the Imam spoke, Parush listened quietly, standing alongside the military personnel. He was not much knowledgeable about any religion. His understanding of Islam was as good or bad as that of any other religion, Hinduism included. Still, his eyebrows couldn't hide the frown when he heard the Imam talking about rebirth. He wondered if Islam too espoused the concept of rebirth and reincarnation, like Hinduism or Buddhism. Or was it, he thought, a wider perspective of a liberal Imam? Nevertheless, he pondered, what actually the Imam might have meant by the thousand gifts of heads and eyes in as many births of a local Prophet.

The term "mulk-e hazar tuhfazat", The Land of the Thousand Gifts, played in his mind several times. Wasn't Hazara the name of an Afghan ethnic group? He tried to recall where he might have heard of it. Soon, he realized there was a Hazara kid in *The Kite Runner*, one of the few books he had read in the past 20 years.

Parush took his phone out and clicked on the icon for ACPS which significantly trimmed the output of a normal Google search based on some parameters. The Hazaras, he found out, were a Persian-speaking people living mainly in Afghanistan. Hazara was also the name of a village in Swat district, a town near Quetta, and a region and erstwhile division and district in the present Khyber Pakhtunkhwa province, all in Pakistan. He added the words "ancient", and "thousand severed heads" to the query string and searched again. He smiled reading an extract from a report prepared by Alexander Cunningham, the then director general of the ASI, and published in 1871.

> *At 2 miles to the north of Taxila there was a stupa of King Asoka, built on the spot where Buddha in a former existence had*

> *made an alms-gift of his head, or as some said of one thousand heads in as many previous existences ... The present name of the district is Chhachh-Hazara, which I take to be only a corruption of Shirsha-Sahasra, or the "Thousand Heads".*

Taxila, Parush checked, was only 80 miles away from Khushawar. It was not unlikely then, he thought, that Khushawar and Taxila had been both parts of the Mulk-e Hazar Tuhfazat. He was amazed that the Imam was actually talking about a very old legend, but the Prophet he had mentioned was not a Muslim hazrat, but the Buddha himself. Not only the carpets, he said to himself, the Imam of Khushawar too was mysterious enough.

The Kilim with Symbols

(Evening, 13 November 2018. Khushawar)

In the evening, the Fareedis assembled at their ancestral house after a very long time. Faraz's brother, presently the eldest member of the Fareedi clan, couldn't remember the last time they all had gathered at this place. The shock that had engulfed them all for the past one day was showing signs of ebbing away, slowly. The questions like "who" and "why" were now being discussed in hushed voices in different groups that the long-scattered Fareedis had uneasily flocked themselves into.

A special investigation team had been formed within the IB, Intelligence Bureau, the previous night, under the direct supervision of the prime minister's secretariat, to investigate the murder of Faraz Fareedi. The team had spent a considerable amount of time talking to Afsar and Kubha, after the funeral. Presently, the other members of the Fareedi fraternity and a few old-timers of Khushawar who were still in the weaving profession, gathered around Afsar. The oldest of the weavers told something that alerted Parush, who had been almost silent all the while, trying to be as inconspicuous as possible.

'Just a few days back, he was enquiring about a carpet,' the weaver recalled, 'which I remember we had last made when I was a kid.'

Parush instantly looked at Kubha, who nodded. Yes, she too recalled the Young Boy telling the same when they had talked, for the last time. That was the same carpet, he had been sure, they had seen at Somak's place, the one with a lot of symbols.

Kubha slid her hand inside the pocket of the long coat she was wearing and pulled her phone out. Hadn't she taken a picture of the rugs piled up on the floor in Somak's drawing room? She scanned through the photos saved in her phone and ran towards the old man, whose bearded round face popped out of a thick blanket that hung from his neck like a sack.

'Is this the one he was enquiring about?' she asked him, showing a zoomed section of the photo she had taken.

His gesticulations left little to anyone's speculation.

'Yes, he had shown me a very similar picture in his computer. It's a round rug—a kilim, a really big one. I was very young and my father was getting old. His eyesight had deteriorated. I had started assisting him. No one dared to do this. It was not easy. My father proudly told we would do it. We used wool. We took

'Is this the one?' she asked him, showing a zoomed section of the photo she had taken.

almost a month to complete. But then there was a big fire in this house and many kilims were damaged badly, along with this one. Father died soon and no one ever made that kilim again in many years. I made it only once later, almost 30 years ago, when I still had strength in my eyes …'

Afsar interrupted him. 'Aba told a hut was constructed at the backside to store the damaged rugs. Do you remember if this particular rug was kept there too?' She paused and stared at the others seated in a semicircle around her. 'I heard Aba wanted to renovate this place. He had got the hut opened. Does anyone know where the damaged carpets are now?'

'They were all dried under the sun for a few days,' said someone. 'Many were in very bad condition. Your father asked me to throw them off. But a few were still good. He asked me to tear off the burnt parts from them and keep aside the good portions. He said the old kilim pieces would fetch good money.'

'Where are those?' Afsar cut him short.

'I kept them in one of the rooms in the backside. But … '

'What?' Afsar was irritated.

'When the police searched all the rooms yesterday, they were missing. I was with the police.'

Afsar dialled a number in her mobile.

'Adab,' she greeted over the phone. 'You didn't mention that a few carpets were missing from one of the rooms.'

She got up and went to the corner of the huge living room and had an animated conversation over the phone for some time.

'I talked to the officer from the IB who's heading the investigation,' Afsar informed, returning to her seat. 'There's nothing unusual, he feels. A rug dealer had come to meet Aba the same evening he died. Aba had talked to my daughter before meeting him. He told my daughter that the dealer was particularly interested in this kilim with symbols. It's possible that the person is interested in old kilims and Aba has sold him the good pieces recovered from the hut. Each of those would be close to 80 years old now.'

Kubha's mobile rang. She picked the phone and checked the number. It was a Delhi number. She could recognize the number. It was the same number she had been repeatedly getting calls from since morning. This time, she took the call.

'Am I speaking to Kubha?' asked a hesitant female voice.

'Yes, I'm Kubha. Who's this?'

'Kubha, I'm Maitreyi,' said the voice from the other side in haste, barely hiding the impatience. It just took a few moments for Kubha to figure out who she was talking to.

'Somak Ajai's granddaughter?' Kubha almost shrieked over the phone, attracting the attention of everyone who had been listening to her mother. She got up and went to one of the many empty rooms in the old mansion.

'I expected you would recognize me. My grandfather has talked a lot about you …' she paused. Kubha sensed she was pondering, perhaps, how to come to the point.

'Maitreyi, I've seen it in the TV. I am really sorry to know that. In fact, had I been in India, I would have been with you now. But … ' now she, too, hesitated.

'You're not in India? I'm so sorry,' she sounded apologetic.

'In fact, my grandfather has died too. Rather, let me put it in this way: He too was murdered, almost at the same time and in the same horrific manner, like your grandfather. We're now in Pakistan, at our ancestral home, where it all happened day before yesterday. The funeral was in this morning.'

The silence on the other side was indicative of the shock Maitreyi was in. But when she spoke, it was Kubha's turn to be stunned.

'I called you,' she said, 'because, I think, his last message for me, just before he would have breathed his last, was to get in touch with you.'

'You talked to him while he was dying? I thought you were travelling.'

'No, I didn't talk to him. He left a cryptic message for me. I'll tell you everything when we meet. When are you returning?'

'Tomorrow,' Kubha replied without thinking any further. 'I'll see you tomorrow.'

☼

Later, in the night, when everyone else had retired to the different rooms of the huge haveli, Afsar, along with her daughter and husband, went to Faraz's room, which also doubled as his home office. It was one of the larger ones in the corner in the ground floor, the last of the eight rooms which flanked the big central foyer on the either side. The room had been cleansed well to erase all the signs of the ghastliness it had been a witness to. Afsar had come to this room a few times since morning, but never when it had been empty. Presently, the eerie quietness, the pallid, sombre lighting of the room and the emptiness was unbearable. She switched on all the lights of the room. She opened the closed window and a gush of chilly air entered into the room. She stood at the window for some time. Kubha went to the window and closed it.

'You'll catch a cold.'

She pulled her mother back and made her sit on the chair by the desk, Faraz's work place.

'Why didn't you tell us about Somak's death?' Afsar asked Kubha rudely.

'Ammi, do you think we had any time to discuss that?'

There was a knock at the door.

'Come in!' Kubha said loudly.

Parush pushed the door open and entered into the room, closing it behind him.

Afsar looked very irritated.

'Porus,' she turned towards Parush, 'what the hell are you all doing? It's already two days and no one has any idea who did it? What's going on?'

'Don't worry!' Parush didn't say much. 'I'll find them out.'

He appeared very cold, expressionless. It was not that Afsar or her husband, Kratu, were not aware of Parush's mannerisms. This coldness meant all the ruthlessness within him was coalescing into a demon. It was this demon in him that they had feared many a time in the past. It was this demon that had killed him many times, killed his wife, and killed his mother too. No one other than Afsar and Kratu had been mute spectators to each of these in the past two decades, since he had become a part of their family, in unusual ways, under unusual circumstances. Presently, it gave her assurance.

'I've a strong feeling,' Kubha broke the silence, after everyone had suddenly stopped talking, 'the rug with symbols, which someone wanted to buy from Young Boy and the only piece of which was with Somak, holds a key. Somak had showed us that many of these symbols are, in fact, Brahmi letters. He had told cryptically that these symbols comprise an unknown script of some unknown language. He had been researching on it for quite some time. He believed that the rugs have some really earth-shattering mysteries hidden in them. Ammi, you have to decipher the symbols.'

Afsar stared at Parush, as though for an approval.

'Yes,' he agreed, 'Kubha does have a point. Apparently, it looks quite weird, but anyway, we don't have any better lead. The only thing we have got to know till now is that the rug dealer, who had come to meet your father that evening, was not anyone from St. Petersburg, as he had told Kubha, unless the guy is a desi who has settled there. The IB folks have corroborated the same from various sources. If someone has hidden his identity, everything he does is naturally suspicious. So, the rug he was interested in can't be ignored too, especially when Somak had so many things to say about it …'

'I do see the point,' Afsar interrupted. 'I need to get back to deciphering the entire manuscript. It's good that we're here. I need to talk to a few local people to understand some of the local traditions and legends. I feel the manuscript refers to many such things, which would be really tough for an outsider to comprehend.'

'You should talk to the Imam.'

Parush narrated how he had been amazed in the morning to find out that the Imam had actually presented a two-and-a-half-millennia-old Buddhist legend from this region in a Muslim garb. He also mentioned about the report prepared by Alexander Cunningham.

'Did you say Chhach-Hazara?' Afsar ran out of the room and returned in a few minutes with her notebook.

'I was not sure about the places mentioned here.' She read out the English translation of a hymn in the manuscript:

> *The relic of Buddha has been erected at Shira and Matuha-Shisha;*
> *At Chhach-Hajarata, Aro and Pituha-Shisha it has been erected.*
> *The relic of Buddha has been erected at Loura-Shisha;*
> *At Aragana-Garaha and Budha-Garaha it has been erected.*

In the Prakrit form used everywhere in the manuscript, Afsar explained, the first line of the hymn read: "*Babato dato shirae paditthabide matuha-shishe*". It was written in a variation of the Arya meter, which in its original form was the preferred metre for all scientific and secular literature in Sanskrit since the fifth century.

'Many words end with "e",' Kubha observed. 'That's Magadhi Prakrit, right?'

'Good,' Afsar patted her daughter. 'The manuscript, though written in the Magadhi Prakrit of the east, still has some local

Pashto flavour, such as "babato" for "bhagavatah", meaning "of Buddha".'

'What about Chhach-Hazara?' Kubha asked.

'The hymn refers to many places, including one called Chhach-Hajarata. "Shira" is head, so is "shisha", the Prakrit form of the Sanskrit "shirsha". The "sha" sound quite often evolves to "chha". The Sanskrit "shat" or "shash", meaning six, is the source of Hindi "chhe". So, "chhach" or "chhachha" is doubtless a corruption for "shirsha".'

'And "hazar" is thousand,' Kubha added.

'Yes, the Persian "hazar" is akin to Sanskrit "sahasra". The place name Chhach-Hajarata is a very explicit reference to the legend of Buddha's alms gift of a thousand heads.'

All the while, she told, she had been wrongly searching for the places mentioned in the hymn in the ancient Magadha region. Being the Land of the Buddha, that seemed natural as the place where "The relic of Buddha has been erected". Moreover, Budha Garaha, or Buddha Griha in Sanskrit, explicitly meant Buddha's House. But Chhach-Hajarata was confusing. It was a very unlikely name in Bihar in the fifth century, when the manuscript was written. The Persian "hazar" or the Arabic "hazrat" made no sense in the pre-Islamic period. Somehow, she didn't think that the ancient Gandhara region could also be a likely place to search for these names. Gandhara too had been as important a site for Buddhism as Magadha.

'Now that I know it's actually Chhach-Hazara,' Afsar said excitedly, 'the other names should be real too. What's really intriguing though is how the Buddha and his legends, like the one about the Thousand Severed Heads, have been preserved for more than 2,000 years in the names of places, that too, in a country where Buddhism had died long back.'

'Doesn't that give us confidence,' Kubha said, 'that, like the legends, many other things—histories, anecdotes, etc.—could also be preserved for thousands of years?'

'What are you trying to say?' Afsar asked.

'I'm trying to say, we can be more sanguine now that the designs and symbols of our carpets have indeed preserved a trove of information, as Somak believed. It's very much like how the Imam has preserved the Buddhist legends, through regional Islamic folklore.'

'Yes, that's right,' Afsar couldn't but agree. 'I'm also excited that the manuscript is, in fact, a very authentic document.'

Parush got a call in his mobile and he raised his hand, gesturing Afsar to stop for a moment. The abrupt change in the contours of his face was indicative enough of the seriousness of the call. The one side of the conversation that Afsar, Kratu and Kubha listened to with rapt attention was enough for them to realize the gravity of the situation.

> "*What? You tracked a satellite call from here to a place in Delhi, around the time of the murder?*"
>
> "*Can you tell me the exact location in Delhi?*"
>
> "*Are you sure?*"
>
> "*Are you sure that the house belongs to someone by the name Somak Ajai?*"
>
> "*But he was murdered too, at the same time, in the same way.*"

The Last Message

(14 November 2018. Delhi)

Parush was taken to a military base in Mardan. A lieutenant general was waiting for him. As the representative of the Indian Government, he was the easiest target, given the present scenario. It was, as though, Pakistan had caught an Indian spy, red handed.

'So, Janab,' the lieutenant general taunted, 'what does your government have to say now?'

'Say, what?' Parush tried to be as calm as possible.

'That's what India always does,' the lieutenant general scoffed. The three stars on his insignia shone in the dazzling light. 'You always pretend as if you are all disciples of Gandhi and that all the khauf is cultivated in our zamin. What more proof do you need now? We've concrete proof that the people who have killed Janab Faraz Fareedi had made a satellite call from his house to someone in Delhi ... '

'And that someone was also murdered,' Parush interrupted, 'almost at the same time. You know that.'

The lieutenant general didn't say anything for a while.

'Janab, this is not the time for beach volley between the RAW and the ISI. You can give a press release blaming the murder on the RAW and we can blame the ISI. But do you realize that someone is fooling both the RAW and the ISI?'

'What do you mean?'

'You'll never tell me, but I know the satellite phone used to make the call from Khushawar was a clone of that of the director general of the ISI.'

The body language of the lieutenant general made it clear Parush was not joking.

'Where do you get all the nonsense?' he asked, in a not-so-firm voice.

Parush smiled.

'The phone of our chief of army staff was cloned too. It was a serious prank on both of our intelligence systems. So, let us not fight among ourselves. Let the media do that. There's a bigger threat. *Someone very powerful is fooling both of us.*'

☼

Later that night, when Parush had retired to one of the many rooms of the Fareedi haveli, he got a call. The name "Pradhan Sevak" flashed on his screen.

'How is Kubha and her family?' Indar asked him straightaway.

That was how he generally talked to anyone—direct and precise. Parush had once taken Kubha to Indar's official residence for an informal dinner. That was also the only time he himself had had an exclusive dinner with the prime minister. Parush was more than amazed at the way Kubha and Indar had interacted on that day. A totally different façade of Indar's personality had emerged before him. He wouldn't have ever known that Indar too had a frivolous side. Since that day, Indar would often enquire about Kubha. '*The country needs girls like her,*' he said more than once.

'They are fine, but overall, things are getting messier.' Parush too was as direct as possible. He knew Indar hadn't called him at the middle of the night just to ask about Kubha and her family.

'In the last three months,' Indar shifted to a totally different topic, 'there has been a spate of vandalism on churches in all the metros. Suddenly more Muslim girls are being raped. I don't care about the Opposition and the media. I've learned to handle them over the past 20 years. But my sixth sense says there's something sinister going on now.'

'Why're you saying so? You know every time there's an election round the corner, such things increase. For your Opposition and your die-hard haters, the only ammunition against you is this diabolic propaganda that India is becoming intolerant and fanatic with your implicit indulgence. Don't you know who all are behind all these?'

'There's a big difference this time. Even the MoSPI, Ministry of Statistics and Programme Implementation was unaware that across India, in the past six months, there has been a sudden increase in the proportion of Muslims among the rape victims. No one has ever sought this type of information through any RTI. When it suddenly flashed in the media today, I was shocked. I asked for the data and I got the second shock when I was told it is, in fact, all correct.'

'How did the media get the information?'

'A blog was doing the rounds in the social media. It's trending. The mainstream media picked the story from there. It claimed that my government is silently perpetrating crimes against the minorities, and that finally, India would be cleansed of all minorities … '

'Haven't you heard of these before?' Parush interrupted.

'Yes, I've heard these many times, especially before the elections and the next General Election is just a few months away. Every time in the past, I knew what exactly was happening. I knew the people who would do it. Some would be my own people, a few minions who come handy at certain times and whom I can't do away with totally. Others would be instigated by the Opposition. I never reacted to any of these. There are graver things to ponder. Children are dying of malnutrition and lack of basic hygiene; people are jobless; farmers are not getting their dues; teachers are not teaching properly in the government schools; our neighbours are not trustworthy. I can't be fixated with vandalized churches and mosques or a maniac mob lynching someone to death. These have always happened. I'm no God. I don't have a magic wand. I can't control everything … ' He paused to take a long breath.

'What're you implicating?'

Parush knew Indar was not the one to beat around the bush. But presently his thoughts appeared cluttered. It was not clear what exactly he was trying to say.

'No one has been arrested for any of the rapes. The police is clueless. Isn't it strange? For all the other rapes during the same period, the accused were arrested within a few days.'

Parush smiled. He knew the point Indar was trying to make.

'Who else have you discussed this with?'

'No one, okay,' Indar again switched the topic, 'tell me, who you think is behind the dual murders?'

'Some very smart guys, I would say. Cloning GSM phones is not an easy thing. It's still in the realms of serious hobbyists and researchers.'

'I'll tell you something. The mobile phone used to upload the blog that's trending now is also a cloned one. And do you want to know whose phone that was?'

'Don't say it's yours,' Parush chuckled.

'Well, it's yours … '

☼

Afsar and Kratu stayed back in Khushawar. Kubha and Parush returned to India the next afternoon. Maitreyi was waiting at the Indira Gandhi International Airport. Kubha hugged Maitreyi the moment they met. Had she not known that sometime in the long-forgotten past they might have been direct kin, related by blood, staying together at Khushawar, perhaps she wouldn't have felt the special bonhomie she was presently feeling for her. Or was the sudden camaraderie, she pondered, because of the fact that both of them had lost their dear grandfathers in the same horrific way?

Kubha had always wondered why her parents, despite not having any odd provincialism in their behaviour or attitude, would still prefer to dine at a Pakistani or Bangladeshi restaurant in downtown Frankfurt or get elated to see the Bollywood Restaurant at Jungfrau, on the top of the Alps. Did a sense of apparent kinship always add an extra layer of security and comfort? Presently, she did feel comforted, hugging Maitreyi.

'What was the message?' Kubha asked Maitreyi, getting into the Mercedes Benz Sprinter that looked like a normal ambulance, parked with its hazard lights on at the VIP area, just outside the terminal building. They settled inside the van, taking two cramped seats jammed into the hi-tech mobile surveillance centre assembled behind the driver's cabin.

Parush pressed the gas pedal.

'I've to tell you a long story … '

As Maitreyi narrated the story, the melancholy in her voice made Kubha sad. She wrapped her hands around Maitreyi's shoulders.

The first thing that Maitreyi said should have made Kubha shriek. But then, knowing both of them belonged to the same clan, with links to Khushawar, it was not surprising to know that Maitreyi too, like Kubha, was adept in *singing* out words. She too could seamlessly spell out any word in only 14 letters, which, very easily, could be represented by the seven musical notes in two octaves. Thus, each word could be sung.

'My grandfather would sing out entire conversations in Maithili, the language I grew up speaking,' Maitreyi recalled. 'I would call him "Dude", a play on the word "dadu". And, he called me "Sexy".'

Maitreyi's father had never been keen on all these, she said. He would find all these very silly. The relation between the two—her father and her grandfather—had always been very cold. Her father felt that Somak was too hung up with the Maithili culture and tradition, which he believed was anyway dying. He felt ashamed of Somak's deep involvement with the weavers of Kusumpur. 'Pay them some money and get rid of them,' he would often say. He left home quite early and rarely visited India.

'I don't know how and when exactly,' Maitreyi said with sparks in her eyes, 'I fell in love with Dude.' She smiled for the first time. 'I should thank my mother that she allowed me to spend so much time with him. I've been spending the winters with Dude since I was in high school. Dude was so proud of me. Most of the times, we would sing, rather than talk. We played with numbers. He taught me so many number games. One of them was with watches.'

'Watches?' Kubha sat straight. 'What's that?'

Maitreyi pulled out two wrist watches from her bag and placed them on her lap. One of them was old fashioned, with

Maitreyi pulled out two wrist watches from her bag and placed them on her lap.

its narrow leather band untied. The other one was quite stylish, very contemporary, with a thick cuff band. She looked around, searching for something. She got up from her seat and unclipped a writing board from a small desk flushed against the wall of the van. She placed the board on her lap and displayed the two watches on it, side by side.

Maitreyi smiled, having realized how surprised Kubha would have been.

'Dude had left these two watches for me on the desk of his living room, before he died.' She turned serious again.

'What do you mean by that?' Kubha was more perplexed than surprised. 'How do you know those were for you?'

'These watches don't have batteries. They don't work. We have plenty of them. Each shows a different time. These are the props for one of our number games.'

'I'm really not getting anything, Maitreyi,' Kubha sounded impatient.

'Let us go to our place.'

☼

Dumbfounded, Parush and Kubha stared at the eight wrist watches, without their leather bands, displayed on the desk of the living room where Somak was found dead three days ago.

Dumbfounded, Parush and Kubha stared at the eight wrist watches.

Not many things in the world could be more amazing than what Maitreyi had told them just now.

The eight watches showing eight different times, Maitreyi had said, represents the eight notes of music—Sa, Re, Ga, Ma, Pa, Dha, Ni and the Sa, an octave higher.

'When the time is twelve o'clock,' she had explained, 'the two hands of the watch form a zero degree between them. That's Sa, the first note. When the time is six o'clock, the two hands form a 180 degree. That's the Sa in the higher octave, with a frequency exactly twice of the lower Sa.'

If a change in 180 degree means doubling the frequency of the note or, in other words, increasing it by one whole time, she elaborated, a change in 90 degree should be equivalent to increasing the frequency by a half. Likewise, a change in 45 and 60 degrees would mean increasing the pitch by a fourth and third respectively.

'The fifth note of the octave,' she had said, 'is called a perfect fifth because its frequency is exactly halfway between the first and the eighth note. So, when it's three o'clock in the watch, and the two hands make a 90 degree, or half of 180 degree, the corresponding note it denotes should be Pa, the perfect fifth. The major third note of a scale is one-fourth time higher in pitch than the first one. When the time is eight minutes past twelve o'clock, the hands make close to 45 degree. So, that's the third note, Ga.'

Maitreyi explained the rest of the notes too, in the same manner. When she completed, she couldn't but laugh staring at the faces of Parush and Kubha.

'Guys,' she tried to shake them off, 'I've a lot more to say.'

'You use the watch bands,' Parush spoke after a while, coming out of the awestruck state, 'to differentiate between the octaves, don't you?'

'You're as smart as my Dude,' Maitreyi smiled. 'Generally watches with cuff bands are used for the notes on the higher octave and those with untied leather bands for the lower.'

'Are you sure the two watches you showed me some time back,' Kubha asked, 'were deliberately kept by your grandfather, before his death, to send a message to you?'

'It can't be anything else,' Maitreyi asserted. 'Dude never plays with the watches,' she stopped abruptly, and took a deep breath. 'I mean, he never *played* with the watches without me,' she corrected. 'I would keep all of them in one of the drawers under his writing desk in the living room before I left for the US. And I would take them out when I returned the next year. He never touched them in my absence.' She stopped talking, looking at the floor.

Kubha got up and stood behind her, placing her hands on Maitreyi's shoulders.

Maitreyi's relationship with her grandfather, Kubha felt, was very much like hers with her Young Boy. That she had already started to see Maitreyi as a mirror reflection of her own self was doubtless because of their grandfathers, who had connected the two girls under such an unusual circumstance. It was as though, the price of connecting the two sides of the long-separated Khushawari clan was their own lives.

Maitreyi touched Kubha's hands and looked up at her. 'Lately, Dude has been very excited about his research. He would often tell me, "Sexy, we've a great lineage. We're no ordinary people. Just wait for some more time." He was on the top of the world when he discovered the connection with Khushawar. "I knew it," he told me many times. And he talked about you too. He was eager to introduce me to you. Dude always had a grudge against my father that he never took interest in our family's heritage. The last time I talked to him, just before boarding the flight from the SFO, San Francisco International Airport, Dude told me, "You and Kubha will do what my son didn't do. Our big clan will live through you. You have lot of responsibilities." Isn't it so ironic, Kubha? It's really on us now to find out everything—what Dude was working on, what he has left behind, what he was so excited about, why they were killed.'

Maitreyi didn't speak for a few moments. Neither did Parush or Kubha.

Maitreyi herself broke the silence. 'You were saying something,' she said to Kubha.

'I was asking about the two watches … '

'Yes, I remember,' Maitreyi didn't allow Kubha to complete. 'Let me show you those watches again.'

She looked for the bag she had been carrying with her. She pulled the two watches out and placed them on the desk, pushing the other watches to the side.

She pulled the two watches out and placed them on the desk.

'The first watch shows four past 12:00. The hands make 22 ½ degrees. It's one-eighth of 180 degrees, so it should denote the second note, Re, whose pitch is an eighth higher than Sa. The watch has an untied leather band. So, the note is actually in the lower octave. The other watch shows the time three o'clock, the hands make 90 degree, half of 180—the note is a perfect fifth, Pa, halfway between two octaves. The second watch has a cuff band, meaning the note Pa is in the higher octave.'

'Re in the lower octave and Pa in the higher octave,' Kubha said excitedly. 'That's Ka-Ba. Yes, it can be Kubha as well.'

'Girls,' Parush smiled, 'I don't belong to your clan and I don't know how to *sing*. Can you please write me down the mapping between the letters and the notes?'

'Sorry, Porus,' Kubha winked at Parush. 'I'll write it down.'

She took a paper from the desk and jotted down the mapping table which she never had to memorize. It had been always so obvious to her.

	Lower Octave							Higher Octave						
Musical Notes	Do	Re	Mi	Fa	So	La	Ti	Do	Re	Mi	Fa	So	La	Ti
	Sa	Re	Ga	Ma	Pa	Dha	Ni	Sa	Re	Ga	Ma	Pa	Dha	Ni
Letters	e	ka	cha	ta	pa	na	sa	a/u	ga	ja	da	ba	ma	la

She took a paper from the desk and jotted down the mapping table.

Parush took the paper and studied it for a while. 'How do you remember the entire table?' he asked Kubha, not taking his eyes off the piece of paper.

'Porus,' Kubha laughed, 'we don't have to remember anything. It just comes naturally to us. It's like reading a staff notation and singing a song or playing the piano. The key is to reduce any word to the 14 letters. Once that's done, it's nothing different from a simple staff notation.'

'Re in the lower octave and Pa in the higher octave,' Parush repeated it a few times, looking at the table. 'Yes, that's Ka-Ba. How do you know it's Kubha? It can be anything else too.'

'Yes, technically, it can be many things. We've 26 letters in English and we're using only 14 here. Both the "ka" and "kha" sounds are reduced to "ka". All the vowels are also ignored. So, Ka-Ba can be many things. But then, the decoding can't be context free,' Maitreyi said.

'Dude has mentioned Kubha's name a few times recently and under the present scenario, Ka-Ba doesn't seem to be anything else,' Maitreyi added.

Suddenly, everyone fell silent.

'Why do you think your grandfather took my name before dying?' Kubha broke the silence.

'I can't say. But knowing what happened to your grandfather, it's doubtless Dude wanted to say something about him. He might have attempted to alert you, sensing your grandfather's life was in danger too.'

☼

While Kubha and Maitreyi talked, Parush went around the house, checking each room. He returned in a while.

'Kubha, you mentioned Somak had shown you many carpets. I didn't find any in the house.'

'I too didn't find a single one in the house,' Maitreyi conceded. 'That's very strange.'

'Now, I'm sure it's all about those carpets,' Kubha got up. 'The murderers have fled away with the carpets from both the places. All the carpets went missing from Khushawar too.'

'It's not that easy, Kubha,' Parush seemed worried. 'You don't have to kill to steal carpets. Both were old people and it would have been much easier to just break into the houses and steal the carpets. Such elaborate plans to murder hints at something else. It's doubtless the murderers needed the carpets. But, they also needed Faraz and Somak to keep quiet about something related to the carpets … something both of them knew … something no one else knows about …'

Parush didn't complete. He ran towards the corner of the room and bent down to pull out something from under a well-crafted corner table.

'Two more …'

He placed the watches on the desk. Both had broken glasses, not impossible to guess why. The watches would have fallen from Somak's hands, during the last few moments of his life, when he was writhing in pain, struggling to breathe, struggling to send a last message for Maitreyi.

Maitreyi took the watches in her hands and broke down. 'He didn't deserve such a death.'

When she calmed down, she placed the watches on the desk.

'One is "ja" and one is "ta",' she said, looking at Kubha. 'I don't think Ja-Ta makes any relevant word. But Ta-Ja is nothing but the Taj.'

'*The Taj Mahal?*' Kubha shrieked.

The Prime Meridian

(14–17 November 2018. Delhi and Khushawar)

Parush had asked Rakesh, his trusted aide, to come along with him to the India International Centre on the inaugural day of the International Renewal Energy Meet. He, along with a few others, had helped Indar to prepare the inaugural speech. More than listening to Indar, Parush's interest was mainly to keep a close eye on a few people he had been lately cautious about.

Indar's Opposition and fierce critics never left any stone unturned to exploit such international congregations, mainly to reach out to the international media and highlight the *total failure* of Indar's five-year term, which was coming to an end in a few months. As though playing with fire was a passion for Indar, he himself had given enough such opportunities to the cynics to attack him viciously. Parush's focus was on Rahul Gupta, the leader of the Opposition in the parliament and the general secretary of the Indian Party, the main Opposition to Indar's Bharatiya Party.

Parush was surprised to see Rahul engrossed in an animated conversation with a round-faced, bearded man wearing a skullcap and short pyjamas.

'Who's the person he's talking to?' Parush asked Rakesh, gesturing towards Rahul.

'He's Shamsur Ali, a new import to the Opposition squad.'

'What do you mean?'

'He's an ex professor of physics at the Dhaka University and a former president of the Bangladesh Academy of Science. He's a visiting lecturer at the Jamia University. I'm not sure how exactly he managed to hobnob with the politicians. He seems to know a few folks in the Rashtriya Dalit Party too.'

'Does he know anyone from the Bharatiya Party?'

'No. And I'm not surprised at that.'

'Why?'

'The Bharatiya Party with its strong pro-Hindu façade is very unlikely to attract someone like him. Let me show you something … ' Rakesh pulled out his tab and searched for something. 'Have a look, sir,' he passed on the tab to Parush.

> *Bangladeshi religious scientist, Professor Shamsur Ali, the chairman of the Committee on Science in Al-Quran Islamic Foundation, said, 'Anybody is welcome to use the Quran as a test for our scientific principle and not vice versa.' Quoting from Maurice Bucaille's book,* The Quran, the Bible and Science, *he asserted, 'There is not a single verse in the Holy Quran which is assailable from a scientific point of view.' He strongly believes that many modern-day scientific discoveries were accurately predicted in the Quran.*

'He seems to be a strong proponent of Islamic Science,' Parush said, browsing through a few pages in the tab. 'I'm wondering since when has Rahul started taking interest in all these.'

'It may be, the other way round,' Rakesh threw the words slowly, not removing his stare from Shamsur. 'Rather, Shamsur might have started taking an interest in Indian politics.'

☼

Parush walked over to Rahul and greeted him. To his surprise, Shamsur turned towards him and said in a typical Bangladeshi accent, '*Ki bhaigyo amar aiz*. I'm finally meeting the most trusted person of, none other than, the *Prodhan Montri* himself.'

Parush wanted to respond, "I don't think your luck is that good today …" but instead, he said, as calmly as possible, 'The pleasure is all mine.'

Parush could barely suppress the surprise that Shamsur already knew about him. More surprises awaited him.

'I've always wanted to meet the *Big Bong*,' Shamsur said next, referring to Parush by the name "Big Bong", which had been a popular epithet in the American press to designate him by, a decade ago, when he had been embroiled in a very nasty, but high-profile IP theft case in the US.

'You seem to know a lot about me,' Parush smiled, shaking hands with him.

'I'm just a visitor, *a guest of your country*,' Shamsur stressed on the last few words, doubtless to assert the special position and status he enjoyed as a guest in India. Parush didn't let the smile he had draped his face with fade away, something that was already putting stress on his orbicularis oris muscle that controls the movements of one's mouth and lips.

'How could I miss the opportunity to meet a *special guest*?' Parush conceded.

'But no one is more special a guest than you are,' Rahul butted in, directing his implicit taunt towards Parush. 'Even the top-notch folks at the Bharatiya Party are surprised at the special status enjoyed by a guest like you.'

'Rahul, you're forgetting one thing …' Parush patted him on his back and said, 'India believes a guest is like a God, *atithi devo bhava*.'

Parush broke into laughter.

'Carry on, guys,' he again shook hands with Shamsur and patted Rahul once more. 'I want to attend the next session. One of my friends is the speaker. You want to join?'

Parush knew very well neither of them had really come to the conference for any enlightenment about renewal energy. He didn't wait for any response from them either. As he walked away, he didn't miss Raju Salim of the Rashtriya Dalit Party waving at Shamsur.

When Parush met Rakesh, waiting a little away, he couldn't but express his surprise. 'Looks like, Shamsur has united two staunch enemies—the Indian Party and the Rashtriya Dalit Party,' he said, walking with Rakesh towards the C.D. Deshmukh Auditorium, the venue of the next session after the short break.

'I too didn't expect Raju Salim to be here, in this place,' Rakesh acknowledged. 'He doesn't understand a word of English. But sir, there are rumours that the Indian Party is frantically looking forward to creating a grand alliance with anyone who sees Prime Minister Indar-ji as the main enemy.'

They had almost reached the auditorium. Rakesh slowed down. 'Indar-ji has decimated the warring Opposition to such an extent that the only way for them to survive is to fight unitedly,' he continued in a hushed tone. 'In my assessment,' he sounded very serious, 'uniting all of them is just as impossible as uniting India and Pakistan, unless, *someone really smart makes a fool of both of them*.'

Parush entered the auditorium. Rakesh stayed behind, to keep an eye on the different people who had assembled at the conference with disparate intentions.

Rakesh was, indeed, a smart fellow, Parush thought, taking the seat designated for him at the front row. His friend, presently a reputed professor at the Berkeley University, was already behind the rostrum. He waved at his friend and settled in his seat.

Someone had already fooled both the Indian and the Pakistani establishments at the highest levels, Parush reminded himself. He was not at all paying any attention to his friend's speech. Cloning the phones of senior-most defence personnel of both the countries was no small thing. Rakesh might not have inconsequentially likened the prospect of a mega alliance of the entire Opposition to uniting India and Pakistan, even if he hadn't thought so deep. Both were possible indeed, Parush felt strongly, if they were duped or fooled by someone really smart.

Given the present condition of the Opposition parties, all fighting with each other on petty things and reeling under the fear of being wiped away soon, it was not impossible that someone had duped them all with the assurance of toppling Indar Sinha and his invincible Bharatiya Party. Was it the same force, Parush pondered, that had duped the military establishments of India and Pakistan and was behind the heinous murders of Faraz and Somak? Was the same force also behind the meticulously planned rapes of Muslim women over the past few months? Was it a big game, being played at various levels? In all the scheme of things, where did Shamsur Ali fit into? Was he at all a player in the whole game, or was it all just a figment of Parush's imagination, in a desperate attempt at connecting some seemingly disconnected dots?

Parush got up from his seat and left the auditorium. He felt as though a barrage had suddenly collapsed and that a gush of thoughts was breaking out forcibly through the innumerable clefts. He had to wait and see how the violent streams eventually merged into a single flow of thought.

☼

Later that day, Rahul was seated in the front yard of his sprawling bungalow on Akbar Road. The tired, late-afternoon sun was fading fast into the smoky evening haze of Delhi. There would soon be a chill in the air. Rahul looked at his watch a few times. He got up and walked towards the gate. The security rose to their feet and saluted him. He returned to the lawn and took his seat on one of the old colonial-style chairs arranged around a highly ornamented low teak wood table. He wrapped the shawl around his shoulders and sat cross legged, reclining on the chair, looking once more towards the gate. It was doubtless he was getting impatient.

A little later, the security opened the gate and let an old yellow Ambassador taxi in. Once the gate was closed behind the car, another security opened the door of the back seat of the ramshackle vehicle. Shamsur Ali and Raju Salim alighted from the car and walked towards Rahul.

'Taking a taxi from the Juma Masjid was a good idea,' Raju Salim said, settling on the cosy chair. 'Indar and his hawks are too dangerous. They are all harami.'

'Doesn't matter, Raju,' Rahul cut Raju short, 'who's a bastard and who's not. It's not wise to let others know what we're planning. Indar and his people are all smart folks. We shouldn't underestimate them at all. They are keeping an eye on us. They shouldn't know you have been here.'

Rahul didn't want to waste a single moment. He allowed Shamsur to speak. He listened to Shamsur intently, the frown on his face never disappearing even for a moment, his looks affixed on the grass, his locked hands tapping on the knees of his crossed legs.

'All we have to do is to use the Indian intellectuals,' Shamsur said towards the end. 'Muslims are the safest in India. They are also among the most educated here. Out of the 1.6 billion Muslims worldwide, around 60 per cent or close to a billion are illiterate. But in India, only 40 per cent Muslims are illiterate. There are less than 600 universities in all the 57 Muslim-majority countries in the world and India alone has more than 8,000 universities …

'I'm not talking about the films and music, where the Khans are the kings. Even in business, education, jobs, Muslims are everywhere. And yes, who can forget the Indian politics? It doesn't move without the Muslims. Countries such as Bangladesh and Pakistan should take lessons from India …

'But still, you see, the Indian intellectuals always find reasons to complain that India is intolerant. You've to use these brilliant people of India for your purpose. To your benefit, most of the ire of these people is directed towards Indar. Let them speak more. Give them the chance to speak more. You just keep quiet. Let them do their job. And trust me. They are already at work.'

'But, professor,' Rahul asked him, 'what's new about it? They have been always like this.'

The professor smiled; it was quite a sly one. 'It's just the beginning. They will get a lot more to shout about. They will get a lot more to protest against. You all have to be united. You all have to be always with them, on their side, and against Indar. *And, the forthcoming General Election is all yours.*'

'What exactly are you trying to say?' Rahul sat straight.

'I've to take a leave.'

Rahul understood Shamsur was in no mood to talk more. He got up. 'You people keep talking. You've to walk a long way together.'

As Shamsur got into the yellow Ambassador, Rahul wondered why he was taking so much interest in Indian politics. Who was he and what was he talking about? Rahul couldn't but think …

☼

Afsar was getting used to the life in Khushawar. She would wake up early, open all the windows and doors of all the rooms of the ancestral mansion of the Fareedis and let the morning sun sweep the house that had seen better times.

Once the centre of all activities in Khushawar, this house had suddenly fallen quiet. Before Faraz decided to stay there a years ago, the house had been locked for some time, after the last few of its residents had shifted to Lahore. Faraz reinstilled life into the century-old mansion; he started opening the rooms which had been locked for years, cleared the sprawling campus. He also wanted to revamp the place totally, and upon his death, the responsibility of completing his unfinished tasks, Afsar felt, had been bestowed on her. It was not that she wanted to shy away from it. On the contrary, she took the reins from the very next day. A day after Faraz's funeral, immediately after Kubha and Parush had left for India, she called for the architect who had been entrusted by her father to refurbish the home.

Afsar, along with her loving husband Kratu, decided to stay back at Khushawar for some time, at least till the funeral reception she was planning for in a big way.

Bahnaz and Bahrukh, her twin sisters, who had arrived a day after the funeral, wanted to stay back too, with their elder sister.

Afsar was sitting in front of an open window, the fresh morning air lapping on her face. Bahnaz hugged her from behind. 'Do you remember the last time we all were here?' she said.

'You two never wanted to be here,' Afsar pulled her young sister and made her sit in front of her. She took Bahnaz's face in her hands. 'It's so nice here,' her words trembled. 'I wish we all came here, and stayed like this, when Aba was alive.'

It was not that she was seeing her sisters after a long time. They would talk over the phone and Skype, almost daily, often with Kubha joining them through video conferencing. The big screen in Afsar's home office had been mounted on the wall essentially for this purpose. Powered with Cisco TelePresence SX20 Quick Set, Kratu had created a virtual reality where the sisters felt at home, together, *virtually*. Still, she had realized over the past few days that *actually* living with her sisters was an altogether different experience, the thrill of which she had forgotten, perhaps. More than that, suddenly she felt as though she was their only guardian. They had always been kid sisters to her. Even with Kubha's birth, the status had remained unchanged. Sometimes she felt, they were more of sisters to Kubha than to her.

☼

Sitting at her father's desk, where he had breathed his last a few days ago, Afsar opened her notebook. Kratu had settled on a couch, trying to connect his tab to the Wi-Fi someone had set up the previous day. Faraz would use an old-fashioned desktop and never really needed the Wi-Fi.

'I'm taking too long to decipher the manuscript,' Afsar regretted. 'I don't know what has happened of me.'

Kratu didn't say anything. He just stared at his wife, who looked as gorgeous as she had been the first time he had met her at Stanford, more than two decades ago. He remembered that wonderful night, when he had taken her out, for the first time. That night was memorable to him for one more reason. When he had returned to Stanford, he had heard that his uncle was dying. He had rushed to Calcutta, arriving just in time to see his uncle for the last time, lying lifeless on the hospital bed. Very soon he died. The previous year, Kratu had lost his elder sister, the only other person who too had played a major role in shaping his life and thoughts. The next few days after that brought him closer to Afsar, who unknowingly filled the sudden void in his life. Had it not been for her, he wouldn't have coped with the two deaths.

To a great extent, Kratu thought presently, the death of Afsar's father and that of Kratu's sister and uncle were similar. All were heinous murders, pre-planned and immaculately executed with precision and gory grotesqueness.

It had taken a while for Kratu and the others to realize what had led to the murders in his family. That his grandmother's bedtime stories he had grown up with could be the reason for the murders was, indeed, a shocking revelation. For thousands of years, the seemingly harmless fantasy tales had been hiding behind them such explosive facts about Hinduism and its origin that a nondescript fanatic group espousing a very radical view about Hinduism felt it necessary to suppress the stories forever. What ensued was a series of killings.

Presently, an apprehension troubled Kratu a lot. The background of Faraz's murder seemed much like that of his own family members. Here too, he was doubtless, there was something about the rugs which Faraz had known and which the murderers wanted to suppress, at any cost. Here too, he couldn't but think, a chain of murders had already ensued. Who would be next? Was Afsar safe? Was Kubha safe?

Kratu got up from the couch and hugged Afsar from behind. 'You will decipher the manuscript soon,' he assured her. '*We will do it soon*. We have to get to the bottom of it.'

☼

Kratu was checking his mails.

'Is the net working?' Afsar asked him.

'Yes, it's quite good.'

'I need help. I'm stuck with a few lines of the text in the manuscript which I'm not able to decode fully. They're in plain Magadhi Prakrit, but words often undergo so much transformation that, at times, tracing the original Sanskrit form is quite tricky.'

'Are you expecting me to trace back the Sanskrit originals?' Kratu laughed.

'No, sweets,' Afsar sounded frivolous, 'I know you're linguistically challenged. I want you to search the online Sanskrit database.'

'Give me a moment,' Kratu opened the Cornell University Library app Afsar had helped create. 'It's asking for quite a few things.'

'Ya, I know. It needs some parameters to fine tune the search. We've to specify the type of texts it should look for.'

'Type of texts?' Kratu asked. 'What do you mean by that?'

'The entire Sanskrit literature can be classified into various categories. We've the Vedic corpus. Then there are the epics, *Ramayana* and *Mahabharata*; the Buddhist and Jain texts in a form of Sanskrit which is highly influenced by Pali and Prakrit; the classical works by the likes of Kalidasa; then, we've the scientific or secular works on astronomy and mathematics from the same period by the likes of Aryabhata, Bhaskara. What are the different categories available in the app?'

Kratu passed on the tab to Afsar. 'The couplets are in a variant of the Arya meter,' she said, checking the various options in the app. 'Each line comprises 18 syllables, with a caesura or pause after the eighth syllable.'

The Arya meter, she explained, was widely used in the Prakrit texts of the Jains. It was used in a lot of secular texts too. The entire *Aryabhatiya* by Aryabhata was written in the Arya meter.

'The couplets I'm working on seem to be about music,' she said. 'I see the Prakrit term "chhuti-chchhala", which must be the Sanskrit term "shruti-swara", pitch and note, in Indian music.'

Afsar gave the tab back to Kratu. 'Choose "Secular Text",' she said.

'What should I search for?' Kratu restricted the scope of the search to the "Secular Text of the Classical Period".

Afsar passed on her notebook to Kratu and showed him the text she wanted to search for in the online database.

'*Shruti-swara-madhyat shadja mandalaya bhavet-chatur-bhage*,' she read out the lines in Sanskrit.

The manuscript though, she said, has the same text in Magadhi Prakrit, with most of the words ending with "e": "*chhuti-chchhala-maddhe chhajje mandalae habe chaul-bhae*".

'What do these couplets mean?' Kratu asked.

As he typed the text on an empty form in the app, Afsar explained the meaning of the first couplet, 'From the centre of *shruti* and *swara*, the pitch and notes, *shadja* or the first note Sa is at one-fourth of the *mandala*, the circle. From Sa, *rishabha* or the second note Re is located to the north at its one-fourth.'

'What the hell is this?' Kratu laughed. 'Anyway, I'm done.'

He clicked the "Search" button of the app and waited for the results to appear on the screen.

'The text matches to a great extent with the 14th couplet of the fourth section of *Aryabhatiya*, written by Aryabhata,' he said, scrolling the page, browsing through what all had been thrown by the search engine of the app.

Afsar snatched the tab from Kratu and soon her eyes glowed. 'This is incredible. The fourth section of the *Aryabhatiya* is called Gola, or the Globe; and the couplet says: "*sthala-jala-madhyat-lanka bhu-kakshyaya bhavet-chatur-bhage*". From the centre of *sthala-jala*, the land and water, Lanka is at one-fourth of *bhu-kakshya*, the earth's orbit. From Lanka, Ujjayini is straight north, at its one-fourth.'

'Is this Lanka same as Sri Lanka?' Kratu asked. 'The modern-day Ujjain is, indeed, straight north of Sri Lanka.'

Afsar stared at Kratu. 'As far as I remember, in ancient Indian astronomy, Lanka had a much greater significance. Wait a moment!'

She spent a few moments on Kratu's tab, and then, suddenly, a broad smile appeared on her face. She looked up at Kratu. 'The *Monier Williams Sanskrit-English Dictionary* says, "the first meridian of longitude, or the Prime Meridian, which passed through Ujjayini is supposed to pass through Lanka also". Then, one of the translations of this couplet says, "Lanka is 90 degrees from the centres of the land and water, the north and south poles; Ujjayini is straight north of Lanka by 22½ degrees".'

'The north and south poles are the centres of land and water?' Kratu was doubtless not satisfied. 'Is that a metaphor or a general belief?'

'I would like to believe it's the former. But do you realize the significance of the couplet?' Afsar was excited. Her eyes sparkled.

'So, 90 degrees from both the poles is nothing but the equator,' Kratu said. 'And Sri Lanka is, indeed, very close to the equator. But what's more interesting is how "90 degrees" has been referred to.'

'Exactly,' Afsar agreed. '*Bhu-kakshya* or the earth's orbit comprises 360 degrees, and a fourth of it is 90.'

'And I'm sure Ujjayini's latitude would be close to 22½, one-fourth of 90, isn't it?'

'I've already checked. Present-day Ujjain is exactly at 23.18 degree north of the equator, which has been approximated to 22½. Lanka is 90 degrees from the poles, and from Lanka, Ujjayini is straight north, at Lanka's one-fourth, or at one-fourth of 90 degree, which is 22½.'

'Now, it would be quite simple to explain the couplets from the manuscript. Can you read those for me once more?'

'From the centre of *shruti-swara*, Sa is at one-fourth of the circle. From Sa, Re is straight north at its one-fourth.'

'The circle comprises 360 degrees and a fourth of it is 90. So, Sa is at the diameter of the circle, at 90 degrees from both the poles; and Re is 22½ degree north of Sa. What's the next couplet?'

'From Re, Ga is straight north at its same angle. From Sa, Ma is straight north at its two-third angle.'

'Re is 22½ degree north of Sa. From Re, Ga is straight north, at its same angle, which is 22½. So, Ga is 22½ degree north of Re.'

'Ma is north of Sa at its two-third.'

'Two-third of Sa is two-third of 90, which is 60. So, Ma is 60 degrees north of Sa.'

Kratu looked around the room and grabbed an A4-sized paper from the paper tray of the printer kept at a small desk at the corner of the room. He drew a circle with two perpendicular diameters and three radial lines at 22½, 45 and 60 degree from the horizontal diameter, marking them Re, Ga and Ma respectively.

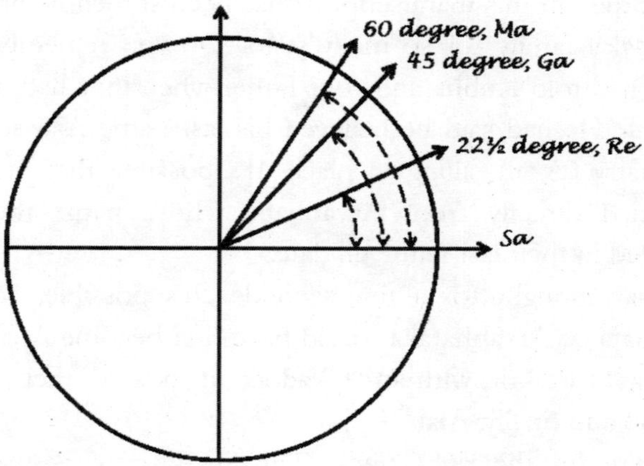

He drew a circle with two perpendicular diameters and three radial lines at 22½, 45 and 60 degrees from the horizontal diameter.

Staring at the paper, Kratu suddenly jumped onto the couch and grabbed his phone. While he dialled Kubha's number, he asked Afsar, 'Do you remember what Kubha said about Somak and his watches?' Before Afsar could say anything Kratu had already got Kubha on the other side.

'Sweetheart, do you remember the eight clock angles Somak used to denote the eight notes by?' he asked.

'Are you fine, Baba?' Kubha was totally confused.

'Darling, I'll call you later. Don't worry. We're all fine. Tell me, if you remember.'

'If I remember correctly,' she tried to recall, '0, 22½, 45, 60 and 90 denote Sa, Re, Ga, Ma and Pa.'

'That's enough, sweetheart. Take care. I'll call you later.'

He ended the call and came running to Afsar. He hugged her tight and said, 'It's no coincidence that Somak denoted the eight notes of music by eight different angles in the watches. It's a very old trick, perhaps invented by none other than Aryabhata himself. It's recorded in this manuscript. It has been somehow preserved by Somak's family for so many years. Do you remember what Somak had told Kubha and your father when they had met him in Delhi? He had said he believed his last name Ajai stood for Aryabhata. It's all falling in place. It's possible that his family descended directly from Aryabhata, whose name they have preserved in their last name till date.'

Afsar thought for a few seconds. 'It's possible,' she said. 'Aryabhata or Aryabhataka would have first become Ajjabhatake in Magadhi Prakrit, with an "e" added at the end, then A-ja-ha-a-e, Ajae and finally, Ajai.'

'We're on the right track. This manuscript is the prime meridian for us. Once we get it right, the rest of the world will fall in place.'

That would soon seem like a prophecy.

The Kilim of Troy

(18–19 November 2018. Khushawar)

Bahnaz and Bahrukh were serving lunch when suddenly, Afsar got up.

'Get up,' she pulled Kratu.

She pushed her chair aside and ran towards Faraz's office on the other side of the long corridor, at the corner. Kratu followed her.

'You carry on …' he turned back and told his two puzzled sisters-in-law.

Afsar opened her laptop and kept it on Faraz's desk.

'*From the centre of shruti-swara, Sa is at one-fourth of the circle. From Sa, Re is straight north at its one-fourth.*' She stared at Kratu.

'What?' Doubtless, Kratu hadn't grasped the reason for the sudden urgency.

'Remember Somak's cryptic way of communicating through watches? The other day, Kubha explained everything so well.'

'Yes, I do. Every note in an octave is higher in pitch from the first note Sa by a fraction. The second note Re is higher by one-eighth and is depicted by the clock angle of 22½ degree, which is one-eighth of 180 …'

'So, degree is essentially another way of representing a fraction. Isn't it?' Afsar interrupted him.

'Yes, that's true,' Kratu said.

'And what do you have in the manuscript?'

Afsar was well aware that the abrupt change in the size of Kratu's eyes indicated the intensity of his awe or jolt, or perhaps both. Presently, his eyes were certainly at their maximum permissible sizes. Even before he said anything, Afsar passed on her laptop to him.

'Almost all the numerals in the manuscript are in the form of fractions.' As she spoke, Kratu browsed through the digitally enhanced images of the fragile pages of the Khushawar Manuscript in the laptop.

'Give me some time,' Kratu threw the words, not taking his eyes off the screen. 'Why don't you go and complete your lunch? I'll be done by then. You can send my grub here.'

Afsar knew presently he wouldn't bother for anything else. Neither would he tell what exactly he was trying to do. She had no other option than to leave him alone. Bahnaz asked if she would get him some food.

'He will not eat now,' Afsar replied curtly.

When Afsar completed her lunch and went back to Faraz's office, she found Kratu reclining on the chair.

'Now you can decipher the entire manuscript,' he smiled, turning the laptop towards her. 'Isn't this really cool?'

'I too expected the same,' Afsar said, looking at the laptop.

	Lower Octave							*Higher Octave*							
Fractions in Manuscript	●	[illegible]	[illegible]	[illegible]	[illegible]	[illegible]	[illegible]	[illegible]	[illegible]	[illegible]	[illegible]	[illegible]	[illegible]	[illegible]	[illegible]
Musical Notes	0 Sa	1/8 Re	1/4 Ga	1/3 Ma	1/2 Pa	2/3 Dha	7/8 Ni	1 Sa	1/8 Re	1/4 Ga	1/3 Ma	1/2 Pa	2/3 Dha	7/8 Ni	
Sanskrit Letters	e	ka	cha	ta	pa	na	sa	a/u	ga	ja	da	ba	ma	la	

'Now you can decipher the entire manuscript,' he smiled, turning the laptop towards her.

'I parsed all the Sharada numerals in the manuscript,' Kratu said, 'and did some simple analysis. Six fractions comprise more than 99 per cent of the numerals, and you don't need Einstein's brain to guess what they could be.'

'I don't really remember the ratios between the different notes of an octave. But, I believe you would have done due diligence.'

'Yes, of course I did.'

The second note Re, Kratu explained, had a pitch one-eighth higher than Sa. Expectedly, one of the six most frequently used fractions in the manuscript was ⅛. The short lines under the fractions perhaps represented the notes in the lower octave.

'*Shruti-swara-madhyat-shadja*, from the centre of *shruti-swara,* Sa is at one-fourth of the circle. From Sa, Re is straight north at its one-fourth,' Afsar repeated the verse once more. 'That's how the notes have been described in the manuscript, plagiarizing a verse originally composed by Aryabhata.'

'Thank God,' Kratu joked, 'the IP protection laws were not strict 1,500 years ago. Otherwise, this case of plagiarization wouldn't have happened and we couldn't have deciphered the manuscript.'

'Anyway,' Afsar got back to the discussion on the fractions, not quite appreciating Kratu's jibe, 'one-fourth of the circle is 90 degree, and one-fourth of that is 22½, which is one-eighth of 180.'

'Yes, you're absolutely right!' Kratu said.

Starting from zero, he reiterated, 180 degree comprises a whole octave, during which the pitch doubles itself, or in other words, the frequency of a note changes by one whole time. By the same logic, 22½ degree would mean a change in the frequency by one-eighth. So, Re could be depicted either by the fraction ⅛ or an angle measuring 22½ degree.

'The manuscript,' he said, 'used the fraction and Somak Ajai used a watch, its two hands forming a clock angle of 22½ degree.'

☼

Afsar and her sisters had got into the habit of taking lazy strolls in the alleys of Khushawar. Mostly in the afternoons, when Kratu would be busy with something or the other, the next generation of the Fareedis would venture into self-learning trips in the neighbourhood. She had pondered many a time in the past few days why she had been suddenly taking so much interest in the people of Khushawar. Was it just a sense of responsibility she had inherited from her father?

There was no doubt her father's sudden death had brought in a sea of change within her, especially in her thoughts and feelings for Khushawar and its people. Was it because she had finally realized that the same people, who had been an integral part of the Fareedi household for so long, were actually carrying the batons of the millennia-old legacy of the Fareedis? Was she getting too emotional with the thought that this very legacy of the Khushawari rugs had been the closest thing to her father? He had, indeed, lived his whole life for it, and perhaps, it was quite apparent now, his life had also been sacrificed at its altar. Perhaps the reason behind her new-found interest in knowing the people around was this thought that her involvement with them would keep her father and his legacy alive. These people had been making the rugs for their family forever. For thousands of years, they had preserved the ancient carpet motifs and designs, which now held the key to something really big—something she was yet to decipher.

As Afsar and her sisters walked leisurely in the narrow lanes, waving at people doing their daily chores in their modest houses, many would come and talk to them, sharing tidbits about their father, the person they all remembered with a lot of reverence and fondness. She entered into the small workshop at the backyard of a house and checked the half-made rugs. Bahnaz picked up a colourful rug and rubbed her hand on it.

'It's so pretty!' she exclaimed.

'Sahibah, these are Farsi knots,' an old person working on the loom explained. 'We have to tie each knot carefully. It's not easy.'

Bahnaz took the piece of rug closer to her eyes and wondered at discovering how the thousand tiny knots created the exquisitely colourful designs on the soft surface of the rug.

The old man got up and brought a different rug, a smaller one, something like a mat on which people knelt at prayers in a mosque.

'Sahibah, this sajjada is made of Gordes knots. They are different. This kind of knots is a specialty of the Turki carpets.'

At some other house, a young lady brought her young son and requested Afsar to ask him to study well. 'Your father told me he is intelligent. But you see he is so naughty. He never sits quietly. His teachers in school complain about him. He listened only to your father. Now that he …' she didn't complete, perhaps feeling sorry to have brought the topic of his undeserving death.

An old man sitting in the sun at the front yard of his house called them inside. 'Your father was our guardian. Now you have to take care of all of us.'

Afsar held his hands. 'Don't worry,' she assured, 'hum hain na … we are there.'

Her own words reverberated in her head. She felt as though she *really* had the responsibility of the entire village.

They walked through sugarcane fields, towards the Balar River. The narrow stream meandered through the seemingly endless sugarcane and wheat fields, strewn scarcely with small hamlets of Pashto people, one of them being Khushawar. As though they were kids, the three Fareedi sisters took their sandals off and ran towards the water. They shivered as the cold waters washed their feet, wetting the folded edges of their salwars.

'Aba had to die to get us here, like this,' Bahrukh suddenly sounded serious. Afsar hugged her and Bahnaz embraced both of them together. They remained like that for quite a few moments. Afsar recalled that was what they would always do as kids. Whenever Afsar would hug one of the twin sisters, the other one would jump on them and try to embrace them tight. They could actually do it much later, only when their hands were long enough.

Afsar remembered fondly how Bahnaz and Bahrukh, the adorable and cuddly dolls, gradually grew up to be two beautiful and naughty girls. Afsar had been always the striking element of contrast in every aspect, from looks to behaviour. She had sharp features, and they, roundish. Even at her present age, she looked 10 years younger, perhaps because of her well-chiselled physique, whereas they were happily plump and looked older. And when they were with Kubha, the trio could put everything on fire, literally and metaphorically.

On their way back home, Bahrukh asked Afsar, 'I've been hearing in bits and pieces about the manuscript; the designs of the rugs; about the other person who was also murdered, at the same time and in the same way; about his research on our rugs. Do you really believe that the motifs used in our rugs could be really so old?'

'The earliest known kilim,' Afsar spoke as they slowly walked side by side, 'was discovered by James Mellaart in 1960 in a king's tomb at a place called Dorak, near the ancient city of Troy. It's dated to 2500 BC. The structure shows that kilims haven't changed much in more than 4,000 years.'

'*Kilim of Troy*?' Bahnaz broke into laughter. 'Don't you think Homer could have written one more epic?'

Afsar slapped Bahnaz gently, making a loving gesture.

'Sorry,' Bahnaz apologized, holding her ears like she would do as a kid, 'please continue. I'm skeptic about the antiquity of the motifs of our rugs.'

'During the late '50s,' Afsar continued with her narration, 'Mellaart carried out many excavations at a place called Hacilar in southwestern Turkey. He discovered interesting pottery of the Late Neolithic Age dating to 5600 BC. The boldly painted red-and-white relief decoration on the pottery was doubtless derived from the contemporary kilim motifs. Present-day carpets still have traces of those prehistoric motifs …

'Many motifs, still in vogue in Iran and Pakistan, can be traced back to the Central Asian civilization of the third and second millennium BC. It's possible that our rugs have also preserved some really old designs …'

'Not only old,' Bahrukh interrupted, 'our motifs are sinister too. Two old men had to give up their lives.'

Afsar stared at Bahrukh. 'I too felt the same, at the beginning. But then, once I came here, and started learning more and more about our rugs, I've changed my opinion. Yes, Homer could have really written an epic on it, even if it were not the *Kilim of Troy*.'

☼

By evening, Kratu had already transliterated most of the fractions of the manuscript, which were all in Sharada numerals, into their corresponding Devanagari letters. He called for Afsar and showed her the first transliterated text from the Khushawar Manuscript.

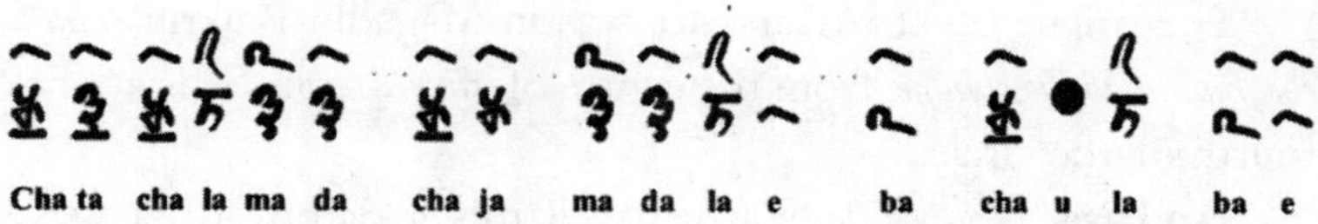

He called for Afsar and showed her the first transliterated text from the Khushawar Manuscript.

'I'm sure you wouldn't be surprised.' Kratu leaned back on the chair and locked his hands behind his head. Afsar supported herself against the edge of the table, holding the tab.

'*Chata-chala mada chaja madala-e ba chaula ba-e*,' Afsar read the line from the tab. 'Cha-ta-cha-la, that's Ga-Ma-Ga in lower octave and Ni in the higher.' She hummed a few notes and then sang loudly, 'Ga-Ma-Ga-Ni Dha-Ma Ga-Ga Dha-Ma-Ni-Sa Pa Ga-Sa-Ni Pa-Sa'.

'Kubha is so good at this,' Kratu said.

Kubha was really an expert, he knew, in this kind of reduction of any sentence in Hindi or Bengali to just 14 letters, and then singing them in 14 notes, like a song.

'I've been so used to it that I always fell short of appreciating the ingenuity of such a thing. But if you think about it, it's such an incredible, but simple way of encrypting a language.'

'And equally incredible is the way the musical notes have been represented in the manuscript. Neither the eastern nor the western notations explicitly give away the pitches of the notes. We just represent a note by a symbol or a letter. But here, each note has been depicted precisely by its pitch.'

Kratu got up and stood beside Afsar, glancing at the tab. '*Chata-chala mada chaja madala-e ba chaula ba-e*,' he repeated the line from the tab. 'Isn't it the reduced form of the parody of an Aryabhata verse?'

'That's amazing!' Afsar quipped. 'I see, you're no longer linguistically challenged. Chalo, these many years of togetherness have yielded something.'

The original text, Afsar said, was in Magadhi Prakrit: *chhuti-chchhala maddhe chhajje*; from the centre of *shruti-swara*, Sa is at one-fourth of the circle.

'And yes,' she said, 'you can call this a parody of a verse from *Aryabhatiya* that talks about the equator and the location of Ujjain.'

Afsar spent some time studying the transliterated texts as Kratu went out for a while, stretching his arms and chitchatting with his sisters-in-law.

'So essentially,' she said, when Kratu returned with two cups of tea, 'some of the texts in the manuscript have been presented in two ways: one in normal Magadhi Prakrit, written with the Sharada letters of its time; and the other one in the encrypted reduced form, depicted through the fractions in Sharada numerals. I've a feeling the manuscript was meant to be a manual to teach the reduction technique.'

☼

The next morning, Kratu found Afsar in her father's office, sitting in front of her laptop.

'Didn't you sleep the whole night?' he asked.

'From the centre of Ma-e-pa mapa-e, Chachajala-e is at 11¼,' she said, not responding to Kratu's query. 'This is one more Magadhi Prakrit text from the manuscript. It's written in Sharada numerals. Chachajala-e is, doubtess, Chhach-Hazara, with the Magadhan "e" added to it. But what's Ma-e-pa mapa, from where Chhach-Hazara is at 11¼? I'm stuck with this. The mixed fraction 11¼ is perhaps one of the very few instances, where the numerals actually denote numbers, and not the musical notes.'

She turned the laptop so that Kratu could have a look. 'That's how a mixed fraction is represented in the Bakhshali Manuscript, by placing the integer, and the numerator and the denominator

'That's how a mixed fraction is represented in the Bakhshali Manuscript.'

of the fraction, all one below the other. That's $11\frac{1}{4}$. In the Khushawar Manuscript too, it's written almost in the same way, sans the casing.'

'*Kilim of Troy*', Bahnaz's comment echoed in Afsar's mind. The Khushawari kilims, she told to herself, were in no way less important than the Kilim of Troy, the oldest one to have been discovered. Now that she had deciphered most of the manuscript, she felt confident that she would soon decipher the designs and motifs of their kilims, something Somak and Faraz had to give up their lives for.

Thinking of Somak, Afsar's thoughts drifted to the kilim Kubha and Faraz had seen at his place, a few days before his death. It was the same kilim with a lot of symbols, she recalled, which someone had wanted to buy from Faraz and which hadn't been made in Khushawar for decades. Many of the symbols were similar to Brahmi letters. Hadn't Kubha taken a picture at Somak's place? She pulled Kratu's hand.

'Do you have the pictures Kubha had taken at Somak's place?'

'I should have them. Kubha had mailed me all of them.' Kratu took the tab from Afsar and browsed through the folders he had organized the pictures into. 'Is this the one?' he showed the tab.

Afsar jumped to snatch the tab from his hand.

'Is this the one?'

'Yes, this is the one. Thanks!'

Her excitement dwindled as fast as it had ascended.

'What happened?' Kratu asked.

'I'd expected fractions here too,' she sighed. 'I remembered vaguely this one had symbols one below the other. Had these been numerals, it would have made sense. They could have been fractions, like what we've seen in the manuscript. But these look like letters, not numerals.'

'Can you identify the letters?'

'Some look like Brahmi. But I'm not an expert in scripts.'

'Wait a minute,' Kratu took the tab and started working on it. 'I'm feeding these symbols to my programme. If they match with any of the scripts already available in the memory, we will know it soon.'

When the search ended, Kratu showed it to Afsar.

'Some symbols are very close to Gupta Brahmi script!' she said. 'It descended from the Brahmi script used by Ashoka. The Guptas used it from the fourth century. So, what we've been thinking as Brahmi is actually the little younger Gupta script, contemporaneous to Aryabhata.'

Afsar fell silent, staring at the picture of the rug which was perhaps at the centre of the two gruesome murders. *I've to decipher the symbols*, she asserted to herself.

It wouldn't be long before they would get to know of the third murder, and there too, the same rug would be at the centre.

PART-III

Lanka

(20 November 2018. Delhi)

Kubha and Parush had accompanied Maitreyi to the Indira Gandhi International Airport in Delhi to receive Maitreyi's parents, who had arrived from the US more than a week after Somak's murder. Kubha didn't have to be told any further about the relationship Somak's only son had shared with him during his lifetime. More unusual, Kubha felt, was rather Maitreyi's relationship with her parents. Having heard quite a bit about Maitreyi's father and his apathy towards everything Somak would do, Kubha hadn't expected any melodrama at the airport, the moment he would meet his daughter. But she hadn't expected either the sort of emotion, or rather the lack of it, when the nearest kin of Somak greeted each other at the airport, in a way as though nothing unusual had happened in their family. It pained Kubha that even the horrific death of Somak had failed to thaw, even a bit, the frozen relations.

After the formal exchange of pleasantries with Maitreyi's parents, Kubha and Parush left them and walked slowly towards the parking area of the airport.

'It's too late,' Parush said, looking at his watch. 'You don't have to return to your hostel now.'

Kubha held Parush's hand and walked beside him. Was she excited that it would perhaps be the first time she would stay over at Parush's place, alone? She tried to recall if ever, since the time she had memories of, Parush had asked her to stay with him, during the night. It was strange, she thought, that though they had spent so much time with each other, they hadn't ever spent a night together.

Despite being the closest friend of her parents, Parush would rarely stay back at their house, either in the US or now in India. Parush would often come to Kubha's room directly and stay there for hours, without evoking any reaction from anyone at home. It was, Kubha had realized over the years, something which, either her parents ignored totally despite knowing it was unusual, or perhaps overlooked.

For all practical purposes, Kubha and Parush had been, since long, very much like a *couple*, an unusual one though, separated by a generation. But she had never felt anything unusual about it. She recalled, during the ballroom dancing performances at elementary school, she would always think of him as the one to dance with. She recalled, on the Valentine Days in high school, when she would perhaps receive the most number of gifts in the class, she would still wait for the evening when Parush would come to their house with something very insignificant in comparison to everything she had received throughout the day. She recalled the day of the commencement ceremony at the Cupertino High School, the inaugural programme of which she had somehow convinced the principal to delay by more than an hour, just to ensure that Parush could reach on time, to see her performance.

Kubha tried to recall if there had been any single moment in her life, special or insignificant, happy or sad, delightful or traumatic, which Parush hadn't been a part of. She tried to remember if she had ever thought of any boy, guy or man, over the years, other than Parush. A collage of memories, all centered around Parush, from every stage of her growing up, passed through her mind.

☼

Around the same time, Vishnu Godse was waiting in a clumsy and claustrophobic attic atop an old silverware shop on the Paranthe Wali Gali. Vishnu had come only once before to this narrow and dingy bylane in the Chandni Chowk area of Old Delhi and he had sworn not to come here again, come what may. Doubtless to say, he didn't like the oily parathas at all. They were prepared on thick iron pans, large enough for him to sit on and practice sitting yogas, and which seemed to have been in uninterrupted use, without much cleaning, since the time of Shah Jahan. He wondered what exactly could be the claim to fame of this filthy place which had been doling out the most unhygienic food since ages.

Vishnu had been advised by his father to maintain a very low profile in India. Born and brought up in the US, Vishnu had recently joined JNU for a grad course in the Special Centre for Sanskrit Studies.

Vishnu's father, along with many other affluent and well-connected diaspora in the US and elsewhere, had been spontaneously working together for a cause, which they all felt, had been neglected for quite long. They got a shot in their arm by the sudden increase in popularity of the Bharatiya Party and the astronomical rise of a strong nationalist leader like Indar Sinha to the helm of India's political affairs. They considered the swearing-in of Indar Sinha as a new epoch in the annals of Indian history. The Hindu heritage and identity of India, which had been denigrated by all the predecessors of Indar in the independent India, and by the Colonial and Muslim rulers in the previous centuries, had to be revived. They strongly believed that Indar's Bharatiya Party, with its right-of-the-centre approach to everything and strong affiliation to many Hindu organizations worldwide, would extend all support and legitimacy to them.

'This is the time,' Vishnu's father had excitedly said to a closed gathering at their home in New Jersey, 'to set things right. Worldwide an aura of Hinduphobia has been created, very cautiously, of course with an agenda. It's as though, to counter the Islamic jihad, it was necessary to cook up something called Hindu fanaticism, or Hindu terror, just for the sake of secularism.'

'Why do you think the Western academia and media have been always so lenient on the Muslims and extra critical about the Hindus?' Vishnu had enquired, helping his mother arrange the plates on the dining table.

'When you yourself speak ill of your own mother,' his father said, 'what do you think others would do? But if they knew you would cut them into pieces and feed the dogs whenever they said anything derogatory about your mother, would they dare to do the same? The Hindus are their own enemies.'

'That's exactly why the Western academia and media have the guts to say anything about India and Hinduism,' an *uncle*, a friend of Vishnu's father who had a repository of statistics for every occasion, pitched in. 'But the same folks turn a blind eye to the Muslims,' he carried on. 'There is a very powerful, sustained and unrelenting cultural and intellectual attack on Hinduism everywhere at the moment. Writers such as Wendy Doniger liken the ancient Hindus to the cowboys who had destroyed the Native Americans, and even to the Nazis who had persecuted the Jews in the Second World War. Hindus are being called prudes, nasty, militants and fundamentals, but the Muslims are always the victims.'

'That's true,' Vishnu couldn't but agree. 'The secularists have always maintained that the ISIS is the outcome of the US aggression in Iraq …'

'Not only that,' the uncle interrupted Vishnu and added immediately, 'the Western media had even relegated the 26/11

Bombay massacre by Pakistani militants to a mere reaction to things like India's policy on Kashmir, the rise in Hindu extremism and the appalling state of poverty among the Muslims in India.'

'It's time to set things right,' Vishnu's father reiterated firmly. 'Indar is a stern task master and a no-nonsense person. He is an inspiration to us. I'm sure he will help us in all ways possible. We don't want to propagate lies. We just want the truth to come out. If the Muslims had, indeed, demolished our temples and persecuted us for centuries, let us not shy away from saying the same to the world. *We can't reclaim all our temples, but we can at least rebuild a few, the most important ones.*'

A few days later, on a long weekend, Vishu and his father drove to Boston. Vishnu asked his father many times whom they were going to meet, but his father wouldn't divulge anything.

'Don't be impatient,' he said with a cryptic smile on his face, when they were not very far from Boston. 'It will be a special day for you.'

Soon, they drove into the sprawling campus of MIT, the Massachusetts Institute of Technology.

They parked the car in front of the Building 31 on Vassar Street and went directly to the Sloan Automotive Laboratory. Vishnu was surprised to see the uncle who always threw statistics, sitting at a corner, beside something which appeared to him like a dismantled car engine, with its inside out.

'Welcome to the core group of Hiranyagarbha Bharat,' the uncle greeted Vishnu and gestured him to sit on the only chair lining his cluttered desk.

More surprises awaited Vishnu. In the next few hours, his father and the uncle talked at length about Hiranyagarbha Bharat, the most secretive and radical Hindu organization of the world. For more than a century, they informed him, the mostly underground group of only a few exclusive people, had always had only one agenda.

'*Anything that's a threat to Hindu culture and civilization must be eliminated*,' the uncle said forcefully in a hushed voice, not to attract any attention in the lab which was anyway very sparse, due to the ongoing long weekend.

He narrated how ruthlessly the members of the organization had eliminated almost a whole family that had preserved a lot of ancient anecdotes in the form of folklore, which went against what they believed was the true story of the origin of the Indian civilization and culture. Shankar Ranade, a young member of the organization and a bright researcher of this lab had died 20 years ago, while attempting to kill one of the members of the family.

'You need drastic steps to counter the systematic propaganda of the West against everything about us,' he justified. 'How dare they create concocted stories about our history, our ancestors, our culture? *It's time to strike back, again.* My young friend Shankar's life shouldn't go in vain.'

Presently, waiting in a poorly lit small room overlooking the Paranthe Wali Gali, still bustling at the wee hours of a cold and foggy November morning, Vishnu felt a rush of adrenaline within him. '*Yes, it's time to strike back, again*,' he said to himself.

☼

Kubha wanted to take a bath. She knew where Parush kept his casual clothes. She opened the cupboard and pulled out a white ribbed tank top. Before entering into the bathroom, she looked for Parush.

'Hope you don't mind if I use this.'

She showed him the tank top. Parush made a gesture which made her laugh.

'What?' she teased him. 'Does that mean "yes"?'

'Why do you ask? Just use whatever you like.'

Parush seemed embarrassed. Kubha cherished the expression on his face.

Kubha spent almost an hour in the bathroom, lying submerged in the hot water of the tub, adjusting the shower to spray the piercing jets of water directly on her face. She realized she hadn't taken such a leisurely bath since the murder of her grandfather, more than a week ago. The steam filled the bathroom and created a dense haze all around her, giving her the feeling that she was in a sauna. Parush would have knocked on the door of the bathroom quite a few times, but its sounds sunk in the echoed buzz of the constant whizz of the shower. Kubha heard the sound when Parush banged hard on the door. She got up from the bathtub in a hurry, splashing water all over and drenching her undergarments she had left behind on the floor. She walked cautiously towards the door, not to skid on the slippery floor, opened it a bit and peeped through the narrow opening.

'What?' she asked a perplexed Parush, as though it was a usual thing to bathe for an hour at two in a wintry night.

'Are you okay?' Parush asked.

'I'm fine,' Kubha shook her hand, spattered a few drops of soapy water on Parush and shut the door.

Kubha turned off the shower, drained the water from the tub, and dried herself with the towel which might have been dry before an hour. That was when she suddenly looked at the wet floor and saw her undergarments lying there, in a puddle of water. She picked up her brassiere and thong in her hands and stared at them for a while. She threw the bra back on the wet floor and pulled the dryer off the hook. She dried the thong for some time till it was no longer too wet to wear. She slid herself into Parush's loose white tank top, which ended a little below her waist, barely covering the black mesh underwear. She opened the door and emerged out of the bathroom, still rubbing her hair with the wet towel. She came to the living room, looking for Parush.

Parush was sunken into the warmth of the sumptuous cushions of the plush, overstuffed leather sofa, sipping tea. The way he stared at her made her conscious, but not uncomfortable. Slipping the towel slowly on the wooden floor of the living room with minimalistic décor, she came close to him. Parush kept the tea-cup on the side-table and sat erect on the sofa, as Kubha moved even closer and cuddled his hair.

The fragrance of the freshly bathed Kubha filled the warm air of the room. A few drops of water dripped down her long and slender legs. The fine fabric of the white top subtly revealed the whirlpool of her belly button, suddenly sucking deep inside it the curvy waves of her carved stomach. Parush's eyes were riveted to the small, black piece of silky netted cloth that hung below her sculpted waist. He felt a euphoria that reminded him of his long-forgotten days of dope. In all these years, it had seldom bothered him that he had been deprived of the physical touch of a woman for more than a decade. Ruthlessly, he had kept himself barren, devoid of any warmth and tenderness. Perhaps he enjoyed the pain inside—the pain of emptiness, the pain of loneliness. He had disrupted the natural flow of his life many a time with huge dams and Kubha had been there more like the water that naturally filled into every crevasse and chasm of the empty catchment area of a dam. But presently, the placid water seemed like hot lava, flowing over him, burning him.

Parush dragged Kubha towards him and pulled the top up, exposing her bare stomach, moving up and down with her breaths. He wrapped his hands around her waist, slithering his tongue into her belly button. His heavy breaths fell on Kubha's bare body. She pushed Parush behind, throwing him into the sofa. She sat on his lap, her legs bent backward on his two sides. She pulled her tank top and threw it on the floor. Parush embraced her tight as she rubbed herself hard against his crotch, his head sunken into the calmness of the abyss between her breasts.

'Why can't you just forget everything, everything that has happened to you?' Kubha whispered, as she stroked Parush with an iambic rhythm. 'Why can't you just forget the girl, the girl who ditched you even before I was born? *I'll make you forget everything …*'

She threw Parush flat on the sofa.

☼

Vishnu checked the time on his mobile. It was already two in the morning. He felt restless, a little worried too. He had been waiting in this small room, alone, for more than an hour. Had it not been for his father, who himself had mediated this meeting, he wouldn't have agreed to it at all. Apparently, Vishnu had gathered, someone had contacted his father and claimed he had in his possession something which could be of great use in accentuating the agenda of the Hiranyagarbha Bharat. The person was tightlipped and declined to divulge anything over the phone or email. That was when Vishnu's father asked Vishnu to go and meet the person.

'How can you trust this person who has been stalking us?' Vishnu had asked his father.

'He has gathered a lot of information about us,' his father had argued. 'He wouldn't do it unless he too had an interest, a common interest. *We can help each other.*'

Vishnu didn't have much to argue with his father. But, he was, indeed, surprised when he was told about the venue of the meeting.

Presently, waiting eagerly at the scheduled place on the Paranthe Wali Gali, Vishnu wondered what he would hear from the unknown person who had contacted his father.

The door of the room opened with a lengthy screeching sound. Vishnu was alerted. The sight of the person who entered into the room evoked a feeling of utter dismay. He had least expected a bearded person with a pair of light-blue pyjamas, a little short of his ankles, and a loosely fitted long kurta of the same colour. His rounded countenance was bedecked with a pair of antique specs with rectangular frames and thick glasses, which were perhaps the most prominent feature of his demeanour. The rough and wrinkled skin of his face was prominent, even in the darkness of the poorly lit room. He sat on a wooden chair in front of Vishnu, hanging his thick shawl on the stripped backrest of the chair and placing the folded skullcap on his lap.

'I can say you never expected me, or rather a Muslim person, isn't it?' he initiated the conversation. 'Let me come to the point,' he continued, without allowing Vishnu to respond. 'You want to cleanse your Bharat of the filth left behind by the centuries of Muslim rule, don't you? And I want to create an Islamic State, ad-Dawlah al-Islamiyah. I, too, want to cleanse Hindustan of the filth left behind by the Muslim rulers, especially the Mughals. In the name of art and architecture, not only did they vandalize your temples and bring dishonour to your religion, they have also brought disgrace to Islam by doing things forbidden in our religion. For the sake of ad-Dawlah al-Islamiyah, *we've to do away with anything that's haram* ...'

'I don't think I'm getting what you're saying,' Vishnu had to interrupt.

The bearded person, who looked like a Muslim cleric, smiled a bit.

'I read your articles. I read the one you wrote about the temples destroyed by Shah Jahan. I believe you're a well-read person. That's why I wanted to meet you.'

The mysterious bespectacled person waited for a few moments, perhaps to read Vishnu's reaction. Vishnu was so perplexed, or rather overwhelmed, at everything that he was rendered speechless.

'You may be wondering,' continued the person, 'how the Mughal architecture, the crowning glory of which is the famous Taj, which is held as the epitome of exquisite Islamic art and artistry, can be haram. Yes, that's what we're fighting against. We want to reintroduce the pure form of Islam, in which building a tomb is forbidden.'

He got up from the chair and brought the side bag he had hung on a hook on the wall. He took out a tab from the bag and searched for something for a while.

'Here it is,' he looked up at Vishnu. 'I know you care for facts and figures; your articles are well researched. So do I.' He looked at the screen of the tab and read out:

> The Messenger of Allah, may peace be with him, said, '*When a pious person amongst them dies they build a place of worship on his grave, and then decorate it with such pictures. They would be the worst of creatures on the Day of Judgment in the sight of Allah.*'

'That's from Hadith number 1076, Chapter 47 and Book 4 of *Sahih Muslim*,' said the person, putting aside the tab.

'So, you're saying that a building like the Taj Mahal, which is nothing but a place of worship built on the graves of Mumtaz Mahal and her husband Shah Jahan, is forbidden as per Islam?'

The person smiled. He looked at his tab again. 'The 18th verse of Surat al-tawbah, the 9th chapter of the Quran about repentance says very clearly, only he will build and maintain the Masjida Al-lahi, the masjid of the Allah, who believes in Allah and Yawmi Al-akhiri, the Day of Judgement, and who gives al-zakata, the compulsory religious tax in Islam.'

'That's ridiculous!' Vishnu was irritated. 'Are you saying you would demolish everything the Mughals built?'

'Not everything, only the mosques and tombs. The thousands of craftsmen, artisans, masons and sculptors who constructed the mosques were not all Muslims. All those mosques are haram. *They have to be done away with.*'

'I can't believe I'm talking to you,' Vishnu couldn't control his anger. 'You're a psycho!'

The person smiled, not showing any sign of excitement. 'So are you … ' he said in a cold but firm voice, without any emotion. 'For you, the Babri Masjid was haram because you believe it was built with the bricks of a Hindu temple. For us, the Taj Mahal in Agra, the Jumma Masjid in Delhi and many other mosques and tombs around the country are haram too, as they were built by the Hindus, the kafirs, the non-Muslims. We destroyed the Al-Qubba Husseiniya Mosque in Mosul. We destroyed the Jawad Husseiniya Mosque and the Saad bin Aqeel Husseiniya shrine in Tal Afar. We destroyed many more mosques and shrines, as they were all haram.' He paused for a while. 'So, you and I are practically the two sides of the same coin. *We both have the same agenda—to get away with things which are haram. Let us work together.*'

He extended his right hand towards a stunned Vishnu.

☼

Parush had been awake the whole night, feeling Kubha, lying on him, her hands wrapped tightly around his neck, her face sunken into the sofa beside his head, her one leg hanging from the edge of the sofa. Shutting his eyes and resting his hands on Kubha's bare back, Parush was cherishing every moment, every aspect of the sensation aroused by her bodily movements as she breathed—the sound of her heartbeat, her smell, her touch and her thoughts. His mobile would have rung a few times and he would have heard it too, but he was barely in the right senses to realize what it meant in reality. The constant ringing finally broke his trance. He slid Kubha down his body and laid her tenderly on the sofa. He walked languidly towards the phone, ringing on the bar cabinet. Maitreyi's name flashed on the screen. Before taking the call, he checked the time. It was 10 in the morning.

'Good morning!' he greeted Maitreyi. 'Sorry, I was asleep.'

'I got a call from Kandy in the morning and I've been trying to reach you and Kubha for the past one hour,' she said in a single breath, her voice barely concealing her nervousness. 'There's one more murder. Exactly the same time. The same way.'

'What are you talking about?' Parush was not able to grasp anything.

'Dude was working very closely with a professor from Kandy.'

'Kandy?' Parush was even more confused? 'Where's that?'

'Kandy, in Sri Lanka,' Maitreyi clarified. 'The professor's wife had called me. From what she told me, I could gather the professor was killed around the same time as Dude, and exactly in the same way. Apparently, the last call he had made from his phone, before his death, was to Dude. Once everyone got a little acclimatized to the initial shock, his wife managed to call Dude's number. I couldn't tell her anything about Dude. I just told he would call her back. What should I do now?'

'Did you talk to your parents?'

'They are sleeping.'

Parush knew she wouldn't talk to them. 'I'll go and pick you up, now …'

Keeping the phone down, Parush stood in front of the bar cabinet, fiddling with an empty wine glass. The phone beeped. His attention went to the screen which was scrolling with the latest international news from round the world, culled from the live feed he received at regular intervals throughout the day. When he was almost leaving the phone and moving ahead, he suddenly took it back, clicking on a particular news item which had just flashed on the screen. The news was about a recent video released by the ISIS.

As Parush read the news on his phone, he stood stunned. Like a reflex action, he clicked on the "play" button of the video. It started with a commentary in Arabic with English subtitles, quoting a verse from the Quran:

> *The righteous Muslims will be given the Paradise, wherein are rivers of unpolluted water, tasty milk, delicious wine and purified honey. The nonbelievers will be given to drink boiling water, so that it cuts into pieces their intestines.*

Parush reduced the volume of the phone, in case Kubha woke up, hearing the sound. The more he watched the gruesome killing of the Yazidi men by the ISIS, the more he could visualize the unbelievably agonizing last moments of Kubha's grandfather and Somak Ajai and, perhaps, that of the professor from Kandy too. He could clearly see how they would have writhed in unbearable pain when a fatal mixture of sodium hydroxide and methanol had been forced into their mouths; how they would have frantically run around, trying to escape in vain from the hands of their killers; how they would have gradually lost their vision and finally, collapsed to death, their intestines bursting out of their bodies, their throats swollen and their skins perforated in a grotesque manner. It was doubtless, Parush was convinced all the three killings had the irrefutable signature of the ISIS. What could be the relation then, he pondered, between the ISIS and the three people killed?

☼

The same evening, when Parush, Kubha and Maitreyi were waiting at the Indira Gandhi International Airport to board a flight to Colombo, Parush talked to Afsar.

'Lanka is not only the prime meridian,' Afsar said cryptically, 'it's also the crime meridian.'

'What do you mean?' asked Parush.

It was, doubtless, not for Parush to understand what Afsar would have meant. But for Afsar, who had very recently deciphered a text from the Khushawar Manuscript, with striking similarities to a verse written by Aryabhata, the term "lanka", indeed, had a greater significance. Very soon, when another manuscript recovered from the Royal Library at Kandy, an ancient city in Sri Lanka, would become the epicentre of a very important discovery with far-reaching repercussions, Afsar wouldn't be surprised at all. After all, she knew Aryabhata had already identified Lanka as the prime meridian, an epicentre in an altogether different sense though, more than 1,500 years ago.

The Rosetta Stone

(21 November 2018. Kandy, Sri Lanka)

The Ministry of External Affairs had made all the travel arrangements in half a day. Parush, Kubha and Maitreyi would stop over in Colombo for the night. They would stay at the Indian Embassy on the Galle Road, in the heart of the city.

Parush's sixth sense said, the three murders, with an irrefutable signature of the ISIS or its likes, needed to be investigated together, as a single case. The only connection between the three people, murdered exactly at the same time but in three different countries, was something as seemingly irrelevant and unrelated as the Khushawari carpet. That very connection, and the recent revelation that the people behind the murders were perhaps directly affiliated to or were strongly inspired by the actions and ideologies of the ISIS, made the case not only very complex but a very sinister one too. That something dire and menacing was being planned had already been evident when Parush had realized, just a few days back, during his short trip to Pakistan to attend the funeral of Kubha's grandfather, that his phone and that of the director general of the ISI too, had been cloned.

'*Things are getting really messy*,' Parush said to himself.

Parush's phone rang, when they were just proceeding to board the Sri Lankan Airlines' flight to Colombo from Delhi.

Someone had called from the Indian Embassy in Colombo to ensure everything was fine with them.

Walking through the aerobridge, Kubha by her side and Maitreyi behind, Parush said, 'I didn't know that Sri Lankans also have a typical Bong accent.'

'How do you know that?' Kubha asked, turning back to check Maitreyi was not left too far behind.

'Someone by the name Mahinda Weerasinghe called me just now from the Indian Embassy. Had he not introduced himself, I would have taken him for a Bong settled in Colombo.'

'Well, you're not completely wrong,' Kubha smiled.

They had already boarded the flight. Putting their hand luggage in the overhead compartment, they took their seats side by side, Maitreyi taking the window, Parush the aisle and Kubha the middle.

'You guys may not know,' Kubha said, once they had settled in their seats, 'Bengali and Sinhala are sister languages. Both originated from the same colloquial form of Sanskrit spoken in the eastern part of India, in the present-day Bengal and Bihar, some 2,000 years ago.'

'How's that possible?' Maitreyi asked.

'Someone by the name Vijaya Sinha took a few Bongs from southern Bengal on an adventure trip to Sri Lanka. When their visa expired, they managed to stay back there,' Kubha joked, trying to lighten up the mood a bit—it had been quite a hectic and gloomy day since the morning, since they had found out of the third murder, at Kandy. The trick worked. Parush and Maitreyi joined her in laughter.

Kubha continued, 'Mr Sinha made it really big there. The country took his last name and came to be known as Sinhala and Ceylon.'

☼

On the way to downtown Colombo, in an embassy vehicle bearing a diplomatic registration number plate, Mahinda informed them that the wife of the murdered professor had been waiting at the Indian Embassy since afternoon, to meet Maitreyi.

'Does she know that her grandfather was also murdered?' Parush asked.

'Yes, the DIG of Kandy has already informed her, after his discussion with you in the morning.'

'Why does she want to meet me?' Maitreyi asked.

'She feels you may know something about her husband's death …' Mahinda paused and then spoke again, hesitantly. 'I really feel sorry for her. She was carrying. Hearing the news of her husband's death, she fell from the staircase. The doctors couldn't save the baby. She forcefully left the hospital this morning and travelled from Kandy to meet you.'

'How old was the professor?' Maitreyi asked.

'Less than 30.'

'Where was he murdered?'

'In Kandy, in the Sri Dalada Maligawa.'

'What's that?'

Sri Dalada Maligawa in Sinhala means the Temple of the Sacred Tooth Relic, Mahinda said. Presently, a World Heritage Site, it is one of the most sacred Buddhist shrines in the world. One of the Buddha's canine teeth is enshrined there. The tooth is believed to have been taken from the ashes of Buddha's cremation and brought to Sri Lanka in the fourth century from the ancient Kalinga kingdom, in present-day Orissa and Andhra Pradesh. Very close to the main shrine is a raised octagonal structure with tented roof, perhaps the most conspicuous element of the external façade of the Sri Dalada Maligawa.

'It's called the Pattirippuwa,' he said. 'In the earlier days, the king would use it as a podium to address his people. It's now a part of the temple complex, accessible from the main shrine. It has a good collection of old manuscripts on palm leaves.'

Apparently, Mahinda narrated, lately the professor would spend a lot of time in the Pattirippuwa, after the visiting hours, studying the manuscripts. Last week too, he had been there, when he was murdered.

'But, how can anyone enter into a World Heritage Site and murder someone?' Kubha asked.

Parush had already had a long discussion with the DIG of Kandy on this, over the phone.

'Kubha,' he said, 'they have a very strict procedure for allowing any visitor after the visiting hours. The killers dodged the security at every possible checkpoint. They used perfectly forged diplomatic identity cards of people with consular immunity issued by the Thai and Burmese embassies. *They are no ordinary people. It's not a simple murder.*'

☼

Kubha hugged the wife of the professor and allowed the new widow to wet her shoulders with her tears. Her hair hadn't been made in a long time. Her sari was worn clumsily, her eyes were kohled in black rings, her cheeks were sucked inside and her sandals were torn. Knowing that she was the widow of the slain professor, she felt an inexpressible kinship with her.

'Three people were murdered at the same time, including your husband,' Kubha said, once she had composed herself. 'Our grandfathers,' she said, pointing to Maitreyi, 'were also killed in the same way as your husband, and at the same time, we all have to know why. You're not alone. We all are with you. *We all have just one thing in life to do.*'

'He had … very high respect … for your grandfather,' the lady said to Maitreyi, in a heavily accented English.

All that Parush, Kubha and Maitreyi could gather from her was that the professor would often refer to an old palm-leaf manuscript, kept at the Pattirippuwa, as the Rosetta Stone. It was the same manuscript he had been working on when he was murdered.

As the professor's wife talked, Kubha noticed Parush had already started working on his phone. She wouldn't have to be told that he was looking for the Rosetta Stone.

'He was an expert in old manuscripts. He knew by heart almost every page of all the manuscripts at the Pattirippuwa. People would come to him from all round the world, especially from Thailand and Burma. He would just look at a manuscript and correctly say when it was written. His mind has filled only with old alphabets.'

'Yes, we know your husband was an exceptional palaeographer,' Maitreyi acknowledged. 'He was helping my grandfather a lot in his research …'

'What was the research about?' the professor's wife interrupted. 'Do you think they were killed for that?'

'Why do you say so?' Parush asked, suddenly taking his eyes off his phone. Kubha too sat straight.

The frail lady became conscious at the sudden attention from everyone.

'Just a day … before his death …' she spoke in staccato, 'he had mentioned … Dr Somak could be in trouble.'

'Why did he say that?' Maitreyi asked.

'He said Dr Somak believed that when the research would be completed, many people would feel very uncomfortable.'

She looked at Maitreyi, perhaps for a response. Suddenly, she turned towards Kubha. 'Was your grandfather involved in the same research as well?'

'Not exactly,' Kubha gave a very short answer. 'He too was helping Dr Somak in some way, like your husband.'

Parush got up from the sofa. He leaned against the wall and stood cross legged. 'You should take some rest,' he said to the professor's wife. 'I assure you, we will do whatever it takes to get to the bottom of it. We will, for sure, find the murderers of your husband, even if they are hiding under the sea or on the top of the Himalayas. And, these two fiery young ladies,' he pointed towards Kubha and Maitreyi, 'haven't come here for nothing. *They too are burning in the same fire as you*. Trust them. Trust me.'

When the lady had gone, Parush came back and sat on the sofa.

'We're on the right track,' Kubha said firmly. 'Even the professor's wife was aware that Somak's research was not a normal one and that it could make a lot of people *uncomfortable*.'

'What's the Rosetta Stone?' Maitreyi asked abruptly.

Mahinda had just appeared in the room, requesting them to proceed for the dinner with the High Commission. As they followed Mahinda, Parush narrated the story of the Rosetta Stone.

After Alexander's death, one of his bodyguards, Ptolemy, was made the satrap of Egypt. Soon he declared himself the King of Egypt. The Egyptians too accepted him as a successor of the pharaohs. His family ruled Egypt for a few hundred years.

'It could be said,' Parush explained, 'they were quite respectful of the language and culture of the natives. Otherwise, a decree issued by Ptolemy V wouldn't have been inscribed on a stone in three different scripts: the famous Egyptian hieroglyphs; the Demotic script, another ancient Egyptian script popular in the Nile delta; and finally, the ancient Greek.'

Parush explained that many centuries later, the Ottomans built a fort near the town of Rashid or Rosetta in the Nile delta, using the same stone with the inscription of the decree as a construction material. After Napoleon's conquest of Egypt, this dilapidated fort was being reconstructed. That was when, in 1799, someone discovered the stone.

'As the stone essentially had the same text in three different scripts,' Parush elaborated, 'out of which the classical Greek was already known, it soon led to the deciphering of the other two ancient Egyptian scripts. That was how the Egyptian hieroglyphs were deciphered. It opened a whole new gateway to a wealth of information and knowledge about ancient Egypt, totally unknown to anyone till then.'

'So, essentially,' Kubha observed, 'calling a manuscript a Rosetta Stone means, it too has led to the deciphering of something, the opening up of some new gateway.'

Kubha remembered her only meeting with Somak, just a few days before both he and Faraz had been killed. She recalled what Somak had said about the symbols in their carpets: '*All the symbols made a new script. They all expressed a language.*' Somak's words reverberated in her mind. Somak had proudly announced, she recalled, that he was very close to deciphering the symbols in the carpets. He had also mentioned that his findings would *rake the world.* It was all falling in place now.

Something that could rake the world, she asserted to herself, could very well make a few people very uncomfortable. But how uncomfortable could they be, she pondered, that they had to resort to such ruthless murders? She felt excited that they were very close to the place which had supplied the Rosetta Stone to the deciphering of the symbols of their carpets, something which had eventually led to the present trail of murders.

Kubha felt grateful to Dr Sanath Wickramasinghe, the slain professor of the Department of Classical Languages at the Faculty of Arts in the University of Peradeniya. Perhaps, she felt, he too, like Faraz, like Somak, had given up his life to uphold a truth that had been hidden in their carpets for thousands of years.

Kubha remembered the words of the old Fazal, her great grandfather, who would talk to a 10-year-old Kubha as though she was the sole heir to the ancient legacy of the carpets in their family …

> *These rugs have been carrying the pulse beat of our family. I'll die. Your grandfather will die. The pulse beat of our family will never stop. We have to keep the rugs alive.*

☼

On the way to Kandy, the next morning, Maitreyi asked, 'Do we expect to see the manuscript which the professor's wife referred to as the Rosetta Stone?'

'It's possible,' Parush responded. 'The DIG of Kandy told me nothing is missing from the library.'

'Isn't that strange?' Kubha said. 'All the rugs from both the places, Delhi and Khushawar, were stolen at the time of the murders.'

'Yes, it's indeed strange,' conceded Parush. 'But remember, this is a World Heritage Site and one of the most sacred shrines for the Buddhists. People come to visit this place from round the world. Whoever possesses the tooth, I heard, is believed to be the ruler of Sri Lanka. So, it's very likely that the security would be quite heavy. It may not be easy for someone to steal a whole book and run away. The very fact that they managed to sneak into the high-security zone and murder the professor is a feat by itself.'

A senior monk from the nearby Asgiriya Maha Viharaya Buddhist monastery, involved in the administration of the Sri Dalada Maligawa, the Temple of the Sacred Tooth Relic at Kandy, received them at the vahalkada, the main entrance to the shrine. They walked across a short bridge over the moat separating the two walls that ran along the perimeter of the shrine like an open-roofed ambulatory. The vahalkada, a square, flat-roofed structure with pointed finials and arched openings on all sides, was on the other end of the bridge. Dressed in a customary saffron monastic robe, the short and stout monk with a clean-shaven head had been very conspicuous from a distance.

'Let us pay a visit to the Sacred Tooth and then go to the Pattirippuwa,' the monk said, leading them inside the shrine complex. He thanked Parush for the help the Indian Government had already extended towards investigating the shocking murder inside the Sri Dalada Maligawa.

On the way, he provided little tidbits about the temple, about its history and architecture. As they went through the huge Makara Torana, an archway with two large dragons, he explained, 'The dragon you see here is a creature with crocodile's jaws, lion's legs, mouse's ears and peacock's tail; and its body is shaped like an elephant's trunk.'

When they passed through a tunnel, attractive lotuses and creepers painted in resplendent colours on its arched roof, the monk stated it was called ambarawa, the sky-going tunnel.

Crossing a courtyard and then entering into the lower level of the main shrine, they took a staircase to the floor above. They came to a long, wide hall teeming with people, moving at a snail's speed in a long, winding queue. The multitude of people would have come from places all round the world, bearing their diverse cultures and ethnicity in their looks, attires and behaviour. They were all waiting patiently for a moment's deliverance. Given the crowd, the place appeared too quiet to Kubha. There was a certain solemnity in the bustle which added to the inviolable sanctity of the place.

A long table at the centre of the hall was filled with lotuses left behind by the visitors as humble token of their obeisance. 'This is the uda maluwa, the upper terrace of the shrine,' the monk continued with his narration. 'A Buddhist monastery or shrine is often built with multiple levels of terraces, each in the form of a roundish garland, malaka. The lower level is called palle maluwa.'

Cutting short the long queue of visitors, the monk took them directly to the main chamber that housed the tooth relic. 'The Sacred Tooth is encased in seven gold caskets studded with precious stones,' he said, bowing in front of the object that had been venerated by the people of Sri Lanka for millennia.

Kubha—being the daughter of a Muslim mother and a Hindu father—and having grown up with an adequate dose of indulgence and influence from the grandparents of both sides with not-so-convergent views on many things, had an eerie feeling. She stared at the monk, and the others, many devout Buddhists among them and many perhaps curious visitors. Many of them, she knew, did believe that was indeed a real tooth, belonging to the Buddha Himself, who lived more than two and a half millennia ago. Ever since she had heard of the Sacred Tooth, she had been more dismissive than skeptic. But presently, standing in front of the dazzling golden casket, amid so many bowed heads, somewhere her logic, her skepticism, seemed to be fizzling out fast. It was not that she hadn't been to a temple before, though neither of her parents had ever asked her to go to any, still, she felt, here, it was something different, something unexplainable. Without bothering what could be the right way, she sat down before the casket, folded her hands and shut her eyes.

☼

This part of the shrine had been sealed since the gruesome murder of Dr Sanath Wickramasinghe and the Pattirippuwa was presently out of bound to the visitors. The not-so-big octagonal room, with a balcony running along its perimeter, was rather claustrophobic, with too many things packed into it. One wall was lined with a closed wooden cupboard stuffed with palm-leaf manuscripts. At the centre was a big wooden table with a replica of the golden casket, secured inside an octagonal glass casing, and a white idol of the Buddha. A few other pieces of furniture and the Buddha memorabilia occupied some more space.

The monk opened the cupboard and took out the old, fragile manuscript. A thick bunch of dried, polished and flattened palm leaves, around four-inches wide and 10-inches long, were stored between two wooden panels richly decorated with exquisite ivory and mother-of-pearl inlay work. He placed the manuscript on a clearance on the central table. This was the manuscript, he confirmed, the professor would be engrossed with most of the times, before his death.

'The manuscript is essentially a commentary on *Mahavamsa*,' he said, as he turned the delicate leaves carefully.

Written in the fifth century, more than 1,500 years ago, *Mahavamsa* is the most important epic poem in Pali language, the monk informed. It contains an authentic history of Sri Lanka and India from the time of the Buddha till the third century.

'Dr Sanath Wickramasinghe believed,' the monk said, 'this particular commentary was written in the fifth century, around the same time *Mahavamsa* was written too. This manuscript is but a much later reproduction of the original text, not older than 300 years …

'It's a unique manuscript, as it's an illustrated one. There are not many manuscripts like this in Sri Lanka …

'The illustrations were done with pen or brush, as done on paper. The text was written by incision, with a pointed metal stylus. First, grooves were made on the palm leaves with the stylus. Then, a paste of charcoal powder mixed with oil was smeared on the leaves and wiped off. The black mixture deposited on the grooves, thus making the letters stand out …

'We use natural herbs such as sweet flag or margosa leaves to keep the insects away.'

Kubha and Maitreyi both shrieked, almost in unison, seeing the illustration on a page. The partly blackened illustration was almost like a facsimile of the rug with a lot of symbols, the one which hadn't been made for many decades in Khushawar and which someone was eager to buy from Faraz.

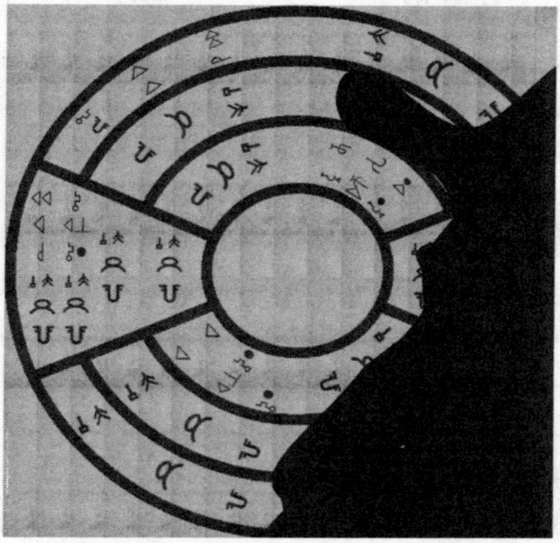

The partly blackened illustration was almost like a facsimile of the rug with a lot of symbols.

'How did the blackening happen?' Parush asked, staring intently at the illustration. 'Is it a common thing for manuscripts?'

'I don't remember seeing this kind of blackening,' the monk replied, trying to recollect something. 'But some ink spilling over a page shouldn't be unlikely …'

'That's a theoretical possibility, but may not be the reality,' Parush interrupted. 'Someone has intentionally spilled the ink on it to damage the illustration,' he asserted. 'Can I do a forensic test?'

'No,' came the curt reply from the monk. 'We don't allow any such thing. Whatever happened to the Shroud of Turin, in the name of investigation, shouldn't happen to anything related to the Sacred Tooth.'

The sudden firmness in the monk's voice made it very clear what the stand of the monastery could be in a scenario like this. Parush was aware that the scientific tests on the shroud, believed by many to be the burial shroud of Jesus Christ, yielded in many contradictory results, not palatable to the orthodox Christians. It was clear the Buddhist monasteries in Sri Lanka were very particular that a similar situation, where the core belief of many people about the Sacred Tooth could be shaken, should be resisted, come what may. It was understandable they would never allow any test, just to be on the safe side.

But then, Parush pondered, how he could prove that the illustration had, indeed, been tampered with, intentionally, perhaps by the murderers of the professor.

'You can take pictures of the manuscript, if that helps,' the monk offered, as a compromise.

Leaving Kubha and Maitreyi at the Sri Dalada Maligawa, Parush went to meet the DIG of Kandy at his office.

☼

Sujeewa Dissanakaye, the DIG of Kandy, was a very sharp guy, Parush realized soon. He had convincing answers for almost everything Parush asked. Parush had been curious how the murderers could have managed to kill the professor within the shrine, without attracting the attention of anyone.

'The professor was heavily doped,' the DIG informed, pushing back his seat.

The DIG would be in his late fifties, Parush guessed. Though a little hefty, he looked quite fit. His military haircut complemented his no-nonsense style.

'The chemicals had the desired effect on him, but he was saved from the pain. He had a quiet death. Whatever, the professor didn't deserve this kind of death.'

'Have you guys got any lead?' Parush asked.

'I've good confidence that I've identified the suspects. I checked the video grabs from the Sri Dalada Maligawa.'

'Can I see the video clips?'

'Yes, why not? Give me a minute.'

The DIG was already on his heels. He returned in a short while with a laptop and played one clip.

'This one is the clearest. The faces of all the three people with forged IDs are visible distinctly in this clip.'

The moment Parush saw the clip, he jumped to his phone and called Rakesh, his go-to man.

'Rakesh, I'm sending you a clip. Confirm that the man in the middle is same as the one we've been keeping a watch on, the one that often drives Shamsur Ali around in Delhi.'

He thanked the DIG.

'You're right. I'll surely give you some good news,' Parush said.

He left the DIG's office in sometime, having taken all the relevant information. The DIG himself drove him back to the Sri Dalada Maligawa, where Kubha and Maitreyi had been taking the pictures of the whole manuscript.

While waiting for someone to receive him and take him to the Octagon, Parush got a call from Rakesh.

'Sir, he's the same person, Mushtaq Shaikh,' Rakesh began the conversation without any introduction or exchange of pleasantries. 'On 10th November, he travelled to Kathmandu from Delhi. The same afternoon, he flew to Bangkok from Kathmandu and returned on 12th afternoon. He was back in Delhi the next day. We were tracking him all along. He had a valid passport and visa. He had confirmed return tickets for Bangkok. Nothing looks suspicious.'

'Why would someone go to Bangkok via Nepal?' Parush interjected. 'Isn't that suspicious?'

'I verified that too. He bought the tickets online at the last moment and that was the cheapest option available.'

'What did he do at Bangkok? Do you know?'

'He had a Thai Airways flight from Kathmandu, reaching Bangkok at 6:30 pm on the 10th. He didn't have any check-in luggage. He left the airport an hour later. Then, he checked-in for the return flight on 12th morning, at round 7:30 am.'

'What did he do at Bangkok?' Parush asked again, the irritation evident in his voice.

'Sir, I don't have any information about what he did the whole of 11th.'

'Why can't you guys say a simple "NO"? It's absolutely fine not to know everything in the world. Thanks for all the information. Call me if you find out anything more.' He disconnected the call.

He called the DIG. 'I'm sending you a better picture of one of the persons in the clip you showed me. Is it possible to find out if he had come to Colombo on 11th November, from Bangkok?'

'That's not easy, but possible,' the DIG assured. 'We need to check the video grabs from the gates where the flights from Bangkok had arrived on that day. But, how did you get the picture? And how do you know he came from Bangkok? Anyone can forge the ID of a diplomat working at the Thai Embassy. You don't have to go to Thailand for that …'

'I'll tell you,' Parush cut him short. 'Please call me back.'

Lord of the Animals

(21 November 2018. Kandy and Khushawar)

On the way back to Colombo, Parush got a call from the DIG.

'We couldn't find the person in any of the video grabs from the Bandaranaike International Airport,' the DIG said. But the records of the immigration authorities at the airport, he informed, seemed to have the picture of the person Parush was looking for. Apparently, the person had come to Colombo from Bangkok on the morning of the 11th, on a Sri Lankan Airlines flight, and returned early next morning, on the 12th November.

'I would assume, the name of the person is not Mushtaq Shaikh,' Parush said. 'And, I would assume this too, that his name is same as that in the ID he had used to enter the shrine.'

Parush didn't have to be told how surprised the DIG must have been on hearing that.

'Yes, you're, in fact, correct,' the DIG exclaimed. 'His name mentioned in the records is Satit Krikul. The real Mr Kirkul is a diplomat working at the Thai Embassy.'

Parush knew Mushtaq, Shamsur's driver, had fooled his people by not taking a direct flight to Colombo from Delhi. The plan to go to Bangkok from Kathmandu, Parush realized, was the masterstroke—it made his trail to Sri Lanka almost impossible to discover.

☼

When Kubha and Maitreyi had fallen asleep, Parush took a stroll on the Galle Face Green, a sprawling urban park in downtown Colombo, along the coast of the Indian Ocean. The pleasant breeze from the waters soothed him. He walked alone on the promenade, skirting the ocean. He watched the last few street-food vendors covering their carts tightly with plastic sheets, at the end of one more day of great business. The smell of fried fish lingered in the air. He stood at the edge of a promontory, a wide courtyard that projected into the ocean from the sidewalk. He leaned back against the railing precariously and suspended his head down, seeing the dark waters merging with the horizon. The constant sound of the waves breaking against the narrow shore and the intermittent sound of the cars zipping along the Galle Road had the meditating effect of a hymn on him. The scattered thoughts in his head seemed to converge gradually. He called Indar.

'Why can't you just arrest Shamsur?' Parush asked directly. 'Now I have solid proof that he is directly involved in the three murders. Indar, he also has very close links with the Islamic State.'

Parush explained that Shamsur's driver, Mushtaq Shaikh, had actually gone to Kandy and killed the professor.

'I've all the proof. What are we waiting for?'

'Porus, it's not that easy. The crime happened in a different country and we can't link things together and arrest someone like Shamsur, especially when the Opposition parties are hobnobbing with him. You don't understand politics. That will ruin me.'

'I thought the country comes first to you. Isn't that what you told me when we had met for the first time?' Parush was seemingly irritated.

Indar smiled. 'Do you think arresting him will save the country?'

'Your Opposition has joined hands with the Islamic State, just to put you down! Do you understand that? I don't know what exactly their plan is, but it's surely going to be a sinister one.'

'So you want me to arrest a person you think is behind the murders of three people, who were all connected in some way or other to a particular type of carpet? What do you think the press would do with such a story?'

'Make it covert. Why should the press know?'

'This is democracy. I don't resort to such tactics.'

'Even if that leads to disasters?'

'*Porus, taking the right action is my responsibility*. Trust me.'

'Okay,' Parush replied. '*I trust you.*'

'Tell me one thing … Even if I believe my Opposition has, indeed, joined hands with the ISIS, how would that help them? Wouldn't that go against them? Wouldn't the people of India throw them out for such a heinous thing?'

'Yes, that's true!' Parush turned back and faced the dark frothing waters of the Indian Ocean. 'But …' he paused, took a long breath, and then spoke again, 'what if the people don't even realize the Opposition is in collusion with the Islamic State?'

'What do you mean?'

'The ISIS is an expert in creating mayhem. They can kill people, bomb buildings, demolish historical sites. They can do anything under the sun. And in India, any such thing will have a cascading effect. There can be communal riots, public outcry, dharna …'

Parush paused again, perhaps allowing Indar some time to frame the rest of the story in his mind by himself. Indar didn't have to be told anything till the end. When he didn't respond, Parush continued, 'In Bangla, there's a saying, "*udor pindi budhor ghare*", Udo's head on Budho's shoulders. You do something, I get the blame. *The ISIS does something, you get the blame …*'

'Have you guys figured out,' Indar interrupted, 'what is it about the carpets they're so desperate to erase all traces of?'

Parush smiled. Indar had, indeed, understood what he had been trying to lead at.

'I think it's all related to one particular carpet, which was in the possession of Somak.'

'You mean the professor from the Delhi School of Economics?'

'Yes, that's correct. Kubha's grandfather might have had a very old piece of the same carpet in Khushawar. Both the pieces were gone after the first two murders in Delhi and Khushawar. An illustration of the same carpet in an old manuscript at Kandy was found blackened after the third murder.'

'What's so special about the carpet?'

'I believe we don't yet have any clue about that. It's a peculiar carpet with a lot of ancient symbols. Kubha's mother is trying to decipher the symbols … '

'Wait a minute,' Indar interrupted again.

Parush had been used to Indar's behaviour by now. He knew something had been already playing in Indar's mind.

'What could anyone gain by erasing the traces of a carpet?' Indar asked.

Parush didn't have any readymade answer.

Indar waited for a few seconds. 'What do you think?' he asked again.

'I don't know … exactly … Indar …' Parush stammered. 'A very similar thing happened in Kubha's father's family.'

Parush narrated in short how a Hindu fanatic group called the Hiranyagarbha Bharat had tried to eliminate all the members of Kratu's family for decades. Kratu's grandmother, the enigmatic and extraordinary Kubha, he had named his daughter after, had a basketful of stories she had inherited from her forefathers. Her folks in her ancestral home in some remote valleys of the Hindukush mountains had preserved the family lore for thousands of years. The apparently fairy tale-like stories were found to be real anecdotes and authentic historical records, which contradicted the partisan view the radicals espoused about Indian history.

'Professor Somak Ajai believed,' said Parush, 'the carpets too had a trove of incredible history hidden in their symbols and motifs.'

'Porus, I haven't heard of the Hiranyagarbha Bharat, but many people from my party do have a radical Hindu nationalistic view of everything. It often borders fanaticism. Many of our actions and gestures do expose our tacit support to many such people and you know very well we're always criticized for that. From my interaction with them, I've realized they wouldn't stop at just eliminating the source of something they feel could go against their views. They would even go to the extent of manipulating things, misinterpreting facts and figures, forging documents and records just to establish their viewpoint. *My sixth sense says a fraud carpet will emerge soon.*'

☼

The Conqueror of the World, the sublime Gotama Buddha,
The Supreme Lord of the Grand Vehicle of the Animals—
The Naga peoples have carried the doctrines of the Conqueror
To every corner of all the nine regions of Jambudipa.

Seated in her father's chair in his home office, a corner room in the ground floor of the palatial Fareedi mansion in Khushawar, Afsar was staring at the four lines she had just translated from the Pali text of the manuscript. Kubha had, in fact, mailed her the digitally enhanced images of all the pages of the palm-leaf Kandy Manuscript the slain professor would refer to as the Rosetta Stone.

Understandably, it wouldn't have been possible for Afsar to read the 300-year-old Sinhala script of the manuscript with ease, had it not been for the transliteration application Kratu had created some time back. Afsar had fed the images of the manuscript to the programme and instructed it to transliterate the Pali text in Devanagari and Roman scripts. She was sure it would identify the old Sinhala script correctly. Expectedly, she got the Pali text, written in the two scripts known to her. Knowing that the manuscript was a very elaborate commentary of the Sri Lankan epic poem *Mahavamsa*, it was not that daunting a task to make sense out of the text.

Most of the illustrations that resembled their rugs were in the 12th chapter, The Converting of Different Countries, which enlists the names of the various foreign countries such as Bali, Java, Cambodia, Thailand, China and Vietnam and local kingdoms in the Indian subcontinent where Buddhism spread. What had attracted her attention was a long verse in the same chapter that talked about the Nagas, their countries, their mountains and their goddesses. The Khushawar Manuscript too, she recalled, had a verse about the Nagas, a part of which was yet to be deciphered.

Not very comfortable dealing directly with Pali, Afsar translated the verse, line by line, in English. She floundered with the expression "magebha maha potaka". The word "potaka" or "pota", akin to the English boat, she felt, would rather mean a vehicle. In the context of Buddhism, where Maha Yana or the Great Vehicle referred to a particular system of Buddhist teaching, she was convinced "maha potaka" too should have a similar connotation. "Magebha", she argued to herself, would be the simplified form of the Sanskrit "mrigebha", which in the current context would mean animals. The Supreme Lord of the Grand Vehicle of the Animals, she wrote on her notebook.

Rocking gently in her father's chair, Afsar repeated the expressions, "The Supreme Lord of the Animals" and "The

Grand Vehicle of the Animals", a few times in her mind. She didn't notice when Bahnaz, one of her twin sisters, had appeared behind her. More than 10 years younger than her, Bahnaz and Bahrukh shared a very special relationship with her and Kubha, often acting as go-betweens, bridging the two generations of the Fareedis.

'Naz,' Afsar pulled Bahnaz, when she saw her, 'don't we have a rug with a man sitting in a yogic posture, surrounded by animals and birds?'

'Ya, we do have. It's not a popular one though. We would have sold only a few pieces in the last 10 years.'

'Can you show me the design?'

Bahnaz got her iPad and passed it on to Afsar.

'Is this the one you're looking for?'

Afsar looked intently at the image on the screen, a smile lingering on her lips. Though the person in the rug was nowhere

'Is this the one you're looking for?'

close to how the Buddha had been usually depicted since the beginning, the epithet "The Supreme Lord of the Animals", she felt, did match with the iconography of the rug.

'Can you please call Kratu?' Afsar requested Bahnaz.

When Kratu came a few minutes later, she asked him straightaway, without providing any background, 'Can you do a picture search on the central figure of this man sitting on a yogic posture?'

She passed the iPad to him. 'The animal and bird motifs are all Central Asian in origin and I would expect the same for the human figure too.'

Kratu transferred the image of the rug to his phone. He cropped out the human figure and fed it to the picture search app Parush had developed. He was going to ask something, but he stopped abruptly, his eyes stuck on his phone, his frowning eyebrows well indicative of his amazement, or rather bewilderment.

'What?' asked Afsar, running towards him. She snatched the phone from his hand. She too gaped at what she saw on the screen.

She too gaped at what she saw on the screen.

'This is just unbelievable!' she exclaimed. 'Our rug is just a facsimile of the four-millennia-old Pashupati seal of the Indus Valley Civilization?'

Pashupati, Afsar knew anyone would realize, also meant The Lord of the Animals.

☼

In the initial excitement, Afsar had totally ignored, perhaps, the most striking feature of the Indus seal. When Kratu pointed that out to her, she was rendered speechless.

Kratu showed her the single-line text at the top of the Indus seal, as well as that at the top of the rug, displaying both the texts side by side on his mobile screen.

'Do you realize what you're seeing?' he asked her. 'Barring that fish sign in the Indus seal, the rest all are essentially the same symbols in both the places. The only difference is in the order of the symbols. The first letter in the rug, seen from the left, looks like an alpha sign. A similar sign is the last one in the Indus seal, the rightmost one. Similarly, the U-shaped symbol is the last one in the rug, but the first one in the seal … '

'Do you realize what you're seeing?' he asked her.

'The Indus script is read right to left,' Afsar interrupted, looking up at Kratu, 'but the Brahmi the other way. That explains the opposite orders in the rug and the seal.'

She paused for a while, as though trying to recollect something, and then continued excitedly, 'This means the unknown symbols in our rugs, the ones that are not Brahmi or its later variants, may be all Indus letters. God! I should have cracked this. I was aware there is evidence that some, if not all, Brahmi letters evolved from the Indus symbols, which were in use in the northwestern parts of India in some form or other, for a very long time.'

'But why would someone do a mix-n-match of the two?'

Afsar stared at Kratu and smiled. 'Do you remember how Kubha would write Bengali at the beginning? Wouldn't she mix some of the Hindi and Bengali letters which looked similar?'

'Yes, that's true. But later, when she learned Bengali properly, she never did that.'

'So you understand how old our rugs are? They date back to an era when Brahmi was perhaps not yet fully developed, when it still used some of the original Indus letters. The scripts evolved, but the rugs preserved the old scripts for millennia.'

'Isn't it too far stretched to believe that your carpets have preserved the Indus symbols in their original forms for so long?'

'In the past few days, I've done quite a bit of research on carpets. I figured out many motifs, still in use in the traditional carpets of Central Asia, are older than four millennia and they have changed very little during this long period. *Our carpets seem to have preserved much more.*'

Tic-Tac-Toe

(22–23 November 2018. Delhi and Khushawar)

The District & Sessions Court Agra has admitted a plea filed by Shankar Dubey stating that the Taj Mahal is a Lord Shiva temple (Tejo Mahạlaya) and Hindu devotees should be allowed to offer prayers there …

In the plea, Dubey has sought direction from the court to remove all alleged burials in the Taj Mahal as well restrain Muslims from offering prayers there. Interestingly, he has named Lord Agreshwar Mahadev Nagnatheswar Virajman as main plaintiff to claim the ownership of the property. Dubey has claimed to be the plaintiff's next friend.

Shamsur Ali stared at the newspaper in the morning and smiled. That was what he liked about India. The politicians here, and not the common men, he had always felt, were the most gullible. The common men on the road could be helpless and despondent, they could be cheated for the slightest things, but they could rarely be deceived into doing something that would devastate their own folks, their own villages, their own country. It was not that they were all very patriotic, or rather nationalistic, but what would amaze Shamsur was that they all had a conscience, a feeling of right and wrong, which prevented them from turning en masse into terrorists. The Muslims round the world were being deceived into joining the jihad for the establishment of the Islamic State, but here in India, Shamsur knew, they wouldn't be dragged into it so easily. There was something in the genes of the Indians, he would often ponder, which made even an illiterate poor man more aware and enlightened compared to one in many other countries.

He called Rahul Gupta, the general secretary of the Indian Party who had lately become a stooge of the Islamists, or possibly even a closet Muslim.

'Congratulations,' he lauded Rahul, 'your work is done.'

Rahul was indeed in a great mood. 'Don't miss the press release I give in sometime.'

The media, another of Shamsur's loyal stooges, had been anyway barking aloud since the previous afternoon, when the breaking news of the plea had been flashed for the first time. The tag line, chosen by Shamsur himself and passed on to the media by none other than Rahul, read "*Is Taj the new Babri*?"

Expectedly, a few hours later, Rahul was facing a battalion of reporters. He was confident. A benign smile lingered on his face.

'What happened yesterday,' Rahul said unexcitedly, 'is far and away the biggest bloat on the face of India. I'm speechless. I don't have words to express my feelings. Like you, my brothers and sisters, my countrymen, I too am reeling under the shock. Such intolerance is all your prime minister has delivered to you. Yes, these are indeed great times, as he had promised to you all …'

Not far from Rahul's press conference, Parush leaned back on the sofa in his living room. He called up Maitreyi. Since they had returned from Sri Lanka a few days ago, he hadn't talked to her.

'Are you sure,' Parush asked her, 'your grandfather indeed wanted to say "Taj" with the watches?'

'It's very unlikely to be something else,' Maitreyi said firmly. 'The clock angles of the two watches depicted the letters "ta" and "ja", which can be only Taj.'

"Taj" was one of the last few things Somak could think of before his death.

'The carpets had something to do with the Taj,' Parush said to himself, 'something that led to the three murders, something that was certainly connected to the press conference the whole nation was presently glued to.'

☼

The same afternoon, Shamsur was making a presentation to a motley group of people. They had all assembled covertly in the attic of a silverware shop at the crowded Paranthe Wali Gali, the bustling food street in the Chandni Chowk area of Old Delhi. Among them was Vishnu Godse, who had met Shamsur only once before, at the same place.

There was something about Shamsur, Vishnu felt. Despite developing a deep hatred for him after their first meeting, Vishnu couldn't resist coming to meet him, again today, overcoming the irritation of the odour of the burnt parathas and tangy spices hanging in the air of the filthy neighbourhood. Presently he, along with the others he hadn't ever met, were huddled in the small room, watching a PowerPoint presentation on Shamsur's laptop and listening to something as unthinkable as what he had heard the last time he had been here.

'Most of the Mughal architecture is non-Islamic,' Shamsur was talking calmly, perhaps trying to gauge everyone's reactions. A very interesting thing about the Mughal architecture, he highlighted, is the *hasht bihist*, the eight heavens. In many structures, he elaborated, a central big room or dome is surrounded by eight other in eight directions—the four cardinal ones, east, west, north and south; and the four intermediate ones in the four corners.

'The eight directions and the eight gods guarding them is a purely Hindu concept,' Shamsur stressed. 'It has nothing to do with Islam. Its origin is non-Islamic. Its wide usage over the past thousands of years is non-Islamic. The next few slides will clarify what I'm trying to say.'

He clicked on the keyboard and allowed his select audience some time to grasp what they were seeing on the screen of the laptop.

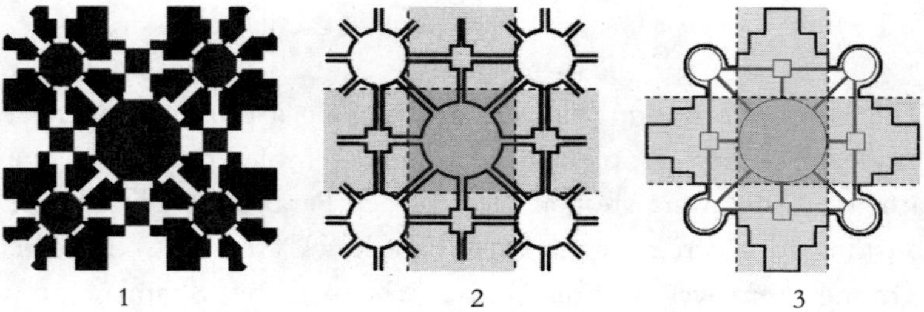

'The next few slides will clarify what I'm trying to say.'

'The first one,' Shamsur said, pointing to the diagram to the left, marked "1", 'is the ground plan of the Taj Mahal. The huge octagonal cenotaph hall, the hujra, is in the centre. The gumbad-i azam, the great dome you identify the Taj with, is atop the hujra. Four square rooms lead into the hujra from the four directions. Each of these square rooms opens outward into a huge, rectangular vaulted gateway, the pish-taq. The hujra is also connected to four octagonal dalans in the four corners.'

The second diagram, Shamsur explained, is a simplified ground plan of the Taj. It clearly depicts the hujra is at the centre of the nine sections a paper could be divided into, by the four lines of a tic-tac-toe game. The other eight sections encompass the four square rooms and the four octagonal dalans, which encircle the central hujra, like a continuous ambulatory.

'This very system of dividing the ground plan into nine regions can be seen in many ancient Hindu temples,' Shamsur pointed to the diagram marked "3". 'See for yourself how well the ground plan of the Taj superimposes with that of the temple complex on the Hemakuta Hills in the World Heritage Site of Hampi.'

Shamsur moved on to the next slide. The same ground plan, he continued, was the fundamental concept behind the "cross in a square" plan of the Byzantine architecture, seen in so many churches. The plan originated 4,000 years ago in the form of primitive Hindu temples, remnants of which were discovered sometime back at Dashly in Northern Afghanistan.

'The first one is the plan of the temples discovered at Dashly,' Shamsur said, pointing to the four diagrams on the screen, 'and the last one is a Byzantine church.'

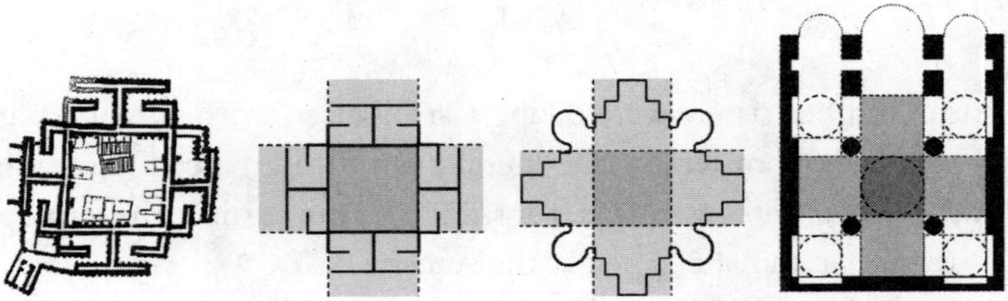

1 2 3 4

'The first one is the plan of the temples discovered at Dashly …'

He smiled at Vishnu. 'How do you feel,' he asked, 'when you realize the designs of your ancient temples have been copied by the Christians and then by the Mughals, but no one gave you the credit?'

It was understandable Vishnu wouldn't have words to express his feelings. Despite his disgust for this hardline Muslim fanatic, he was rather getting attracted to his personality. Not a towering figure that would loom large on others, Shamsur had something which couldn't be ignored either. And more than everything, he sounded very much like his father.

'*No one gave you the credit.*' Shamsur's words echoed in Vishnu's mind.

'Anything that's non-Islamic is not worth preserving,' Shamsur thundered, leaning back against the backrest of the unstable wooden chair, shutting the lid of the laptop. 'The Islamic State can do well without any of the Mughal architecture. And … ' he looked at Vishnu again, 'those are non-Hindu too. Many of them were built on the carcasses of thriving Hindu temples … ' He paused, his intense stare piercing through Vishnu. 'But none of the previous governments had the guts to accept that. They all needed the Muslim votes. But not any more. I believe if you want to do anything, you've to act now. *Your prime minister now is your biggest strength and ours too.*'

☼

Afsar and her sisters were taking a stroll after lunch, when Afsar got the call from Kratu. She literally ran to the Fareedi mansion and dashed into her father's study. Kratu turned the laptop towards her and she gaped at the screen.

Afsar could identify the picture of the pile of rugs. Kubha had taken the snap at Somak's place when she had been there with her grandfather, just a week before his death. Beside the picture, Kratu had put up a chart.

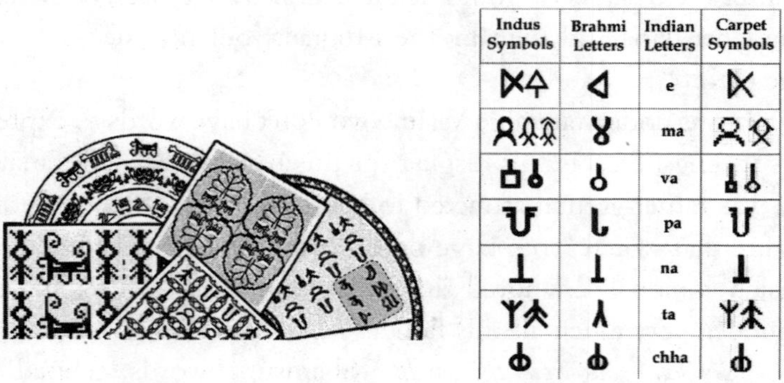

Kratu turned the laptop towards her and she gaped at the screen.

'You took so long to do this!' Afsar teased Kratu, knowing very well it couldn't have been trivial to identify all the Indus symbols from their rugs. Bahnaz maintained a fairly exhaustive digital repository of the motifs and designs of almost all the rugs they had sold in the past many years, and presently, it had really come in handy.

Afsar smiled, looking at the chart Kratu had put in place. 'I was expecting the Indus signs in our rugs would be related to Brahmi letters. In fact, your chart makes it quite clear that some, if not all, of the Brahmi letters actually evolved from the much older Indus signs.'

'But the Indus script is yet to be deciphered, isn't it?' Kratu asked.

'Yes, that's true!' Afsar agreed. 'Some Indus symbols were, indeed, adapted in the Brahmi lettering system, but it's not necessary that the symbols carried the same value in both the places. It's something like the symbol "8", which as a numeral is present both in English and Bengali, but in English its value is eight and in Bengali four. But …' she paused, and looked at the chart very closely. 'There's a very striking thing though … '

The Indus crab sign in the second line of the chart, Afsar pointed out, had a very similar counterpart in Brahmi, where it had the value "ma". Alexander Cunningham, the first director general of the ASI and an authority on Brahmi script and Ashoka's inscription, believed each Brahmi letter, like the Egyptian heliographic, was essentially a pictorial depiction of a word related to the letter.

'For example,' she explained, 'the letter "ma" may stand for "makar", the crab, or "matsya", the fish, both of which can be represented by similar looking symbols. Accordingly "ma" in Brahmi is basically an inverted crab sign. Ditto in the Indus script, where "ma" perhaps implies the Dravidian word "meen", meaning fish, again. There's a school of thought that believes proto Dravidian was one of the languages of the Indus Valley Civilization.'

☼

Vishnu was going through the material Shamsur had mailed him. He had returned to JNU early in the morning after the night-long huddle with Shamsur and had slept off immediately. When he had woken up, it was afternoon. He took bath, had lunch and returned to his room. After lying down on his bed for some time, he opened his laptop and checked the mail Shamsur had said he would send.

Had the Taj really been a Shiva temple a thousand years ago? Vishnu couldn't but ponder over the thought as he went through Shamsur's mail.

> *The term "Taj Mahal" itself never occurs in any Mughal court paper or chronicle, even in Aurangzeb's time. The logic that the Taj stands for Mumtaz, Shah Jahan's wife, sounds ridiculous. Would Shah Jahan distort the name of his beloved wife for whom he made such a magnificent mausoleum? In reality, the Taj Mahal is the Tejo Mahalaya, one of the five temples of Teja Linga, the name by which the Jats of Agra have worshipped Shiva since the eleventh century. Four of those five temples exist till this day. For the past few centuries, the Jats have lost track of the fifth one.*
>
> *In 1652, Aurangzeb wrote a letter to his father Shah Jahan stating that many structures at the fancied burial place of Mumtaz were so old that they were leaking and that the dome had developed cracks. If Shah Jahan had indeed constructed the Taj, how could Aurangzeb call it old? In reality, Shah Jahan never constructed the Taj. He just vandalized and remodeled an existing marble palace and a Shiva Temple. The ground plan of the Taj resembles a temple.*

Vishnu was perhaps absent-minded, as he suddenly discovered he had drawn four lines on a blank paper, as though for a tic-tac-toe game. He couldn't recall though when he had drawn the lines …

The Nine Regions of Jambudvipa

(25 November–5 December 2018. Khushawar)

When it was getting dark, Kratu got up from the chair he had been sitting on since the afternoon. He wrapped a shawl and came out of the house. Afsar and her sisters were sitting on the sprawling and well-attended lawn, which spread like a thick green carpet around the Fareedi haveli.

Bahnaz waved at him. 'Sweetie, you're totally ignoring us this time,' she teased. 'You're getting old!'

Kratu sat with the sisters and took a long breath. 'Now-a-days you don't have time for me, sweetheart,' he said, stretching his hands. 'There was a time when two young girls wouldn't even wake up unless I wished them good morning. And now … ' he paused, as though to recall something, and then spoke again, 'after 20 years, I go to their room, to wake them up even before the sun and the birds can do so, I push them, sing a song I suddenly remember I would wake them up with, but neither of them wakes up.'

'Oh, sweetie,' Bahnaz came and hugged him from behind, 'our bad. Not you darling, I think we've become old. When we were rabbits, we would get tickled even with a feather. Now we're elephants. Even a javelin can't poke us.'

Afsar looked at Kratu lovingly. 'You remember all these little things!'

Kratu smiled back and held her hands. 'I woke up early today and while passing by their room, I remembered something. *When someone leaves you, he brings back a lot of things and leaves them behind, on his way as parting gifts.* Today, after a long time, I remembered a lot of things about Kubha, about Bahnaz and Bahrukh, your grandmother—the tough lady who would scrutinize my every move and gesture every time I went to meet you. Your father has suddenly taken us back by many years.' He stopped abruptly, as though he had suddenly remembered something new.

'Sorry ladies,' he got up, 'we should get back to work. Afsar, there are a lot of things for you.'

As he hurried towards the haveli, Afsar looked at her sisters. Both of them hugged her.

'He is right,' Bahnaz said firmly. 'You have a lot to do. We all have to know who all are behind everything. *Aba didn't deserve to die like this.*'

When Afsar entered her father's office, she figured Kratu had already set up the projector he had managed to get from someone in the evening.

'Afsar, I've found something really interesting.'

As he spoke, he projected on the wall a section of the rug with a lot of symbols. It was the same one, a part of which was visible in the picture Kubha had taken at Somak's place.

'In this entire section,' he pointed out, 'apart from the highlighted part, which I believe comprises all Brahmi letters from the Gupta period, the rest is essentially filled with a four-sign combination of purely Indus symbols. Of course, each of them has a Brahmi equivalent.'

A closer look at the Indus letters, he explained, shows that they comprise two words, "vata" and "mapa". Pulling out the chart he had created for the Indus symbols used in the Khushawari rugs, he corroborated his point.

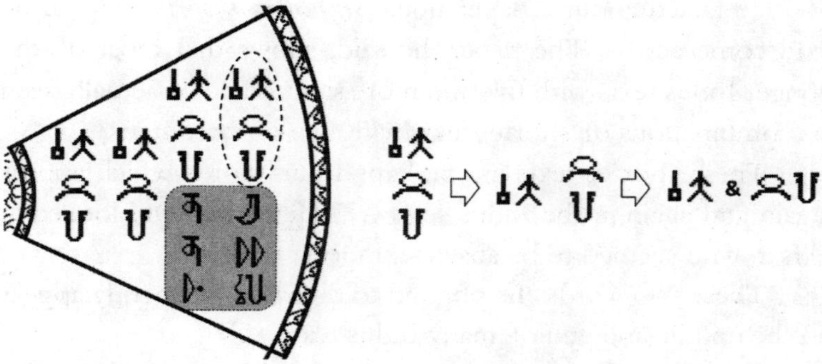

'... the rest is essentially filled with a four-sign combination of purely Indus symbols.'

'The crab symbol in the Indus seals is essentially the Brahmi "ma",' he said, 'and the decorated "U" sign is very close to the Brahmi "pa". So, you get the second word as "mapa". As the Indus symbols are always written left-to-right in the rugs, like Brahmi, whereas in the Indus seals they are right-to-left, the two words from the rug would look different on the seals.'

He projected the words in both the orientations.

He projected the words in both the orientations.

'Wait a minute!' Afsar gestured at Kratu to pause, as she looked at the symbols projected on the wall. 'The Indus script is yet to be deciphered, isn't it? How do you know these are valid words in the Indus language?'

'I was getting at that,' Kratu smiled. 'Yes, you're correct! There's no way to say if these are valid words in the Indus language.'

He talked about a paper titled *Segmentation of Indus Texts* he had come across. The paper, he said, shows that most of the longer Indus texts with five and more signs could be actually seen as combinations of shorter texts with two or three signs.

'These shorter texts are perhaps Indus words which appear again and again in the Indus seals … ' He paused and looked at Afsar, who seemed to be absent-minded.

'These two words,' he pointed to the wall, 'frequently appear in the middle and end of many Indus texts …'

'Show me the Pashupati seal,' Afsar interrupted. 'Display that along with the rug with a person seated in the centre in a yogic posture, surrounded by animals. I want to see the texts you showed me earlier on your mobile.'

Kratu was prompt enough to display both the images side by side. He cropped the text from both and projected them on the wall.

He cropped the text from both and projected them on the wall.

'What would they mean?' Afsar asked, looking at the texts. 'The crab sign is "ma". The "U" sign is "pa". What's the second sign that looks like a triangle with two extended arms?'

Kratu referred to the chart and said, 'The second sign is "e".'

'It's "ma-e-pa-ma-pa",' she mumbled and ran out of the room.

☼

Afsar returned with her notebook and sat on the chair she had pushed off just a while ago. She leaned back and took a long breath. She got up abruptly and hugged a perplexed Kratu from behind.

'Would you mind saying something?' Kratu asked, dragging her from the back. She sat on the table in front of Kratu and read out from a page from her notebook:

> *The Conqueror of the World, the sublime Gotama Buddha,*
> *The Supreme Lord of the Grand Vehicle of the Animals—*
> *The Naga peoples have carried the doctrines of the Conqueror*
> *To every corner of all the nine regions of Jambudipa.*

'That's a verse from the manuscript Kubha saw at Kandy, isn't it?' Kratu asked.

'Yes, you're right, it's from the Kandy Manuscript. I have translated the phrase "mrigebha maha potaka" as the Grand Vehicle of the Animals. I just figured out "mri-ge-bha" would be "ma-e-pa" in our code language with 14 letters.'

'And "ma-pa" is "maha potaka"?' Kratu seemed to have snatched the words from Afsar's mouth as he stared at the two texts projected on the wall.

'It can be "ma-pa-e" too, from "maha potake". Ending words with the "e" of the locative case is rampant in Magadhi Prakrit. Reducing the Sanskrit "maha" to "ma" is not uncommon in Persian or Pashto. China is called Macheen, akin to Sanskrit Maha Cheen.'

She turned the pages of her notebook. 'If you remember,' she spoke again, looking at another page of the notebook, 'I was stuck with a line from the Khushawar Manuscript: "From the centre of Ma-e-pa mapa-e, Chachajala-e is at 11¼". Now I know what "ma-e-pa mapa-e" means. *Mrigebha maha potake.*'

Afsar had always found Kratu's certain gestures and behaviour very adorable. Presently, when the various muscles of his face contracted randomly, and his eyebrows danced subtly, she couldn't but laugh. 'At times I feel we are still in the '90s and I've just met you. You have changed so little in all these years. Your expressions are still the same.'

Kratu was perhaps not in a mood for nostalgic ruminations. 'What do you think is actually meant by "mrigebha maha potake", the Grand Vehicle of the Animals?'

'Given that Maha Yana or the Great Vehicle refers to a branch of Buddhism, The Great Vehicle of the Animals could mean the religion of the animals, or perhaps metaphorically, the religion of all the living beings.'

'Can't it also mean the country where this great religion thrives?' Kratu said abruptly.

'Why do you say so?' Afsar didn't seem to be convinced.

'Chachajala or Chhach-Hazara is said to be at 11¼ from the centre of the Great Vehicle of the Animals. Then, the Buddha is referred to as the Supreme Lord of the Grand Vehicle of the Animals. The very next line in the Kandy Manuscript says the Naga peoples have carried the Buddha's teachings to the nine regions of Jambudipa. The Great Vehicle of the Animals must be a country, and more specifically, the Indian subcontinent, the land where Buddhism was born and has thrived for a very long time.'

'*Kratu, I think you're not wrong*,' Afsar concurred. 'A Grand Vehicle can be the metaphor for the land that has sheltered Buddhism and its peoples for thousands of years, like how a mega boat, *maha pota*, shelters people in the ocean, saves them, protects them from the storms. The legend of Noah's Arc in the Genesis chapters of the Bible has a similar connotation. God saves Noah's family and the rest of the animals of the world from the Great Flood in a boat.'

In Indian scriptures, Afsar explained, Jambudvipa or the island abounding with jambu trees is the name given to the central one of the seven continents comprising the earth. It is often identified with the Indian subcontinent.

'Referring to a continent as a big boat is indeed metaphorical,' she said. 'A continent is like an island floating in the middle of an ocean. So is a boat.'

☼

One afternoon, a few days later, Kratu pulled out an image from his laptop and projected it on the wall.

'Let me show you this … I've tried to complete the partially blackened illustration from the Kandy Manuscript. I cropped the visible part of the rug out of the picture Kubha had taken at Somak's place. I superimposed it on the blackened illustration,' said Kratu.

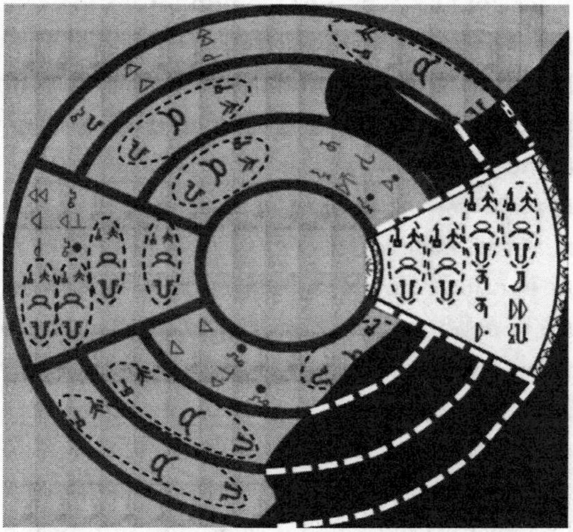

'I've tried to complete the partially blackened illustration … '

Afsar went close to the wall and studied the image for some time. She threw a thankful glance at Kratu, her husband of so many years, who had always helped in her research in many an unassuming way. Being technologically naive, or rather challenged, she couldn't have achieved much in linguistic palaeontology without the support from her geeky husband and Parush. Her multi-disciplinary domain of interest often needed the aid of sophisticated machine learning and a humungous amount of data processing to solve seemingly simple problems.

Had it not been for Kratu's involvement, it wouldn't have been easy to figure out that the purely Indus signs, highlighted with dotted lines, appeared only in the words "vata mapa". The rest of the symbols were predominantly Brahmi letters from the times of Ashoka and the Guptas.

'A circle is divided into nine sections,' she observed. 'The words "vata mapa" are repeated in each section.'

'"Mapa",' she mumbled to herself, 'is Maha Pota, the Great Vehicle. What could "vata" be? Couldn't it be the reduced form of "vrita", which meant concealed or surrounded by?'

'Oh my God!' Kratu exclaimed. 'This is just unbelievable.' He was staring at Afsar's notebook, an open page of which had the verse from the Kandy Manuscript she had been working on.

'What?'

'"The Nagas have carried Buddha's teachings to the nine regions of Jambudipa".' Kratu repeated a line from the verse from Afsar's notebook. 'The nine sections of the rug are the nine regions of the Jambudipa.'

Afsar's eyes sparkled.

'"From the centre of Ma-e-pa mapa-e, Chachajala-e is at 11¼",' Kratu recalled the line from the Khushawar Manuscript Afsar had been stuck with. 'There's no doubt it means Chhacha-Hazara is at 11¼ from the centre of Mrighebha Maha Potake, the Great Vehicle of the Animals, which is nothing but the Indian subcontinent. Isn't it similar to an Aryabhata verse? If I remember it correctly, Aryabhata specifies the location of a place in terms of its latitude from the equator, which he refers to as Lanka.'

'*Ujjayini Lankayah tad chatur-amshe samottarata.* From Lanka, the centre of the world, Ujjayini is at 22½ to its north,' Afsar paused and looked at Kratu.

'Similarly,' Kratu stressed, 'each of the nine sections of the circle is very likely to contain some numbers, which could refer to the location of each of the nine regions of Jambudipa with respect to a place called Vata Mapa. What else do you think could be the reason behind the words "vata mapa" appearing in each section?'

'Wait a minute!' Afsar took the laptop.

A few minutes later she looked at Kratu.

'You do have a point,' she said, relaxing on the chair, stretching her arms. '"Vata Mapa" can't be anything but "Vrita Maha Pota", which literally means the Great Vehicle which is concealed or central, surrounded by others. In the context of the nine regions of Jambudvipa, it may also mean the central region, or the centre of the Indian subcontinent.'

'Is there any significance of the nine regions?'

'Yes, that's what I've checked just now. As per Indian scriptures, the earth is divided into nine regions, called varshas, one of which is Bharata. I think this concept of nine regions of the earth has been superimposed here on Jambudvipa. Such overlap and ambiguities are not uncommon in the ancient Indian books. The interesting thing is that the central region is called Ila-vrita Varsha, which seems to have been referred to here as the Vrita Maha Pota.'

Afsar pulled her notebook. 'I think the Khushawar Manuscript mentions about the nine varshas somewhere ... ' She turned the pages of the notebook fast. 'Yes,' she smiled soon, 'this is what I was looking for.' She read out the English translation of a verse she had noted from the manuscript:

This Takkariya manuscript has been written by the Naga Kings,
They have created the nine Varshas of the Naga Island.

'What are the names of all the nine varshas?' Kratu asked.

'The central one is Ilavrita. Ketumala is to the west and Bhadrashva to the east.' Afsar took the laptop and searched for the remaining names. 'Kuru and Bharata are to the north and south.' Suddenly, she pushed the laptop aside and grabbed her notebook back.

'What happened?' asked Kratu as Afsar frantically turned the pages of the notebook.

'Ketumala and Bhadrashva …' she mumbled, not taking her eyes off the notebook. Kratu stared at her, perplexed. 'Yes,' suddenly she blurted out so loudly that Bahnaz was stupefied; she stopped by the door, holding a plate full of kebabs on her hands. 'Oh, don't scare me!' she fretted.

Afsar read out the two lines from her notebook:

> *The nave of Ketumala is the City of the Severed Heads of the Conqueror.*
> *The nave of Bhaddassa is the City of Bali, the king of wondrous power.*

'The nave of Ketumala,' she repeated, 'is the City of the Severed Heads of the Conqueror. That's how I had translated the Pali text of the Kandy Manuscript.'

'The City of the Severed Heads?'

'That must be Taxila or rather Taksha Shila. I've a gut feeling, the verse from the Khushawar Manuscript too talks about the same place.'

'Which verse?'

'From the centre of Ma-e-pa mapa-e, Chachajala-e is at 11¼.'

'Chhach-Hazara?'

'Chhach-Hazara and Taxila are quite close by. The *nave* or the centre of Ketumala, the western province, can very well be Taxila.'

'In that case,' Kratu hastily pointed out, 'we can expect to see the mixed fraction 11¼ in the blackened illustration too.'

He immediately took the laptop and projected a part of the image he had reconstructed from the tampered illustration of the Kandy Manuscript. He added a small note to the right of the image.

Kratu explained, 'This section is to the left. It should correspond to Ketumala, the western region. The words "vata mapa", written in pure Indus signs, appear four times. The Brahmi letters are arranged very much like how mixed fractions are depicted in the Bakhshali Manuscript: the integer, the numerator and the denominator, all written one below the other. The problem is that, we should have had numerals, not Brahmi letters.'

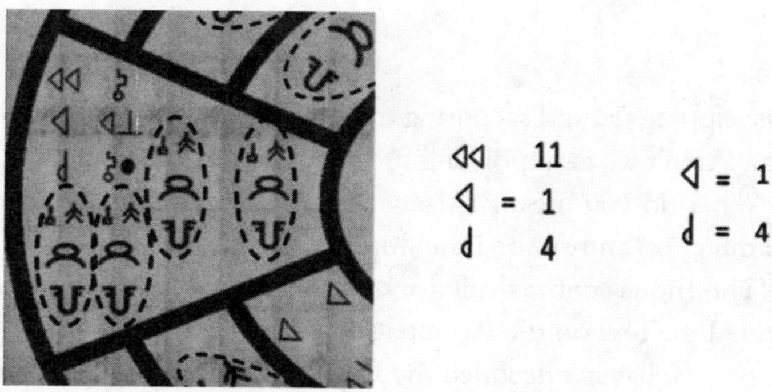

'This section is to the left. It should correspond to Ketumala … '

Kratu opened the chart of Indus symbols used in the rugs. 'The triangle sign,' he said, consulting the chart, 'is the Brahmi "e". It's perhaps used to depict the numeral "1". The numeral "4" is depicted by the "d" symbol, which is the Brahmi "cha". We have to figure out why and how Brahmi letters have been used instead of numerals.'

'We've to also figure out the identity of the centre of the Ma-e-pa mapa-e, from where Taxila or Chhach-Hazara is at 11¼.

If Ujjayini is at 22½ from Lanka, Taxila, which is further north, can't be at 11¼.'

'The centre of the Great Vehicle of the Animals and Lanka may not be the same place. In fact, if our assumption that the Great Vehicle of the Animals is nothing but the Indian subcontinent, then its centre is most likely not Lanka. We've to figure that out …'

Bahnaz had already kept the plate of kebabs on the desk and had started eating one. 'You have to figure out a lot of things in your lives,' she interrupted, tapping on the desk. 'For now, can we all take a snacks break? *Jhindri bhaag nahi rahi.* Nothing is running away guys, except for the aroma of the kebabs.'

☼

While sipping tea and savouring the delicious kebabs, Kratu asked Afsar, 'Aren't we extrapolating too much in our excitement?'

'What do you mean?' Afsar took a bite of a succulent piece of lamb chop and rubbed the dripping oil from her chin.

'The Indus script is still not deciphered and we seem to have decoded the text on the Pashupati seal!'

'No, we haven't decoded the Indus seal,' Afsar argued. 'We've just decoded a text from our rug with similar symbols. Though the meaning of our text matches very well with the context of the Indus seal too, we still can't claim the symbols there had the same meaning.'

It was possible, she argued, the creators of the rugs might have been using the Indus symbols for long without knowing the true meaning, and later someone might have come up with an interpretation. The fact that the Indus signs did match with the Brahmi letters made the task even easier.

Afsar continued, 'It's like superimposing the Buddhist interpretation of Taksha Shira, the City of Severed Heads, on the existing name Taksha Shila, which means the City of the Takshas.'

Kratu wasn't convinced. 'I can understand someone dividing a circle into nine regions. But is it reasonable to assume in ancient times, people knew that north should be upward in a map, south downward and so on?'

'I understand your apprehension,' Afsar smiled. 'The Sanskrit term "uttara" for north comes from the root "ud", which means upward. It is so because the entire northern boundary of the Indian subcontinent is raised upward, guarded by the mighty Himalayas.'

'What do you think is the significance of depicting the nine regions of Jambudvipa in the rugs?' Kratu asked sometime later. 'I mean, there must be some reason or intention behind that, isn't it? And what's so explosive hidden behind all these, that it could lead to such a bloody trail?'

Afsar stopped munching. She drank some water and stared at Kratu. Bahnaz and Bahrukh too looked at Kratu. 'I don't think we know that yet,' she said. '*We'll find it out ...*'

The Confluence

(9 December 2018. The Karakoram Highway, Pakistan)

Holding the cricket series had been Indar's idea. One night he had called Parush and mentioned it.

'You want to call it the Subcontinent Series?' Parush had asked.

'Whether you say Bachchan or Amitabh Bachchan, it's all the same, isn't it?' Indar had quipped.

Parush had smiled. He had already become a great admirer of the subtleties in Indar's actions. It was quite apparent Indar was very implicitly, and perhaps slickly, pushing forward his agenda of establishing India's hegemony in the subcontinent. Parush knew Indar always thought of Pakistan and Bangladesh as extensions of the Indian markets.

'I don't care if we hate each other,' Indar would often say. 'As long as they add to our coffers, I'm fine. Remember, Ashoka had one of the largest empires of the world more than 2,000 years ago. He didn't politically control every country between Central Asia and China. He controlled the trade. No doubt, Ashoka got his trainings in Arthashastra from none other than Chanakya, the greatest prime minister India ever had.'

Presently, waiting at the Old Delhi Railway Station to board the Samjhauta Express with the rest of the Indian delegates going to Lahore to watch the final ODI between India and Pakistan, Parush checked the headlines of the major newspapers in the

West. "The Indian Subcontinent Cricket Series," read one of them, "is a masterstroke by Prime Minister Indar Sinha." Parush smiled. Indar had just called it the Subcontinent Series, but the Western media had already added the "India" to it, making it clear that the subcontinent and India were the same.

Parush saw Shamsur, walking into the platform with Rahul Gupta, the leader of the Opposition. Shamsur waved at him and he waved back.

The next morning, when the Pakistani counterpart of the train chugged into the Lahore Junction Railway Station, least did he expect Shamsur to go and greet Afsar and Kratu. The previous night they had arrived from Khushawar and since morning they had been waiting at the station, along with a big contingent from the Fareedis' present home in Lahore, to greet the Indian delegates.

'Dr Fareedi,' Shamsur gestured an adab and spoke in the Bangladeshi dialect so typical of Dhaka, '*aapni amare sinben na* … but I know you very well. I'm Professor Shamsur Ali. I heard about you a lot in Dhaka. Your work on linguistics is well known even in Bangladesh.'

Parush wondered how many people addressed Afsar as Dr Fareedi. He winked at her. She smiled and shook hands with Shamsur.

'Please accept my condolences on the loss of your father,' Shamsur continued, walking by her side, Parush and Rahul following them.

Half an hour later, after the completion of some customary exchanges of pleasantries between the officials of the two countries, Bahnaz pulled Parush by his hand. 'Why the hell are we waiting here?' she whispered. 'Chalo, let's go.'

The Fareedis had come to the station in a Mercedes van. Parush had already greeted a few of Afsar's cousins he knew. Walking towards the van, Afsar asked Parush, 'Who's this Shamsur?'

'It's a long story … ' Parush replied. 'I'll tell you. I'm surprised that he knows about you and your work.'

'How does he know about my father?'

'I'm not bothered how he knows. I'm bothered, why he knows.'

'What do you mean by that?'

Parush didn't reply.

Bahnaz started talking …

☼

Shamsur bid farewell to Rahul. 'I'll see you soon in Delhi,' he said, getting into the car he had been guided to by a highly decorated official of the Pakistan Army. 'Anyway, Bangladesh is not playing and I can't miss this fabulous opportunity. I've always wanted to see, with my own eyes, the amazing graffiti and art work of the ancient petroglyphs, pecked into the sun-varnished rocks by the unknown travellers, some thousands of years ago, all along the desolate turns and corners of the Silk Route.' His over dramatization attracted the attention of a few of the uniformed people, who couldn't but stare at him with suspicious looks.

Rolling down the window of the car, Shamsur threw the words, 'Karakoram Highway … '

No one else would have noticed, but it didn't elude the hawk-eyed Shamsur that there were frowns on Rahul's face. He himself had told Rahul all about the upcoming trip he had been so excited about. 'Travelling for miles alongside the Indus on the Karakoram Highway and seeing the Nanga Parbat from such a close distance,' he had said excitedly, 'is a once-in-a-lifetime experience. My friends in Pakistan have organized everything.'

As the convoy of cars carrying the green ensigns started moving slowly, Shamsur didn't remove his eyes from Rahul as long as he could see the Indian delegates, still waiting at the cordoned entrance of the station. Had Rahul suspected anything, he pondered, realizing how close he might be with the Pakistani military establishment?

Soon, Shamsur reached the non-flying Pakistan Air Force Base at Lahore. An Aérospatiale Alouette III helicopter was waiting for him. It took him directly to the Chaklala Air Force Base in Rawalpindi. It took less than an hour to cover the distance of 150 miles. As the fuel tank was being filled, Shamsur waited inside the chopper. When it was again ready for the final lap of the journey to Jaglot, some 250 miles away, he welcomed his four co-passengers aboard. 'It's my privilege to welcome you to this special chapter of Majlis-e Muqaddis-e Hind, the Council of the Purifiers of Hindustan,' he said to them. None of them, he knew, had ever met each other and they had been strictly instructed not to interact among themselves either. Neither did they know who Shamsur was.

The helicopter jerked into motion as the blades whirred noisily. When it had been airborne for some time, Shamsur looked below. 'My comrades,' he attracted the attention of his co-passengers, 'we're now flying over the Margalla Hills, just north of Islamabad. Do you know how the name "Margalla" came about?'

Shamsur, of course, didn't wait for any response from the four stern-faced, bright, young men, recently indoctrinated into the radical ideology of recreating an Islamic Caliphate, an Islamic State comprising most parts of the world. They had been chosen for their brilliant academic record and their ability to influence many other young minds. They were internet geeks and technology savvy. All four looked almost similar to Shamsur. With their well-built physique, sharp features, chiselled bodies and piercing looks, they gave enough confidence to Shamsur that it had, indeed, been a wise choice. Barely in their early twenties, these young men of Pakistani origin had been raised affluently in the West and recently brought into Pakistan.

"'Mar-galla" literally means to kill someone by his neck. It can also mean severing the head from the neck. It's a sad vestige of the Buddhist past of your country. The Buddhists, like the Hindus, were kafirs. They worshipped idols and believed in silly stories about their prophets and gods. Pakistan is spewed with innumerable Buddhist memorabilia which you never bothered to eliminate. Mar Galla is connected to a legend which says the Buddha had cut his neck and severed his head hazar bar, thousand times, in as many as thousand births and gifted it to his followers. In fact, this region was part of the old Hazara division. The name Hazara is also reminiscent to the same silly legend of the Buddha's hazar heads. Such legends are blasphemous. Worshipping the idols of Buddha was so rampant in Pakistan that soon his shortened name "but" happened to mean idol and "bhoot" came about derogatorily to mean a ghost. You have to cleanse your country. *You have to eliminate all traces of "bhoot".'*

☼

The chopper flew low over the richly wooded, lush and leafy terrain of Azad Kashmir. Shamsur and the four young boys gaped at the sceneries below with wide open eyes. Perhaps for the time being, all of them would have forgotten where they were heading to and what they had been chosen for. Perhaps the idea of jihad, the thought of the ensuing violence and blood bath, all for the noble and pak intent of creating an Islamic State, ad-Daulah al-Islamiyah, would have been lost temporarily in those sprawling green meadows punctuated carelessly by steep ridges and cascading waterfalls; the deep gorges thrown haphazardly into the landscape, as though to create those alluring curves and crevasses; and the enticing hillsides decorated with colourful hamlets.

The landscape changed abruptly. A wide valley suddenly dashed against a sheer wall, bigger than anything they could think of. They were awestruck by the suddenness of the blinding sight of the huge, naked vertical rock, too steep for snow to stick, blocking the horizon. Perhaps, they were suddenly shaken off so hard that they emerged out of their mesmerized state in no time.

'That's the Nanga Parbat, the symbol of nakedness, ruthlessness, firmness,' Shamsur uttered every word discretely with a sly smile on his face. 'It falls by 14,000 feet, flat, on your face. *You all have to be like the Nanga Parbat.* But remember, the name "Nanga Parbat" again is a sinful remnant of your blasphemous past. Can you believe such a magnificent and grand thing is named after Naga, the snake? The Hindus and the Buddhists are both fascinated by serpents and trees. *You've to cleanse your land of the serpents and demons and ghosts.*'

Soon after they had landed at a makeshift helipad at Jaglot, Shamsur and his chosen champions were led to an army vehicle. A short drive on the Karakoram Highway skirting the Indus river, and the vehicle came to a halt in front of a whitewashed monument on the right side of the road. They got down from the vehicle and followed the driver to the monument which had been cordoned off for them. Climbing a flight of stairs, Shamsur appeared on the flat terrace and walked towards the broken wall that ran along its edge. He looked ahead at the site of the confluence of two rivers, the Gilgit, flowing from the left, and the Indus, from the right. He took a long breath, inhaled a big dollop of air. He looked around. It was not for nothing that he had chosen this particular place to ignite the fire in the chosen four.

The black Karakoram Highway pierced through the brown and barren earth like a directionless arrow, as though chasing desperately an erratic target in a whimsical landscape. Shamsur leaned over the wall and looked at the two rivers merging and flowing as one, the one that wouldn't tell it was indeed the mighty Indus, the identity of many civilizations for millennia, *none of which had been essentially Islamic.*

Shamsur gestured the driver to leave them alone. He waited for some more time till he saw the driver getting into the car.

The air was chilly, even in the afternoon. Shamsur turned towards the four boys. 'In front of you is the confluence of two rivers, the Indus and the Gilgit,' he addressed the boys. 'This is also the place where the Himalayas, the Karakoram and the Hindukush meet. To your right, on the right side of the Indus is the Himalayas. The Karakoram is on the other side of the Indus and to your left is the Hindukush …

'Before Islam came to your country, it was the confluence of the three peoples—the Hindus, the Chinese and the Farsis. What is now the Karakoram Highway used to be the Silk Route in the ancient times. The three cultures would flow along the Silk Route and congregate at this very place you're standing at. Going ahead, there wouldn't be any trace of those three cultures …

'It would be only Islam that would flow out from here, in three different directions, to India, to China and to Iran. Though Iran is an Islamic State, it still carries the sins of its non-Islamic past. Do you know the word for religion in Farsi is "din", which is related to "dhenu", the holy cow of the Hindus? *Snakes and ghosts and cows, all should go.*'

☼

Shamsur was taking a stroll along the Indus in the evening. He had had a great experience with the four young men he had chosen for the orientation programme. He was sure these boys would do all the right things. He noticed the two men in arms keeping an eye on him from the army jeep, parked on the Karakoram Highway cutting through the crest of a ridge some hundred feet above the Indus. The wind was getting colder with every moment. The sun had already disappeared behind the Hindukush, to the left. The night was descending fast, perhaps like a bomb falling freely from a bomber plane—the moment it would hit the earth, it would shatter the ground. Shamsur had been to the highlands of PoK, Pakistan-occupied Kashmir, many times and he had always felt here the nights landed like exploding bombs, releasing a chill suddenly, unfathomable even a moment before.

Shamsur got a call. He listened to the caller quietly. The army men keeping a watch on him might not have noticed the signs of worry on his forehead. He sat on a boulder and wrapped the shawl tightly around him. He thought about the plan he had been hatching for the past few months and considered the various possible repercussions of what he had heard just now.

He had learned from the caller that the Turkish Police were frantically looking for a Sanjeev Raina, who had suddenly gone missing from the Ankara University in Turkey a few weeks ago. It had so happened that Sanjeev had been conspicuous by his absence from a recently held conference in Delhi, organized by the Kashmir Hindu Organization. One of the conveners of the conference was a close friend of Sanjeev and he knew someone influential at the Ministry of External Affairs. Soon, there were interactions between India and Turkey at the diplomatic level and the General Directorate of Security, the High Command of the Turkish Police situated at Ankara, had to swing into action. Shamsur rebuked himself that he had underestimated a Kashmiri Pandit whose parents had been murdered in the Valley in the early '90s and who had been raised as an orphan by various not-so-caring relatives.

Somak Ajai, a professor of mathematics at the Delhi School of Economics, had handpicked Sanjeev from JNU to assist him in his research. Sanjeev had already completed his PhD in linguistics from JNU and was looking out for a job. He soon became Somak's Man Friday, doing all the painstaking work of going through old manuscripts, studying the ancient scripts and deciphering the symbols of the intriguing carpets Somak possessed.

Somak had cursorily mentioned the carpets and his research work to his acquaintance Muhammad Basha, a senior professor of history at JNU. Basha was a key node in Shamsur's network, working stealthily towards infiltrating Shamsur's doctrines into the premier institutes of India. Another important node in his network was a professor at the Jadavpur University in Calcutta, the other institute in India that had nurtured the best minds in various fields of humanities, over the years.

Basha had seen huge prospects with Somak's works. '*His research, when tweaked a bit, will be like an atom bomb*,' he said excitedly to Shamsur the same evening, when they met. He knew, asking the tightlipped Somak wouldn't yield any result. So, he contacted Sanjeev, whom he had known since his JNU days. Basha promised him to liaison, on his behalf, for a position in the Department of Linguistics at the Ankara University. Sanjeev was aware that Basha, indeed, knew a few people in Turkey. Basha told Sanjeev that his friend at the Ankara University was looking for someone with commendable knowledge in ancient Indian scripts, especially Brahmi. 'The work you're doing for Somak will come handy,' he assured Sanjeev. When Sanjeev actually got the offer from the Ankara University, he started sharing more and more details about Somak's research with Basha, least suspecting anything.

A month before Somak would be murdered, Sanjeev left India. Somak was very happy about Sanjeev's sponsored trip to Turkey.

Sanjeev went missing from the university campus within a week of his arrival in Turkey. A fake mail was sent from Sanjeev's hacked account to Basha's acquaintance, through whom the position at the university had been arranged, saying that Sanjeev had to suddenly travel to India for personal reasons.

Shamsur started trekking up to the Karakoram Highway as it was getting dark. He knew it was time for the next step.

Around the same time, the match between Pakistan and India was underway in Lahore.

Shamsur returned to Lahore a few hours later.

☼

Shamsur knew Rahul would be watching the match. He waited till the match ended. He called Rahul quite late in the night. 'Do you know that Yakub Memon got his first master's degree from jail in 2013?'

'What are you talking about? Who's Yakub Memon?'

'He is your golden goose that gives eggs even after his death,' Shamsur laughed.

'Are you talking about that guy who was hanged for his role in the 1993 Bombay Bombings?'

'Yes, that's true. He got two degrees from jail, before his death. The first one was in 2013, in English, and the second, the next year in political science.'

'Why are you telling me all this now?' Rahul sounded irritated.

'See the symbolism: a Muslim, hanged for his alleged role in terrorism, pursuing knowledge and enlightenment from jail. He knew that he might be hanged and still he wanted to enrich himself. Isn't that a good theme for the fifth anniversary of his post-graduation?'

Rahul didn't have to be told anything further. It was not for any reason that he tolerated Shamsur. He knew Shamsur always came up with something no one else could think of.

'Ask your guys to seek permission from the JNU authority to hold an event for recital of Ghalib's poems. Ask the media to be alert so that they can descend on the campus in no time. Make sure there is enough sloganeering such as *Hindustan ki barbaadi*; *We will finish India*; *Death to Indian Judiciary*, etc. At least hundred students should be shouting at the top of their voices. Create enough ruckus for the institute authorities to panic and call for the cops, who will have no other option than to arrest the unruly students. Get the intellectuals, writers, painters, theatre persons and NGO workers. *They will liken the arrests to the highhandedness of a fascist regime.* They will complain that freedom of speech is under threat. Someone will say Yakub Memon was hanged because he was a Muslim. The media will hound Indar. By then, those arrested will get bail. Your law says, unless sloganeering reaches the level of incitement of violence, everything is fine. *The whole of India will start boiling and Indar will be in a soup.*'

Shamsur always felt the Indian intellectuals were among his best weapons. He was confident as long as they had their say in the mainstream media and academia, people like Indar had little to do. He knew most of his work would be anyway executed by them. It was like scoring same sides in football. He had to just watch and see, without scoring any goal.

Rahul had a smile on his face. '*Where will you go now, Indar?*' he muttered.

The Khushawar Numerals

(12 December 2018. Delhi and Khushawar)

After staying in Lahore for one more day, Kratu and Afsar returned to Khushawar. From there, it was decided, they would directly go to Kalash the next week, to participate in the traditional new year festival on the winter solstice. For the past two decades, visiting Kalash regularly during this time of the year had become a habit they never thought of changing. Since their first trip to the Kalash valleys, sunken deep into the high altitudes of the Hindukush, in search of the Urheimat, the original homeland of Kratu's grandmother, the original Kubha of their family, they had never missed returning to the roots, once a year, every year.

One afternoon, when Afsar and her sisters were busy addressing some concerns raised by the last few weavers of Khushawar, Kratu was essentially working on "Computational Linguistics", a term he had taken fancy to lately. The Brahmi symbols of a particular Khushawari rug, depicting the nine regions of the Jambudipa, were yet to be deciphered. An illustration of the rug had been recently found in an old manuscript in Kandy. The arrangement of the symbols in the illustration made it very obvious they were numerals, but it was still not clear how the Brahmi letters could actually signify numbers. To find an answer to it, he was painstakingly feeding each symbol from the rug into the various programmes he had created over the years in the field of Computational Linguistics. By mistake, he fed a page from the Khushawar Manuscript into a programme which threw up a very interesting thing about the manuscript.

When Afsar returned, he asked her, 'What is Kharosthi?'

Afsar looked at him suspiciously. 'Where did you hear about Kharosthi? It's another ancient script of India, alongside Brahmi. It was mainly used in the Gandhara region in the modern-day Pakistan and Afghanistan. One of the rock edicts of Ashoka, at the nearby village of Shahbaz Garhi, is in the Kharosthi script. Sadly, there's no successor of Kharosthi.'

'Are the Indian numerals related to Kharosthi?' Kratu asked.

Afsar was now even more suspicious. 'What's the matter? Where are you getting all these from?'

'I was analyzing the symbols in the illustration from the Kandy Manuscript, hoping to find some clue as to how they could be numbers.' He explained how he had mistakenly landed up analyzing the Sharada numerals from a page of the Khushawar Manuscript. 'The programme,' he said, 'ran into an error. While debugging I realized the programme crashed because it confused the Sharada numerals with the letters of the Kharosthi script. When I had made the programme, I never considered the case where the numerals of one script could be the letters of some other. It's like having a script where a few letters look like the digits from one to nine.'

Kratu displayed the Sharada numeral "4" from the Khushawar Manuscript and the lookalike Kharosthi alphabet side by side in the laptop.

Afsar looked at the laptop and stared at him. 'Does your programme account for the changes in the letters between rock inscription and freestyle handwriting?'

Kratu understood what she was hinting at. He took the laptop and edited the Sharada "4", removing one of the strokes. He had indeed accounted for the variation Afsar was referring to.

She had explained to him that letters in handwritten manuscripts generally have more strokes than in rock inscriptions. 'In freestyle handwriting,' she had said, 'the pen must be constantly kept in touch with the palm or birch leaves of the manuscripts, unlike when you're inscribing on a rock with a chisel.'

Presently, Kratu inserted the edited Sharada "4" between the original and the lookalike Kharosthi alphabet.

Afsar looked at the three symbols on the screen as Kratu talked. 'The right one is the Kharosthi "cha" from a rock inscription and the left one is the Sharada numeral "4" from the Khushawar Manuscript. If you have to write the Kharosthi "cha" in freestyle, it would exactly look like the Sharada "4". The middle one is the same "4", sans one particular stroke, which makes it apparently look different from the Kharosthi letter. *I do take care of these differences.* My programme does correlate between the two and read them as one.'

Afsar looked at the three symbols on the screen.

Afsar turned her face from the laptop and looked at Kratu.

'What?' Kratu asked.

'The numeral "4" is the Kharosthi letter "cha",' Afsar muttered a few times. Kratu kept quiet, knowing very well any enquiry presently wouldn't be dealt politely. 'Give me the laptop,' she took the laptop from Kratu and in a short while showed him something that rendered him speechless.

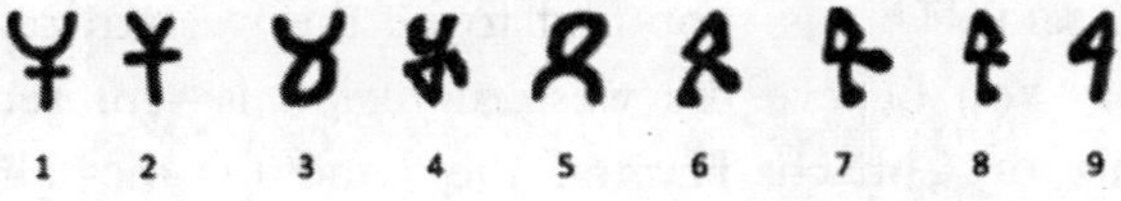

She showed him something that rendered him speechless.

'The third one is the Devanagari "4", we use in Hindi, and the last one is the "4" in English!' Kratu exclaimed. 'So, "4" is essentially the Kharosthi "cha".'

'You're correct. The first one is the Kharosthi "cha" from Ashoka's time, third century BC; the second one is the Brahmi "4"; the fourth one is Sharada, around the ninth century; the last four symbols are the various forms of "4" used in Europe since the twelfth century. Not only "4", all the numerals from three to nine have descended from Kharosthi letters, more precisely, the first letters of the Sanskrit words for those numerals …'

'Wait a minute,' Kratu interrupted, 'the symbol for "4" is the letter "cha", which is …'

'The first letter of the Sanskrit "chatur", meaning four,' Afsar completed.

Apparently, she mentioned, as early as the 1880s, the famous philologist Isaac Taylor had observed that the Hindu-Arabic numerals from four till nine were essentially the first letters, in Kharosthi script, of the corresponding Sanskrit words—"cha" for "chatur", four; "pa" for "panchan", five; and so on.

'So, when we write any numeral in English or Arabic or Hindi,' Kratu said in a frenzy, 'we are actually writing the first letter of the corresponding Sanskrit word, and that too in an ancient Indian script!'

'So now you can guess what the Brahmi letters of the rug could be.'

'Khushawar numerals!' Kratu had already pulled the laptop. He displayed a portion of the illustration from the Kandy Manuscript.

Kratu said, 'This is supposed to be the western region of Jambudipa. You believe the western region is represented by Takshashila or Chhacha-Hazara, the Land of the Thousand Severed Heads, isn't it?'

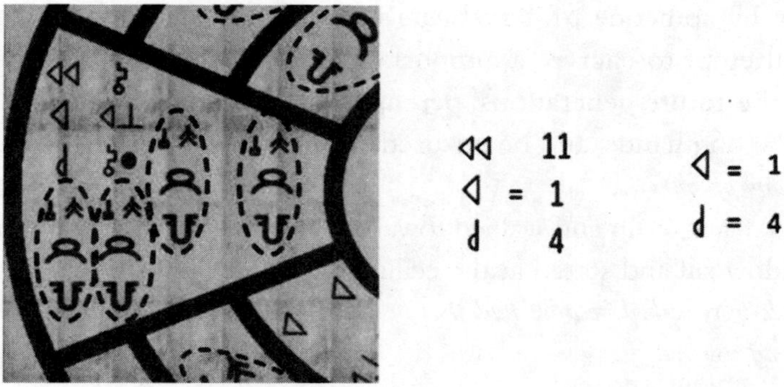

He displayed a portion of the illustration from the Kandy Manuscript.

'Yes, I do! The Khushawar Manuscript refers to Chhach-Hazara as something that's at 11¼ from the centre of the Great Vehicle of the Animals.'

Looking at the laptop, Kratu said, 'The numeral "1" is depicted by the triangle-shaped Brahmi "e" and "4" by the Brahmi "cha", a lookalike of the English "d".'

'And,' Afsar added, '"e" stands for "eka", one in Sanskrit, and "cha" for "chatur", four.'

She took her stare off the laptop and looked at Kratu. 'Do you realize the significance of this?' she asked him after a few moments, during which she hadn't taken her eyes off Kratu. 'Someone has tried to create a new system of representing numerals. Who do you think could do that?'

'How am I supposed to know?'

'You can guess,' Afsar smiled. 'He must be a maverick of numbers.'

'Aryabhata?'

'Who else?' Afsar's eyes sparkled. 'In the Khushawar Manuscript, numbers and fractions are used to depict letters, and in the rug, letters are numbers. Such number-play is possible only by someone of Aryabhata's stature. At the core of it is an attempt to encrypt an important message, preserve wisdom for the future generations, perhaps in a way it shouldn't fall in the wrong hands, and be misused. *Someone wants to misuse this old wisdom of ours …*'

Afsar got up and walked towards the window. She sat on the window sill and stared at the ceiling of the room, blankly. '*Three people were killed because had they been alive they wouldn't have allowed this misuse …*'

☼

Kubha and Parush came to Somak Ajai's house to meet Maitreyi. Kubha got down from the car as Parush drove it back, looking for a convenient parking space up the narrow lane. Somak's house was at the dead end of the lane which seemed to have abruptly stopped on its way, perhaps at the sudden sight of the relics of the Aravalli Hills of the Northern Ridge. Kubha stood in front of the wooden gate of the low boundary wall of the white bungalow, nested inside the lush green surroundings. She remembered the first time she had been here, accompanying her grandfather, to meet Somak.

Neither of them had survived beyond a week.

After staying at her grandfather's house for a few weeks, all alone, Maitreyi was finally travelling back to the US. Kubha and Parush had come to see her off. They had wanted to drop her off at the airport, but she had insisted she better go alone. 'I don't like people seeing me off at the airport,' she had said.

Kubha hugged Maitreyi for a long time. Perhaps the circumstance, under which they had met, had played a big role in fostering a peculiar camaraderie, a unique bond of affection and attachment between them. Kubha had often wondered if the knowledge that somewhere in the distant past they might have shared the same ancestry, or rather they might have been related, made any difference in their present relationship.

Maitreyi looked very dull.

'Are you sad?' Kubha asked, pulling her by her hand as she sat on a chair in the disorganized living room with things scattered everywhere.

'Sanjeev is missing.'

'Who's Sanjeev?' Parush asked, dragging a stool.

'My grandfather had picked him from JNU to assist him in his research. A month back, Sanjeev got a good position in the Ankara University and moved to Turkey.'

Sanjeev had had a thing for her, Maitreyi said, but she had never given it any indulgence. Over time, they developed a relationship which Sanjeev hoped to turn romantic someday but Maitreyi didn't. Nevertheless, she too developed a sort of attachment with him and she felt uncomfortable if he didn't ping her in a few days. When he was incommunicado for more than a week after he had reached Ankara, Maitreyi became restless. Not having his phone number, the only way to reach out to him was through emails and messages on Facebook, all of which went unanswered for weeks. Neither did Somak get any message from his Man Friday, which he attributed to Sanjeev's being extremely busy in settling down in a new country, in a new environment. Maitreyi, not convinced with the argument, didn't have anything else to do than wait.

With Somak's murder and the subsequent turn of events, Maitreyi remained busy with a lot of things, but still she could never come to terms with Sanjeev's silence. 'Then yesterday,' she said with mist in her eyes, 'I saw a post on FB from the only friend he had ...'

'What was the post?' Kubha asked, sitting erect. Parush looked serious, staring straight at the messy floor.

'"*Please let us know where you are. We haven't heard anything from you in more than a month.*" I messaged his friend. He told me that he had confirmed from his sources in the Ministry of External Affairs that Sanjeev was indeed missing. The Turkish Police has been searching for him for more than a month now.'

Parush got up and pulled his phone out. 'Rakesh,' Kubha heard him speak over the phone, 'I need some information from the Ministry of External Affairs.'

The Naga Realm

(14 December 2018. Delhi and Khushawar)

Article 19(1)(a) of the Constitution of India states, all citizens shall have the right to freedom of speech and expression ...

Article 19(2) states, nothing shall prevent the State from making any law, in so far as such law imposes reasonable restrictions on the exercise of the right conferred by Article 19(1)(a) in the interests of the sovereignty and integrity of India ...

This leads us to a discussion of what is the content of the expression "freedom of speech and expression". There are three concepts which are fundamental in understanding the reach of this most basic of human rights. The first is discussion, the second is advocacy, and the third is incitement. Mere discussion or even advocacy of a particular cause howsoever unpopular is at the heart of Article 19(1)(a). It is only when such discussion or advocacy reaches the level of incitement that Article 19(2) kicks in ...

Parush was listening to a heated discussion on a news channel in the context of the recent arrest of a few students who had organized a function in JNU condemning the hanging of Yakub Memon, a convict in the 1993 Bombay Bombings. Apparently, the students had raised very hateful slogans against India and the supreme court, leading to a scuffle with the security personnel and finally the arrests, when they resorted to violence.

The entire media had got anonymous calls at the last moment, asking them to go to the Committee Hall of the Convention Centre, if they bothered for the next big headlines. The hall which could barely accommodate a hundred people, and which had been booked for a low-key Urdu seminar on Ghalib's poetry, suddenly overflowed with people, jamming the entire Convention Centre. What transpired was nothing related to an Urdu seminar. The media was clueless at the beginning, but soon realized they had an interesting story.

Kubha, who happened to be there at the Convention Centre, attending some other seminar, landed up in the Committee Hall out of curiosity, seeing the commotion outside. She was the first one to raise her voice against the hateful sloganeering. One of the students shouting at the top of his voice pushed her and she fell on the ground. The security had arrived by that time.

It didn't take much time to figure out that the arrested students had all enrolled in the past few years, mainly in doctoral programmes, and showed no signs of leaving the campus soon. The police were perplexed that they had always kept a low profile and very few people had, in fact, seen them anywhere in the campus. Kubha, who filed the FIR against them, confirmed the same.

The next day, Parush got to know the Article 19(2) had been applied on the students. They had been slapped with charges of threatening the interests of the sovereignty and integrity of India, the security of the State, and inciting to an offence. All hell broke loose with the Opposition, bolstered by the intellectuals and freethinking citizens of India, accusing the ruling Bharatiya Party of fascism and likening Prime Minister Indar Sinha to Hitler. Slapping Article 19(2) on the students, just for sloganeering, they claimed, was against the basic tenets of the freedom of speech.

As Parush watched an eminent historian quoting from Justice R.F. Nariman's judgement in the "Shreya Singhal versus the Union of India" case, he wondered who could be behind this sinister plan of putting Indar in trouble, suddenly, out of the blue. He changed the channel. He heard Rahul saying, '*This represents centralized despotism and it is talking about a rigidly unitarian imperial state …*'

Parush's phone rang. He was expecting the call from Indar.

☼

'You could have easily avoided making a hero out of these useless students,' Parush said directly. 'Don't you realize these are all age-old tactics to tarnish your image? You've just fallen into the trap.'

Indar didn't speak for some time, during which Parush wondered what could be playing in his mind. 'I don't care if people call me a fascist,' he said firmly. '*For me, the country comes first.*'

'What are you talking about, Indar?' the tinge of irritation in Parush's voice couldn't have eluded the erudite Indar. 'I can't believe you could sound like one of your illiterate minions who find anything and everything as a threat to India …'

'Porus,' Indar interrupted. 'Oh, that's what you think about me?' he laughed over the phone. 'Good, if I can fool you, I would be fooling the whole world.'

'What are you trying to say?'

'Just consider this. Fifteen Hindu students from across India graduate from the Sher-e-Kashmir University of Agricultural Sciences and Technology of Kashmir in the May of 2014. All of them get masters in Statistics from the Faculty of Postgraduate Studies from their Shalimar campus in Srinagar …'

'What university did you say?'

'Sher-e-Kashmir University of Agricultural Sciences and Technology of Kashmir,' Indar repeated. 'All of those students, who hadn't found any other place to go to in the whole country and who had finally chosen that very university which rarely enrolls Hindu students, eventually landed at JNU and Delhi University in Delhi and Presidency College and Jadavpur University in Calcutta in May 2016. It so happened that their passports were also made in May 2014. Three of them actually joined the School of Computational and Integrative Sciences at JNU for doctoral programmes in the Sports and ECA Quota, something unheard of in the history of JNU. Rule books were suddenly changed in May 2014 to make way for their admissions …'

'Were they among the ones arrested for that event in JNU?' Parush asked hastily.

'Good that you got my point,' Indar didn't speak much after that.

Parush called his trusted lieutenant Rakesh. 'Didn't you say some time back that Shamsur Ali is often invited to Kashmir to give guest lectures at various colleges?'

'Yes, sir,' Rakesh confirmed. He checked his records and called back in a few minutes. 'In the past few months, he has been to SKUAST Kashmir the most number of times …'

'What's SKUAST?'

'Sher-e-Kashmir University of Agricultural Sciences and Technology.'

Parush disconnected the line and turned on the TV, not listening to anything though. He wondered how deep the tentacles of Shamsur Ali had reached. More than four years back, Parush joined the dots, when it had been imminent that the previous government led by Rahul's Indian Party would lose the General Election in May 2014, Shamsur had trapped the desperate and helpless incumbent. That he had infiltrated into the Opposition was evident from the rapport he maintained with the likes of Rahul. But it was more dangerous, Parush realized, that he had infiltrated into the educational institutions too. *What was he up to*? Parush felt restless.

☼

Kratu was going through the various illustrations and slides he had created over the past few days, in the course of deciphering the Indus and Brahmi symbols of a Khushawari rug, which was, doubtless, at the centre of the murder of his father-in-law.

The Kandy Manuscript had a neat illustration of a similar rug, a good part of which had been blackened. The remaining un-blackened portion was filled with mixed fractions comprising zero and seven numerals from one to nine, barring six and eight. Kratu had created a chart of the rug-symbols and the numerals, he believed, they depict. Presently, he studied the chart closely, trying to be a devil's advocate, suspecting his own logic. The

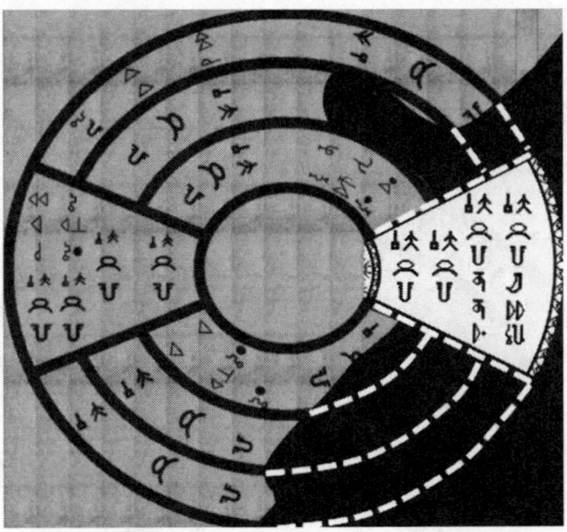

e *eka* one	**dva** *dva* two	**tra** *tra* three	**cha** *chatur* four	**pa** *panchan* five	**sa** *saptan* seven	**na** *navan* nine	zero

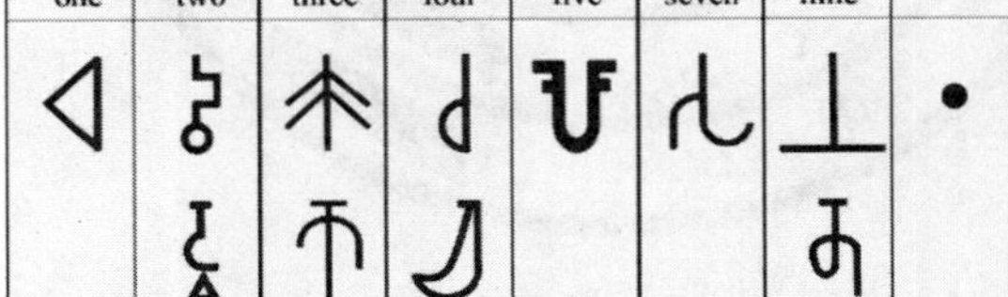

Brahmi/Indus Non freestyle Rock Inscription

Gupta Brahmi Freestyle Manuscript

Kratu was going through the various illustrations.

entire foundation of the logic rested on the hypothesis that the symbols—a combination of Brahmi and its lookalike Indus signs—depict the first letters of the Sanskrit words for the numerals. The fact that the rug had only seven numeral-signs and that each of the signs actually matched with the first letter of the seven words "eka", "dva", "tra", "chatura", "panchan", "saptan" and "navan"—one, two, three, four, five, seven and nine—he found no ground to refute the logic. As he looked at the chart, he couldn't but revel in his own discovery that the Brahmi symbols showed some variations—some were in freestyle handwriting and some not.

Later, when he was studying the slide in which he had replaced the Brahmi symbols of the rug with the corresponding numerals in English, Afsar entered hastily into Faraz's study.

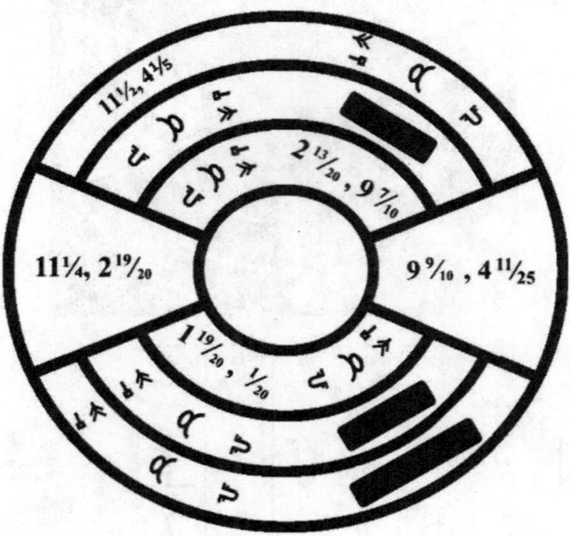

He had replaced the Brahmi symbols of the rug with the corresponding numerals in English.

Afsar looked at the laptop screen and then went and sat on the window sill, keeping her open notebook beside her. She was panting.

'What happened?' Kratu asked her.

'All these days, I've been wondering about the significance of the Nagas, referred to so many times in the Kandy and Khushawar manuscripts.' She closed her eyes as she spoke, sliding her head between the iron grills of the open window and inhaling the chill air of the evening. 'I had a feeling The Naga Country, The Naga Realms, The Land of the Nagas wouldn't really be a country or kingdom per se. Rather, I was thinking, it would be a concept. But I'm more inclined to believe now that it's nothing but the Indian subcontinent.'

'India, the Land of the Nagas,' Kratu broke into a laughter. 'We're all snakes, and we never knew.'

Afsar got up from the window sill and sat in front of Kratu on a revolving chair. 'Yes, darling, you're correct! I don't know about myself, but being a Bong, you are very likely a Naganvaya, a descendant of the Nagas, the serpent peoples.'

What Afsar narrated henceforth was very incredible. She had been researching a lot in the past few days about the ancient Nagas, one of the most prominent indigenous peoples of India.

'The original homes of the Nagas were perhaps Tibet and Burma,' she began the long narration. 'How exactly the Tibetans and Burmese were related may be a matter of conjecture. But the fact that their languages belong to the same family tells they are indeed related. And if that's so, the northern India, and especially the ancient Magadha, the present-day Bengal and Bihar, was the region which would have connected them, brought them together. It's not surprising then, that the impact of the Nagas would be more prominent in Magadha, and also in the Himalayas that adjoin Tibet. Like most other ancient tribesmen, they too had a totem and it's a no brainer that their totem was *naga*, a serpent. They were a *naga*-worshipping race …

'At the same time, I feel, the Nagas were technologically, intellectually, culturally and even, spiritually quite advanced. The footprints of the Nagas are visible to this day. "Nagara", the Sanskrit word for city, is of uncertain origin. It may be connected to the Nagas, the master city-builders. Nagari or deva-nagari, the name of the script in which Sanskrit has been written for centuries, may have been derived from "nagara", for it might have originated in some city of the Nagas. It's possible the Brahmi script was also introduced by the Nagas.'

The Nagas might have been so important and powerful, Afsar said excitedly, that the Aryans, who were doubtless much lesser in number than them, would have adopted many of their customs and rituals. The Aryans might have even adapted to the Naga way of life, to a great extent. The impact of this, she argued, was perhaps the innumerable references to the Nagas in the *Mahabharata*. Nagas were shown as descendants of the sage Kashyapa. Two of Arjun's wives, Chitrangada and Ulupi, were daughters of Naga kings. Arjun's grandson, Parikshit, was coroneted at Takshashila, the modern-day Taxila, the city of the Takshas, a Naga people. The *Mahabharata* was first recited at Takshashila too, at a snake festival.

In the documented history too, Afsar asserted, the Nagas were quite prominent. Magadha was ruled by them for a long time. Prior to the Mauryas, the Shishunagas and the Nandas were at the helm.

'"Sishu-naga" means a young snake,' she said, 'and Nanda has been often referred to as a snake in ancient Sanskrit literature, including the *Mahabharata*. The symbolism clearly means both the Shishunagas and the Nandas were Naga peoples. Chandragupta Maurya, the grandfather of Ashoka, was mentioned in the Sanskrit classic *Mudrarakshasa* as Nandanvaya, a descendant of the Nandas, thus making the Mauryas also one among the Naga peoples …

'It may not be a coincidence that Magadha and Gandhara, the two frontier regions of the Indian subcontinent, one to the east and the other to the west, were the centres of power and knowledge for a long time. Both were peopled predominantly by the Nagas. I don't think the designation "Nagas", as used in the Khushawar and Kandy manuscripts, refers to a separate race. I would rather like to believe it encompasses a wider group of the indigenous peoples of the subcontinent, the Nagas being the most dominant among them. With the South Indian Dravida peoples too believed to have originated from the Nagas of the ancient Magadha, a major part of India can be truly called a Naga Realm …'

'The Dravidians have a Bong connection?' Kratu interrupted.

Afsar took her notebook and read from a page. 'The Kandy Manuscript has this line: "The illustrious father of the Bang peoples, who having travelled from Damalitti, has founded Naga realms in Damila and Lanka and also in Champa faraway".'

Damalitti, Afsar explained, must be Tamralipta or Tamraliptaka, the ancient port city and the modern Tamluka, on the Bay of Bengal, in southern Bengal. In Pali, it was known as Tamalitti, which is doubtless the origin of "Damalitti". *Mahavamsha*, the Sri Lankan epic in Pali, talks about "damila", which is believed to be the source of the terms "dravida" and "tamil". But what is interesting is the Bong connection that "damila" derives from "damalitti".

'Equally interesting is another Bong connection, you'll be happy to know of.' Afsar smiled, patting Kratu. 'The ancient Indian name for Vietnam was Champa and it can be conjured from Chinese records that Vietnam was peopled by the Bang tribes, coming from a faraway country known as Bang Lang, which perhaps we know as Bangla or Vanga.'

Afsar didn't allow Kratu to react.

'It is very likely,' she continued, 'that at some point of time, the Aryans, and especially the upper-caste Brahmins, would have started envying the Naga peoples. That perhaps explained the Nagas of the Gandhara and Magadha being relegated to the ranks of outcastes, the ill-spoken and uncultured peoples. That the same peoples were the early adopters of Buddhism told a lot about their broad-mindedness and dexterity. They were among the first to have realized the need of reforming the old Indian or the Hindu way of life that was based on the tenets of the ancient Vedas and the diktats of the Brahmins. It was not for no reason that the Buddhists often referred to their fraternity as Nagas.'

'Given the friction between the Nagas and the Brahmins,' Afsar concluded, 'The Naga Realm or The Naga Country in the manuscripts would typically refer to the portion of the subcontinent which was relatively free from the puritan Brahmanical influence.'

'What does that mean?' Kratu asked, crossing his hands behind his head.

'Wait a minute …' Afsar got up from the chair. 'Let me get my laptop.'

She left the room and returned soon with her laptop, a picture displayed on the screen. She placed the laptop on Faraz's writing desk, in front of Kratu. She opened a particular page in her notebook and read out four lines from the Kandy Manuscript:

The Jambudipa is guarded by the mighty Naga countries.
Starting with Kasmira-Gandhara, Aparantaka comes next;
Then Maharattha, Damila and Kalinga come in the right order;
How can you forget Suvannabhumi and Himavanta, the abodes of the Nagas?

'This is the realm of the Naga countries,' she said, looking at Kratu. 'One of my research scholars has made an interesting observation about the places mentioned in the manuscript.'

She pointed to the picture on her laptop. 'Are you getting the point?' she asked.

'This is incredible!' Kratu exclaimed, looking at the picture. 'The Mighty Naga Countries comprise most of the Indian subcontinent, leaving aside just a central portion of North India, like a doughnut.'

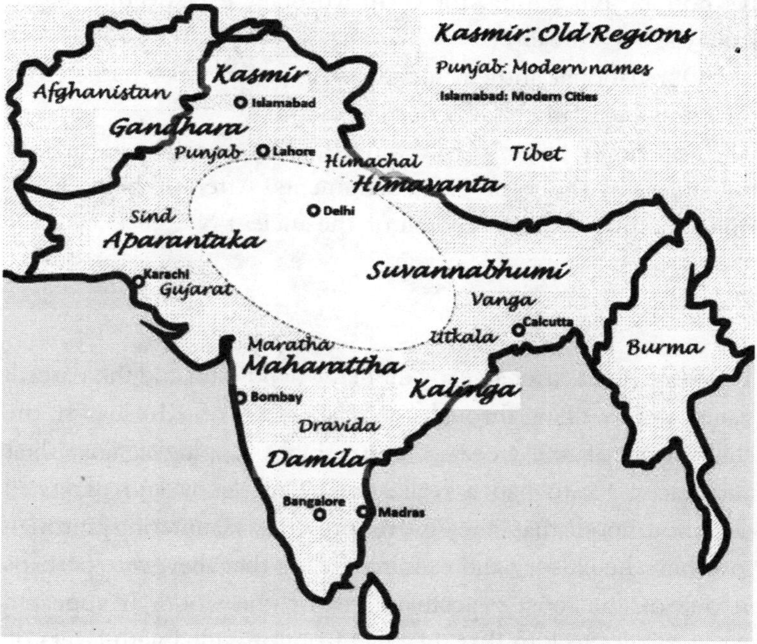

'This is incredible!' Kratu exclaimed, looking at the picture.

'In fact,' Afsar added, 'the hole in the doughnut is the present Hindi heartland, comprising the states of UP, Delhi, Haryana and parts of Rajasthan and Madhya Pradesh …

'This entire region is seen as the epicentre of power since the antiquity. Starting from Ayodhya, Kashi, Mathura, Vrindavan, Hastinapur and Kurukshetra of the epics, till the New Delhi of today, the whole of India is often believed to have been controlled by this region, both in terms of religion and politics. Even now, no political party can come to power in Delhi unless they have a strong hold in this region. This very region is also the symbol of the Aryan hegemony that the non-Brahmins and the large number of the backward castes in India often complain about. The Naga peoples too were against the same hegemony. It's nothing but natural for them to totally exclude this region from the Naga Realm.'

'Our national anthem too doesn't mention any name from the Hindi heartland,' Kratu observed.

'You never know,' Afsar winked, 'Tagore might have been influenced by the same Naga sentiments. After all, being a Big Bong, he too was a descendant of the ancient Nagas.'

☼

The same night, after an early dinner, when Kratu and the Fareedi sisters were walking through the misty alleys of Khushawar, the chilly wind of the freezing wintry night lapping against their bare faces, Kratu had a realization. The sleepy and darkened neighbourhood that they were presently sauntering through gave him the illusory and calming feeling that they were perhaps in one of the most peaceful places of the world. It appeared extraordinary to him that they had been provided with layers of security for this very place, because the Taliban had created a totally different perception about this entire region. Just a few days ago, they had killed some 20 girl-students in the Bacha Khan University at the nearby Charsadda.

Kratu had fallen behind Afsar and her sisters. He took a deep breath. 'Afsar,' he called out to his wife.

Afsar turned back and waited for Kratu to catch up. 'What?' she asked him.

Kratu glanced at the few hazy lights coming from the houses around them; the heavy mist made the lights flicker like stars.

'Ever since we've been here, have you ever felt it's the most dangerous part of the world?' Kratu asked.

'That's exactly what I've been thinking too,' Bahnaz acknowledged. 'People in the US make too much fuss about Pakistan. I'm not saying there's no problem in this part of the world, but it's surely not as bad as what it has been made to look like.'

'Perceptions are mostly like that,' Afsar responded. 'It's not necessary they are always correct,' she turned towards Kratu. 'Some time back, we were discussing about the Naga peoples and their conflict with the Aryans.'

Bahnaz and Bahrukh walked ahead, letting Afsar and Kratu talk.

'There's a strong perception that a few Aryans and upper-caste Brahmins had imposed their culture and language on the millions of hapless natives,' Afsar continued. 'It sowed the seeds of the irreparable North–South divide in India. The entire North India was perceived as the symbol of Aryan imperialism on the Dravidian peoples of the South. Something called a Self-Respect Movement catapulted in the South during the 1920s. It aimed at restoring the individuality of the Dravidian peoples. Eventually, it digressed into a movement against the Hindi-speaking North Indians, against the Brahmanical system …'

'Doesn't the concept of the Naga Realm, excluding North India,' Kratu interrupted, 'speak of the same thing?'

'There's a difference,' Afsar argued. 'The Naga Realm essentially comprises most of the Indian subcontinent. Remember the verse from the Khushawar Manuscript? "They rule over the world, from Gandhara to Magadha". The Nagas represent the common men of the entire subcontinent, the real sons of the soil, the resilient, dexterous, broad-minded and pragmatic Indians, whose influence in shaping the Indian culture has been as much as that of the Aryans.'

Afsar suddenly stopped talking. Kratu held her hand and walked fast to catch up with her sisters whose silhouettes were visible through the thickening mist.

'The manuscripts tell us of an incredible thing,' Afsar spoke again. '*Most of India is same.* The Aryans might have brought a new language, but the Indian culture is essentially indigenous, the progeny of her own soil, not a forceful imposition of the imperialist Aryans.'

'Such a theory would be disastrous to our politicians, isn't it?'

'Exactly!' Afsar asserted. 'Politics thrives on divide and rule: the divide between the North and the South; the divide between the languages; the divide between the ethnicities. But here is someone who says, "*We're all the same, irrespective of what we speak, what we wear and how we look like. We're the Naga Peoples.*" Yes, that's disastrous.'

'This is, indeed, an earth-shattering revelation in a country that's divided in so many ways, but do you think the three murders were just to stop Somak from declaring this to the world?'

Afsar fell silent.

The Deceit

(16–26 December 2018. Khushawar and Delhi)

Shamsur made a call. 'The time has come now,' he said over the phone to the person on the other side. 'Afsar is an internationally acclaimed academician with impeccable credentials. Something coming from her wouldn't be questioned. She will be our champion at the World History Association 2019 Calcutta Conference.'

The same afternoon, Afsar got a mail from an Ataulla Bayazitoz, the deputy dean of Teaching and Methodology at the Faculty of Philology in the St. Petersburg State University. Afsar read the mail many times. It was written in a very weird form of English, perhaps a heavily Russianized English, she thought. What perplexed her was not of course the language, but the content of the mail. She showed the mail to Kratu.

> *Dear Afsar,*
> *The sudden demise of your father has brought me great deal of sadness. Please accept my condolences. I pray for his well-being in the seventh heaven.*
>
> *From the earliest beginning of collecting oriental carpets, my mentor asked me to engage with your father. I first saw few of your father's carpets at St. Petersburg Mosque. Someone got those carpets from Bukhara. I personally got in touch with your father in early*

> *seventies and I bought many carpets from him in next few years. I was not in touch with your father after that.*
>
> *Few months back, I saw picture of a carpet at an agent's place. I was especially fascinated because the carpet had lot of ancient symbols. I was happy to learn that the carpet was originally sold by your father. I wanted to buy it but the agent was not premised to sell it to anyone. I asked him to get in touch with your father. I was also looking for another carpet, which was planned to make from combining with rich oriental ornaments and mosaic of turquoise-blue colour. The agent personally met with your father. He brought few old pieces of carpets from your father. Later, I learned about your father's death from an article on* Antique Rugs and Textiles *by Thomas Cole.*

Kratu took his eyes off the laptop and stared at Afsar. 'This mail practically leaves nothing to suspicion about the identity of the person who had come and met your father just before his murder,' he observed. 'It's also proved beyond doubt that the old rugs which went missing after his murder had been given to the person by none other than your father. One thing which still remains murky is the fact that no one saw any foreigner coming to your Khushawar mansion and meeting your father on that day. This means, the agent doesn't look like a foreigner.'

He paused and looked at the laptop, scrolling down the long mail. 'What else does the mail say?'

Afsar realized Kratu had lost interest in reading the entire mail.

'Ataulla Bayazitoz has requested me if I could somehow get him the rug he's interested in. Apparently, Ataulla claims, Aba had promised he would get it woven especially for him …'

'It's the same rug with the symbols, isn't it?' Kratu interrupted.

'Yes, it's the same one we've been trying to decipher.' Afsar took the laptop and clicked on an attachment in the mail. 'He has sent me the design.'

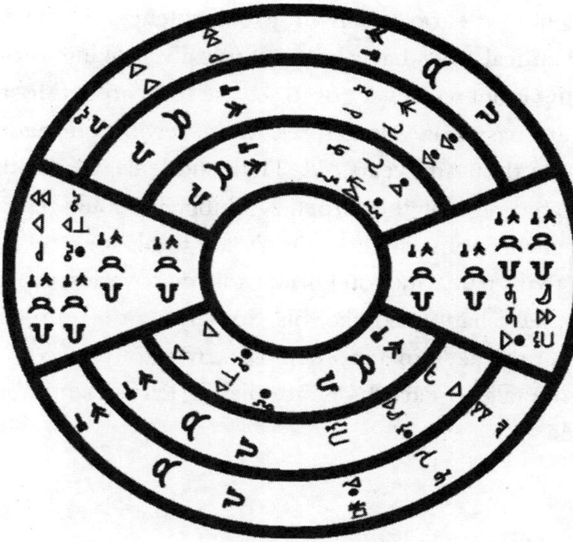

'He has sent me the design.'

Kratu noticed the sparkles in Afsar's eyes. 'The darkened portions of the illustration from the Kandy Manuscript are revealed in this design … ' she extolled.

'But are you sure,' Kratu interrupted again, 'the two are same?'

'Yes, I've compared the two. The non-darkened portions match perfectly. There's no reason why the darkened portions wouldn't … ' Afsar paused.

Kratu appeared absent-minded.

'What happened?' Afsar asked.

'How did this person get your email?' Kratu asked suddenly.

Afsar thought for a few moments. 'Is it too tough a thing? Getting my email is so easy, especially when I've never made any attempt to keep it classified. Moreover, he has sent the email to my official address. All my papers have it. You can get it from the internet.'

'Somehow it's too much of a coincidence,' Kratu was, no doubt, skeptical. 'We have been frantically looking forward to deciphering it but we never got to see the real carpet. Most of our findings are based on conjectures. We're relying on manuscripts more than a thousand years old. Then suddenly, we get this mail with a clean design of the carpet. Nothing else could have helped us more, at this point of time. Don't you think so?'

'Yes, that's true. But you know, most discoveries, especially in our areas, have happened like this. Something pops up suddenly, and you get the keys, in a moment of serendipity.'

'Let me talk to Parush.' Kratu dialled Parush's number from his mobile.

☼

Since that night when Kubha had stayed back at Parush's place for the first time, the state of affairs between them had become very easy, rather natural. All these years, Parush had thought many times later, there had been a certain barrier, a certain kind of uneasiness in their relationship, which prevented them from talking about certain things, behaving in certain ways, even when there wouldn't be anyone else around them. That particular night shattered an invisible thin glass between them. They started behaving like a couple, perhaps more in a visible way.

Kubha often stayed back at Parush's place. She never forgot to lap her hands around his waist as they walked. She jumped on him and hugged him whenever they met. The way she dragged his face and planted a goodbye kiss on his lips turned many an eyeball. It never bothered her that people around looked at them in suspicion, the huge age difference between them not eluding anyone's eyes.

A few hours earlier, when Kratu had called Parush in the afternoon, Kubha had been with him. She didn't move from over him as he talked to her father. She cherished how Parush had to put effort to talk normally over the phone as she slithered on his bare body, like a snake. Once Kratu hung up, Parush dragged her up and enmeshed his face in her thick long hair. As she stroked him, her breath becoming heavier, her heaving faster, her moaning louder, her bites more piercing, her embrace tighter, he suddenly loosened himself, drooping like a big drenched tree, splashed with rains.

Putting Kubha to sleep, Parush got up. They had been awake the whole night, taking a stroll on the lonely alleys of an otherwise bustling Delhi, sitting on the near-frozen footpath, leaning against each other, shivering in the biting cold of late December.

Parush stared at the sleeping Kubha. He pulled the comforter over her and looked at her face, closely.

In no time, Parush confirmed Ataulla Bayazitoz had indeed sent the mail from a genuine email address. When he was going to call up Kratu and inform the same, he recalled something Indar had said. '*My sixth sense says a fraud carpet will emerge soon.*'

Indar's words appeared like a prophecy. He went out and stretched his arms. He called Kratu a little later. 'The email seems to be genuine.' He didn't say anything else.

☼

Kratu replaced the mixed fractions in Brahmi-Indus symbols with the corresponding Hindu-Arabic numerals. The term "va-ta ma-pa" appeared in eight of the nine sections of the circle, except the central one.

Afsar had conjectured "va-ta ma-pa" was perhaps the reduced form of "Vrita Maha Pota", meaning the central region, or rather the centre of Jambudipa, the Indian subcontinent.

'Expanding the same line of thought,' she had stressed, 'va-ta ma-pa along with the two mixed fractions $11\frac{1}{2}$ and $4\frac{1}{5}$ in

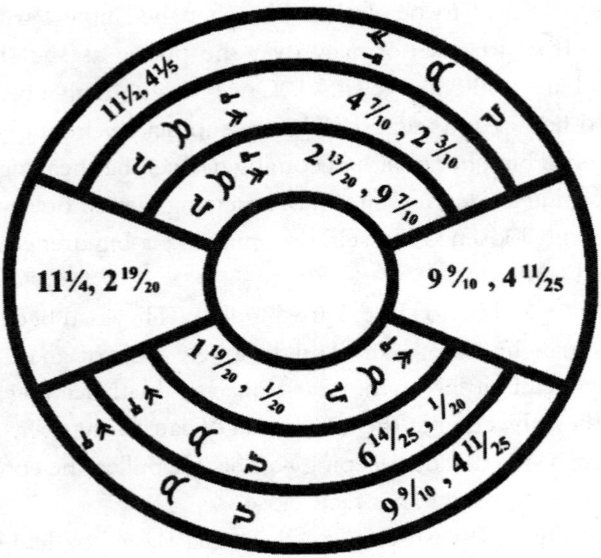

Kratu replaced the mixed fractions in Brahmi-Indus symbols with the corresponding Hindu-Arabic numerals.

the top section could mean the northern country is at 11½ and 4⅕ from the centre of Jambudipa.'

Kratu had been quite confident the two mixed fractions for each region actually referred to the latitude and longitude of the capital, or rather the most important place of the region.

Afsar was skeptical though. 'Were latitudes and longitudes in vogue,' she had asked, looking at the laptop screen, '1,500 years ago, during Aryabhata's time?'

'I understand,' Kratu had argued, 'Aryabhata defined the location of Ujjain quite precisely in terms of its latitude. Moreover, the reference to Lanka as the prime meridian makes it very clear that Aryabhata was very much aware of longitudes too.'

Afsar's expressions revealed she was still not convinced. She stared at the ceiling, tapping the desk with her fingers.

'Taxila is at $11\frac{1}{4}$ from the centre,' Afsar spoke after some time, pointing to the leftmost section of the circle, corresponding to Ketumala, the western country. 'I figured out the latitude of Taxila is $33\frac{3}{4}$, not $11\frac{1}{4}$.'

'Wait a minute,' Kratu said. 'Are you sure Taxila is at $33\frac{3}{4}$ degree north?'

'Yes,' Afsar asserted.

Kratu got up from the chair. 'Afsar,' he shouted in excitement, 'Ujjain is the Vrita Maha Pota, the centre of Jambudipa.' He paused to gauge Afsar's reaction. Afsar appeared confused. She stared at Kratu's face with a blank look. 'It's so simple,' Kratu said. 'We shouldn't have taken so long to figure this out. Ujjain is at $22\frac{1}{2}$ degree north and Taxila $33\frac{3}{4}$. The difference between the two is essentially the position of Taxila with respect to Ujjain, That is precisely $11\frac{1}{4}$, and that is what you see in the manuscript, and in the carpet too … '

Afsar was speechless for a while. 'Ujjain is the Vrita Maha Pota,' she mumbled a few times, looking straight into Kratu's eyes. She pulled Kratu and hugged him tightly. 'We're quite close now,' she whispered and suddenly pushed him off. 'Let us find the other places too,' she said firmly. 'Which place is at $11\frac{1}{2}$ and $4\frac{1}{5}$ from Ujjain?' she asked, pointing to the topmost section of the circle.

It didn't take long for Kratu to figure out that Peshawar's coordinates—latitude and longitude—were 34 degree north and $71\frac{3}{5}$ degree east. 'That's nothing but $11\frac{1}{2}$ north and $4\frac{1}{5}$ west with respect to Ujjain,' he said, his eyes sparkling.

'We now know three of the nine countries or the Nava Varshas of Jambudipa—Ujjain, Taxila and Peshawar,' Afsar said, once Kratu's excitement had subsided a bit.

In the next half an hour, Kratu decoded the capitals of the remaining six countries. He simply used the coordinates derived from the mixed fractions associated with the corresponding

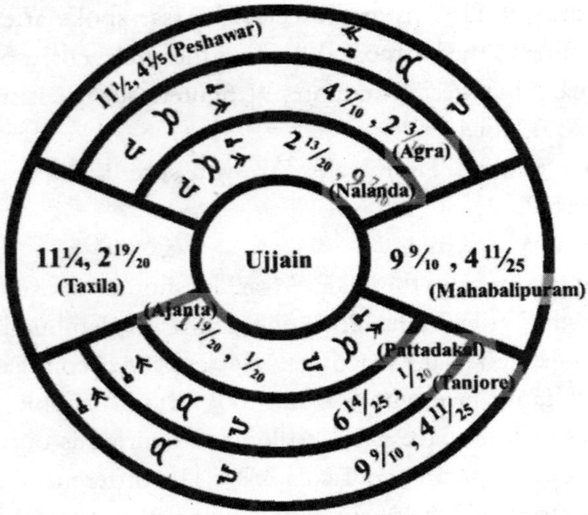

He added the names of the places on the diagram …

sections of the circle. He added the names of the places on the diagram displayed on the screen and passed the laptop to Afsar.

Kratu noticed the frown on Afsar's face. 'Are you sure of Agra?' she asked him, not taking her eyes off the laptop.

'Yes,' Kratu replied with confidence. 'The coordinates are quite accurate and each of them precisely corresponds to a real place …'

'Nalanda has been recently included in the UNESCO World Heritage list,' Afsar interrupted. 'Each of the other seven places—Taxila, Peshawar, Agra, Ajanta, Pattadakal, Tanjore and Mahabalipuram—have been already there in the list. So, not only are the places real, but they all happen to be sites of extraordinary historical significance. *Still, can't you see Agra seems to be the odd one here?*'

'Why?' Kratu seemed clueless.

Afsar stared at him for a few moments. She took her notebook and flipped through the pages. 'There are enough indications that the design of the rug was conceptualized by Aryabhata,' she said, not taking her eyes off the notebook. 'Only the maverick himself could have played with numerals like this. The places such as Mahabalipuram, Pattadakal and Tanjore are posterior to Aryabhata and are very likely later additions.'

'What do you think the original design by Aryabhata would have been like?' Kratu asked.

Afsar looked up, tapping the desk with her fingers a few times. Suddenly, she turned the pages of her notebook hastily as though searching for something, frantically. 'Yes,' she almost screamed, 'here it is.'

She read out four lines from the Kandy Manuscript:

The Jambudipa is guarded by the mighty Naga countries.
Starting with Kasmira-Gandhara, Aparantaka comes next;
Then Maharattha, Damila and Kalinga come in the right order;
How can you forget Suvannabhumi and Himavanta, the abodes of the Nagas?

Afsar was going so say something, when she abruptly grabbed her mobile. 'Give me a minute,' she mumbled, as she browsed through the contacts in her phone in a frenzy.

☼

Shamsur Ali looked around him, studying the reaction of everyone huddled in the claustrophobic room on the Paranthe Wali Gali in Old Delhi's Chandni Chowk area. His audience was a homogeneous group of young people, all in their early twenties. If seen in a crowd, none of them would attract the attention of anyone. They would merge easily into the crowd, as one of them, as insignificant, and more importantly, as harmless as anyone else. Perhaps that was the main reason why they had been chosen to be the part of one of the many batches of young people Shamsur had been meeting lately on a regular basis.

The only thing that made these young people useful to Shamsur, or rather worthy of his time and effort, was their tacit support for the Islamic State, ad-Daulah al-Islamiyah. Their internet footprint had been tracked closely for quite some time before they were approached by Shamsur personally. He knew his academic background would come in handy. He also knew precisely how to subtly flaunt his status of being in the inner circles of many political heavyweights in Delhi. All these, along with his personality, he was sanguine, would be enough to get the young people attractedto him.

'Yes, my young friends,' Shamsur thundered, 'you've heard it right, *Christianity is nothing but repackaged Hinduism and Buddhism*. These two religions of the Aryans have propagated the haram cult of idol worship throughout the world.'

More than a hundred years ago, Shamsur said, Nicolas Notovitch, a Russian journalist wandering in the wilderness of Ladakh, was recuperating from a broken leg in a Tibetan monastery at a place called Hemis. The monks there showed him an old Tibetan manuscript, about the life of a saint called Issa. Mysteriously, the manuscript went missing in the 1920s, only after Nicolas' story had created a flutter.

'It can't be a mere coincidence,' Shamsur said, 'that in Arabic the name of Jesus is Isa. It's doubtless a corruption of the Sanskrit word "ishwar", meaning God. Even the name Christ derives from Krishna, the biggest of the bigots of the Hindus. In Bengal, Christ is referred to as Krishto and Krishna as Keshto.'

It so happened, Shamsur elaborated, that Jesus had spent a good amount of his growing years in Kashmir, studying Buddhism. Many of the teachings of Jesus, he claimed, had surreptitious similarities with that of the Buddha.

'If we want to eliminate all traces of Hinduism and Buddhism from the earth,' he roared, 'we can't spare Christianity. And the very symbol of Christianity is Rome, from where it spread like a wild fire, and keeps on spreading till date. Interestingly, Rome had always been a bastion of the Aryans, long before Jesus was even born. The most popular God of the ancient Romans was Jupiter. It's nothing but Dyuspitar, the father of Indra, the king of all gods of the Hindus. The Pantheon is one of the biggest temples dedicated to all the Aryan gods. Not many cities in the world would have as many temples as Rome has had since antiquity. We've demolished temples in India and elsewhere in the world, but somehow Rome has been spared. *In the Islamic State, the existence of places like Rome is a matter of sheer blasphemy.*'

☼

Afsar took much more than the minute she had asked for when she had called the research scholar who had previously pointed out a very interesting thing about the Naga Countries mentioned in the Kandy Manuscript. The research scholar had graphically shown the Naga Realms or the Naga Countries comprised almost the entire Indian subcontinent, except for a central region—the Hindi belt or the Hindi heartland, as it's often referred to now—forming a doughnut hole in the map. When Kratu returned to his father-in-law's home office close to an hour later, Afsar was still on the call, this time on Skype, studying the images shared on the screen.

'Come here,' Afsar called Kratu the moment he appeared at the door. 'Do you now realize that Agra couldn't have been a part of the Naga Countries? This is deceitful. Doubtless.'

Kratu turned the laptop towards him as Afsar carried on with her conversation with the research scholar. Kratu was stunned too, seeing the nava varshas, the nine regions, demarcated on India's map, along with their capitals.

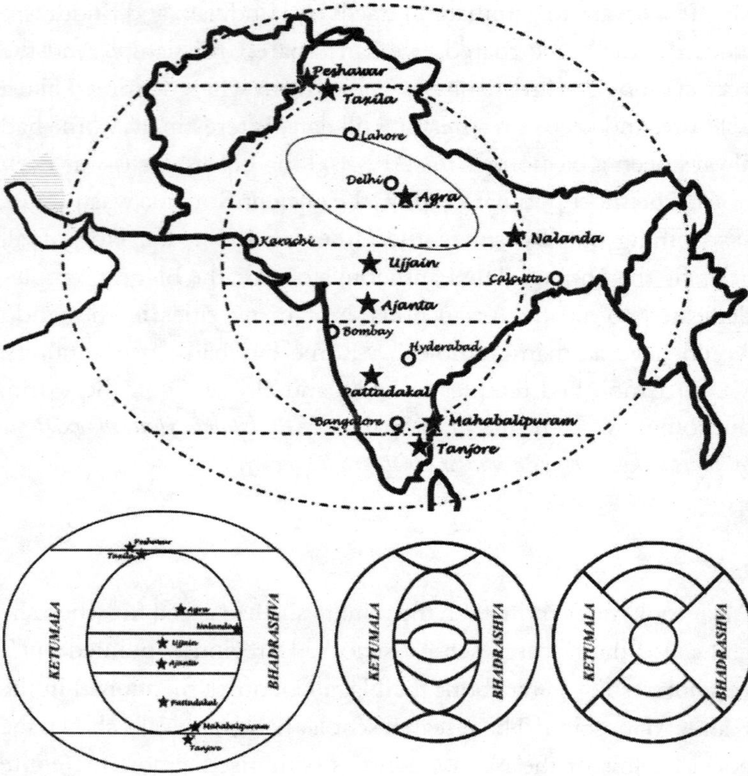

Kratu was stunned too, seeing the nava varshas.

'*Agra falls deep inside the doughnut hole!*' Kratu exclaimed.

Afsar thanked the research scholar and ended the call. 'Do you realize why Agra can't be a Naga Country?' Her excitement was presently both audible and visible. She pulled the laptop back. 'Agra is perhaps the only place which doesn't have a strong association either with the Nagas or with Buddhism.'

'I remember you mentioned that the Buddhists referred to an ordinary man as Naga.'

'That's correct,' Afsar said. 'It may refer to the historical fact that the non-Aryan Naga peoples of the Magadha region were among the first to embrace Buddhism.'

Peshawar, which represents the northernmost country, had been a very important Buddhist centre in the past. The Kushan Emperor Kanishka, Afsar said, had enshrined the begging pot of the Buddha there in a huge dagaba 2,000 years ago. Some 400 years later, the Chinese traveller Fa-Hien extolled it as the highest tower in India.

'The dagaba doesn't exist now,' she said, 'but during Aryabhata's time, it did exist, and going by Fa-Hien's description, it was a very important monument. Many Buddhist monasteries have survived till date around Peshawar. Takht-i-Bahi is listed as a UNESCO World Heritage Site.'

'"Taxila", I understand, derives from "Taksha", the name of a snake,' Kratu said, as Afsar took her notebook and turned its pages. 'The Naga connection is very obvious.'

'It has close to 70 Buddhist topes, all in ruins though,' Afsar said, taking her eyes off the notebook, looking at the laptop screen. 'It's also connected with the legend of the Thousand Severed Heads of the Buddha …

'Nalanda's Buddhist connection is also quite direct. The monastery and the university exist till this day. It's the Monte Cassino of India, or rather I would say, Monte Cassino is the Nalanda of the Holy Roman Empire. Moreover, Nalanda derives from Naga Nanda …

'Ujjain was Aryabhata's karmabhoomi, his work place, and also the prime meridian. Ajanta is famous for the 2,000-year-old cave-shrines, modelled on Buddhist chaitya or prayer halls. I would believe they were very much in use during Aryabhata's time.'

Afsar paused, staring at Kratu, inquisitively, perhaps expecting him to say something.

'And, what about the other three places in the south?' Kratu asked. 'Pattadakal, Mahabalipuram and Tanjore are famous for their Hindu temples.'

Afsar replied, 'Mahabalipuram is named after Bali, a mythological character, a demon, who is said to have fathered the Naga peoples of Anga, Vanga, Pundra, Sumha and Kalinga, the five contagious ancient regions comprising entire Bengal and parts of present-day Bihar and Orissa ...

'Mahabalipuram has more Naga connections. There's a huge bas-relief on rock, with a Naga wearing a crown surrounded by a seven-fold hood ...

'Tanjore is a Chola bastion and my assistant told me there is evidence that the Cholas, along with the Cheras and the Pandyas, the three most powerful Dravida peoples of South India, were all Nagas who moved from Bengal ...

'The central square of the roof of the hall or the mandapa of the eighth-century Virupaksha Temple at Pattadakal is filled by a great coiled Nagaraja, the Naga King with five hoods. He is protected by a chhattra ... Two naginis, female snakes with triple hoods, intertwined with his tail.'

As Afsar spoke, Kratu could feel that she had again become absent-minded.

'What's bothering you?' he asked her directly, without any pretense.

'Kratu, I'm wondering why someone would even attempt at inserting the name of Agra fraudulently.'

'Are you sure this is a deceit? We may not know, but there could have been something very important in Agra in the ancient past, something that has been erased with time. Ajanta was lost in the jungles for thousands of years. There have been reports that the Taj Mahal was built on the foundations of a much older Shiva temple.'

'*That's what makes me suspicious*,' Afsar got up from the chair. 'I'm very confident Agra has no Buddhist or Naga connection, like any of the other places in our list. The grand dagaba erected by Kanishka 2,000 years ago in Peshawar no longer exists, but we know of it, we've heard about it from multiple sources. We haven't heard of anything like that about Agra. Putting Agra in the same league as the other places seems to me like a sinister plan to create a credible and glorious pre-Islamic antiquity for the city which is best known for the Taj. *But why would anyone do that?*'

Kratu and Afsar stared at each other, their looks blank.

It wouldn't be long before they would find out the main intention behind the deceit.

Parush wouldn't be surprised then. Neither would be Indar, the prime minister of India.

☼

A few days later, Parush got a call from Rakesh in the morning, immediately after Christmas. He had just woken up and had put his hands on his mobile, checking the scrolling updates from across the world, culled from various classified and unclassified sources and sent to him regularly through a highly secured application in his phone. Kubha was still asleep, lying on the bed, curled like a "S" in a way that Parush had become so fond of. Since Kubha had virtually started living together with him, many subtle gestures and mannerisms of hers he hadn't noticed till now had captivated him a lot. He stared at her for some time, his attention drifting away from the news scrolling on the screen of his mobile. Rakesh's call jerked him out of his musing.

'Sir,' he said excitedly over the phone, 'I'm sending you the image of some pamphlets. The streets of Agra have been littered with them since early morning.'

'Pamphlets?'

Parush was perhaps not in the right mood to suddenly appreciate Rakesh's excitement. He didn't stretch the call, but did get an idea of what had happened. A few hundred thousand pamphlets had been strewn all over the roads of Agra, perhaps during the previous night. Everyone was shocked to see those in the morning. In no time, there was a commotion of sorts everywhere in Agra. By the time it was brought to the notice of the police, uneasiness had been already brewing up in various parts of the old city. The Ministry of Home Affairs was contemplating on imposing prohibitory orders in most parts of Agra. The areas around the Taj were slowly converting into a fortress, with more and more armed guards pouring in from wherever possible. Parush was quite impressed with the promptness shown by the government machinery in such a moment of sudden crisis.

Parush clicked on the image Rakesh had sent him. A flood of thoughts inundated his mind as he stared at the screen of his mobile for a long time, not exactly reading the English text of the bilingual pamphlet:

> *Hindustan, the Holy Land of the Hindus, has been the hiranyagarbha, the Golden Embryo, for many millennia. The Sacred Womb has given birth to the richest of the peoples, the grandest of the civilizations and the most profound of wisdom. But our Mother has been repeatedly raped by the unholy Musalmans and the Golden Womb has degenerated into a filthy abyss. It's time for abhigamana, the act of cleansing and smearing with cow dung the path that leads to the temple, the act of purifying the hiranyagarbha. And it should begin from here, the Abode of the Splendorous and Majestic Shiva, Tejo Mahalya, which was defecated and slyly converted into the Taj Mahal by the slanderer Shah Jahan. Shrinvantu vishve, amritasya putrah, arise, awake, oh the people of Bharata Varsha, the progeny of the hiranyagarbha, the children of the Immortal Bliss, listen to me, cleanse the Tejo Mahalaya of the excreta of the Musalmans.*

As though some inconsequential leader of a never-heard-of organization called Majlis-e Munazzim-e Muslimeen, The Council of the Organized Muslims, had had an inkling of what would happen in Agra, he had called for a meeting the same day at Nirmal, a small town in the Adilabad district of Telangana. When Parush saw the live coverage of the huge gathering at Nirmal, he wondered how and from where such a large crowd had suddenly assembled there. 'When a Musalman dies,' the leader thundered from a high rostrum, 'he is interred into the soil. He remains there, forever. And when a Hindu dies, he is burnt down. His ashes vanish in the thin air. We're here to stay forever and the Hindus will disappear, like the ashes. How dare they talk about cleansing the Taj Mahal? The day we all will become munazzim and muttahid, well organized and united by the laws of Islam, the day we all will possess the right mix of jasba and iman, the passion and faith in Islam, we will be the writers of the mustaqbil-e mulk, the history of this country.'

The TV channel suddenly switched from Nirmal to Delhi, where Rahul Gupta, the leader of the Opposition, began his press conference. 'As if the Babri episode wasn't enough,' Rahul roared, 'now they want to demolish the Taj Mahal. I would like to ask our prime minister that doesn't his party and its affiliates have a tacit support for everything we're seeing? My countrymen, do you think the lakhs of pamphlets could have been distributed in each and every street of Agra if not for the support from the government machinery?'

Parush's phone rang. He switched off the TV and greeted Indar over the phone.

'Do you have any doubt Rahul is organizing all these?' he asked Indar directly.

'Overestimating your enemy is also not a good thing,' Indar smiled. 'It's not always true that only the paranoids survive.

It's not Rahul. It's someone else, someone very powerful, very resourceful, very intelligent.'

Not far from Indar and Parush, Shamsur kept his specs down, rubbing his eyes, as he switched off the TV at his temporary residence in Delhi. He took a deep breath and smiled a bit, stretching his hands.

Parush got another call from Rakesh. 'Sir, already there are news of riots from many parts of the country.'

PART-IV

The Conference

(Morning, 5 January 2019. Agra and Calcutta)

It might have been quite a while, Kubha felt, since she had fallen asleep in the tunnel. As she lay semi-awake, in a kind of state of drunken stupor, the first thing that soothed her was a familiar smell. Some memories passed by her mind, like the passing landscape seen from a moving train. Like a slide show of pictures, played fast on the laptop, the moving landscape often evokes a sense of incomprehension, not because it changes fast, but, perhaps, for the inattentiveness of the leisurely passengers of the train. Kubha often felt the transition between sleep and waking up passed through such a phase of leisure when the surrounding sounds and smell are consciously kept incomprehensible. She was presently in such a transitional state when the familiar smell lingered too long to be ignored. That was when she realized it was the sonda smell of the soil after a splash of rain. She liked this smell so much that she always wanted to fill a small bottle with it, if at all it were possible. She often wondered why English hadn't had a word for such a wonderful thing before the term "petrichor" was coined only 50 years ago.

Haphazard broken images of the past, not in any particular chronology, flashed before her, momentarily, and faded away sooner than they had appeared.

Kubha saw a rainy evening at Khushawar, the ancestral place her mother hailed from. It was a pretty, little hamlet she had grown up thinking of as a fantasy land. In one of their unwinding vacations to Khushawar, when she had perhaps just crossed the age of total incomprehension, she had first fallen in love with the smell of the soil just after a sudden rain.

A few splashes of that rain-soaked evening flashed before her, like a sparkle. Kubha could almost smell the moist earth …

Kubha saw a night at the JNU caves, when the sudden rain after a long spell of hot and dull days had brought a soothing charm. She had been with Parush, at her favourite place in the university campus, in front of one of the caves, in the middle of the night. She had lain down on the uneven wet ground, resting her head against a rock, allowing the raindrops to fall on her face.

'Can you get me this smell of the soil,' she had asked Parush, 'whenever I want, whenever I feel lonely, whenever I would like to see you but you wouldn't be around?'

For a moment, Kubha felt, she was there, at the JNU caves, and it was raining. That smell of the soil soothed her.

Kubha couldn't be in that state of virtual reality for long. Suddenly, she felt the severe pain in her body, and the biting cold. She opened her eyes. A strong light fell on her eyes. Like a reflex, she pulled her hands up and guarded her eyes. She looked around. In no time, she knew where she was. More importantly, she realized what she had to do.

'I don't have time,' she reminded herself. *'I've to get out of this tunnel.'*

She didn't take more than a minute to reorient her thoughts and crystallize her strength, whatever she was left with. When she tried to get up, she realized she was shivering badly. She dragged herself on the almost-frozen, uneven rocky floor. She grabbed the torch and flashed it forward, lighting up the dark, narrow alley with an arched top, appearing like an arrow. She switched the torch off, immediately, realizing how precious each second of light could be for her presently. She allowed some time to get accustomed to the darkness. She pushed herself up slowly, pressing against the floor with one hand as she held the torch tightly with the other. Supporting herself against the plastered wall of the tunnel, bruising her bare back, she pulled herself up, finally.

Suddenly, horrid images from the previous day or two appeared in her mind, like a deluge, like an instant cloud burst, and wanted to sweep her away. She tried to fend herself off the gushing waters.

She closed her eyes and tried to meditate. She took some deep cleansing breaths, inhaling the stuffy air slowly through her nose and exhaling through her mouth. As she made her breaths normal, she closed her lips and repeated the word "strength", gently, every time she exhaled. Gradually, the rhythm of the utterance fell out of synch with her breaths as her mind wandered less, and her attention drifted less into other thoughts.

☼

Parush was taking a stroll in the lanes of Kachhpura, still lazy on a wintry morning. He was perplexed that the satellite calls were repeatedly originating from a dilapidated ruin which looked like a remnant of an old structure, the thick wall of a building with wide arched openings, built in typical Islamic style. It was not possible for anyone to sneak into that place during the night, especially when it was guarded by four men. He himself had inspected the place just a while ago. He was convinced that no one could hide anywhere around that place and make the satellite calls. It was also not possible that the GPS tracker was failing repeatedly and showing up the wrong location of the calls every time.

Parush had a gut feeling, somewhere around would be the Hasht Bihisht at Bagh-i Filhal, the names deciphered from an intercepted call the night Kubha had been kidnapped. Nearby, he repeatedly told himself, there must be a hasht bihisht, a Mughal-style building with a central big room surrounded by eight smaller ones, symbolizing the eight paradises of Islam.

He called Rakesh and asked if he had managed to get any information about Bagh-i Filhal, in the context of the present scheme of things.

'Let me talk to the superintending archaeologist once more,' Rakesh said.

When he had come quite close to the Yamuna, at a place from where the dargah and the mound of bricks behind it were visible clearly, Parush chanced upon a termite mound. It adjoined the last house of the neighbourhood, beyond which the river bank turned into a wasteland. Parush stopped walking and stared at the mound. He knew termites mostly constructed underground colonies, unlike the mounds that he was presently staring at.

Parush saw one of the four guards in casual clothes keeping an eye on the place. He came forward and greeted Parush. 'We've been here since last morning,' he said. 'Nothing is suspicious, sir.'

'You all can take a break for an hour. I would be here for some time.'

Parush moved slowly along the shore, absent-minded, coming quite close to the waters to avoid walking on the plastic waste the whole region was strewn with. When he reached the exact location from where the calls had been originating, barely a few tens of yard away from the dargah, he looked at the vestige of the erstwhile building. The battered and crumbling ruin presently didn't look much different from a huge termite mound. Standing in front of a mound that protruded from the ground, he thought, no one would have an inkling of the activities deep inside, underground.

Parush ran towards the broken structure, trampling over knee-deep plastic waste and suddenly fell into a pit, hitting its uneven bottom with a thud. His ankles pained instantly and he found himself waist-deep into the pit. As he tried to balance himself, he slid deeper inside, drowning more into the plastic. As he struggled to get a stable footing, he abruptly hit against something hard and fell down on his back. That was when he realized he had landed at the base of the derelict brick structure standing in the middle of a depression created around it, like a sort of moat, into which he had fallen. He could feel the ground under him was not hard. Rather, he felt, it was too soppy, filled with slush.

Already neck-deep inside plastic, Parush sunk deeper into the muck as he pressed against the slush with his hands and tried to get up. The stench of the plastic waste mixed with the wet mud suddenly made him feel uncomfortable. He dragged himself slowly towards the broken wall and tried to get up, holding onto a brick that protruded. Once he stood erect, he looked around him carefully. What had remained of the structure was a portion of a few metre-thick wall punctured by three vaulted gateways which opened only outward. It was not hard for Parush to guess that in its full glory, the wall and the arched forms with their hemispherical domed roofs would have made a sort of an ambulatory, a closed passage or aisle, running around a room.

Parush tried to walk towards the vaulted chamber when he suddenly slipped inside a deep pit. No sooner had he realized that he was sinking fast into a dark void, than his hands, both raised up, held onto the edge of something, like a reflex action. It took a few moments for him to realize that he was actually hanging from the edge of a deep and narrow trench. One of his hands slipped from the edge, and before he knew the other one would slip too and he would have a free fall, he supported himself by pressing his knees hard against the muddy wall of the trench. He released his hands and ascended slowly, like a lizard, crawling vertically, keeping his weight on the knees and augmenting the upward drag by pressing his hands against the slippery edge of the trench, as hard as possible. Once his elbows were out, he pushed them against the slippery ground and dragged himself out of the trench. He stood up carefully, not slipping again.

He tapped the ground a few times with his boot before taking any further step and walked cautiously around the broken wall. He smiled when he figured out there were more such camouflaged trenches. The trenches and the mud and the slush, he realized, were not natural. They were all cleverly put in place to ensure no one reached the broken wall, even if someone came close to it by sheer accident or chance.

Termites, he reminded himself, mostly constructed underground colonies …

'There's something inside,' he whispered a few times.

When he was looking for something to hold onto and climb up the pit he had fallen into, his phone rang. He pulled it out from the secured pocket of his trousers.

'Where are you, sir?' asked Rakesh, his trusted assistant. Parush could sense from Rakesh's voice that he was panting.

A few minutes later, when Rakesh pulled him out of the pit, the first thing Parush asked Rakesh was, 'Have they left for the conference?'

A perplexed Rakesh, Parush sensed, was eager to know how he had landed up in this mess. But Parush's reaction—he pretended as though nothing unusual had happened, and that his falling into a pit and coming out of it, totally covered with plastic and slush, was like anything else that could have presently happened to him—didn't give Rakesh a chance to ask anything about it.

'Not yet, sir,' responded Rakesh. 'Someone has called Afsar a few minutes back. He would be collecting the original manuscript from her. The moment he called, he was under our radar. A full team is following him in stealth mode. They can't run away from us.'

Parush had started walking fast towards the old white Ambassador parked on the road. Rakesh had to struggle to keep pace with him.

'Update me on everything,' Parush said, brushing off the slush from his shirt.

'Enough mobile jammers have been installed to cover the entire old building of the Asiatic Society and the adjoining areas of the Park Street. Anyone who enters the Asiatic Society can't leave till we allow them. Whatever happens inside remains inside. Nothing goes in. Nothing comes out.'

'Great,' Parush commended Rakesh, getting into the car.

☼

Afsar was ready with the packet which contained the dilapidated birch leaves of the Khushawar Manuscript. She would have to hand over the packet to someone who could arrive anytime soon. It was quite clear that without the original manuscript, whatever claims she would make at the WHA 2019 Calcutta Conference would not have any credibility, especially when one of the dual themes of the conference was Mistake, Misinterpretation and Monomania in World History.

It had so happened that a few weeks earlier, she had got a mail from an Ataulla Bayazitoz, the deputy dean of Teaching and Methodology at the Faculty of Philology in the St. Petersburg State University. Like a providential help, just on time, he had supplied her with the complete design of the Khushawari carpet, which was doubtless at the centre of three gruesome murders, including that of her father. The deciphering of the cryptic symbols of the carpet motif had become very essential to solving the motive behind the murders. But she was yet to recreate the complete motif authentically. That was when the sudden mail from the deputy dean and the subsequent unravelling of the obscure information buried in those carpet symbols appeared like a fluke.

Kratu, Afsar's husband, did ponder over the uncanny coincidence of receiving the mail, just at the right time, as though someone really wanted Afsar to solve the mystery. Afsar was not surprised though. Most historical discoveries, she asserted, appears to have happened by fluke.

A few days later, when Afsar got another mail, this time from Prof. Dr Berahitdin Albayrak, the president of the WHA, asking her if she would be interested in delivering a keynote speech on "Deciphering the Ancient Carpet Symbols" at the Calcutta Conference, Kratu was more suspicious than surprised.

'How do they know about the ancient carpet symbols?' he asked Afsar.

'Looks like,' Afsar replied, not very convincingly though, 'Somak Ajai would have presented his findings in the well-publicized keynote address, had he been alive. He was a good acquaintance of the president of the WHA. A day before he was murdered, he had talked to the president about his meeting with my father, the Khushawar Manuscript and also about me.'

'But how does the president know you too are working on the same thing?'

'He said he had heard a lot about me. He thought I would be aware of Somak's work on the carpet symbols. When he found out about Somak's death …'

'How did he get to know of Somak's death?' Kratu interrupted.

'His granddaughter used to manage his emails and social media interactions,' Afsar smiled. 'She has informed everyone who would send him mails. The president was constantly in touch with him …'

'Carry on,' Kratu interrupted her again. He was still not convinced that everything was natural. 'You were saying something. How did the president get the idea of asking you to speak at the conference?'

'He felt I could cover for Somak, in his absence. Somak had sent him an abstract of the speech. He thinks it could be a significant highlight of the conference which is being held for the first time in Asia. They have heavily promoted the event. I'm quite impressed with the list of the speakers they have lined up.'

Afsar accepted the invitation to deliver the inaugural keynote address at the conference. It was decided she would speak on the first day, on the main theme—Surviving Ancient Forms of Art in World History.

Two weeks later, just a few days before the conference—by then Afsar and Kratu had returned to Calcutta after a month-and-a-half-long stay in Pakistan—the secretary of the Executive Committee of the WHA sent a mail to Afsar with a brief that would go to the media at an upcoming press release about the conference. Afsar was quite agitated when she read the blurb about her keynote. Neither had anyone asked her for it, nor would she have ever approved of the same.

> *The late Professor Somak Ajai, in his seminal work spanning many decades, has ushered in an epoch in the annals of digital epigraphy and palaeography. Deciphering the cryptic signs and symbols, preserved for millennia in distinctive carpets, under the tutelage of his illustrious clan that shares the ancestry with the great Indian mathematician Aryabhata, he unravells the hitherto unheard-of aspects of Indian history, the most controversial of which is that of the forgotten temple of Agra that was eclipsed by the Taj Mahal. Renowned linguistic palaeontologist, Dr Afsar Fareedi, will do the honour of presenting Prof. Somak Ajai's fundamental works, which she has brought to a final closure, posthumously.*

By the time Afsar had received the invitation from the WHA, it was quite clear to her that the carpet design sent from St. Petersburg by the deputy dean couldn't but be a big deceit. She was surprised that someone of the stature of Somak Ajai had totally failed to see the fraudulence.

'How do you know Somak had indeed failed to see the deceit?' Kratu contradicted.

'What do you mean?' Afsar seemed to be quite irritated. 'How would they even know of the Agra connection of the rug, unless Somak himself had told them?'

'Why do you think your father and Somak were eliminated, if not for the direct threat that they would have easily caught the trickery?'

'*What do you mean*?' Afsar asked again, firmly, the folds in her forehead quite prominent and indicative of the irritability in her countenance.

'Don't you think the rug is being fraudulently used, stealthily, perhaps to create a strong case for a Hindu legacy of the Taj Mahal? I believe Somak didn't even have any idea of it, and the conspirators didn't want him to know of it either.'

Afsar's irritation subsided to a great extent. She was indeed getting the point Kratu was trying to make. She knew a similar claim—a Hindu legacy of the Taj Mahal—by the minions, the types of which had been lately raising their voices significantly, wouldn't evoke any sense of trustworthiness. But the same thing, coming from the WHA, would be very credible.

'On the basis of whatever we've learned,' Kratu continued with his argument, 'the only plausible reason behind the three murders seems to be the absolute need to silence the three upright people on *something* related to the rug Somak had been researching on. What could be that "something"?'

'*It could very well be the deceit*,' Afsar nodded her head in affirmation.

'Just think of the coincidences,' Kratu said. 'The initial promos of the conference don't have any reference to "the forgotten temple of Agra that was eclipsed by the Taj Mahal".

Then, last week, there was this mysterious event of the Agra pamphlets, wherein a very direct premise was being created for the demolition of the Taj; it was claimed without any ambiguity that the Taj Mahal is the defecated Tejo Mahalaya, a Shiva temple. Parush told me yesterday they are still clueless as to who was behind this; it could very well be the Hiranyagarbha Bharat, that deadly fanatic Hindu group who has eliminated so many people of my family over the past hundred years. Now, the sudden inclusion of the "forgotten temple of Agra" in the promos of the conference doesn't seem to me as a mere coincidence. It's, as though, a concerted effort is being made, at various levels, to legitimize a theory.'

It was exactly what Afsar had been thinking too. She kept quiet for a while, staring blankly at the screen of her laptop. Then, suddenly she looked up.

'So, are you saying the Hiranyagarbha Bharat is behind the triple murders?' she asked, the frowns in her face divulging her suspicion and surprise in no indirect way. 'Isn't it some fanatic group affiliated to the Islamic State? I believe that's the conclusion Parush thinks everything is leading to.'

'That's the most confusing thing,' Kratu conceded.

Afsar replied to the mail she had got from the secretary of the Executive Committee of the WHA, articulating the seriousness of her concerns about the real intent and agenda of the organizers of the conference, as directly as possible, without mincing any word.

'I can be a part of the conference,' she wrote, 'only if all the references to the "forgotten temple of Agra" are removed from all the promos and abstracts, and if I'm allowed to speak on the theme Mistake, Misinterpretation and Monomania in World History. I've very credible proof that the whole theory about the "forgotten temple of Agra", built upon the interpretation of the symbols and signs of one of our carpets, is a big deceit …'

As Afsar typed the mail, Kratu called Parush. 'Can you check the background of the organizers of the conference?' he asked, giving him the précised context.

Parush called back in the evening. 'Dr Berahitdin Albayrak,' he informed, 'the president of the WHA, is the head of the Department of Linguistics at the Ankara University. He has an impeccable reputation in the university and is very popular, both among the professors and the students. All the other members of the Executive Committee of the WHA are equally reputed. There's nothing suspicious about anyone. The WHA conferences have become quite popular and prestigious over the years. This is the first time they have organized an Asian edition of it. It is being very well covered in the media. It has got a good traction from the academia too. But …' he paused, 'there are some interesting connections.'

'Interesting connections?'

'Berahitdin is well connected to Ataulla Bayazitoz, the deputy dean of Teaching and Methodology at the Faculty of Philology in the St. Petersburg State University …'

'Ataulla?' Kratu shrieked.

'It's the same Ataulla who has been under our surveillance since he sent that mail to Afsar with the design of the rug …' Parush paused for a while, perhaps allowing Kratu some time to assimilate and arrange everything in the right perspective. It was, indeed, mysterious that all the connections and coincidences, which apparently appeared quite natural, were somehow linked either to Somak or to the rug which was at the centre of everything.

'There's something more,' Parush said. 'I don't think you know Somak Ajai's research assistant, Sanjeev Raina had recently got a good position at the Ankara University under the same Berahitdin. Very suspiciously, Sanjeev went missing soon after he had landed in Turkey. The Turkey Police hasn't yet traced him; it's been more than two months since he has gone missing.'

'Really?' Kratu was surprised.

'Now that could have been an unrelated incident or rather a mere coincidence. But what's intriguing is that the liaisoning for Sanjeev's job at the Ankara University was done by a professor from JNU, Muhammad Basha. *Basha is on our radar.* He has been spotted a few times in the company of Shamsur Ali ...'

'Who's Shamsur Ali?' Kratu asked, interrupting Parush. 'Is he the same person you talked about, who's a darling of the Opposition parties, especially Rahul Gupta?'

'Yes, that's true. I haven't told you everything. He is, no doubt, a kingpin, involved in too many suspicious things and perhaps, linked to the triple murders too, in some way.'

'Why are you not arresting him?'

'It's not that easy,' Parush paused.

Kratu realized, presently Parush didn't want to divulge anything more about Shamsur.

'On one hand, the WHA can be indirectly connected to Shamsur, through Muhammad Basha,' Parush continued, 'and on the other, it seems to have a scathing agenda same as that of the Hiranyagarbha Bharat. Shamsur espouses the radical views of the Islamic State and the Hiranyagarbha Bharat, by construction, is just the opposite of that. If brought together, both would first kill each other, rather than collaborating on anything. I can't think of a common ground for them. *This has brought in a totally new dimension to the problem.*'

No sooner had Kratu completed the call with Parush, than Afsar came running to the living room.

'I think there's something fishy about the WHA,' she said to Kratu, throwing herself on the plush sofa. 'The president himself had called me and apologized for everything. He will send me the modified text by tonight. He assured me he would set things right in tomorrow's press conference. When I asked where they had got the previous content from, he claimed that was what Somak had sent them.'

'In the overall scheme of things, such a scenario is absolutely impossible,' Kratu said. 'Either the president is lying blatantly, or he has been tricked into saying this.'

A day later, when Afsar and Kratu were having dinner, Afsar's mobile rang. It displayed an international number with the country code 284. The caller identification application in her phone identified the call to have originated from the British Virgin Islands.

'Dr Fareedi, we would advise you to stay away from the WHA conference,' said an unknown voice curtly over the phone, without the exchange of any pleasantries. 'You've no business slandering someone who is dead.'

'Who the hell are you?' shouted Afsar.

'Who we are is of no relevance to you, Dr Fareedi,' came the firm response. 'This is for your own good that we repeat again: *we ask you to stay away from the conference*. And we also ask you to give us the original manuscript your father had given you.'

'How do you know about the manuscript?'

The phone went silent. When Afsar tried calling back on the number, she figured out it was bogus.

Afsar called Parush immediately. 'What should we do now?' she asked him.

Given the fact that the press release earlier the same day had been extensively carried on the electronic media, Parush argued, there was no strong reason to suspect that the WHA had leaked the latest information about Afsar's keynote address. 'Let us wait for some time,' he suggested. 'Let them call you again.'

The second call did come, a day before the conference, in the morning, not to Afsar, but to Kratu.

'Is it Mr Kratu Sen?' someone asked in English.

'Yes,' replied Kratu.

'*Your daughter is in safe hands. Don't worry. We'll take good care of her as long as you agree to listen to us.*'

The call dropped.

The turn of events over the next one day would have forced Afsar and Kratu to, indeed, listen to the callers, if not for Kubha's cryptic message: '*Do not listen to them*'.

Presently, Afsar and Kratu were counting every passing moment, awaiting the conference to commence. Parush had a plan which he had explained in details when he had called them sometime back and insisted they follow it, blindly. 'Do exactly as I say. Trust me,' he had assured, 'you know, *I'll save Kubha, at any cost*, come what may.'

Someone would come soon to Afsar's house in Calcutta and collect the dilapidated birch leaves of the Khushawar Manuscript. She was supposed to hand it over to the unknown person.

☼

The white Ambassador Parush had got into a few minutes ago, after being rescued by Rakesh from the pit he had fallen into, reached the constable's house in Kachhpura. Parush realized he was shivering badly, being covered with the icy sludge. Rakesh took him inside the house, trying best to avoid anyone else getting curious about what had happened.

Once inside the house, Parush asked Rakesh, 'By the way, why did you call me some time back?'

Finding Parush in the pit, Rakesh had totally forgotten to inform him why he had called him. Presently, he thanked God that he had indeed called, for Parush would have otherwise had a really tough time getting out of the pit.

'Sir, Mohit Sharma, the superintending archaeologist of the Agra Circle of the ASI had called me,' Rakesh said, as Parush proceeded towards the bathroom. 'He says he has some information about the Bagh-i Filhal. I've asked him to come here. He is already on his way. It's nine o'clock now. He'll reach here in 15 minutes.'

Bagh-i Aqsa-i Filhal

(9:00–10:00 am, 5 January 2019. Agra and Calcutta)

Mohit Sharma, the superintending archaeologist of the Agra Circle of the ASI had a short structure, most of which was covered with various forms of warm clothing when he appeared at the constable's house, a little after nine o'clock in the morning. Parush had already cleaned himself and got into the constable's clothes. Wrapped in a thick, coarse shawl, he sat in front of Mohit in the small living room. Rakesh sat on a stool beside him.

'What have you figured out about the Bagh-i Filhal?' Parush asked directly, immediately after Rakesh had introduced him to Mohit.

'Since the time Rakesh told me about the Bagh-i Filhal,' Mohit said, 'I've been wondering where I have heard about it. The whole of yesterday I was restless. Finally, early this morning, I remembered someone had come to me a few years back. He sought my help in creating a digital database of all the old manuscripts lying unaccounted in private possessions in the various homes in Agra.'

The ASI had been aware of such manuscripts for more than 150 years, said Mohit. A report on Agra dating back to the 1870s, prepared under the superintendence of Major General A. Cunningham, the former director general of the ASI, had talked about many such manuscripts, which were actually bogus.

'That was the reason I didn't take much interest in digitizing the manuscripts,' Mohit said. 'But the person was relentless. I knew Daulat Parwar had in his possession many such manuscripts, written mainly in Persian. I had myself checked some of them and figured out that they were not original and that they were mostly bad copies of others' works. I sent the person to Daulat … '

'Is it the same Daulat,' Parush interrupted, 'who has been missing for the past few days and who seems to know of every old building in Agra?'

'Yes, it's the same Daulat. His family has been working for the ASI since many generations. I sent the person to him and a few days later, he came running to me. He claimed he had found a few couplets in one of Daulat's manuscripts which referred to a hidden underground tunnel that ran along the Yamuna. There have been so many spurious claims of hidden tunnels from the Mughal era that I couldn't but laugh. I told him the ASI hadn't yet come across any such tunnel. Nevertheless, he worked diligently for a few months. Before leaving Agra, he handed over to me all the manuscripts he had collected, along with a searchable digital database of the same. Later, he translated a few couplets from some of the manuscripts to English, from the original Persian, and emailed them to me. The term "Bagh-i Filhal" was there in one of the couplets which talked about the underground tunnel.'

'How did Daulat get those manuscripts?' Parush asked.

'He claims they were written by his ancestors,' said Mohit.

'Did you by any chance check with him if he knew of the underground tunnel?'

'He appeared quite tightlipped about it. I felt he was reluctant to talk about it. Given his knowledge about old buildings in Agra, I would have done something had he told he knew of it. I kept the manuscripts in our archive. No one has asked for them in the past few years, till this morning when I wanted to see them. I was surprised to see they are all gone.'

'What do you mean?' Parush sat erect.

'Yes, the original manuscripts are all gone. But I've the digital copies of the same though.'

'How often do things go missing from the ASI archive?' Parush asked.

'It's very rare. I didn't get the time to probe into it. I wanted to check the original Persian couplets in the manuscripts. Thank God, I still have the scanned copies. I feel I should have given more attention to them.'

'Why do you say so?'

'I can't say anything about the underground tunnel, but the other things mentioned there are quite authentic, though very cryptic. Perhaps, someone wanted to say something in such a way as to keep it out of reach of the common people. This very aspect of conveying something in a veiled way, maintaining a high degree of vagueness, makes me think it was perhaps a conscious effort to keep the information about the underground tunnel secretive.'

Mohit had already opened the lid of his laptop. He turned the laptop towards Parush. 'This is the English translation of the couplets I was talking about,' he said. 'The term "Bagh-i Filhal" appears as "Bagh-i Aqsa-i Filhal", which has been quite correctly translated as the Park Far and Sudden … ' He read out:

Here he'd created one of Kabul's grand gardens:
The first having made as the "Park Far and Sudden" …

☼

Afsar received the call she had been eagerly awaiting for. She took the packet and came out of her house. A car was parked on the road outside. She opened the iron gate on the boundary wall. She could clearly see the person seated in the back seat of the car, by the window. He had very normal looks, the sort which could very well mix in the crowd without attracting the attention of anyone. As Afsar came close to the car, the glass window rolled down. The person stretched his hand out of the window. Afsar placed the packet on his hand. He took the packet inside and opened the cover to peep into it. He would have surely noticed the delicate fragments of the birch leaves of the Khushawar Manuscript. He kept the packet beside him. The car started moving, leaving behind a perplexed Afsar standing at the gate, speechless.

The person inside the car wouldn't have noticed someone kick-started a ramshackle scooter, a little ahead of him, the moment he had left Afsar's house. He wouldn't have realized too, that he was being tailgated, at a distance, by an auto-rickshaw which had been idling in the road for quite some time. As the car moved slowly along the busy Diamond Harbor Road in South Calcutta, the auto-rickshaw stopped at multiple places, like any other auto would do, and every time, someone got in or out. There was no reason for the person in the car to know that each of the passengers getting in and out of the auto was actually a resourceful sleuth in plain dress.

Back home, Afsar was waiting for someone else to arrive anytime soon. Close to nine o'clock, there was a sound of the opening of the iron gate. Afsar stayed inside. A mid-aged lady, who looked very much like a maid servant, rang the bell of Afsar's house. Kratu opened the door and allowed her in. Once inside the house, she removed the 3D-printed resin mask from her face. In no time, she fitted the same mask on Afsar's face and made her up to look exactly like the woman who had entered the house a few minutes back. Half an hour later, when Afsar left her house, someone keeping an eye on the house from a taxi parked nearby would have, for sure, mistaken her for the maid servant. Someone keeping an eye on him didn't fail to notice that he made a phone call.

As Afsar waited at the iron gate, an auto with just one empty seat passed by. She shouted at the auto and it stopped. She ran a bit and got into it. Once inside the auto, one of the two other ladies in the back seat spoke to her in hushed voice. 'Don't worry,' the lady assured her, 'our people are everywhere. Everything is under control. You just do whatever you've been told.'

The car with the person who had the Khushawar Manuscript reached 1 Park Street and stopped in front of the old building of the Asiatic Society. He got down from the car and walked into the 200-year-old heritage building, the venue for the WHA 2019 Calcutta Conference. He knew that Afsar wouldn't attend the conference but still, he had been asked to attend the same. He wouldn't have realized that the moment he had entered the old building his mobile phone had stopped working; the entire area was heavily covered with mobile jammers.

Afsar arrived at the same place close to 10 in the morning. Her keynote address was scheduled at ten o'clock. She directly walked into the rest room and removed the mask. She also removed the sari, revealing the formal dress she had worn underneath. When it was time, she walked into the main hall on the ground floor and directly went to the podium.

'I'm Afsar, Afsar Fareedi,' she introduced herself to a hefty person whose badge read "Dr Berahitdin Albayrak, president, WHA". She might not have realized that Berahitdin was suddenly rubbing his forehead, a little too frequently, with the tips of the fingers of his left hand. Afsar would have totally ignored such an action, while Berahitdin shook the other hand with her, but few others in the audience, who had known him from before, knew he was nervous. Afsar exchanged pleasantries with him and enquired about a few common acquaintances she hadn't heard about for a long time.

In a few minutes, the president took the centre stage. 'The late Professor Somak Ajai,' he started speaking, 'in his seminal work spanning many decades, has ushered in an epoch in the annals of digital epigraphy and palaeography …

'Renowned linguistic palaeontologist, Dr Afsar Fareedi, will do the honour of presenting Prof. Somak Ajai's fundamental works, which she has brought to a final closure, posthumously.'

As Afsar stood behind the podium, three people in the audience stared at each other. One of them, the one who had collected the manuscript from Afsar, tried to make a call in haste, but realized immediately there was no signal. He wanted to run out of the hall. Apart from the two other he had exchanged glances with a moment back, no one else in the conference noticed someone who had suddenly run towards the gate was swiftly frisked away by three security men.

'One of the themes this year,' Afsar began her keynote address, 'is Mistake, Misinterpretation and Monomania in World History. Here, I stand before you to talk about one of the worst examples of the 3Ms in World History: Mistake, Misinterpretation and Monomania ...'

☼

'T'is the place where, on a victorious new year,
Fell the "Light of Faith", shimmering and clear.

Many years ago the glorious emperor,
Inspired by the charm of the "Heaven of the World",

Here he'd created one of Kabul's grand gardens:
The first having made as the "Park Far and Sudden" ...

'The English translation appears cryptic,' said Mohit Sharma, the superintending archaeologist, once Parush looked up from the laptop, 'but a close look at the original Persian couplets made things very clear.'

"Nur-i Din", translated as the Light of Faith, Mohit said, is the Persian form of Jahangir's honourific title Nur-ud-Din. In the context of the "grand gardens" of the couplets, Nur-i Din couldn't but be the present Aram Bagh, one of the oldest surviving riverfront gardens in Agra. The original name of Aram Bagh, also known as Ram Bagh, was Bagh-i Nur Afshan, the Garden of the Sparkling Light. The component "nur", light, alludes to Jahangir's title Nur-ud-Din, and that of his wife, Nur Jahan, the Light of the World.

'The garden was constructed by Nur Jahan,' Mohit said, 'probably on the foundations of an even older garden built by Babur. In his autobiography, Jahangir specifically mentions a ceremonial visit to this garden after his conquest of the Kangra Fort. It's also mentioned that his wife celebrated Nauroz, the Persian New Year, at the same place, later that month …

'This is the place where the Glorious Emperor, inspired by the charm of Bihisht-i Dunya, the Heaven of the World, had built one of Kabul's grand gardens.'

'What's the significance of Kabul?' Parush asked.

'This is again an interesting trivia we can gather from Babur's autobiography. Once settled in Hindustan, he was missing the gardens of Samarqand, which was often allegorically referred to in the Persian literature as Bihisht-i Dunya, the Heaven of the World. He wanted to recreate those beautiful terraced gardens with flowing waters in Agra, on the Yamuna riverfront. He did construct many gardens on the left side of the Yamuna river. We learnt from various sources that people would often refer to that side of the river as Kabul, the other city he had decorated with similar gardens …'

'What about the Bagh-i Filhal?' Parush interrupted Mohit.

'Yes, I was leading to that,' Mohit assured a visibly restless Parush. 'The third couplet says the first garden constructed by the Glorious Emperor was the Bagh-i Aqsa-i Filhal, which literally means the Garden Far and Sudden. The word "filhal" may mean both temporary and sudden.' Mohit paused and looked around. 'I can't say if I've heard of a Bagh-i Filhal, but I'm aware of an Achanak Bagh, which literally means the Sudden Garden, and the site of the garden and a palace within its premise is not far from where we are sitting …'

'Does anything exist of that any more?' Parush asked, getting up abruptly. He stood in front of Mohit, his hands forming triangles at his waist.

'Very little of it exists today,' Mohit sighed. 'It's not even in the ASI's list of protected monuments and we don't have funds to restore the ruins at all. Daulat had once taken me there. That was one of the many ruins he would visit regularly and take care of, in whatsoever ways possible to him, without any support from anyone. He would say something about this place which I suddenly find very relevant …'

'What's that?'

'He would say "*everything started from here …*"'

'What's the relevance?' Parush put his hands on his head and played the fingers through his hair. He looked at Rakesh who was very well aware of this particular body language of Parush which meant he was getting irritated now.

'There's nothing called the Achanak Bagh now, but the old ASI report on Agra dated 1874 and prepared by someone called A.C.L. Carlleyle refers to this area as the Achanak Bagh. Carlleyle believes it was the first place where Babur would have encamped after his arrival at Agra. He would have then constructed here a temporary palace and a garden, in haste. He would have had elaborate plans of building grander palaces and gardens later, leisurely. That's what, Carlleyle argues, is the origin of the Achanak Bagh, the Sudden Garden, the name which was still in vogue during his time. The Bagh-i Aqsa-i Filhal, the Garden Far and Sudden is, doubtless, the more literary and Persian term for the Achanak Bag. I couldn't connect the two when I had heard about the Bagh-i Aqsa-i Filhal a few years back.'

Parush sat down on the decrepit sofa covered with an old and overused bedcover. He pulled the laptop on his lap and stared at the screen that had the English translation of the couplets Mohit had been talking about. He read out the last two couplets:

> *With eight moon-seats 'round a domed house small,*
> *On the other side of earth that a "Sword of Flesh" they call,*
>
> *Through the apex of which runs the "Safety Street Down",*
> *Joining the two ends of two "Sparkling Garden-Crowns".*

'Safety Street Down,' Parush uttered the words discretely, staring at Mohit. 'Does that mean a tunnel?'

'The Persian term is "kucha-i salamat",' Mohit said, 'which literally means a narrow passage for safety.' This particular term, he explained, can also be used in the context of a military entrenchment. In the overall scheme of things, kucha-i salamat is indeed an underground tunnel.

Mohit took his laptop and opened another file. 'Now consider this,' he said, looking at the laptop. 'This is what Carlleyle had to say of this place, some 150 years ago … ' He read out:

> *A wall, having a tower at each of the four corners, of which the remains of two are still standing at the river side … At the centre of the river frontage, on a square raised mound, the traces of the walls of a large building, or palace …*

Parush got up and ran out of the house, Rakesh and Mohit following him, perplexed.

'I know what you're talking about …' Parush had already got into the driver's seat of the Ambassador parked in the narrow, dingy lane in front of the house. Rakesh took the front seat beside Parush, gesturing Mohit to get into the car too. Mohit silently followed the instruction, keeping the laptop beside him, on the back seat of the car.

☼

When Kubha opened her eyes, she was calm. She felt she was no longer restless. Her thoughts were no longer drifting. She had acclimatized herself to the darkness around her. She felt confident. She had heard people say meditation did wonder in times of crisis. Presently, no one perhaps would know that better than her. She switched on the torch for a few seconds and lit the tunnel in front of her. She took a deep breath and started walking, slowly, through the darkness. She held the torch in one hand and used the other to drag it against the wall of the tunnel, thus maintaining her direction forward.

Kubha would have walked for a good 10–15 minutes when she suddenly felt, with her hand, that she had come to a dead end. Immediately, she switched on the torch. She was pleasantly surprised to find what she had thought of as a wall was, in fact, a low and narrow archway punctured into a thick wall. She bent down and passed through the arch, entering into a small, roundish room. As she looked around the room, the oval beam of the light emanating from the torch sweeping its wall, she realized the room was actually octagonal, not round. Suddenly, she felt excited. She counted the eight identical arched gateways of the room, and figured out the third one to her left. She recalled the 313 rule the mysterious person had taught her during her captivity.

Entering into an octagonal room with eight doors, she reminded herself, *she should exit from the door number "3" to her left and go straight.* Then, entering into the room number "3", she should leave "1" door to the right and exit from the next. Finally, when she would again arrive at the room number "3", she should exit again through the door number "3", to the left. One wrong exit, the person had warned, and she would be lost forever in the intricate mesh of the interconnected identical rooms.

Kubha recounted the doors a few more times and exited from the one which she was sure was the third one to her left. Passing through a narrow corridor, she entered into a square room, with four identical doors. She instantly realized the room was very similar to the one she had spent a good amount of time in, in the recent past. She tried to recall if the person had mentioned anything about a square room. All he had talked, she conjured, was about octagonal rooms. She looked around and leaned against the wall, shutting her eyes, trying to think about each and everything the person had told her. '*Go straight, never taking any left or right till you enter into the third octagonal room.*' Wasn't that what the person had said? Didn't it imply that she should discount anything she passed by, unless it was an octagonal room? She pointed the torch to the door opposite to the one she had entered through. The light illuminated a continuous pathway, passing through a series of doors, all in a straight line. She resumed her walk. She exited from the square room, in the direction of the light, passing through another narrow passage and entering into an exactly similar octagonal room she had passed by just a while ago. She felt confident. She counted "1" in her head. She walked straight, exiting the octagonal room through the door directly opposite to the one she had entered it through. She crossed a narrow aisle, identical to the ones she had by now encountered twice, and appeared inside another octagonal room, which she counted as "2". By now, she was confident enough that she would be next encountering the third octagonal room.

Staring at the identical eight doors of the room number "2", Kubha remembered something Parush had taught her a long time back, about probability, when she had been in high school. Had she not known which door to exit from in the first octagonal room, the probability of her choosing the right one in the first attempt would have been one-eighth. Subsequently, her chance of identifying the right way out through one of the four doors in the square room would have been only one in 32, and that in the room number "2" a meagre one in 256. She couldn't but thank that unknown person, who had taught her the 313 rule. Presently, he appeared to her like a messiah, without whose help her chance of coming out of the bhulbhulaiya would have been zero.

Not much later, Kubha was back into the tunnel, emerging out of the mesh. She switched off the torch and walked in the dark.

☼

'The remains of one of the two corner towers mentioned by Carlleyle exist till today, doesn't it?' Parush asked Mohit, turning back. He pressed the gas pedal of the old Ambassador harder than it had been perhaps built to endure, jerking the ramshackle vehicle into an unsteady motion. Visible signs of surprise appeared on Mohit's roundish face, peeping out of the monkey cap he had covered his head with. 'And little away from the ruins of the tower,' Parush added, even before Mohit could respond, 'the mound is still there.'

The car cut through the few people and cycles in the clumsy lanes, passing through the sleepy hamlet waking up lazily from the slumber of a chilly wintry morning.

'Daulat had shown me the tower and the mound,' Mohit said. 'There's now a small dargah in front of the mound, I believe.'

Parush had already come quite close to the river, beyond which the narrow road vanished in the piles of plastic waste. He got out of the car and ran in the direction of the pit he had fallen into sometime back. The four guards, who had returned to their duties already, came running towards Parush. He gestured them to be at ease.

'This is indeed the southwestern tower of the garden-palace complex,' Mohit said, pointing to the dilapidated wall they were approaching fast. 'It was perhaps a multi-storied watch tower. What we see today is the remnants of the outer wall of the structure.'

The four sides of the ground floor of the octagonal tower, he explained, which were visible from the river side, had interconnected vaulted rooms with domed roofs and arched openings in the front. 'One of the arches is recognizable even today,' he pointed to the gap in the thick broken wall that stood in front of them. 'There was a pish-taq, a rectangular frame, around each of the arched openings.'

As Parush looked around, at the gaping hole in the wall, the pit he had fallen into and the mound close by, he had a strong feeling that the kucha-i salamat was, indeed, an underground tunnel and that the access to it lay somewhere hidden inside the ruins of the tower.

'There was something about a Sword of Flesh,' Parush recalled. 'What's the significance of that?'

'I should get the laptop,' Mohit said, turning back.

'I'll get it.' Rakesh ran towards the car and got it in no time. He opened the lid and held the laptop in front of Mohit.

'The Yamuna takes a sharp U-turn near the Agra Fort,' Mohit said, browsing through a folder in the laptop. 'If you see the map of the entire region bounded by the U-shaped river, it actually looks like a tongue, which in Persian is allegorically referred to as tegh-i goshtini, a Sword of Flesh.' He had already clicked on an image. He turned the laptop towards Parush. 'This is an old map from our archive showing some of the riverfront gardens since Babur's times. I've added the two gardens—the Aram Bagh and the Achanak Bagh.'

These two gardens, Mohit said, as Parush studied the map, were among the first to have been built by Babur. They could be rightly called the Sparkling Crowns, Munauwara Afsari. They lay on the two sides of the tongue-shaped land bounded by the Yamuna river. The apex or the tip of the zamin-i tegh-i goshtini, marked by a star-sign in the map, lay to the east of the Agra Fort.

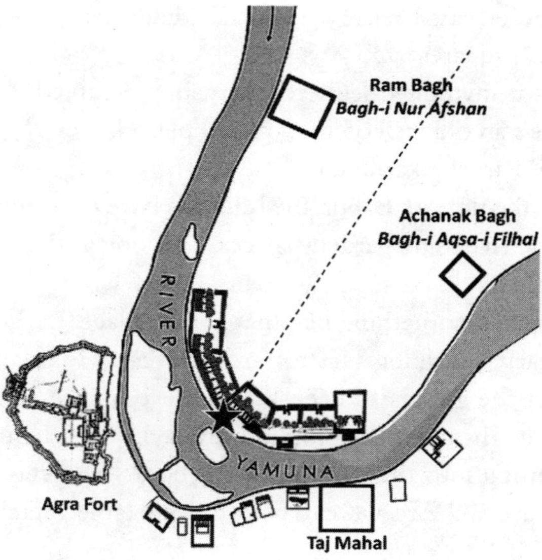

'They lay on the two sides of the tongue-shaped land bounded by the Yamuna river.'

'The kucha-i salamat connects the two gardens on the two sides of the tongue-shaped land and passes through its apex,' Parush looked up at Mohit.

'Through the apex of which runs the "Safety Street Down",' Mohit repeated the last couplet, 'Joining the two ends of two "Sparkling Garden-Crowns".'

'Is there anything at the apex?' Parush asked.

'That entire region is where Babur had constructed a garden known as the Chahar Bagh or the Bagh-i Hasht Bihisht. Chahar is four, the Hindi "char", and "hasht" is eight, the symbol of paradise in Islam. Babur introduced the concept of constructing the river-side gardens comprising symmetrical blocks of four quadrants each. The gardens were divided and subdivided into multiples of four and eight by cross axial walkways called khiyaban, or water channels, nahr. The gardens don't exist today, but most of the walkways have survived. If you go around, you can see the elevated narrow paths dividing this entire area into symmetrical squares …'

'Is there anything else there?' Parush interrupted.

'There's an old well of the Mughal period.'

'Well?' Parush exclaimed.

'Since the time of Babur, the Mughals have constructed many wells in the river-side garden-palaces. The one at the apex is the best preserved.'

'I expected something like that at that place. Let's go there,' Parush started walking fast towards the car. He asked Rakesh to instruct the guards to keep a closer eye on the ruins of the Achanak Bagh and the adjoining areas, in stealth mode. Just before getting into the car, he turned back. 'You stay back,' he ordered Rakesh. 'Are we carrying the portable metal detector with us?'

'Yes, sir,' Rakesh confirmed. 'We've procured the latest Pulse Induction detector. I have it in my tool kit.'

'How far can you detect a metal with it?'

'It can detect correctly within 50 metres.'

'Use the maximum power to generate the strongest possible current pulse. I've a gut feeling, there's a repeater, somewhere inside the debris of the ruins of the watch tower. The repeater is interacting with the satellite phone which, I'm sure, is located somewhere else. Locate the repeater. Use the detector from a distance. Don't go too close to the pit I'd fallen into. It's a dangerous death trap.'

Parush turned back again, gesturing Mohit to get inside the car. 'One more thing,' he moved closer to Rakesh and whispered. 'Scan the entire region. You'll find interesting things below.'

☼

As Parush was manoeuvring the car through the narrow alleys of Kachhpura, he got a call from Rakesh. 'All private channels have been denied permission to cover the conference,' he informed. 'Apart from the few DD staff, there wouldn't be anyone else from the media.'

'Didn't the private media create any fuss?' Parush asked.

'Our people would have handled it well.'

'Make sure the news-story looks credible. *It shouldn't look fake.* Are you sure the DD staff will pull it off properly?'

'Don't worry, sir,' Rakesh assured, 'I've taken care of everything. The entire building will be sealed. No one can enter or leave once the conference starts. Mobiles will be jammed. Anything that happens inside can never go out of the four walls of the building. Whatever we broadcast through DD is what the world will know about the conference.'

Mount Kaushiki

(10:00–10:30 am, 5 January 2019. Calcutta and Agra)

To the south of the Naga Mountains is the nave of a northern region,
Where the Yakshini and the Naga goddesses dwell on the Mount Kaushiki.
Further south is the abode of Naga Nanda, where people come from faraway places,
To walk on the path created by the sublime Gotama Buddha.

Halfway through her keynote speech, during which Afsar had talked about the Aryabhata Clan and the cryptic symbols of the Khushawari rugs they had preserved for millennia, she projected a verse from the Kandy Manuscript on the screen.

'These four lines,' she revealed, 'hold the final key to the exposing of a very well-planned and immaculately executed fraud, with a sinister agenda behind it.'

Afsar had already introduced the concept of the Nava Varshas, the nine Naga Realms of the ancient Indian subcontinent, and their relevance in the context of one particular Khushawari rug, which was at the centre of the three murders. Presently, Afsar drew the attention of her startled audience to the Northern Region, mentioned in the verse. Her firm voice showed no signs of her shattered heart, bleeding for her daughter.

'Someone with a very perverse agenda,' she asserted, overcoming a heavy lump in her throat, 'has left no stone unturned to eradicate every trace of an original rug which depicted the Nava Varshas very authentically …

'The very idea behind the Nava Varshas is to celebrate the indigenousness of the Indian subcontinent, the cultural homogeneity of the autochthonous peoples, not divided by their ethnic and provincial diversities, but united by their common resilience to the external forces. A few millennia later, now we may not even discern each and every individual component of the bhumiputras, the real sons of the soil, but they are all around us, in ever newer garbs. Once we realize this very idea of Indianness, understanding the composition of the Nava Varshas will become very straightforward …

'The northern region, mentioned in the verse, is very likely Almora, the lone representative in the list from the Himalayas, whose association with the Naga peoples is, perhaps, the most conspicuous. The Naga Mountains could be either the Nanda Devi or the Nanga Parvat, two of the highest peaks of the Himalayas—the terms "nanda" and "nanga" both being common corruptions of "naga". But in the overall scheme of things, it's more likely to be the former. To the south of Nanda Devi is the Kashaya Hills, the horseshoe-shaped ridge of Almora, referred to in the Manas Khanda chapter of the *Skanda Purana*, one of the post-Vedic treatises of myths, legends and traditional lore from ancient India. The Kashaya Hills, we learn from the *Purana*s, is the site where Durga, the quintessential Indian Goddess of strength and power, took the form of Kaushiki and annihilated the demon, Shumbha. It's said that Durga, in her Kaushiki-avatar, derived the power from the kosha or the body of Parvati, the mythical daughter of Parvata, the mountain. The name Kaushiki has survived in the present-day Kosi river that flows through the Almora district. The Kaushiki Mountain of the manuscript is very likely the similar sounding Kashaya Hills. It is till date the home to temples dedicated to Yakshini and Nanda, the indigenous demi-goddesses of the mountains, who are worshipped by the local peoples as the various forms of Durga …

'The manuscript also talks about the "abode of Naga Nanda, where people come from faraway places". Naga Nanda is most likely the origin of the name Nalanda, which doesn't have any acceptable etymology otherwise. Nalanda was a famous university of international repute and an acclaimed Buddhist centre for many many years …

'What's interesting is that, the purely indigenous Yakshas and the Nagas have been everywhere in the Himalayas since many millennia, much anterior to the Aryans. They have survived till date in the various rituals and traditions of the mountains, often under the garb of later Hinduism and Buddhism. The Nagas have been everywhere else too, in each of the other eight countries of the Nava Varshas. The indigenous peoples of India are generically designated in the Khushawar and Kandy manuscripts as the Nagas, perhaps due to their predominance at some point of time in the ancient past. The basic premise of the Nava Varshas is, perhaps, the certainty in the belief that India was not colonized either by a few Aryans or Mongols or Europeans, but has been mostly an indigenous culture which has influenced anything external to such an extent as to preserve not much of the latter's original structure. If we take Hinduism as an Aryan import, it is also as much indigenous as are the rivers and the mountains and the peoples …

'This may be a matter of conjecture, or perhaps a thought overstretch. I've a strong feeling, the secretive way of depicting the Nava Varshas, through a totally new system of numerals, was the ingenuity of Aryabhata himself. At the core was perhaps the maverick's plan to encrypt an important message, and preserve for the future generations the rare wisdom that India doesn't belong exclusively to the Aryans or the Dravidians or the Hindus or the Muslims, but inclusively to all the bhumiputras, the real sons of the soil, the real Indians …

'The present-day Hindi heartland, a part of the North India, is seen as the epicentre of power since antiquity. Starting from Ayodhya, Kashi, Mathura, Vrindavan, Hastinapur and Kurukshetra of the epics, till the New Delhi of today, the whole of India is often believed to have been controlled by this region, which has now politically become a symbol of the Aryan hegemony the non-Brahmins and the large number of the backward castes in India often complain about. Such a thing is against the concept of the Nava Varshas and the Naga Realm.'

Afsar projected a map on the screen. 'Referring to this map,' Afsar argued, 'Almora fits very well into the definition of the Naga Realm. It's outside the doughnut hole, the Hindi heartland.

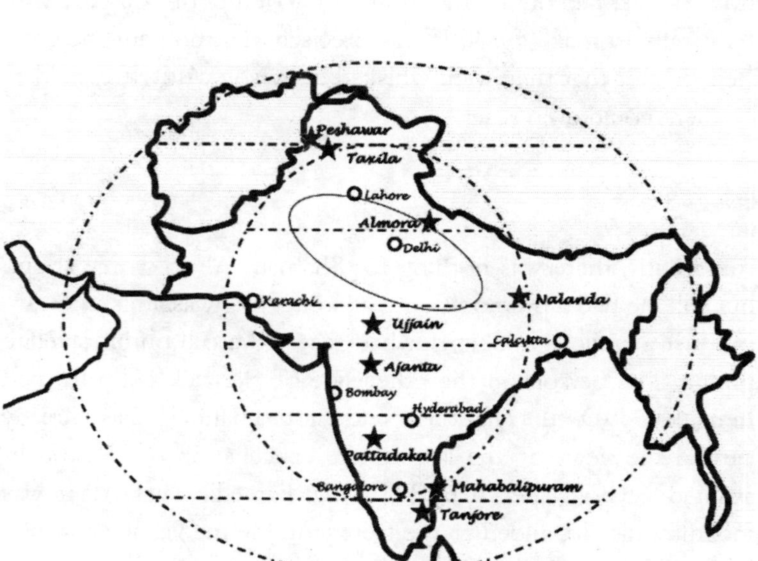

'Almora fits very well into the definition of the Naga Realm …'

But Agra is very much inside. Even without the Khushawar and Kandy manuscripts, which anyway make no reference to Agra, its inclusion in the list of the nine regions of the Naga Realm wouldn't have made any sense.'

☼

While Afsar had been delivering the speech, she wouldn't have noticed that the front chair where Dr Berahitdin Albayrak, the president of the WHA, had been seated was presently empty. She wouldn't have noticed that two more seats were empty too. It was also not possible for her to know that one of these two seats had been occupied by the same person who had collected the manuscript from her a little while ago.

It had so happened that Berahitdin, along with the other two, had stepped out of the room, not together of course, trying frantically to make a call. It was precisely the moment they had stepped out that they were whisked away so swiftly that neither of them could even react.

☼

Apparently, there was nothing for Shamsur Ali to worry about, but still, he had a premonition that something was amiss.

Just a while ago, Shamsur had received a call on his satellite phone. The person on the other side of the call had informed him that DD, the national television channel, had already carried the news of the last-minute cancellation of the much-awaited keynote speech by Dr Afsar Fareedi. That Afsar was incommunicado, added to the frenzy of the media, all of which had picked the story from DD in no time. The conference, especially the topic of Afsar's keynote speech, had been very closely followed by the media, both print and television. It was not though, that no one was surprised why such an event was suddenly getting so much coverage. Very few people would know how much money Shamsur had indirectly pumped into the entire machinery, towards the surrogate advertisements and promotions for the event. The transactions had been so smartly executed that even the most sophisticated system would fail to track the trail, which finally ended at Shamsur.

Sitting alone in one of the rooms of the underground hasht bihisht, just below the mound of bricks at the site of the old palace in Achanak Bagh, Shamsur took a stock of all the events in the recent past. He cursed himself for he had underestimated Afsar's wisdom and intelligence. No one had any idea that she had already figured out the fraud, till she sent that email to the secretary of the Executive Committee of the WHA, claiming she had very credible proof that the whole theory about the forgotten temple of Agra was a big deceit. That was when Shamsur had to make the plan, in haste, to kidnap Afsar's daughter, two days before the conference and blackmail her not to deliver the keynote speech.

Shamsur already had a backup plan and things were going on fine, as planned. Even today, nothing unprecedented had happened since the morning. The early morning video call to Afsar, revealing the gang rape of her daughter in gory details, had its expected result. A few hours later, his person collected from Afsar the original manuscript, without which, he knew, any of her claims would be baseless. Finally, as expected, Afsar *didn't* arrive at 1 Park Street for the conference.

It had so happened that Somak Ajai had himself talked about the manuscript and its connection to the Khushawari rugs to Dr Berahitdin Albayrak, the president of the WHA and the head of the Department of Linguistics at the Ankara University. He had also talked to Berahitdin about Faraz Fareedi's daughter, Afsar Fareedi, an eminent linguistic palaeontologist. Berahitdin was a key person from academia in Shamsur's network. The other key person in his network was Ataulla Bayazitoz, the deputy dean of Teaching and Methodology at the Faculty of Philology in the St. Petersburg State University. Ataulla knew Afsar and he spoke highly about her. It was he who came up with the idea of using Afsar as the medium to propagate the subtle message behind the symbols of the fake carpet in the academic world and perpetuate the theory of the forgotten temple of Agra. A massive campaign through pamphlets, followed by the endorsement of the theory by someone like Afsar Fareedi and the WHA, Ataulla had argued, would suddenly make the theory look very credible.

Moreover, Shamsur knew, the pamphlet-campaign Ataulla was talking about would serve another purpose. Much to the delight of Rahul Gupta, the leader of the Opposition, it would suddenly destabilize the entire country, out of the blue. Shamsur also knew that the Indian media and intelligentsia, much of which he already had control on in some way or the other, would put the blame, as usual, entirely on the prime minister and his Bharatiya Party. Eliminating Somak and the Sri Lankan professor he had taken help from in deciphering the symbols of the rug, had been imminent for a while, for it wouldn't be possible to introduce the fake carpet in their presence. But Shamsur decided to eliminate Faraz too. It was not clear how much Faraz knew of Somak's work and how much chance there would be for him to catch the fraud. *Shamsur didn't want to take any chance.* Ataulla came up with a plan to trick Faraz into falling into a trap. He sent an email to Faraz asking for a particular rug he would be interested in buying. He had once met a small-time Pakistani trader at the St. Petersburg Mosque who had eventually become his accomplice. Ataulla sent him to Khushawar to meet Faraz, posing as a rug dealer, as though he was acting as a go-between.

Along with the elimination of Somak and Faraz, all traces of the original carpet had to be erased, so that the fake one wouldn't have anything to be verified against. Both the unsuspecting old men were tricked into showing their entire collection of the carpets to Shamsur's men. Subsequently, the execution of the rest of the plan was almost a cakewalk. Shamsur was, indeed, impressed with Ataulla's resourcefulness. He patted himself for having decided to extend his tentacles into the world of academia. He had always believed eminent people from the academia would be of great help, especially to reach out to a wider and more literate audience and to add a factor of legitimacy to everything.

Presently, seated on a broken wooden chair and stretching his legs forward, Shamsur stared at the unevenly plastered wall of the square room, insufficiently lit by the white light emanating from the CFL bulb hanging from the domed roof. Something, seemingly as nondescript as which TV channel had first broken the news of the last-minute cancellation of Afsar's keynote speech, brought wrinkles on his forehead. It was not that DD didn't have any reason for showing interest in the conference, especially when all other private channels had been talking about it for quite some time now. But still, Shamsur himself couldn't justify why, he had a feeling there was indeed something behind DD's suddenly jumping into the foray. There was a strong reason why the private news channels had lately been abuzz with tidbits about a conference no one had ever heard about in this part of the world. They had been heftily paid for doing so, though not in a direct way that could raise any suspicion in anyone's minds. The national channel too had been approached for the same, but somehow nothing had worked out there. What had happened then, Shamsur pondered, that the same DD was now in the forefront, covering the conference? Something was amiss, he couldn't but think.

Shamsur felt restless. He got up from the chair and walked up and down in the small room.

☼

'*Monomania is an excessive mental preoccupation with one thing or one idea,*' Afsar said, slowly, stressing each word. 'World history is replete with instances of deliberate mistakes and misinterpretation of facts and figures, to fulfil a veiled agenda. The Nazis misinterpreted Aryan history to establish the myth of the racial supremacy of the Germans. The Communist Party of the Soviet Union attempted in many ways to control the telling of the history of their country. In India, most of the historians in the post-Independence era have been highly influenced by the leftist ideologies, and hence, the history they wrote smacks of monomania too. A few days back, a leader of the Majlis-e Munazzim-e Muslimeen claimed, the day all the Muslims of India would be well organized and united by the laws of Islam, they would be the writers of the mustaqbil-e mulk, the history of this country …

'Fraudulently inserting Agra in the list of the nine regions of the Naga Realm is also an example of monomania, and one of a very loathsome kind. It's another malevolent attempt at rewriting the history of Agra in a way as to perpetuate the very ridiculous theory that the Taj Mahal was actually a Shiva temple, known as the Tejo Mahalaya. Each place in the list is of extraordinary cultural and historical significance. Each place is enlisted as a UNESCO World Heritage Site too. But apart from Agra, every other place in the list belongs to the ancient and medieval eras. More importantly, each other place has a strong Naga connection, something that tells of an astounding achievement of the indigenous peoples of India, something that can't be called hegemonic or Brahmanical. Putting Agra in the same league as the other places seems to me like a sinister plan to create an incredible and glorious antiquity for the city which is best known for the Taj …

'Faraz Fareedi, my father, and Somak Ajai were both members of the Aryabhata Clan, and so have I been too, unknowingly, all my life. Given that we've been the true custodians of the Khushawari rugs for more than a millennia, it's perhaps not for no reason that my father and Somak had to lay their lives, in order to protect the sanctity of the rugs.'

☼

Parush couldn't drive fast through the narrow roads of Kachhpura, which had finally woken up from the slumber of the cold and misty morning. There was still a thin layer of fog, lingering over the river, even at 10:00 am. A few enthusiastic foreigner-visitors had already arrived at the Mehtab Bagh, a river-side garden constructed by Shah Jahan exactly opposite to the Taj Mahal, and perfectly symmetrical in dimension to that of the mausoleum, on the other side of the river. Skirting the western boundary of the garden, Parush drove the car along an unpaved road that ended abruptly in the sands of the river bank. Mohit asked Parush to turn right, into a cordoned off defense land. Parush showed his identity card to the man in green uniform and zoomed through the makeshift road, cutting through the river bank. As the car shook dangerously and skidded a few times on the sand, Mohit held on tightly to the window sill of the car. After a bumpy ride of a few hundred metres, Mohit asked Parush to stop the car. He got down from the car and started walking on the sand, Parush followed him. Soon they reached the point where, Parush was surprised to see, the river actually took a U-turn. Almost at the apex of the "U", stood a structure, which comprised a flight of stairs ending abruptly at a landing.

'There are 11 stairs,' said Mohit, as they came close to the structure. 'Humayun built it as an observatory. It's called Gyarah Sidi, the Eleven Stairs …'

Parush had already moved ahead. He was leaning over a broken roundish wall, quite high to be a parapet.

'That's the well, the Mughal Baoli,' Mohit said, catching up with him from behind. 'I told you, there were many in these river-side gardens. This one is the best preserved.'

Mohit didn't have to say that the broken wall had once been a part of the thick stone casing of the huge and dangerously deep well. The bare edge of well was mostly unguarded, suddenly falling vertically down by at least a hundred feet. The dark and dirty water, littered with plastic, cans, bottles and other paraphernalia of the insensitive visitors, shone from the depth like a piece of black metallic floor. From where Parush stood, at the edge of the well, he could clearly see two storeys of the typical Mughal-style arched gateways, which punctured the otherwise barren and upright cylindrical inside-casing of the well. The lower arch was partially submerged in the water and was dark, being quite below the ground level. The upper arch revealed a part of an underground room. Parush walked to the other side of the well, to get a closer look of the room, which, he figured out, was connected to an open aisle, some 20 feet below the ground level.

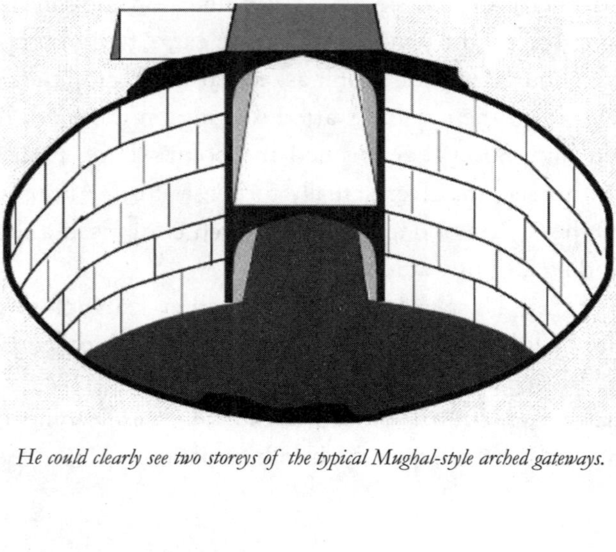

He could clearly see two storeys of the typical Mughal-style arched gateways.

'Is there a way to go to the lower level?' Parush asked Mohit, kneeling and leaning precariously over the edge of the open aisle, trying to peep into the room.

'I'm not sure,' admitted Mohit.

'Through the apex of which runs the "Safety Street" down, joining the two ends of two "Sparkling Garden-Crowns",' Parush paused. He stared at Mohit for a few moments during which a smile of satisfaction appeared on Mohit's round face.

'Are we thinking alike?' Mohit asked.

'Thank you,' Parush got up and shook hands with Mohit. 'I think you're correct. There's an underground tunnel which starts from somewhere near the dilapidated wall in Achanak Bagh, the Bagh-i Filhal, and passes through this place. It can be very well below us, where we are standing. I won't be surprised if the lower level of the well, which is partially submerged, opens up into the tunnel.'

☼

Parush's phone rang. Rakesh's name flashed on the screen.

'Sir, we've found the repeater. You're correct.' His voice did little to hide his excitement. 'The detector gave away the rough location. I scanned the entire region and retrieved the repeater from inside the pit you had fallen into.'

'Did you find anything underground?'

'There's something for sure, deep inside, at a depth of about 50 feet. But the location is changing, quite frequently.'

'That's understandable,' Parush smiled. 'If you're excited, or tensed, or worried, would you sit at one place?'

It was understandable too, that Rakesh wouldn't understand what Parush was trying to imply.

Parush continued, 'There's a room 50 feet below the ground and someone carrying a phone is restless, down there, walking up and down. The metal detector is not able to track down the exact location of the phone.'

☼

Parush and Mohit sat on the ground, beside the well. Parush wanted to know more about Daulat's manuscripts. 'Don't you think the source of Daulat's knowledge about the old buildings of Agra could be the manuscripts?' he asked.

'He doesn't know even a bit of Persian,' Mohit said, 'and neither did anyone in his family in the past three generations.'

'How did he possess the manuscripts then?'

'That's an interesting story. Daulat says his ancestor came to India from Persia, along with a mirza, a learned person. On the way to India, the mirza was robbed of everything and was left alone. Daulat's ancestor took good care of him during those tough times. Later, during Akbar's time, when the mirza became a very rich and important person, he stayed with him, as his trusted servant-cum-caretaker-cum-bodyguard. The mirza entrusted him with the upkeep of all of his properties in Agra. The mirza would call him Daulat Parwar, the protector of the empire. Ever since then, the eldest son in Daulat's family has always taken that name.'

'Do you believe all this?' Parush was visibly irritated.

'I wouldn't, if I didn't know that Jahangir's father-in-law and Mumtaz's grandfather was actually a Persian, and that he was, indeed, robbed off on the way to India.'

'What's his name?'

'Akbar gave him the name Itimad-ud Daula, the Pillar of the Empire.'

'Oh, I see,' Parush nodded. 'That explains the name Daulat Parwar. It's not "daulat", the empire per se, but it indirectly refers to the name of his master.'

'Being so closely connected to the Mughals for three generations,' Mohit added, 'Itimad and his family would have owned many buildings in Agra. Daulat's family, being the caretaker of all those buildings for more than three centuries, would naturally know a lot about the old buildings of Agra.'

'The manuscripts could be then,' Parush conjectured, 'authentic documents about the various buildings of Agra, not necessarily all owned by Itimad & Sons. Somehow, they might have landed in Daulat's family.'

'Earlier, I had totally missed this very point about the authenticity of the manuscripts,' Mohit acknowledged.

Cradle of the Heaven

(9:30 am–12:00 noon, 5 January 2019.
Inside the tunnel, Agra)

Kubha realized she was suffocating. She tried to take a few deep breaths, but there was not enough air in the claustrophobic tunnel. She recalled what the guide had cautioned her about, before descending into an illegal Peruvian gold mine in the Amazon Parush had taken her to a few years ago. It is not the lack of oxygen, she remembered, but the excess of carbon dioxide in the air that suffocates people in such places. With every breath, she knew, she was increasing the proportion of the fatal gas in the air. Even in the cold she felt hot. Was she sweating? She felt as though she had run on a treadmill for a long time. She felt dizzy.

Kubha hit a wall, head-on. The torch fell from her hand. She felt a severe pain on her forehead. She couldn't stay afoot. She fell onto the ground immediately, bruising against the rough wall of the tunnel. The first thing that came to her mind was to look for the torch, without which, she knew for sure, she would be stranded forever in the deadly labyrinth.

The darkness had acclimatized her to such an extent that she barely felt she couldn't see. She had heard many a time that visually challenged people *saw* more without their eyes. Presently, she realized what that really meant. She found the torch quite easily and immediately switched it on. 'Thank God,' she muttered, when the torch lit up. For a moment, she felt she was in a state of spatial disorientation, like the aircraft pilots or deep-sea divers when they suddenly lose the sense of direction and position. She looked around for a few moments, before realizing that the tunnel had taken a sharp turn to the left. What she had hit a while ago was actually a pile of stones used to block the straight way through tunnel, converting the T-junction into a forceful left turn. She switched off the torch and started walking, in the new direction.

☼

Suddenly Kubha felt she was struggling less to breathe. She switched on the torch immediately, frantically searching for the direction from where the fresh air was flowing in. The prospect of finding an opening in the tunnel excited her. She looked around in a frenzy, but she couldn't see an opening anywhere. The tunnel ran straight, like an arrow. She leaned against the wall, a sense of déjà vu abruptly exhausting the meagre energy she had been left with. The torch, held loosely in her hand, shook a bit, casting a jarring vision of the portions of the tunnel lighted up by it. Engulfed in a sudden fatigue, she let her head loose, resting against the wall. As the head leaned backwards a bit, she could see something on the curved ceiling of the tunnel and jerked into motion. She pointed the torch upward and exclaimed at what she saw. The arched roof was punctured by a round opening, not more than a foot in diameter, which went up straight. She realized it was a vertical duct, through which the fresh air was entering into the tunnel. It was not an opening, as she had badly expected it to be, which could have led her out of the tunnel. She closed her eyes, turned the light off and took a few deep breaths, before resuming the walk.

☼

Kubha smelt the petrichor, the sonda smell of the wet soil, soaked in rain. The smell became stronger the more she walked through the tunnel. The dampness increased too. She felt as though a lot of water had sipped in through the walls of the tunnel for years and dampened it permanently. She switched on the torch every now and then to check the surroundings.

A thought had crossed her mind many a time, all the while she had been walking through the tunnel. Wasn't it a well-trodden path? Wasn't it surreptitiously clean and litter free? Who used this path regularly? She couldn't but ponder. And why was it being used?

Kubha would have again banged on the wall, where the tunnel took a perpendicular right turn, had she not become cautious since the last time. She put on the light and checked the narrow passage ahead of her. The beam of light seemed to hit a wall again, not far from where she stood. She didn't put out the torch. She walked faster. Soon the tunnel ended in a round, vertical shaft, some six-feet wide, she guessed. A rusted iron ladder, attached to the wall of the shaft, went up. Looking around the shaft she realized, to her amazement, that its wall was made of massive chunks of wood, a few feet taller than her, arranged tightly like blocks of stones. The façade of the unpolished and uneven surface of the wood was much like that of the ship wreck furniture she had seen at someone's house in the US. It also reminded her of the wooden planks for laying the railways tracks on in the older days. She came close and touched the coarse surface of the wood. She observed the innumerable thin channels that spread across the surface, like arteries and veins, creating its artistic texture. The wood looked very dry and old.

Kubha looked up, trying to guess how far the ladder went. The gap between two steps, she estimated, would be a foot. When she decided to climb up, a practical problem posed a challenge. How would she hold the torch if she had to climb using both her hands? No sooner had the thought come to her mind than she came up with a simple solution too. She held the torch between her chin and neck, lowering her head, so as to press the chin against it. This way, she kept her hands free for holding onto the ladder, and climbing very carefully. She slipped on the very first rung of the ladder, slipping the torch and dropping it on the floor. It hit the ladder and broke the glass, exposing the bulb. She picked it up carefully, heaving a sigh of relief. Presently, it would be the last thing she could afford to lose. When she climbed again, she was very cautious. She didn't slip any more. Wood and stones alternated as the building material of the round shaft she ascended carefully, one step at a time, trying not to look down.

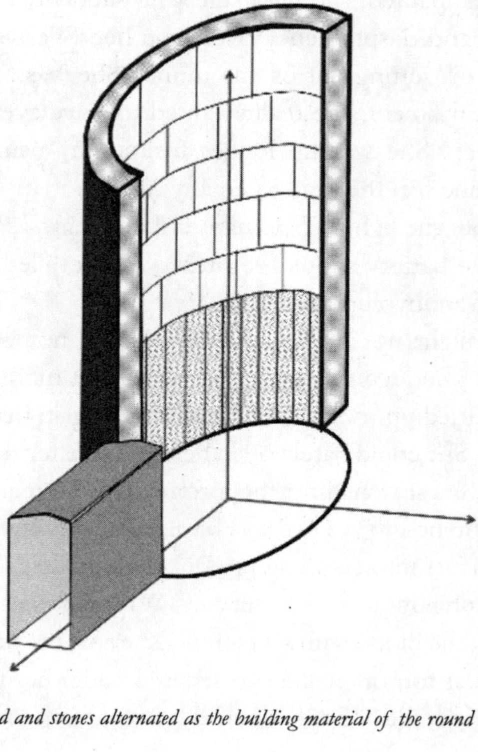

Wood and stones alternated as the building material of the round shaft.

When she had climbed roughly 20 steps, she saw the tunnel again, perforating out of an opening on the vertical casing of the round shaft. Stepping onto the floor of the tunnel, she looked up, trying to guess how much further the ladder went. She would have already climbed 20 feet and the shaft seemed to rise twice as much more. Something told her she should climb further up, till the end of the shaft. Perhaps, she would have thought, she would find a way out of the tunnel, if she climbed up. She set herself for another ascent.

The ladder ended abruptly. Kubha landed on the floor of another horizontal tunnel, similar to the one she had seen some time back. She sat on the floor, keeping the torch beside her, stretching her legs forward, leaning against the wall of the tunnel. As she panted, she felt like crying suddenly. A feeling of helplessness and despondency overcame her. She was gradually losing hope of getting out of the tunnel. She was again feeling sleepy. For a moment, she really wanted to leave everything else and fall asleep. She was no longer feeling any pain anywhere. Neither did she feel the urge to go any further.

Kubha put the light off, perhaps unknowingly, as though, the sense that the battery should be preserved prevailed in this dire situation like an involuntary reflex.

Kubha might not have woken up, had it not been for the sensation of a sudden thirst that jerked her out of the doze. Her tongue had dried up totally. Her breaths had again become heavy and exerting. She could barely open her eyes. She felt a severe pain, down there. She searched for the torch on the floor and put it on. She was frightened to see she was bleeding profusely. She tried to put all her effort into standing up. But she couldn't. The amount of blood oozing out made her nervous. When she was thinking of a way to soak the blood with something, she spat the pulp of paper she had almost forgotten she had secured under her tongue. Lest she would forget the 313 rule she had learned from the mysterious person during her captivity, she had made a drawing on a piece of paper and secured it properly, inside her mouth.

Presently, Kubha picked the tiny lump of paper from the floor and tried in vain to soak the blood with it. Horrid scenes from the recent past, which appeared like a distant ancient age, fluttered in her mind. The more she remembered those, the more she regained the urge to move on. Soon, she was again up, walking slowly, moving ahead through the tunnel. This time she didn't turn off the light.

☼

Just a few steps ahead, and Kubha appeared in a square room with four doors, a little bigger than the ones she had passed through till now in the tunnel. She was a bit confused. As per the 313 rule, she recalled, an octagonal room should appear first, not a square one. Pondering over what she should do next, she decided finally to go straight, for, a square room had to be always walked through straight, if it were a part of the bhulbhulaiya. The door on the other side of the square room didn't lead into any aisle or corridor, like before. It opened into a long and narrow cavity, enough for a person or two to pass by

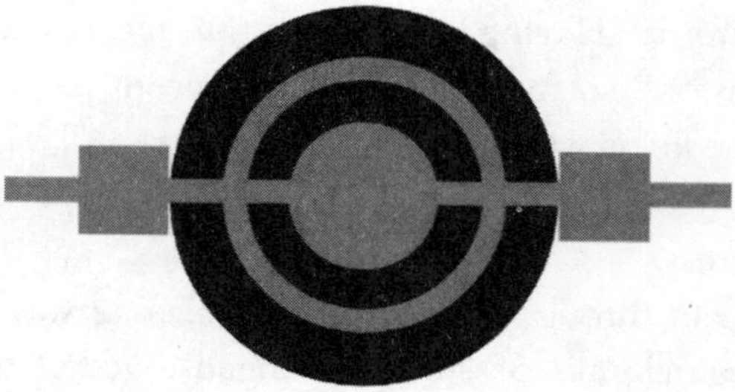

It opened into a long and narrow cavity, cutting through a massive block of stone masonry.

comfortably, cutting through a massive block of stone masonry. As Kubha walked through the cavity, she noticed a number of smooth round holes, a few inches wide, drilled into the masonry at regular intervals. It didn't need any extraordinary intelligence to understand that these holes had been drilled recently. The floor was filled with rock-dust. Some lay on the holes too. Kubha inserted her index finger into one of the holes and pulled out some of the rock-dust.

Walking some 15 feet, Kubha found the cavity trifurcating—one going straight and the other two branching off to the right and left, forming an arc. Flashing the light straight, she could see the narrow passageway opened into a big room, a little ahead. She felt she should go straight, but something pulled her to turn left. What had appeared like an arc, she realized soon, was actually a part of a circle. Given the symmetry of most of the things she had come across today, she knew she was traversing a semicircular path, along the circumference of a huge circle, the diameter of which was the straight path she hadn't taken. The holes were drilled here too, into the masonry, in the same uniformity.

Walking a few steps, she wanted to turn back, when she saw something hanging out of a hole, at the end of her line of sight, beyond which the curvature of the passageway blocked her vision. Upon reaching there, she was stunned at what she saw. From that point, each hole had a narrow cylindrical pipe inserted into it. Having overheard the terms "demolition" and "implosion" so many times in the recent past, during her captivity, she knew what those cylinders were. All of them were wired together. A few lay on the floor, indicating perhaps a work under progress.

Kubha ran through the semicircular passageway, perforated through huge chunks of stones arranged together to form the massive block of solid masonry. All along, cylindrical explosives were drilled into the masonry.

As she had expected, at the other end of the diameter of the circle, she reconnected soon with the two paths she had left behind. She took the straight path backwards and arrived at the big room—had she taken the straight path earlier, she would have arrived at the same room, from the other side. This room was perfectly round in shape, quite big and spacious. To her surprise, there was no explosive either here or in the straight passageway. The explosives, she conjured, were drilled into the masonry only along the circumference of the circle, not anywhere else.

At the centre of the room, was a Persian inscription, engraved on a round elevated marble platform. She knew enough Persian to comprehend the overall meaning of the inscription. The fact, that in high school she had been close to two friends, Nadiatul Mahdi Ulya and Ashiyana Firdaus, came in handy to her now, quite miraculously though.

'Above this lie mahd-i ulya, the cradle of the heaven, and firdaus ashiyani, the one that nests in the heaven,' she muttered.

She exited the room from the same side she had entered it through. As she passed through another square room, at the end of the narrow passageway cut through the stone masonry, she tried to connect the dots. There was no ambiguity about what the professor planned to demolish. While she had been in the hasht bihisht, she had overheard many things he had discussed with his team. It was an eerie sensation to have witnessed that his plan was almost ready to be executed. Once a few more explosives had been drilled into the remaining holes, it would just take the press of a button to detonate them all. She remembered a programme she had seen on the Discovery Channel, about the demolition of an entire building by a process called controlled implosion. When someone detonates the dynamites inserted strategically inside the main load bearing sections of the foundation of any building, she recalled, the entire structure could be brought down by gravity, in a matter of a few minutes.

The very thought of the entire monument crumbling down in a few minutes made her dizzy. That was also when she realized where exactly she was now.

She was right under the monument, deep inside its foundation, directly below the dome …

Scattered bits and pieces of the professor's words played fast in her mind, all jumbled up, like a cacophony:

> *'It took 20,000 workers, 1,000 elephants, untold riches and 22 years to build …*
>
> *'The massive dome weighs over 12,000 metric ton …*
>
> *'Akbar had standardized the measuring yard. It's called ilahi guz, the universal yard. The diameter of the dome is 22 yards. It's approximately 58 feet …*
>
> *'The dome stands exactly above the 32-yard-high hujra, the octagonal cenotaph hall at the centre. It rises a lofty 23 yards above the roof of the hujra …*
>
> *'The entire weight of the dome rests on a massive drum of solid masonry, six-yard thick and 22-yard wide. From the surface of the earth till the base of the dome, this load-bearing colossal cylinder is 69-yard high, out of which 37 yard is inside the solid foundation of sang and saruj …*
>
> *'If we blow off the base of this gargantuan drum, sang bar bala-i sang na mi-manad, no stone remains upon another. Gravity will pull down the entire dome.'*

☼

Kubha was absent-minded as the various thoughts settled in her restless mind. Suddenly, she looked ahead and, to her horror, saw the edge of the tunnel, just a few inches from where she stood. Had she not noticed it at the nick of time, she would have directly fallen into the vertical shaft, similar to the one she had ascended sometime back. The sudden realization of what could have happened to her made her feet tremble. She loosened the grip of her hand and the torch fell into the shaft, hitting the ground with a thud. The instant darkness took some time to spread into Kubha's mind. She took a few deep breaths and closed her eyes. *There would be no light, henceforth.*

Kubha stood calm for a few minutes, trying to get acclimatized to the surroundings and get accustomed to the prolonged darkness. It was not that she would keep the torch on all the time, but the very thought that she could do it whenever she needed to, was a big assurance. *Now there was no assurance of anything.*

Kubha kept one hand on the side wall of the tunnel and dragged her feet very cautiously, inch by inch, on the ground, till she sensed her feet had reached the edge. Turning back a bit, she stretched out the other hand and held onto the iron ladder which, she knew, would be close by. She hung one foot out in the air and looked out for the first rung to place it on. Once she got a firm footing, she took her other foot too off the tunnel and placed it on the ladder. She held the ladder tightly with her hands and started descending. Now that she didn't have the torch any more to hold onto, between her chin and neck, she felt more at ease. She descended the steps, slowly, one step at a time, counting each one. There would be around 60 steps, before she would hit the ground of the shaft.

Kubha hit the ground exactly after the 58th step. She figured out the direction of the tunnel and started walking that way, keeping her hands constantly on the side wall of the tunnel. Just when she felt she was struggling to breathe, she sensed there was a sudden gush of fresh air. She knew she was under another duct which brought in fresh air.

☼

Passing through another region which smelt strongly of wet soil, Kubha entered into a room. Keeping to the left, she walked along the perimeter of the room, touching and feeling each side of it, and keeping precisely a track of the position and the count of the sides. There was no way to confirm if the room was square or octagonal. But, in either case, she knew, she would be back to the same edge she had started from, once she completed counting eight. She assumed it would be an octagonal room. Accordingly, she followed the rule of 313 and identified, on the left, the third exit from the one she had entered the room through.

As though she was possessed by some supernatural power or perhaps, an extra vision with which she could *see* in the dark, Kubha identified the right exit every time and finally, emerged out of the bhulbhulaiya successfully, once more. But she realized she was again collapsing. She couldn't stand on her feet any more. She fell onto the ground. Her mouth had become so dry that there wasn't even a drop of saliva to swallow and quench her thirst. She felt her tongue was swollen. She felt so weak and dizzy that she could barely remain awake. She tried to get up, but couldn't lift herself a bit. She tried to crawl on the ground. She failed. The slumber was again engulfing her. She felt she was panting, her heart was pounding fast. She had visions of the Young Boy. Scattered memories of disjoint events of her growing up in the US flashed in her mind like the fireworks flashing in the sky, for a few seconds and then vanishing into the darkness. Images of her grandfather appeared like a fast-changing, colourful kaleidoscopic collage. She saw the last moments of his life, like a dream. She saw Faraz running around in his home office, blinded, vomiting, hitting the walls, falling down onto the floor, crawling like a baby, trying to stand up, his skin getting perforated by million holes, his intestines coming out of his stomach, slowly. Wasn't he calling out to her?

She felt sleepy. She knew she was hallucinating. Something within her reminded again and again that she couldn't afford to fall asleep now. She had to keep moving. She tried to think about the other Kubha, her namesake, the one she had been named after, the one her father wanted her to be like, the one who had been an invisible guiding power in the family, someone who would say, '*You've to flow, always, like a river* ... '

Kubha started crawling over the floor of the tunnel, slowly. Something told her she was close to coming out of the tunnel. Something, she didn't know what, seemed to be supplying her with an unending provision of hope and optimism she could thrive on, as long as she needed.

Suddenly, she felt a gush of fresh air. She took a few deep breaths and inhaled as much air as possible. The previous two times, whenever the fresh air would suddenly rejuvenate her, there would be air ducts, connected to the tunnel. She assumed this time too, it would be the same. But soon she realized, presently, it was something different. The more she crawled, she sensed, more air gushed into the tunnel. When could that happen? She pondered, and instantly felt a renewed vigour within her. *She was approaching an opening, perhaps the end of the tunnel.*

Did she see a flash of light ahead? Was she hallucinating again? She sat back, leaned against the wall and stared at the direction she had seen the light from. No, she was not dreaming, neither was she hallucinating. She was sanguine about that. What she saw, at a distance, was indeed an opening, through which a stream of light was flowing into the tunnel and submerging the darkness along its way.

Kubha realized the true meaning of the "light at the end of the tunnel". She crawled faster towards the direction of the light. It would be barely a hundred feet, she knew, but still it appeared so distant. Weird thoughts came to her mind. Would she die now, finally, at the end of the tunnel? And then, she shivered in horror, would they really blow up the monument? Would she also be buried here, forever, like the bricks and mortar which had held the monument up for more than 300 years?

She wanted to shout, but she realized her throat wouldn't vibrate a bit.

She sat on the floor and dragged herself, pushing against the floor with her hands and using the legs to create a little pull. Her bare back bruised against the rough floor and she cried in pain every time she dragged herself by a few inches. The only saving grace was the fact that the stream of light was appearing closer, with every passing moment.

When she was barely a few yards from the square opening ahead, the light fell on her directly. She couldn't open her eyes for some time. The dazzle blinded her, like the afternoon sun stared at with bare eyes. She allowed the light particles to spread over her bare body and wrap her up with their warmth. For a moment, she felt as though she had just woken up on a wintry weekend morning and her mother had pulled the curtains down, allowing the morning sun to fall on her, tickle her, cuddle her and put her back into the coziness of the comforter.

Her feet touched the wall ahead. She folded her legs and dragged herself further, so as to hold onto the edge of the square window on the wall, at a height of a few feet from the ground. She could now hear the sounds of life outside, the familiar sounds which assured her that henceforth nothing could be worse.

She tried to pull herself up, holding onto the window sill, clenching her teeth. Her fingers slipped from the sill and she fell on the ground. She stretched her hands up and tried to reach the window again, exerting all the energy she still had within her. She held onto the edge and attempted again to pull herself up. Somehow, she could make herself stand, partially, leaning against the window sill. That was when, for the first time in so many days, she saw the outside world. She saw sunlight. The window overlooked a rectangular room completely submerged with water, which reached almost the level of the window. The room had a big opening, a little ahead, to the left, through which entered all the light. She could now hear voices of people, quite clearly. She tried to shout again, at the top of her voice. But she couldn't produce even the faintest sound. She leaned over the window more, trying to reach the water. She splashed some water with her hand so as to wet her face. It didn't matter to her that the water was black and dirty. She licked the few drops that sprinkled over her face and trickled down to her lips. She splashed more water. The cold water soothed her. It brought back the touch and feel of the life she had thought, perhaps, she had left behind, forever. Suddenly, all the weariness, exhaustion, pain, thirst and hunger seemed to have dissipated and submerged into the opulence of this water. She splashed more water …

☼

'Based on what you can gather from the manuscripts,' Parush asked Mohit, 'can you create a probable map of the entire tunnel?'

'That shouldn't be a problem. We have a software to create and edit maps,' Mohit said, as he pulled out his laptop.

Half an hour later, by when Mohit had already created the map, Parush noticed the small ripples in the dark and stagnant water, coming out of the arched opening in the lower level of the well. 'Stop,' he gestured Mohit. 'Did you see the ripples?' He pointed to the lower arched opening in the vertical wall of the well.

The surroundings were anyway quite calm, removed from the normal bustle of Agra. The ripples were emanating out from somewhere within the room, not visible from outside. Did Parush hear the sound of a splash in the water? He leaned more over the edge of the well. He heard the faint sound again. Without thinking anything further, he dived into the well. A visibly perplexed Mohit jumped up, his laptop falling onto the ground.

Parush had never been an acrobat, but he had taken the advanced course on diving from a professional training school in California. He knew a few tactics to manoeuvre in the air. In the nick of time, he realized he shouldn't have jumped head-on into the water. If the water was shallow, he could fatally hit the ground with his head. Somehow, he managed to curl and make himself upright at the last moment, thus hitting the water with his legs. He sunk quite a bit into the water, as he took a while to stop the inertia with which he had fallen from a good height. That was when he realized the well was very deep. The cold water bit him hard. When he swam up, he was shivering badly. He swam fast towards the arch. It was from the room beyond it that he had heard the sounds of splashing. Once he swam into the room, he tried to gauge the level of the water in it. He sank a bit, trying to reach the floor with his feet. Expectedly, the water was just waist-deep. He walked cautiously on the submerged floor and looked around. The sounds had come from the right side of the room. He turned right and immediately saw the black, long hair, hanging from the edge of a square opening on the wall, a few inches above the water. The ends of the hair floated in the water, completely covering the face, drooping down from the window. One bare arm lay partially submerged in the water.

Parush ran towards the window and pulled the face up. For a while, Parush forgot everything and just stared at Kubha's face, visible in bits and pieces from below the web of her thick, dark hair, like the light that sieved through the maze of leaves in a dense forest. Her eyes were closed. Her lips trembled faintly. Her nose quivered with her breath. A few drops of water lay scattered on her face. She was asleep, so calmly. Parush couldn't but look at her. Suddenly, oblivious of the reality of the prevailing situation, he removed the strands of hair from her face, softly, perhaps to not wake her up. He ran his fingers on her face, his breathing turning heavy, his eyes turning moist. When he heard the loud sounds of splashing in the water, he recovered from the state of his momentary trance. He pulled out Kubha's almost-motionless body carefully through the window. That was when he realized Kubha didn't have a string on her body. He made the senseless Kubha stand on the floor, supporting her against the wall. He took out his jacket and put it on her bare body. He took out his shirt and wrapped it around her waist. He took her on his shoulders and started walking through the water, slowly.

He saw Mohit and two other persons walking through the waters towards him. They guided him towards a narrow staircase which led to the upper level. Parush climbed the stairs carefully, carrying Kubha on his shoulders. Once inside the underground room on the upper level, Parush stopped for a while, making some calculations in his mind. He laid Kubha on the dirty floor of the room. 'Can you arrange for a few blankets immediately?' he asked Mohit.

'I'll get it,' replied one of the two other persons he didn't recognize. He ran out of the room immediately.

'Rakesh ji had sent us here, to guard this place,' said the other one. 'He will be here anytime. Mohit ji has already called him and told everything.'

Parush took the mobile out from the pocket of his wet trousers. He called Rakesh. 'Get an ambulance here, immediately,' he instructed. He came out of the room and talked to Rakesh from the open aisle adjoining the room, his firm voice revealing nothing of the emotions that churned inside him. 'Set up an ICU at the DM's residence. Everything should be in stealth mode. Very few people should know of it. Get an escort for the ambulance. Clear the roads. We don't have time. She needs to be treated immediately. And, pass on the message to Afsar that Kubha is fine.'

The good thing about Rakesh was that, Parush knew, he didn't need to be told much.

The person, who had gone to get the blankets, returned in five minutes. Parush took the blankets and ran into the room. He laid one on the floor, lay Kubha on it and wrapped her with two more. He put his hands inside the blanket and removed the wet clothes from her body. He noticed the stains of blood on his shirt he had wrapped her waist with. He hid the shirt under his wet jacket, as though, hiding the stains of Kubha's ordeal from the three people in the room would reduce her pain. A gush of emotions rushed out of him, as he watched Kubha, lying almost lifeless in front of him. He had never thought this could happen to her, ever.

Parush was restless. He stood up and walked up and down the room. He went out in the open aisle and looked up several times to see if the ambulance had arrived. He returned again to the room and knelt down in front of Kubha. The ambulance arrived in 10 minutes, along with Rakesh. Kubha was laid on a stretcher. Two men in uniform carried the stretcher on their shoulders. They climbed two separate ladders, put side by side against the wall, and lifted the stretcher up to the ground level.

Minutes later, while closing the door of the ambulance, Rakesh asked, 'Sir, do you want me to raid the underground rooms of the well? One regiment of commandos from the Para Special Forces has been exclusively kept ready for you. I'm told the orders came directly from the PMO.'

'Wait,' Parush said. 'It's not wise. Let me talk to Kubha first. We're dealing with dangerous people. Haste is not a good option, at least now. Wait for my instructions. Just make sure no one sneaks in or out of the two places—the well and the river-side place in Kachhapura you had recovered the repeater from.'

Just before Rakesh completely shut the door from outside, Parush shouted from inside, 'I need to talk to Mohit. Get him with you to the DM's place.'

The escort vehicle swept the road ahead, and Kubha was in the makeshift ICU at the official residence of the District Magistrate of Agra in less than 15 minutes.

Connecting the Dots

(12:00–12:30 pm, 5 January 2019. DM's residence, Agra)

The most experienced doctors from the Agra District Hospital had already set up a fully functional ICU in one of the guest rooms on the ground floor of the palatial residence of the DM on the Mahatma Gandhi Road, not far from the Agra Fort.

While the doctors attended to the senseless Kubha, Parush stood for a while, outside the room. The DM requested him to take some rest. He came to the disproportionately large living room and sat in front of Mohit Sharma on one of the many plush sofas, which haphazardly filled a meagre part of the excessive empty space of the room. The courteous DM tried to initiate some useless conversations with Parush, but the decorated officer gave up soon, as he maintained a stoic silence. He would rarely be in such a state that could evoke a totally wrong reaction from others, perhaps who didn't know him well. Not many would know that this sudden silence was nothing but a desperate attempt to put on a fake façade of indifference, as though he was unmoved by anything happening around him. But in reality, he was shattered from within.

When the DM took leave, Parush came out to the sprawling lawn in front of the house, Rakesh following him. When he reached the edge of the lawn, he turned back. 'Have you got all our stuff with you?' he asked Rakesh.

'Yes, sir,' Rakesh nodded his head, 'I've packed everything from the constable's house. What do you want, sir?'

Parush sat on one of the many wooden benches placed along the perimeter of the lawn. 'Can you get my laptop?' he requested.

As Rakesh got the laptop, Parush gestured him to sit on the bench, by his side. He connected the laptop to the personal hotspot of his mobile and logged into the cloud through a highly secured and almost-invincible Virtual Private Network with multiple layers of the best-in-class encryption and firewalls. He opened an online application and worked on it for some time. 'What do you have to say about this graph?' he asked Rakesh, looking at the laptop.

Rakesh had been already quite conversant with this simple but effective way of first representing each individual, connected to a case, by a node in a graph, and then creating a network of the nodes by joining them as per the relationships between the

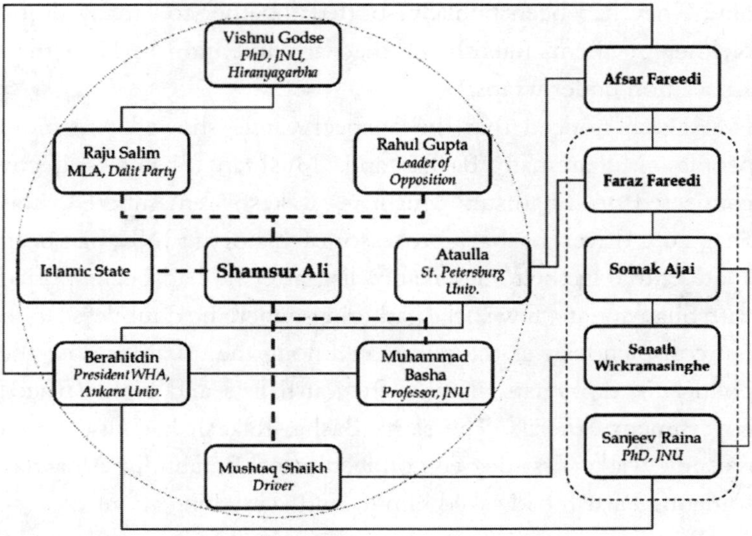

'What do you have to say about this graph?'

individuals they represent. Parush had explained once that it was called Graph Theory, in computer parlance.

Rakesh studied the graph for some time. Shamsur Ali had been at the centre of most of their surveillance for quite some time now, and quite logically, was at the centre of what Parush called a Suspect Circle. The other nodes inside the Suspect Circle comprised people who had also been on their radar for various reasons. They all had, in some way or the other, a connection with Shamsur, even if it were not a direct one. Some of them also had a direct connection with the victims, who were all placed inside the Victim Beat, depicted by a rectangle with dotted lines.

☼

That Shamsur was directly connected to both Raju Salim and Rahul Gupta, the two leaders from the two warring Opposition parties, had already been the talk of the town for quite some time now. They had been publicly spotted together too many times. Neither of them, Rakesh felt, had any intention to keep their association under wraps.

Rakesh noticed that the Suspect Circle showed two more people—Muhammad Basha and Mushtaq Shaikh—directly connected to Shamsur. Mushtaq, Rakesh remembered, was Shamsur's driver. Basha, a professor of history at JNU, had been a late entrée in their surveillance list, after he had been spotted with Shamsur at a few social gatherings where he doubtless stood out conspicuously as the odd man among the usual faces of the politicians, diplomats, flamboyant journalists and highly placed government officials. The same Basha, Rakesh had discovered recently, was a first-degree connection of Berahitdin Albayrak, someone Parush had asked him to find everything about.

Berahitdin was the president of the WHA, the organizer of the conference that Afsar was presently giving the keynote speech at. He, along with three others, had already been taken over by the commandos at the Asiatic Society, where the conference was going on in full swing, completely cut off from the external world. He was the same person, Rakesh recalled, under whom Sanjeev Raina had taken up a position at the Ankara University, just a month before the three murders. Rakesh had learned that Sanjeev had been Somak Ajai's trusted assistant and someone who would have known the most about Somak's research, perhaps after Somak himself. In a very suspicious way, he had suddenly gone completely missing from the university, immediately after his arrival in Ankara. Till date, Rakesh knew, there had been no information about his whereabouts.

Berahitdin, Rakesh had found out, was also a first-degree connection of Ataulla Bayazitoz, a professor at the St. Petersburg University in Russia. Ataulla's email account had been under constant surveillance ever since he had sent a mail to Afsar, presumably with something which happened to be a big fraud, something which was at the centre of a much bigger sinister plan that Parush had only hinted at a few times but never talked about much.

☼

Rakesh looked at Parush, sitting beside him on the wooden bench. 'Berahitdin seems to have the maximum direct connection in the graph,' he said.

'That's true,' Parush said, 'as we haven't yet got any specific evidence of Shamsur's direct connections with the rest of the nodes in the Suspect Circle.'

'Do we have any evidence of Shamsur's direct association with the Islamic State?' Rakesh asked.

'The three murders, I told you, had direct footprint of the Islamic State, and one of Shamsur's associates seems to be directly involved in one of them …'

'Mushtaq?' Rakesh blurted out.

'You're correct,' Parush smiled. 'He established a smart alibi to suppress the fact that he had gone to Kandy to murder Sanath Wickramasinghe. The surveillance cameras of the Sri Dalada Maligawa shrine corroborates very well that he was, indeed, the last person to have met Sanath, before he was found dead.'

'Is that enough to conclude that Shamsur is associated with the Islamic State?'

'No, it's not, I do agree. It's my gut feeling. It may sound like a prophecy now, but I believe the next big step for the Islamic State, in their endeavour to create an Islamic Caliphate in the world, would be infiltrating into the academia and intelligentsia. If you think logically, that's the most dangerous thing. It's more dangerous than the brutal killings and the nonsense demolitions. *It's like stealthily attacking the brain with some deadly, invisible virus and rendering the entire world brain-dead, slowly, seamlessly, without being noticed.* That's what, you see, Shamsur has been doing all this while. He has already infiltrated into JNU, Ankara University, St. Petersburg University.'

In the present scheme of things, Parush elaborated, the three murders, the very intention behind the deceit and the plan to use the esteemed conference to endorse the same, all pointed to a totally different paradigm in the strategy of the Islamic State.

'I'm sorry,' Rakesh interrupted, 'I don't think I know much about the fraud …'

'My bad,' apologized Parush. 'Let me tell you the little bit Afsar has told me a few days back. The carpet Somak was working on has a very cryptic code in its design, a code either created or inspired by the great Indian mathematician, Aryabhata. It's a sort of a mysterious riddle in numerals, something that makes it more likely to be linked with the mathematician.'

☼

The riddle hidden in the carpet, Parush explained, when solved, leads to a very authentic list of nine places in ancient India. Each of these places has a unique and extraordinary significance, both culturally and socially, and a common theme that unites the vast Indian subcontinent from Bengal to Peshawar and from the Himalayas to Tanjore, down south. Remarkably, seven of these nine places already feature in the UNESCO World Heritage list. Someone in the Suspect Circle got the fantastic idea of tweaking this record and fraudulently inserting a new place in the list, so as to attach to it a remarkable history and antiquity, and alleviating it to the same league as the others.

'But in order to tweak the carpet,' Parush said, 'you've to remove all the traces of the original carpet from everywhere in the world, and also eliminate the people who are very closely associated with it. Hence, the murders of Somak, Faraz and Sanath, and the vanishing act of Sanjeev …'

'But, what's the connection to the Islamic State?' Rakesh asked abruptly.

'I'm coming to that,' Parush smiled again, perhaps appreciating Rakesh's impatience. 'Since Indar has become the prime minister five years back, it has become extremely tough for anyone to mess up with India's security and home affairs. There hasn't been any major terrorist attack on the Indian soil for the last five years. It's, doubtless, a very dreadful thing for something like the Islamic State, which has achieved nothing in India in all these years. I believe Shamsur Ali has been sent here by the Islamic State to create prospects for them. What do you think would be the topmost priority then, for Shamsur?'

'To work out a strategy to oust Indar ji in the upcoming General Election,' Rakesh said. He got up from the bench and stood in front of Parush. 'I can connect the dots now. He has joined hands with the Opposition. No, he has actually united the Opposition. He has brought the likes of Raju and Rahul together. I can't believe …'

'He did something even more incredible,' Parush interrupted Rakesh. 'He also got the likes of Vishnu under his aegis. Vishnu belongs to a 100-year-old Hindu extremist group, called the Hiranyagarbha Bharat. It represents the radical and revisionist groups of the extremist Hindus who would be happy to demolish even a Taj Mahal because they believe it's a Shiva Temple. And if they did so, the blame would directly fall upon Indar's Bharatiya Party, as they have a history of hobnobbing with people from that camp.'

'This is such a plan!' Rakesh reacted tensely, holding his head. 'Now, I can arrange the events in the right chronology. We know Raju had been to JNU and met Vishnu a few times in the past one week. Immediately after that, there was the incident of the pamphlets. The media and the Opposition projected it as the handiwork of the Hindu fanatic groups, purportedly reared in the backyards of Indar's party. Soon, the entire country was paralyzed. Vishnu's Hiranyagarbha Bharat would have distributed the pamphlets in Agra, but all the funding and logistical support would have come from Raju, whose party is in power in Uttar Pradesh.'

'That's not all,' Parush said, leaning against the backrest of the bench. 'By that time, a fraud carpet had already been created, with Agra as one of the nine places. The plan was to get an academician of international repute, someone like Afsar, to talk about Somak's research on the deciphered carpet codes at the WHA conference in Calcutta. The surrogate motive was, doubtless, to get a scholarly endorsement of the bizarre theory of an exceptional and glorious pre-Islamic past of Agra, at par with the ancient places such as Taxila, Nalanda, Ajanta and the others.'

'How would that help Shamsur?'

'Such a thing would suddenly bolster the vigour of the radicals, who would then go full throttle in their movement to reclaim the desecrated Shiva Temple, the Tejo Mahalaya, which was allegedly turned into the Taj. *It would be a new Babri Masjid.*'

'The entire Babri Masjid episode had brought the Bharatiya Party to the limelight, 30 years back,' Rakesh argued. 'Had it not been for that, they wouldn't have ever come to power. Don't you think a new Babri may help Indar?'

'Not at all,' Parush denied vehemently. 'Times have changed. Now there is the so-called *liberal* media and the firebrand secular brigade, the intellectuals, the international hawks, the NGOs, and above all, a smarter and younger demography. Indar will be totally finished if the Taj flares up into another Babri. See the timing. The General Election is just a few months away. The country was already paralyzed once last week in reaction to the pamphlets. The conference would have shut it down for many more days.'

'Did Afsar find out about the fraud?'

'Yes, she did and she threatened to expose the fraud at the conference. That was when Kubha was kidnapped, as the last resort to prevent Afsar from attending the conference.'

'If Afsar were allowed to expose the fraud, don't you think that would have further brought the wrath of the media and the intellectuals on the Hindu fanatics? The fraud would have been taken as a desperate attempt of the fanatics to prove their point?'

'Not exactly! It would have tumbled many skeletons out of the closet. The real people behind the fraud could have been exposed too. It wouldn't have been a wise thing.'

Rakesh sat down on the bench and looked at the graph for some more time. 'One thing is still not clear to me,' he said doubtfully. 'Somak is not directly connected to anyone in the Suspect Circle. How did anyone from that circle find out about his research?'

'The connections you see in the graph are based on what we have evidences of. I'm sure there are more connections we're yet to know of …'

'If I'm not wrong,' Rakesh interrupted Parush, 'Somak was somehow connected to Muhammad Basha. They could have been professional acquaintances. Given Somak's interest in history, his knowing Basha from JNU is not something unusual.'

'You're correct,' agreed Parush. 'Somak would have cursorily talked to Basha about his research—the carpet, the mysterious codes and their hidden meanings, his own analysis of the codes, etc. Basha would have instantly realized the potential of Somak's work in distorting history. But he didn't want to enquire more about it, lest Somak got suspicious. His best option was obviously Sanjeev Raina, Somak's assistant. Being a PhD in history from JNU, he would have been surely known to Basha. Luring him wouldn't have been tough. It was understandable that he didn't have a long-term prospect with Somak, who after all was not a historian, per se. Basha and Berahitdin would have then laid a trap for him, by giving the bait of a prestigious position at the Ankara University. The unsuspecting Sanjeev would have taken Basha into confidence and shared with him everything about Somak and his research. The rest, we already know.'

Sanjeev went to Ankara, Parush said, to work under Berahitdin. He was eliminated soon after he reached Ankara. Next, Ataulla created a context to send someone to Faraz in Khushawar, in the pretext of seeing some old carpets. An alibi was established to show that Mushtaq was going to Bangkok, but in reality, he went to Kandy. Then, on the same day, Mushtaq killed Sanath in Kandy, Ataulla's person killed Faraz in Khushawar and someone else killed Somak in Delhi …

Parush paused, seeing the frown on Rakesh's face; he seemed to have some doubt. 'What?' Parush asked.

'If I remember correctly,' Rakesh tried to recall, 'you said that Somak and Faraz met only a week before their death. Then, Sanjeev was no longer working with Somak. So, if Basha got to know everything about Somak and his work from Sanjeev, he couldn't have learned about Faraz from him. Sanjeev would know Sanath, but not Faraz.'

'So, you're not sure,' Parush summarized, 'how Basha or anyone else in the Suspect Circle got to know of Faraz. Isn't it?'

'Yes,' Rakesh nodded.

'All the nitty-gritty detail may be a matter of conjecture. We still don't know a lot of things. We don't know when and how Somak got associated with the conference. It's possible he himself contacted the WHA. Otherwise, Basha could have also asked Berahitdin to send a note to him, soliciting his participation at the Calcutta conference. He would have shown interest in presenting his work on the carpet codes.'

Later, Parush continued, when Somak had been dead and the fraud carpet had been created, Ataulla laid a trap for Afsar. He emailed her the complete design of the fraud carpet, with some pretext, of course. He would have guessed Afsar might not have seen the original carpet, as all traces of it had already been eliminated. Next, Berahitdin contacted Afsar, gave Somak's reference and requested her to present Somak's work at the conference, posthumously.

'You may ponder,' Parush said, 'why Afsar didn't find anything unusual about the entire scheme of things. She did talk to me. There was always some justification behind everything, or at least that was what we all believed.'

Parush took the laptop and worked on the graph for a few more minutes. 'I've numbered the connections between the victims and the suspects, chronologically. The first connection between the two was presumably initiated by Somak, when he would have casually talked about his research to his acquaintance, Basha.'

☼

An attendant ran out of the DM's residence. 'Sir,' he addressed Parush, 'madam is calling you.'

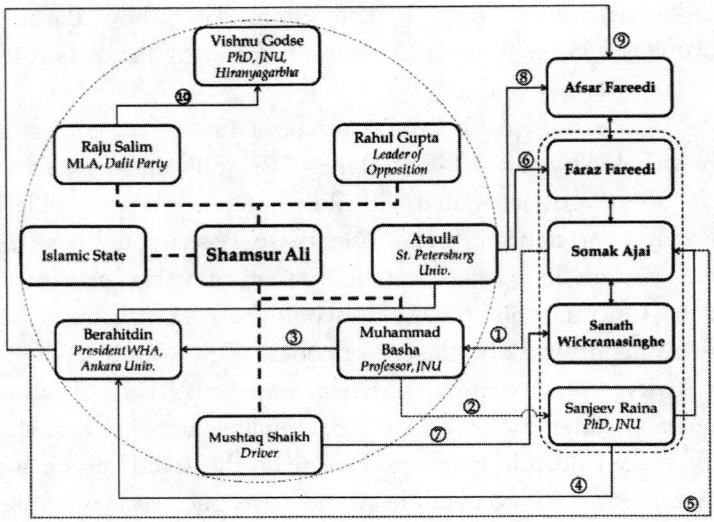

'I've numbered the connections between the victims and the suspects, chronologically.'

Parush left the laptop on the bench and rushed into the house. He saw a doctor waiting in front of the room which had been converted into an ICU. 'She wants to talk to you,' the doctor informed him. 'She's out of danger. She's very weak, though. She should take rest.'

Parush had already reached the bed Kubha had been lying on. He sat on a stool kept beside the bed and held her hands tightly.

'*They are blowing up the Taj*,' Kubha blurted out, trying to get up.

A doctor rushed to her. 'Please don't get excited,' he pleaded to Kubha. 'It's not good for you.'

Kubha brushed the doctor off. 'Porus, don't listen to them,' she mumbled. 'You have to do something.'

Parush asked the doctors to leave them alone. They left the room, reluctantly. He leaned over Kubha, staring at her, closely, their breath touching each other. Kubha dragged his face and broke down.

The Apocalypse

(12:30–2:30 pm, 5 January 2019. Agra and Calcutta)

Mohit frantically searched for something in his laptop. He, along with Parush and Rakesh, had been listening to Kubha, with rapt attention. The more Kubha retold her experiences, the more shivers ran down their spines.

'Do you know the name of the kingpin, the professor?' Parush asked Kubha.

'No, I don't think anyone called him by his name,' Kubha replied. 'But I can say he's a Bangladeshi.'

Parush and Rakesh exchanged glances.

'How do you know that?' Parush asked.

'He spoke English with a heavy Bangladeshi accent.'

'But he can be also someone like my father or your grandfather, who came to India from East Bengal after the Partition. They too have the similar accent.'

'No,' Kubha asserted, 'I have a lot of Bangladeshi friends and I know the difference.'

'*He's Shamsur Ali*,' Parush told her directly. 'He's an affiliate of the Islamic State and the mastermind behind all the three murders. I'll tell you more about him later. Tell us everything you can remember.'

Parush was amazed at the resilience and the sheer grit of the young woman he had known since she had been a kid. Lying on the back-adjustable hospital bed, Kubha looked tired, as she spoke slowly, recalling each and every detail authentically enough for Mohit to reconstruct many things.

'While we were at the well,' Mohit mumbled, browsing through the folders he generally used to keep temporary files in, 'I had created a rough map of the tunnel, based on what we can gather from Daulat's manuscripts. I'm getting old. I keep on forgetting things.'

Mohit looked up at Kubha. 'Didn't you mention there was a point, where the tunnel was suddenly blocked ahead and you had to turn left? And then, you passed through a region which smelt of wet soil, isn't it?'

'That's correct,' Kubha acknowledged.

'*That was when you crossed the Yamuna river, from below*.' He turned his attention back to the laptop.

A doctor administered a few injections to Kubha, requesting her to take rest. Parush gestured to the doctor that he would take care of her. The doctor left the room.

'Here it is,' Mohit announced with a bang, showing a map on the laptop to Parush and Rakesh. 'There are multiple verses which refer to the tunnel in cryptic ways. One says the tunnel joins the two gardens, the Aram Bagh and the Achanak Bagh, on the two sides of the zamin-i tegh-i goshtini, the tongue-shaped land. It also says the tunnel passes through the tip of the tongue. Now, we know there, indeed, exists a tunnel that starts from the Achanak Bagh, the Bagh-i Filhal of the manuscript.'

Like Parush, Mohit too had a strong feeling that the tunnel could be accessed from within the relics of the watch tower on the river side, the only thing that had survived of the Achanak Bag, the first garden built by Babur in haste. 'It was for no reason,' he asserted, 'that Daulat would visit this place so often.'

Another verse, Mohit said, implies that the tunnel passes through the garden which the Queen, Mahd-i Ulya, the Cradle of the Heaven, had gifted to her daughter, Giti Aray, the World Adorning. 'Mahd-i Ulya is a common epithet for Mumtaz Mahal,' he explained, 'and Giti Aray alludes to Jahan Ara, which also means the same—world adorning.' The garden then, he inferred, would be nothing but the Zahara Bagh, the word "zahara" being a corruption of "jahan ara".

'Only the southwest tower of the erstwhile Zahara Bagh exists today,' Mohit said. 'It's broken, but it's still in much better condition than the watch tower in the Achanak Bagh. It was only due to the persistence of Daulat's father that the ASI had to finally declare it as a protected monument. Now, I know why Daulat took so much interest in that river-side tower, little north of Chini ka Rauza. He would access the tunnel through it.'

He turned the laptop back. 'Let me add the detour which runs below the Taj Mahal. I assume this part of the tunnel was added later, posterior to the manuscripts, perhaps during the construction of the Taj.'

☼

When Mohit showed the map again, a few minutes later, Parush pulled the laptop towards him and observed it closely. The start and the end of the tunnel, and the two places it passes through were distinctly marked with star signs on the map.

'Did you say Mahd-i Ulya?' Kubha asked suddenly, trying to get up, pushing against the adjustable slant part of the bed. Parush helped her sit comfortably.

'Yes,' said Mohit. 'It's one of the many titles of Mumtaz.'

'And what's Firdaus Ashiyani?'

'Where did you hear about it?' Mohit was surprised. 'That's an epithet for Shah Jahan,' he said. 'It means one who nests in paradise, firdaus.'

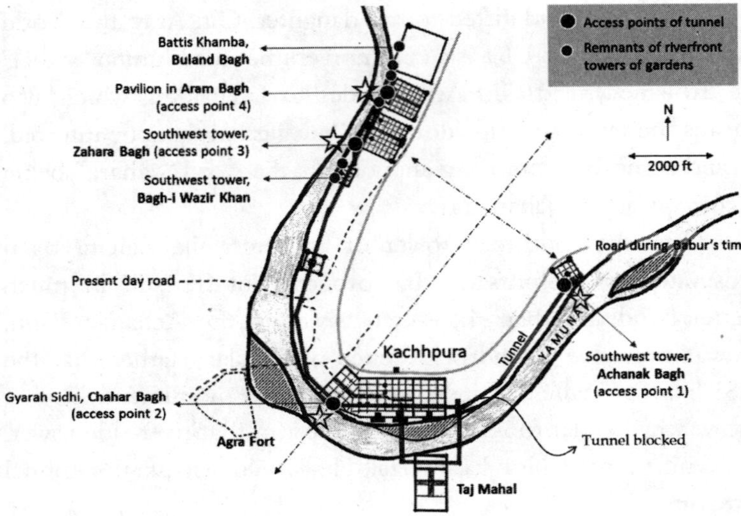

When Mohit showed the map again …

'"Above this lie Mahd-i Ulya and Firdaus Ashiyani",' Kubha uttered each word discreetly. 'I forgot to tell you. There was a Persian inscription on the floor of the room, at the centre of the colossal drum of masonry pierced through with dynamites. I overheard, the professor was repeatedly referring to this massive cylindrical drum, which bore the entire load of the dome.'

'Now there's no doubt,' Mohit said, barely holding back his excitement, '*you were exactly below the centre of the dome of the Taj*, more precisely, directly under the graves of Mumtaz and Shah Jahan, Mahd-i Ulya and Firdaus Ashiyani.'

'Do you have any good diagram of the design of the Taj?' asked Parush. 'I don't need a proper engineering drawing. Even a representative one would do.'

'Yes, there are many in fact,' replied Mohit, 'but they are all in the archives.'

'I'm sure by now the entire archive is online.' Parush had already picked up his laptop. 'Do you remember the site of the archive?'

In a few minutes, Parush was browsing through hundreds of scanned images of the design of the Taj, some very old, some recent, but none seemed quite useful to him. Suddenly, he chanced upon an axonometric view of the Taj from a book called *Agra: The architectural heritage*, written by a Lucy Peck. He also got a decent floor plan of the ground floor of the mausoleum. He displayed both on the laptop. 'Are they any good?' he asked Mohit.

'This is a very accurate depiction of the Taj,' Mohit said. The floor plan of the Taj, he explained, is a typical hasht bihisht. The central big octagonal cenotaph hall is called the hujra. The dome is directly above it, at a height of 85 feet. The hujra is flanked on eight sides by eight rooms, four square and four octagonal.

Kubha was getting a slanted view of the laptop screen from her bed. 'Can I see the floor plan?' she requested. When Parush brought the laptop close to her, she looked at the two diagrams for a while. 'Where is the load-bearing cylindrical drum they plan to blow up?' she asked Parush.

Parush took the laptop back and loaded the axonometric view of the Taj into a basic AutoCAD tool he had used a few times in the past. Soon, he created two more diagrams, trying to depict the load-bearing "drum" of the mausoleum in a simple way. He held the laptop in front of Kubha, so that she could see all the diagrams comfortably.

'The arrangement of the rooms under the Taj,' she exclaimed, 'is very similar to the floor plan of the hasht bihisht of the Taj!'

'*They are exactly same*,' Parush said. 'The entire hasht bihisht was reproduced below the Taj. The room with the inscription is directly below the cenotaph hall. There would be four square rooms, straight below the four square rooms above. You would have passed through only two of them, the ones you encountered straight on your way through the tunnel.'

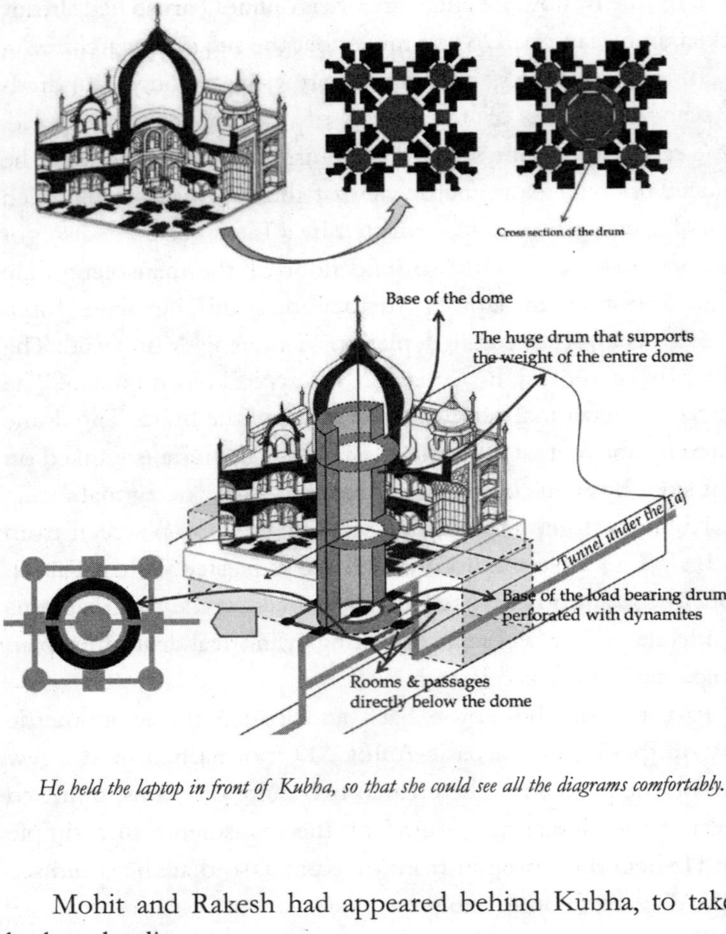

He held the laptop in front of Kubha, so that she could see all the diagrams comfortably.

Mohit and Rakesh had appeared behind Kubha, to take a look at the diagrams.

'You said,' Parush said to Kubha, 'there is a circular passage at the base of the drum. This is from where you saw the dynamites inserted into holes in the wall of the drum.'

'Is there really a drum inside the Taj?' Mohit asked. 'I haven't heard of anything like that.'

'It's not a real drum,' Parush clarified. 'It's the load-bearing section of the walls and the foundation of the Taj. Had it been constructed today, the drum would have been erected first in solid concrete, and then the rest of the structure would have been made of lighter material. Even if you damaged the rest of the foundation of the Taj, the dome wouldn't come down. But if you managed to blow up the base of the load-bearing drum, gravity would pull down the dome in a matter of few minutes. That's how buildings are demolished everywhere in the world. It's called controlled implosion. You don't have to really demolish the entire structure. *You blow up just the load-bearing beams.*'

The Babri Masjid too had been brought down in a similar manner, explained Parush. Structural engineers were consulted to weaken the base of the load-bearing parts of the old mosque, over a long time. Thousands of hooks were then affixed to the dome of the mosque. Finally, a multitude of people pulled the dome with strong ropes attached to the hooks. It came down easily because the load-bearing parts had already been weakened.

As though the realization had dawned on him just now, Mohit shuddered all of a sudden. '*They will blow up the Taj?*' he shrieked. 'Why are we sitting idle here? We should stop them immediately.'

Rakesh knew Parush would be irritated at such abrupt histrionics. In fact, he himself would have reacted the same way had he not known the background. He knew the risk of undertaking a commando attack inside the tunnel would be huge. Shamsur could detonate the dynamites anytime, at the slightest provocation. The collateral damage would be unthinkable.

'We're not sitting idle here,' Parush responded, firmly. 'There's no point in jumping into a well, with eyes blindfolded and the hands tied. Rather, I would take some time and then dive into it with all the needful gears and know-how. We need to know everything about the tunnel under the Taj even before we think of any action. *And we need to know that without going there.*'

'Do you have any drawing of the foundation of the Taj?' Rakesh asked Mohit. 'We need to know precisely the position of the tunnel under the Taj. It's quite clear that the tunnel passes through the foundation.'

'Are you still connected to the ASI archive?' Mohit asked Parush.

☼

It was not that the delegates of the WHA conference hadn't noticed that their mobile phones were not functioning. But Afsar's keynote address was interesting enough for everyone to be oblivious of even the most useful gadget for the entire duration of the speech. When she ended with a thundering applause, many in the audience looked at each other, enquiring about the mobile network.

When Afsar took a seat in the front row, someone from the audience went up to the rostrum. 'Ladies and gentlemen,' he addressed the audience, 'I'm the president of the Asiatic Society. I will take a few minutes of your time before the next speaker takes the stage. I'm really sorry for the inconvenience caused by the mobile jammers. Just a few hours back, we got to know the prime minister would be in Calcutta on an unplanned personal visit. He is scheduled to pass through the Park Street in a few hours, and hence, the entire area is being sanitized. Lately, there have been intelligence reports of a possible terrorist attack in Calcutta. The sudden visit of the PM has put his security in a fix. I've been told our entire building will be sealed for the next few hours, till the PM's cavalcade passes by. Don't worry, we've arranged for a gala lunch. We'll take good care of you all. Stay blessed.'

Rakesh got a call. 'That's good,' he said over the phone. 'Please make sure the entire building is totally sealed until we give you the next instruction. No one inside should panic or have the slightest doubt about anything. If possible, create another fake news item about the PM's Calcutta visit and keep on beaming the same on the internal TVs. You anyway have the DD staff with you.'

Parush showed a thumbs up to Rakesh.

☼

Shamsur got a message on his mobile. He read it, and stared at the curved ceiling of the room he had restricted himself to since the past few hours. The conference was going on fine, he learned from the message, without Afsar of course. Though there was nothing to be concerned about, he knew, but still his sixth sense said something was really amiss.

Shamsur got up from the wooden chair and stood by the cold wall, leaning his head against it. He closed his eyes. "*In a repeat of the Babri Masjid, Hindu fanatics bring down the Taj Mahal,*" he visualized the headlines in the newspapers. How far was he from that morning, when shocked people from across the world would wake up to read the news? Something within him repeatedly told him, it wouldn't be what he was thinking.

Something was amiss …

Hundreds of miles away from the underground hasht bihisht in Kachhpura, a commando sent a few more messages from the mobiles of the five people lying heavily sedated in one of the rooms of the Asiatic Society in Calcutta. Among them were two foreigners: one Turkish, a professor from the Ankara University and the president of the WHA; and the other a Russian, from St. Petersburg. The other three were Indians, one of whom had in his possession a very old manuscript.

Shamsur read the message from the president of the WHA once more. Of course, he had no way to know that the message hadn't been sent by the president himself.

☼

'Abu Talib Kalim, one of the court poets of Shah Jahan, gives an interesting account about the construction of the Taj,' Mohit said, while helping Parush in editing two old drawings of the Taj's foundations and adding the tunnel to it, as per the information gathered from Kubha's description. 'Kalim refers to the well foundation of the Taj.'

Kubha had fallen asleep. Rakesh had gone out to gather the latest updates from the guards placed at the well in Chahar Bagh and at the dilapidated river-side tower in Kachhpura.

It was a common practice for the Mughals, Mohit explained, to use well foundations for the structures built on water or wet marshlands. Deep wooden wells would be first inserted into the water. Then, it would be emptied of the soil and slush, and filled with stones and mortar till the surface of the water. All the wells would be then joined by a platform or kursi of stone, which would form the base of the construction.

'Doesn't the Taj have a wooden foundation?' asked Parush.

'Yes, that's what can be construed from various sources, though we don't have any direct proof of the same. We don't know exactly how the ebony wood was used in the foundation. But something Kubha mentioned may tell us a lot about it.'

'Really?' Parush sounded skeptical.

'You may recall, she mentioned that she had to climb up a vertical shaft before landing at the level of the base of the drum, where she saw the room and the circular passage under the dome. The long tunnel suddenly ends in the vertical shaft, which opens into two horizontal tunnels above, one roughly at 20-feet height and the other at 60 feet …'

'How do you get the heights?' Parush interrupted.

'Kubha mentioned she had climbed roughly 20 steps before she reached the first horizontal opening, which she didn't take. She climbed some 40 steps more to reach the upper one, which took her to the base of the drum. So, there are two tunnels under the Taj, at two levels, one upper and one lower.'

'That's a very smart conjecture,' Parush commended. 'Please carry on.'

'*The wall of the vertical shaft was made up of alternate blocks of wood and stone …*'

'I know what you're leading to,' Parush stopped Mohit, his eyes sparkling. 'The vertical shaft cuts through one of the foundation wells, filled with chunks of stone and wood. It is such a simple and ingenious design! The layers of wood inside the stone act as shock absorbers, like the suspension springs of the cars. The springs absorb the shocks from the wheels and keep the car stable. The wood in the foundation wells also serves the same purpose. It keeps the building above stable, absorbing any shock coming from below. That's how the Taj has been protected from earthquakes and any movement due to the settling of the foundation in the soft soil below.'

'Now I know,' Mohit exclaimed, 'where from Daulat learned of the wooden foundations of the Taj. He would have seen it himself. He would have noticed over the years the wood had dried up, and hence, created the furore over the safety of the Taj.'

'It's incredible that he knows that the wood needs to be wet and moist in order to maintain its structural qualities.' Parush stopped abruptly. 'Who do you think would have helped Kubha with the trick to come out of the bhulbhulaiya?'

'It can't be anyone other than Daulat,' Mohit said, his excitement brimming over his eyes. 'He too is held up inside! How did he land up there?'

'There can be many reasons behind that,' Parush said. Both of them fell silent for some time. Parush concentrated on the drawings of the foundation he had been working on. 'How deep is the tunnel?' he asked Mohit, looking at the scanned copies of the fairly detailed old drawings, with the various dimensions marked in ilahi guz, the measuring unit standardized by Akbar. For a better understanding, he had added the corresponding values in feet in some cases.

'One of the verses alludes to kucha-i salamat, the underground safety tunnel, which runs 21 and a half guz, or roughly 56 feet below takhta-i ab, which is, doubtless, the level of the water, as marked in the drawing.'

The same verse, Mohit said, allegorically refers also to takhta-i khak, which literally means the surface of the earth. In the context of the drawing, he pointed out, takhta-i khak could be the level where the wet and muddy slush of the river bank became harder underneath. The foundation wells cut through the regions of slush and soil, from the level of the water above till the rocky surface below, which provides a strong base for the structure. The main mausoleum of the Taj stands on a square kursi of white marble, some 18-feet thick, sitting atop a massive red sandstone platform, nearly 1,000-feet long and 40-feet thick, which rests on the wells. 'The entire stretch of the red sandstone platform,' he added, 'is visible from the river. I've a feeling, the upper tunnel under the Taj, the one Kubha took, lies exactly at the base of this red sandstone kursi.'

'I agree,' Parush nodded, adding the tunnels in the AutoCAD tool he had loaded the drawings into. 'The term "safety street" seems to have a different significance altogether. The tunnels under the Taj might have been added for the safety and maintenance of the foundation. The two very important aspects of the foundation are the load-bearing drum and the shock-absorbing ebony wood of the wells. You have the circular passage running along the base of the drum and the vertical shaft cutting through the wood. You could easily notice any damage either to the drum or the wood. *Daulat noticed the damage in the wood. And Kubha noticed the damage to the drum* ...'

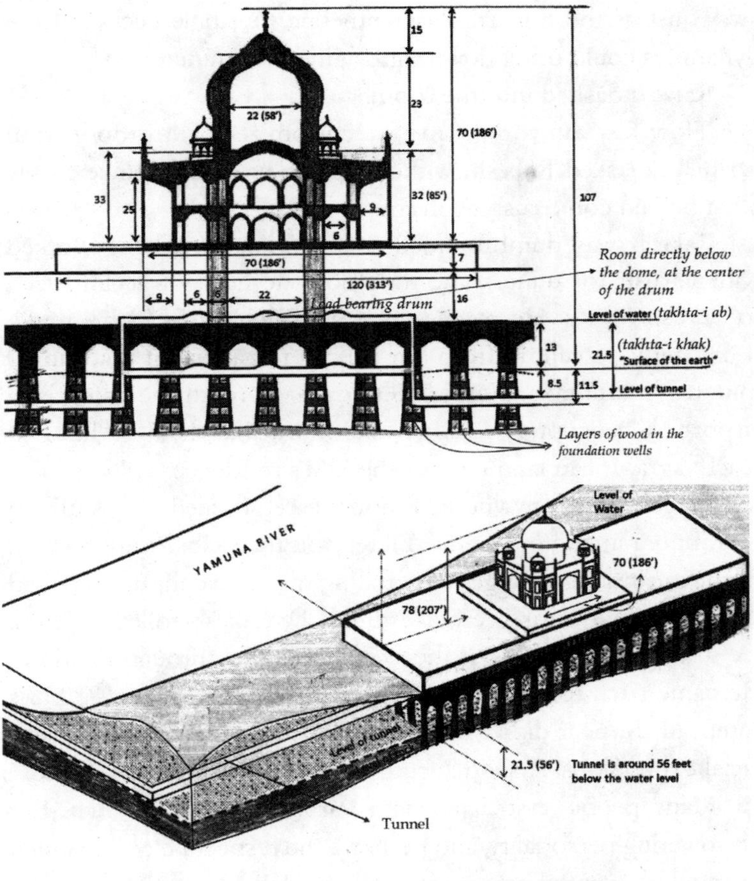

'I agree,' Parush nodded, adding the tunnels in the AutoCAD tool he had loaded the drawings into.

'What irony!' Mohit reacted, abruptly, interrupting Parush, 'the kucha-i salamat, the safety street, has become kucha-i maut, the street of death. *The apocalypse is coming down the street.*'

Parush could feel Mohit's despondency. He knew time was running out fast. He had to act soon, if the apocalypse had to be avoided. The apocalypse, he knew, could be just a few moments away, just at the fingertips of someone. A single click and the dynamites could bring down the Taj in a few minutes.

Rakesh dashed into the room.

'How fast can you get me the customized YuMi robot from Delhi?' he asked Rakesh, without giving him any chance to say what he had come rushing in for.

Rakesh was dumbfounded for a moment. Having worked with Parush for quite some time now, he had got acclimatized to Parush's ways. He made some fast calculations in his mind. 'I can get it picked up from our office in Connaught Place in 10 minutes. It will take another 10 minutes to reach the Safdarjang airport. A helicopter wouldn't take more than half an hour to reach Agra. It can land here, at the DM's residence … '

'It can land anywhere. I don't care. I need the stuff in Kachhpura in an hour's time. I'll tell you the exact location soon. In the meantime, arrange for a drilling rig, at Kachhpura.' He had already come out of the makeshift ICU, Rakesh following him. He turned back, staring at the sleeping Kubha through the door. He came back to the room. As he placed his hand on Kubha's forehead, Rakesh didn't fail to notice the sudden change in his facial expressions. A sudden ruthlessness made him look fierce.

Many people associated with Parush knew of Kubha. But his towering personality, and perhaps, the respect he commanded from all, prevented any gossip or loose talk about their unusual relationship, even behind his back. Rakesh himself had met Kubha a few times, and gradually he had developed a fondness and a very special admiration for the bold and beautiful girl, that she was. Presently, looking at her, sleeping on the bed, Parush touching her forehead, standing still, he too felt a rush of adrenaline within him. *It was time to be ruthless …*

Paradise Regained

(2:30–5:00 pm, 5 January 2019. Agra and Calcutta)

Parush couldn't but commend Rakesh for his organizational skills, or rather the out-of-the-box solutions he always managed to think of for seemingly unsolvable problems. By the time, they reached the spot, a little east of the Mehtab Bagh and diagonally opposite to the Taj on the other side of the river, the Bauer BG 15 H drilling rig had already arrived there from nowhere. 'Where did you manage to get it from in less than an hour?' he exclaimed.

'The Railways are undertaking some construction work at the Yamuna Bridge station. I got in touch with someone. Yamuna Bridge is close by, but getting the machine here, through the densely populated villages with narrow roads, was a challenge indeed.'

'How do you always manage to know someone somewhere every time?'

Rakesh smiled shyly. 'That's my job, sir.'

'Can you get a concrete mixer truck too?' Parush asked apologetically. 'I should have told you earlier.'

'I'll get one.'

As Parush got out of the car with VIP beacon lights on the roof, Rakesh made a phone call, again to *someone* he knew of course. Parush smiled at him and walked towards the river. Quite a few inquisitive and enthusiastic villagers had already poured into the small tract of barren land, very close to the river. The nearest village was less than a mile away, beyond an empty stretch of cultivable field, segmented uniformly into small squares.

Someone came to Parush and greeted him. 'Thank you, sir,' he spoke reverentially. 'We don't get good water in our village. We've requested the local corporators many times for a tube well. No one did anything in these many years.'

Parush understood the context. He felt bad that the villagers would be disappointed again. But presently, he saw it as a great opportunity to keep the entire operation secretive. He smiled at the person and went to talk to the operators of the rig.

'But why are they digging the tube well so close to the river?' Parush overheard a conversation he decided to ignore.

'You have to do it really fast,' Parush said to the person he thought would be the head operator of the rig. 'Are you ready?'

'Please give us five more minutes,' the head operator replied.

☼

Rakesh had already completed his call.

'Get the Pulse Induction detector,' Parush instructed him, and walked closer to the water. 'Find the exact location of the metal wire. The tunnel is supposed to be around 56 feet below the water level. It shouldn't be far from the river. Scan the entire area within a hundred metres of the river.'

Rakesh had already taken out the gadget. 'Are you sure you can cut the wire with the laser cutter?' he asked, selecting the settings for the highest precision.

'We have to do it,' Parush asserted. 'There's no other way out. We can't do an underground implosion to blow up the entire tunnel. That will rupture the wire for sure, but the shocks may detonate the dynamites. We can't take any chance.'

'We're more than a kilometre away from the Taj, aren't we? Can an explosion that far detonate the dynamites?' Rakesh walked along the shore of the river in a straight line, sweeping the ground with the device. Parush walked with him, holding the display which showed the coordinates when the instrument detected any metal.

'The explosive oil nitroglycerine is mixed with an absorbent and stabilizer to render a dynamite moderately sensitive to shocks. But I'm not sure how much vibration the implosion could generate and how much of that could reach the dynamite through the walls of the tunnel.'

Each dynamite had a sensitive blasting cap, Parush explained, which could be set off by a short burst of current released from a blasting machine kept at the other end of the long wire connected to the dynamite. All Shamsur had to do was to just trigger the blasting machine with the push of a button. The easy-to-ignite explosive of all the blasting caps would then explode almost instantaneously, generating the activation energy needed to detonate the dynamite, a few kilometres away. 'If we snap the wire connected to the dynamite,' Parush said, 'the dynamite would never explode, unless you supplied it with the activation energy in the form of physical shocks. *We have to be extremely careful.*'

Parush stopped talking. The display beeped. '*Fifty-four feet below*!' he screamed. 'It must be the metallic wire connected to the dynamites. Keep walking.'

The display beeped constantly as Rakesh walked straight. 'That's good enough,' he gestured to Rakesh and turned back. 'Are you ready?' he shouted at the operators of the rig.

☼

The head operator had already mounted the base carrier of the rig, taking his seat inside the glass enclosure. He positioned the base close to where Parush and Rakesh stood. He pulled the winch and lifted the drill pipe up, to some 10 feet above the ground. Two persons inspected the ground and signalled him to bring the drill pipe down.

Parush shouted at him, 'You'll hit a hard surface at around 50 feet. Don't drill through it. Stop at that level.'

Soon the rotating drill bit pierced through the soft ground of the river bank, the powerful torque from the KDK 150 KL single-gear rotary drive generating the downward thrust to drill into the earth. For the machine which could cut through hard rocks with ease, creating an uncased borehole in the soft and slushy soil seemed like a cakewalk. When the drill bit was pulled up, dumping the muddy slush dredged from within the newly created hole in the ground, Parush inspected the hole. 'It is four-and-a-half-feet wide,' said one of the two persons clearing the drum which had collected the slush. It wouldn't take long to reach 50 feet, he knew.

A police escort vehicle honked from behind the crowd watching the drilling. Rakesh ran to the vehicle and returned soon with a bag. Parush sat on the ground and opened the bag, while Rakesh tried to keep a few over-enthusiastic villagers at bay. Parush assembled the YuMi robot he had got custom-made by ABB, especially for precision tasks involving humanly impossible manoeuvring. It was empowered with Artificial Intelligence, based on the theorized computational principles of the human brain. It was also equipped with the latest 3D Laser Cutter, which could cut through a 10-metre-thick metallic slab in no time.

'Sir, they have hit a slab of rock, exactly at 46 feet,' Rakesh shouted from the drilling site. Parush got up and ran in haste. 'You're absolutely correct, sir,' Rakesh said excitedly. 'We've hit the roof of the tunnel.'

The concrete mixer truck had already arrived. 'Come closer,' Rakesh gestured at the driver.

☼

Parush called for the head operator of the rig. 'I've to insert a machine into the borehole,' he said to him, without giving any context. 'Can you fix it to the tip of the drill bit and take it down?'

'Yes, I can do that,' he nodded. He took his two assistants and immediately got into action. They detached the drum from the long octagonal shaft which rotated along with the drill bit. Parush got the robot and connected one end of a special wire to it. The other end of the wire was connected to a tab. He checked the batteries of the robot and switched the power on. The dual-armed miniature humanoid jerked into life, making a few clicking sounds. The head operator brought the drill bit close to him. Parush noticed the bit had been cleansed off the slush, and dried too. He affixed a thin rectangular box to the drill bit with a strap and attached the robot to the box through a groove. He gestured the operator to lower the bit.

As the robot descended through the round shaft, Parush switched on the camera and the powerful light attached to it. The camera gave a 360-degree view around the robot. When the depth showed 45 feet, he gestured the operator to stop. He focused the camera downwards and looked for the stone roof of the tunnel in the tab. As the bottom of the pit was covered with slush and water, he couldn't see the surface of the stone. He enabled the 3D laser cutter and instructed YuMi to create a nine-inch hole on the bottom. As the laser beams pierced through the hard bottom of the pit, Parush held up his breath and fixed his stare on the tab. In less than a minute, he heard the sound of a thud on the speaker of the tab and saw a portion of the bottom caving in. The water and slush accumulated on the floor of the pit flowed into the cavity, creating a sort of whirlpool, for some time. When the flow of the water subsided, he could see the gaping hole in the floor.

Parush instructed YuMi to descend through the hole. It dislodged itself from the rectangular box, affixed to the drill bit, and hung out from the box with a thin metallic rod, which stretched out more, taking YuMi down, through the hole, slowly. As it entered into the tunnel, cutting through the roof, Parush frantically looked around for the wire. Halfway into the tunnel, Parush stopped the robot. He zoomed into each frame of the high-resolution video stream of the 360-degree view of the tunnel. He saw the wire in the fourth frame, lying on the floor of the tunnel, at the corner. His eyes sparkled, his breaths became faster and he could feel the palpitation within him. Rakesh, standing behind him, had seen the wire too. Without wasting any further time, he selected the wire on the tab, with a stylus. He held his breath as he instructed YuMi to cut the wire with the laser. The robot swung back into action, rotating a bit, and positioning the laser beam such that it hit the wire perpendicularly.

YuMi snapped the wire in a fraction of a second. Like a reflex action, Parush looked up and stared at the Taj, visible beyond the river, quite clear, people walking around it like Lilliput. When it was quite clear to him that the dynamites hadn't exploded, he heaved a sigh of relief, taking a deep breath.

Parush looked at Rakesh. '*We've done it*,' he muttered, handing over the tab to him. '*Paradise regained* … ' He lay on the ground, staring at the gloomy sky, fading with the dwindling sunlight.

Rakesh pulled YuMi up. He got the tunnel totally blocked with concrete filled through the hole created on its roof. He instructed the staff of the drilling rig and the mixer truck to return to the Yamuna Bridge railway station. All the while, Parush lay on the ground, his eyes shut.

After some time, Parush called Indar and talked only for a minute. He lay down again on the ground. He felt exhausted, dizzy. He wanted to run to Kubha …

☼

The last session of the day at the WHA 2019 Calcutta Conference ended at four o'clock in the evening. The president of the Asiatic Society took the stage once more. Thanking all the participants and the audience, for their patience and support all throughout the day, he announced, 'We've a very special vote of thanks from a very special person.'

Indar Sinha, the prime minister of India, appeared on the screen instantly. 'Dear brothers and sisters from across the world,' he began his televised address, beamed live on all the channels in India, 'it's my pleasure to get an opportunity to address you all. History is the best teacher. History is the conscience keeper of the nation, of the civilization, of the peoples. History is the aks, the reflection that is never wrong. We, the mortal people, have wronged many a time, but our aks has been always right. It has been what we were. To err is human. There's nothing wrong in doing wrong. But it's wrong not to accept the wrong. It's wrong not to learn from the wrongs of the past. It's a crime to distort the aks. If you are given a mirror, which shows a different person when you stand naked in front of it, you've been duped. If you want to buy such a mirror to look different, you've been misguided. If you want to sell such a mirror to others, you've been possessed by the devil. It is in this context that this conference, organized by the WHA, is very significant. History shouldn't be retold with an agenda. Monomania is an unpardonable offence in history and I'll keep no stone unturned to punish any such attempt …

'Dr Fareedi, I would like to especially thank you, for delivering the wonderful keynote address. I had the good fortune of going through the abstract of your speech. Despite the fact that your daughter has been in the ICU for the past two days, you still believed it was your responsibility to expose to the world a sinister plan for distorting sensitive historical facts and eventually, paralyzing the country. I learned your daughter is now out of danger. It was really very nice of you to have decided to come to the conference, at the last moment. May God bless you, and your daughter …

'I wanted to visit an old friend of mine, a monk with the Ramakrishna Mission. We have come a long way, working together for the people of the country, in different ways. I wanted to wish him for the last time. He is on a wonderful journey to a new world. I wanted to be by his side, when he sails on the Shonar Tori, the golden crescent. But something unprecedented happened within the confines of the Asiatic Society. At the nick of time, we got to know at least two dreadful terrorists, wanted jointly by India and the US, were hiding here, amongst you. No one knew what they had descended to Calcutta for. Our commandos undertook a covert operation, very swiftly, and caught both the terrorists all the while the conference was underway. I apologize to you all for the inconvenience you all have faced during the operation. As a direct consequence, I was not allowed to say goodbye to my friend …

'I want to send out the message very clearly that in South Asia, and globally, terrorism remains the biggest threat. In the territory stretching from the west of India's border to Africa, it may go by different names, from Laskhar-e Taiba, to Taliban, to the ISIS. But, its philosophy is common: of hate, murder and violence. The fight against terrorism must be fought at many levels. And for us to succeed, those who believe in humanity must come together to fight for it as one, and speak in one voice …

'*Sam gachchhadhvam, sam vadadhvam, sam vo manamsi janatam.* Assemble, speak together and let our minds be all of one accord. *Samano mantrah, samiti samani, samanam manah saha chittamesham.* The place is common, common the assembly, common the mind, so be our thoughts united … Jai Hind.'

☼

While Prime Minister Indar Sinha's televised speech at the WHA 2019 Calcutta Conference was being telecast live on all the channels, and streamed extensively on the internet, Shamsur got a call on his satellite phone. Someone panicked on the other side of the phone. Shamsur silently listened to everything he had to say. 'Don't do anything till you hear from me,' Shamsur instructed him. '*I repeat, don't do anything ...*'

He lifted the M4A1 fully automatic assault rifle the Islamic State had captured from the Iraqi Army. He came out of the room he had restricted himself to for the greater part of the day, carrying the rifle in his hand. His stoic countenance didn't evoke any special reaction from the young people in the central octagonal room of the underground hasht bihisht. The professor, they had come to know, seldom smiled and expressed excitement or emotions. But something in his body language sent shivers through their spine.

Shamsur entered the room Daulat had been confined to. He pressed the trigger of the automatic rifle and Daulat was dead even before he would have perhaps realized anything. The people outside the room were alerted. Shamsur came out of the room and stood at the centre of the octagonal room, the rifle hanging from his hand. Everyone in the room stood in a row in front of him, as they would have done every time Shamsur had wanted to address them.

Shamsur looked up at them. 'Jihad never dies,' he said calmly, 'people do. A true Muslim dies to keep the jihad alive. So would you.' He lifted the rifle up and swept it across them, with his finger pressed hard against the trigger. No one got a chance to escape. The bloody bodies of his carefully chosen and trained jihadists fell onto the floor, like how he had planned for the dome of the Taj to fall too.

Shamsur returned to his room and switched on the display of the portable blasting machine, another coveted war booty of the

Islamic State. It was quite an advanced gadget which had replaced the age-old trigger with a sleek button. Detonating the dynamites was literally a push of a button.

The display of the blasting machine blinked. Shamsur bent down to see the display. *It reported an open circuit.* Frowns appeared on his face. How was that possible? The circuit wouldn't show open unless the wire was snapped. Had Kubha snapped the wire? But why would she do that? She might even not have noticed it.

Shamsur ran out of his room. He dashed into the square room Kubha had been confined to. He kicked open the door that led to the tunnel. The dark tunnel lay ahead of him. He switched on the light of his satellite phone and started running.

☼

Rakesh got a call from the back office. 'There may be more calls,' he said over the phone to the person who had intercepted the most recent satellite call made to Shamsur, just a minute ago.

'Sir,' Rakesh informed Parush, still lying on the ground, 'Shamsur has got to know his plan has failed. We intercepted a call just now. Someone had called him from a place called Raqqa, presently under the control of the Islamic State. He mentioned about Indar ji's speech.'

'How did Shamsur react?'

'He was reactionless. He just asked the caller not to do anything till he gave any further instruction.'

'Where are the commandos from the Para Special Forces?'

'They are at the Yamuna Bridge station.'

Parush smiled. 'Raid the tunnel. Ask them to reach the pit I fell into. The tunnel starts from inside the debris of the broken wall.' Parush got up. 'Let's go.'

☼

The light seemed to fall on a wall ahead. Shamsur had been quite familiar with the tunnel and he knew very well there couldn't be any wall. He stopped running and focused the round beam of the steady light ahead. Yes, it did fall on a rough wall ahead. He started running again. The more he ran, more he got closer to what had appeared like a wall from a distance. Soon, he realized, it was not a wall, but a mound of concrete dumped unevenly into the tunnel. The concrete smelt fresh. He hit it with his fists. It hadn't hardened fully, but was invincible enough for him. The wire lay hidden under the concrete. He bent down and pulled the wire gently. A loose end came out from under the concrete. He held the end and wondered who could have snapped it so precisely. He started running back to the hasht bihisht.

☼

Parush met the commandos at the river side. It was getting dark. 'Hello, sir,' one of the commandos greeted him. 'Don't worry. We've already got the briefing. We have inspected the place many times in the past one day. We know where exactly you fell. We didn't have the orders. Otherwise we would have already figured out the opening of the tunnel.'

'There are hidden trenches … '

The commando smiled. 'We can handle that.'

'I want to come with you,' Parush said.

The commando hesitated a bit. 'I would request you stay here till we capture the target. We are trained to survive Direct Actions like this. First, we will sanitize the place and then someone will get you in.'

'*Don't kill him*,' Parush said firmly. 'Shoot him, but I need him alive.'

☼

The captain of the commando team of five descended into the pit Parush had fallen into in the morning. Very smoothly, he manoeuvred through the booby trap of the deep trenches, clearing off their camouflaged openings, and reached the base of the remains of the watch tower and the wall. Inside there, it was darker. Soon the captain vanished behind the piles of small bricks which made up the relics of the erstwhile watch tower of a garden-palace at the Bagh-i Filhal. A few moments later, he emerged out from behind the wall. 'I've got the opening of the tunnel,' he shouted from inside the pit. The other four commandos slid through the plastic waste and reached the bottom. As the trenches were clearly visible, they didn't pose any threat to them. Soon, they too vanished behind the wall.

The opening of the tunnel lay hidden inside a thick wall, in the form of a gaping hole. The commandos descended into the opening, which led them inside to a steep ramp. As they walked carefully, virtually not making any recognizable sound, they reached a point where the ramp took a perpendicular right turn, at the end of which a closed door was visible at a distance.

The captain was the first to reach the single door made of thick wood. Holding the Glock 17 semi-automatic pistol firmly in his right hand, he tried to sneak peek through the slit between the heavy door and its equally heavy frame. The door appeared to be unlocked. He pushed the door gently and it opened a bit with a screeching sound. All of them were alerted. Instantly, they pushed themselves to the walls of the tunnel, expecting firing through the door. They waited for a few minutes, patiently, but when there was no attack, the captain kicked the door with his leg, all of a sudden and dashed inside the room. He took just a fraction of a second to sweep the room with his hawk eyes and realize there was no one inside, alive. Ten bloody corpses lay on the floor, making a nearly straight line.

The captain stood at the door he had entered through, keeping an eye on the octagonal room, lest anyone attacked from behind any of the seven other closed doors. His four colleagues went ahead and checked each of the 10 dead bodies, fresh blood still oozing out from their wounds. 'They have been shot dead just a few minutes ago!' they exclaimed, almost in unison.

'Check all the doors,' the captain instructed. The four commandos kicked open each door and cursorily scanned each room it opened into, through an aisle. They found none, except for one more person, shot dead in the same way in one of the rooms. Some of the rooms had bare minimum things needed to live: thick blankets, mattresses, clothes and utensils.

Neither did anyone jump on them from any hidden corner nor did anyone fire at them.

The entire commando team assembled at the centre of the octagonal room. 'Eight doors open into eight other rooms,' said the captain, looking around. The austere room had almost no furniture, barring a low quadruped wooden platform and two stools.

'We're surrounded by eight small rooms, square and octagonal, alternately,' said one of the commandos.

'The square rooms have four doors and the octagonal eight,' added another. 'We don't know where so many doors lead to. What do we do? Someone has shot 11 people just a few minutes back. There can be so many ways to get out of here.'

The captain pulled out a paper from one of the many pockets in his trouser and a pen from another. He made a drawing of the layout of the rooms, in less than a minute.

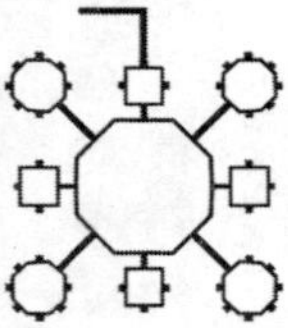

He made a drawing of the layout of the rooms.

'We entered through one of the square rooms,' the captain said, showing the drawing to others, 'and we're presently in the big room in the centre.'

There was the screeching sound of opening of a door. Instantly, all five of them jumped up silently and took positions at five corners of the room. When they heard the screeching sound of opening of another door, they all knew which room it was coming from. All of them targeted their pistols at the door directly opposite to the one they had entered through. The moment the door opened, each one shot a bullet at Shamsur. He fell onto the ground.

Paradise Lost

(Later the day, 5 January 2019. Agra)

Parush looked at the bleeding Shamsur; his legs had been totally shattered by the five bullets fired from close range. He was lying on the floor, writhing in pain. His loud wails reverberated in the closed room. The commandos hadn't touched him. He tried to crawl on the floor but couldn't move much.

Parush could identify the room the moment he had entered. He identified the wooden platform he had seen Kubha lying on, in the morning. He ran to the platform and sat on the ground, touching the rough wooden top with his hands, as though every particle of it still bore Kubha's pain, as though every inch of it wanted to speak to him and share with him how they had struggled to keep her alive, every time she would be laid on them and killed a thousand deaths …

Did Rakesh see a few drops of tears drip on the wood? Were there tears in his eyes too?

Suddenly, Parush got up and kicked Shamsur hard, so hard that he skid to the corner of the room and banged on the wall. He ran towards the wall. He pulled the broken Shamsur up and threw him again. He trampled on Shamsur's mangled limbs. Shamsur cried in pain, like a beast. His shrill voice sent a shiver through the spine of Rakesh.

'Get Kubha here,' he ordered Rakesh.

'But she can't come here,' Rakesh said hesitantly. 'She's still very weak …'

'*Get her here*,' he repeated, firmly. 'Can you get someone here on a stretcher?' he asked the commandos.

'Yes, sir,' the captain assured him.

Rakesh ran out of the room.

☼

The ambulance zoomed through the crowded roads of Agra, escorted and trailed by police vehicles. The entire stretch of the roads from the DM's residence to Kachhpura had been already cleared. It reached the site of the erstwhile Bagh-i Filhal in 15 minutes. Not to attract any attention from the villagers, Rakesh hadn't arranged for any light around the ruins of the river-side tower. The commandos descended into the pit, carrying the stretcher, using their night vision apparatus. They had to do quite a bit of manoeuvring to get the stretcher through the opening of the tunnel. All the while, Kubha kept her eyes closed as she bumped on the stretcher.

She didn't have much recollection of the events since she had been in the ICU. All she remembered was that whenever she had opened her eyes she would see the misty eyes of Parush, hovering over her face. Presently, she knew Parush had wanted to see her.

Soon the jerks subsided. Kubha opened her eyes. She saw Parush. She tried to get up. Parush helped her sit on the stretcher. That was when she realized where she had been brought. Her vision blurred. She looked around the room and instantly saw the professor lying on the floor. Suddenly, she felt as though a powerful devil had possessed her. She pushed Parush and got up from the stretcher, all by herself. She ran towards the fallen Shamsur. She kicked him with all her strength. She kicked him again, howling at the top of her voice. Parush held her from behind. She pushed him so hard that he almost lost his balance. One of the commandos prevented him from falling. Parush ran to Kubha and caught hold of her, strongly. 'Leave me, Porus,' she shouted. *'I'll kill him ... I'll kill him ... I'll kill him ...'*

Parush hugged her tightly. She calmed down a bit, curling herself in Parush's embrace, her deep breaths falling on his chest.

All of a sudden, she released herself. Before anyone could react, she snatched a pistol from one of the commandos and pulled the trigger, pointing at Shamsur's crotch. From such close distance, the bullet couldn't have hit anything else. By the time the commando managed to take the pistol back from her, she had shot two more rounds, one hitting Shamsur on the thigh and one on his stomach. She ran towards Shamsur and crushed his crotch with her bare feet. Parush had to exert himself to pull her back. He laid her on the stretcher and cleaned her bloody feet with the pillow cover.

Kubha fell asleep in a few minutes.

Parush got up. 'Shamsur,' he howled, 'you've lost all the eight paradises, *hasht bihisht*. You're finished.'

Parush called for Rakesh. 'Take him to Delhi. ASAP. I want him alive, without the hands and legs.'

☼

Parush and Kubha took a helicopter from the DM's residence. By the time Parush reached his home, Rakesh had already set up everything there. Round-the-clock doctors and nurses from the AIIMS had been deployed to take care of Kubha in all possible ways.

Kubha had been asleep most of the time. Parush talked to the senior doctors from AIIMS who had come to check Kubha at his place. 'She's a wonder woman,' exclaimed one of them. 'Such grit and courage is rare. Remarkably, her physical injuries are not much. She will recover fast. We will do some tests tomorrow. There may be a possibility of gynecologic hemorrhage. She has been already treated for dehydration. She has caught a severe cold.'

Afsar and Kratu were already on their way to Delhi. Parush had talked to Afsar from Agra. He didn't allow her to talk to Kubha. 'She's fine,' he assured her. 'Let her take rest. She may be too excited talking to you.'

Parush got a call from Indar. 'How is Kubha now?' he asked.

'She's asleep. The doctors say she will be fine soon.'

'When are Afsar and Kratu arriving?'

'In a few hours.'

'Come and see me at my house.'

Half an hour later, Parush and Indar were sipping tea, in Indar's living room.

'So, now can you please do something about Rahul?' Parush asked quite agitatedly.

'I've told him everything over the phone. He will be here any time soon.'

'Are you waiting for his consent before exposing him? He was on his way to get the country sold to the Islamic State, just for his personal gain.'

'Who doesn't do that?'

'What do you mean? Why are you trying to act so magnanimous suddenly? He has gone all the way to finish you. And now you're an epitome of forgiveness. Why suddenly this charity?'

Indar smiled. 'I'm neither being magnanimous, nor forgiving.'

'I don't get you.' Parush was visibly irritated.

'Do you think Rahul knew anything about Shamsur's plan that he was going to blow up the Taj? I don't think so. I know him. He is just an ambitious politician. He wants to become the PM of the country, like I too had wanted to, for a long time. And I too have backstabbed so many people in my career. But, I've never done anything that would demean my country. Neither would Rahul do that. That's my conviction. He can't stoop to that level. He was shattered when I told him everything. If I expose him, he will be finished for now, but he may rise like a sphinx, sometime in future. But if I forgive him now, he will be finished forever. He will live a life of slavery, the slavery of my benevolence, the slavery of my forgiveness, the slavery of the life that I'll give him. He can never rise against me.'

Parush was stunned. He didn't speak for some time.

'And one more thing,' Indar spoke again. 'No one should ever know about Shamsur's plan to blow up the Taj.'

'And why is it so?' Parush was more surprised than irritated.

'The biggest threat to a devil is the threat of being ignored. His strength comes from others' fear. The very fact that the Islamic State had almost blown up the Taj would create fear in the billion minds and that would become their strength. I don't want to strengthen them. Rather, let them know they have lost the paradise, they have lost India.'

The expression "Paradise Lost" reverberated in Parush's mind. He knew Indar didn't know anything about the hasht bihisht, the eight paradises, and its significance in the present scheme of things. It appeared so ironic to him that, in the lure for paradise, people could actually create a hell. It would be better, he felt, to really lose such a paradise.

'I know, they will strike again, somewhere, some other time, to spread fear,' Indar muttered, as though he was talking to himself.

A little later, when Parush was leaving Indar's residence, he bumped into Rahul at the entrance. Rahul stopped by him. 'We've been on different sides,' he said softly, after an uncomfortable silence. 'I wish we all were on the same side.'

Parush patted Rahul.

'*We'll be on the same side now*,' Parush said. As he took long strides, Rahul stared at him, as long as he could see him.

Epilogue

Parush was stunned, looking at the map of the centre of Rome, a small area around the Forum and the Colosseum.

'Are you sure you're not extrapolating too much?' Parush asked Afsar, reclining on the plush sofa in Parush's living room, Kubha's head resting on her lap.

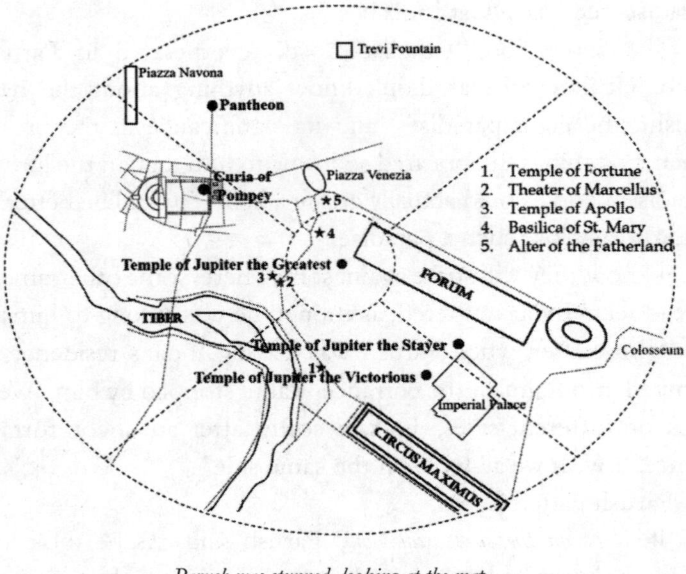

Parush was stunned, looking at the map …

'I don't think so,' Afsar said confidently, playing her fingers through Kubha's hair. The image in Ataulla Bayazitoz's hacked email, she said, had uncanny similarities with Aryabhata's encrypted map of the Nava Varshas, the nine regions of ancient India. It was doubtless, someone had taken inspiration from Aryabhata and had created a similar map, but for five regions, not nine.

'There's something called the Temple of Jupiter the Greatest?' Parush asked, pointing at the centre of the map.

'It was known as Aedes Iovis Optimi Maximi Capitolini, the Temple of Jupiter, Best and Greatest, on the Capitoline. It was the most important temple of ancient Rome. It was situated on the Capitoline Hills, at the northwestern corner of the Roman Forum, the fabled place where the likes of Julius Caesar, Mark Anthony, Augustus and Brutus would meet regularly. It's all ruins now.'

Taking the Temple of Jupiter, Best and Greatest, on the Capitoline as the origin, Afsar elaborated, the latitudes and longitudes of the four places in the four quadrants of the map point to the sites of two more temples of Jupiter in ancient Rome, adjoining the ruins of the Imperial Palace; the back side of Pompey's theatre, the place where Julius Caesar was assassinated; and the Roman pantheon, the best preserved structure of ancient Rome.

'Out of the four,' Afsar said, 'Pantheon is the only one which exists today, in full glory. It's perhaps the oldest surviving temple dedicated to all the Roman gods. It has enormous symbolism, if viewed from the perspective of the Islamic State.'

Afsar fell silent, neither did Parush say anything for some time.

'Pantheon is the very symbol of the ancient Roman civilization.' Afsar spoke again, 'It's the very symbol of the religion of the ancient world. The Romans, along with their older kins—the Indians, the Persians and the Greeks—all had fully evolved civilizations and religions much before the advent of Islam. That's the biggest threat to the Islamic State, for whom nothing can exist, or could have existed outside Islam. They want to eradicate from the earth, each and every symbol that's not Islamic. They failed to eliminate the most conspicuous symbol of India—the Taj. They may not fail again. *Pantheon is at risk.*'

Parush seemed to be thinking something. 'What's going on in your mind?' Afsar asked him.

'Isn't the Taj an Islamic structure? Why would the Islamic State demolish that?'

'Tombs are forbidden in the pure form of Islam. Do you see any such wonderful tomb, like the Taj, anywhere in the Arab world? More than anything, the Taj is the epitome of the confluence of the Indian and Persian cultures, both of which originated much before Islam. *They can't exist in an Islamic State.*'

Kubha had woken up. She would have heard the last part of the conversation. She got up and hugged her mother. 'Ammi, if I could survive,' she whispered into Afsar's ears, 'everything else will survive too. I'm not alone. There would be many more Kubhas, like me. There would be many more Aryabhata Clans, like ours. We will not allow any apocalypse to happen anywhere in the world, in life and in death.'

Afsar broke down, for the first time since the previous day.

Afsar pulled her daughter into her arms and cried loudly, like a child.

Kubha immersed her head into the warmth of her mother's body, like a child.

Parush stared at both of them, and yearned to be a child too …

Addendum

Motifs in Khushawari rugs

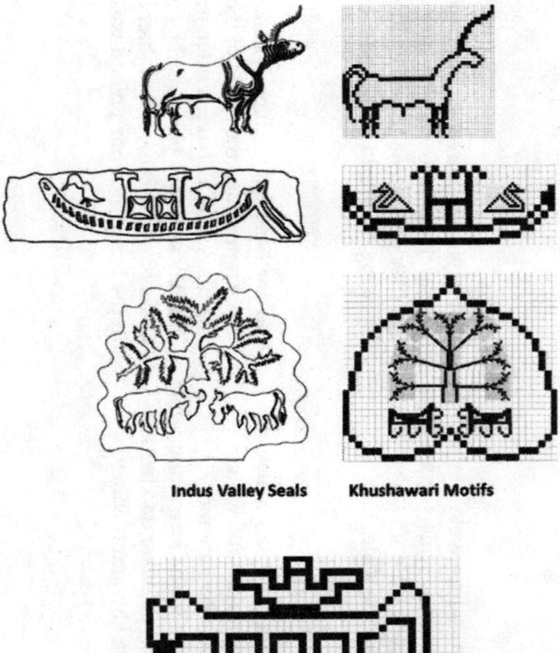

Indus Valley Seals   Khushawari Motifs

Central Asian Goddess mounted on a lion

Animal & Bird motifs from Baluch rugs

Pashto poems on Santis April

Malakul maut ko khatir mein na lene wale	Not paying any heed to the Angel of Death,
Goliyan taney huye seeno pe khane wale	Taking the bullets valiantly on their chest,
Qabr tak sabr ko sehte huye jane wale	Till they go to their graves enduring the patience,
Sabat ka mujiza dunya ko dikhane wale	Showing the world the wonder of perseverance…
Dasey toye karhi hecha nadi da chargano winey	No one has shed the blood of the chickens in the way
Laka toye karhi di angrez da mazlumano winey	The Angrez shed the blood of the oppressed, that day.
Zaka likaley de Santis April harcha pa wino	"Santis April" all have written in letters bloody red -
Che pa de wradz bande werhia we da khwarano winey	The day saw easy blood as the poor died and bled.
Qissa Khana qasab-khana wah pa nazar da khalqo	Qissa Khani became a slaughter's house before our eyes;
Che ye bazar ke bahedalay da khwarano winey	In the bazar the poor's blood was scattered under the sky.

Sanskrit and Magadhi Prakrit verses

स्थलजलमध्याल्लङ्का भुकक्ष्याया भवेच्चतुर्भागे ।	Sthala-jala-madhyat-lamka bhu-kakshyaya bhavet-chatur-bhage |
उज्जयिनी लङ्कायास्तच्चतुरंशे समोत्तरतः ।।	Ujjayini lamkayah-tad-chatur-amshe samottaratah || *Aryabhatiya IV.14*

Khushawar Manuscript (Sanskrit)

श्रुतिस्वरमध्यात् षड्ज मन्डलाया भवेच्चतुर्भागे ।	Shruti-swara-madhyat shadja mandalaya bhavet-chatur-bhage |
ऋषभक षड्जकर्णात्तच्चतुरंशे समोत्तरतः ।।	Rishabhaka shadja-karnat tad-chatur-amshe samottaratah ||
गान्धारक ऋषभकात्तत्समानांशे समोत्तरतः ।	Gandharaka rishabhakat tad saman-amshe samottaratah |
मध्यम षड्जकर्णात्तद् द्वित्रिलवांशे समोत्तरतः ।।	Madhyama shadja-karnat tad dvi-trilav-amshe samottaratah ||

Magadhi Prakrit

छुतिच्छलमद्धे छज्जे मण्डलए हबे चउल् भाए ।	Chhuti-chchhala-maddhe chhajje mandala-e habe chaul bha-e |
लिशहए छज्जकण्णे दे चउलंशे शमोद्दलदे ।।	Lishaha-e chhajja-kanne de chaul-amshe shamoddalade ||
गाद्धालए लिशहए दे शमानांशे शमोद्दलदे ।	Gaddhala-e lishaha-e de shaman-amshe shamoddalade |
मद्धमे छज्जकण्णे दे दुत्तिलबांशे शमोद्दलदे ।।	Maddhame chhajja-kanne de du-ttilab-amshe shamoddalade ||

The Khushawar Manuscript

English translations, with the original Magadhi Prakrit and the corresponding Sanskrit texts

English	**Original Magadhi Prakrit** *Sanskrit*
This Takkariya manuscript has been written by the Naga Kings –	**Ayam takkariyalipi nagannae lajabhe likhapi |**
They have created the nine Varshas of the Naga Island.	
The slang-speaking race, the kins of the Banas, they don't pour ashira, heat kettles;	**Maddhabache banabashe nashire duhe tabadi ghamme |** *Mridhravachah Banavamshah nashiram duhe tapanti gharmam |*
The despised race, the kins of the Banas, they don't pour ashira, heat kettles.	**Bashalae banabashe nashire duhe tabadi ghamme | |** *Vrishalakah Banavamshah nashiram duhe tapanti gharmam | |*
They have created the nine Varshas of the Naga Island,	
They rule over the world, from Gada to Gada.	

Original Magadhi Prakrit	*Sanskrit*
Babato dato Shirae paditthabide Matuha-Shishe Chhach Hajarate Aroe Pituha-Shishe paditthabide	Bhagavatah dhatu Shirshake pratishthapita Matrika-Shirshake Shirsha-Sahasrataye Arjikiyayam Pitrika-Shirshake pratishthapita
Babato dato Shirae paditthabide Loura-Shishe Aragana-Garahae Budha-Garahe paditthabide	Bhagavatah dhatu Shirshake pratishthapita Lauha-Shirshake Arjikiya-Grihe Buddha-Grihe pratishthapita

English

The relic of Buddha has been erected at Shira and Matuha Shisha,
At Chhach-Hajarata, Aro and Pituha Shisha it has been erected.

The relic of Buddha has been erected at Shira and Loura Shisha,
At Aragana Garaha and Budha Garaha it has been erected.

At the Takas, this stupa was erected in the glory of Buddha.	**Takaeshu aye thuve paditthabide Bude puyae |** *Takshakeshu ayam stupa pratishthapita buddhasya pujayam |*
Buddha's eyes were enshrined by Kanishka Namavara.	**Kanikki namabarena paditthabide bage chakabe | |** *Kanishki Namavarena pratishthapita bhagasya chakshavah | |*

Haro (Aro), Garhi Afghanan (Aragana Garaha), Buddho (Budha Garaha), Taxila, Margalla Hills and Islamabad

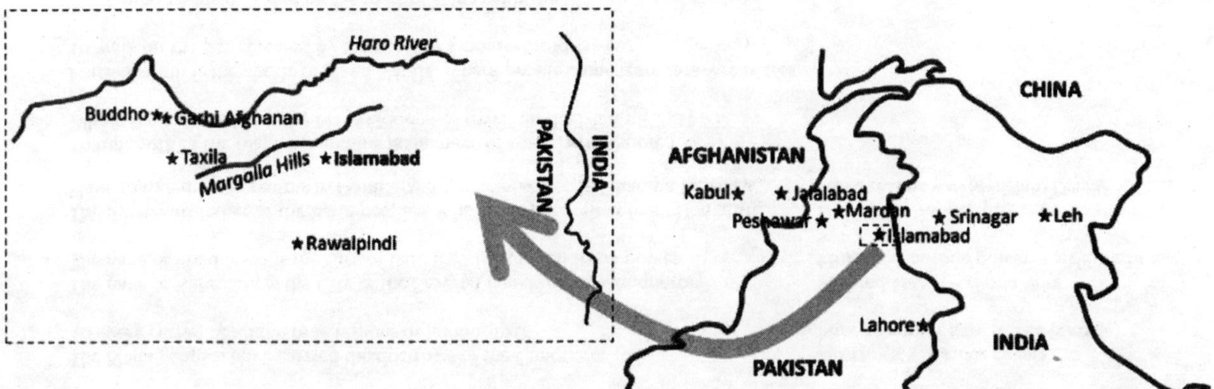

The Kandy Manuscript

English translation, with references to the original Pali words

The Conqueror of the World, the sublime Gotama Buddha, The Supreme Lord of the Grand Vehicle of the Animals.	Conqueror = *jina;* sublime = *uttama* Vehicle of the Animals = *magebha potaka*
The Naga peoples have carried the doctrines of the Conqueror To every corner of all the nine regions of Jambudipa.	Doctrines = *dhamma desana* Nine regions = *nava vasaka* (varsha)
The nave of Ketumala is the City of the Severed Heads of the Conqueror. The nave of Bhaddassa is the City of Bali, the king of wondrous power.	Severed Heads = *chutta shira* king of wondrous power = *mahiddhika raja*
The illustrious father of the Bang peoples, who having travelled from Damalitti, Have founded Naga realms in Damila and Lanka and also in Champa faraway.	*Damalitti* = Tamralipti/Tamluk Naga realms = *naga nibbiti; Damila* = Tamil
To the south of the Naga Mountains is the nave of a northern region, Where the Yakshini and the Naga Goddesses dwell on the Mount Kaushiki.	
Further south is the abode of Naga Nanda, where people come from faraway places, To walk on the path created by the sublime Gotama Buddha.	
The Jambudipa is guarded by the mighty Naga countries. Starting with Kasmira-Gandhara, Aparantaka comes next;	 *Aparantaka* = Sind/Gujarat
Then Maharattha, Damila and Kalinga come in the right order; How can you forget Suvannabhumi and Himavanta, the abodes of the Nagas?	*Maharattha* = Maharashtra; *Damila* = Dravida *Suvannabhumi* = Suvarnabhumi (Bengal)

Daulat's Manuscript

Translation of the Persian verses

This Land of Peace is well-known, as is Jamshid's Council.
Here, there's a city and a Heaven of the World
In every nook and turn, every corner of a field.
And here his glorious forefather had unfurl'd

Land of Peace = *alam-i aman;*
Jamshid's Council = *arish-i Jamshid*
Heaven of the World = bihist-i dunya

A Kabul on the other shore of Sea of Pleasantness.
The Queen, the endearing, the Bilqis of the Age,
The Exalted Lady of the World, Her Highness,
To the Garden of Iram here, She added one stage.

Sea of Pleasantness = *darya-i khurram*
Bilqis of the Age = *Bilqis-i Dauran*
Exalted Lady of the World = *afraz-i zan-i alam*
Garden of Iram = *Bagh-i Iram*

Nothing like this has ever been laid.
This Place Like Heaven and this centuries old
Wondrous pavilions, each with lofty pillars eight,
Making a distinct quadrangular mold,

Place like Heaven = *bihisht-i sawad*
badi nashiman-i hasht-imadi tarbi

The Queen, the endearing, the Cradle of the Sky,
She gifted to her daughter, who they call World Adorning,
Who kept the flowers alive, lest the roses droop and dry,
From the black locks of the dusk to the white blaze of the morning.

The Cradle of the Sky = *mahd-i ulya*
World Adorning = *giti aray*, Jahan Ara
az ṭurra'i mushki sham ta ghurra'i baiẓa'i bam

Right beneath this place runs the Safety Street small
That joins the two ends of two Sparkling Garden-Crowns,
And opens through the vault below the minaret tall
In front of the Sea of Pleasantness profound.

Safety Street = *kucha-i salamat*
Sparkling Garden-Crown = *bagh-i munauwara afsari*
minaret tall in front of the Sea of Pleasantness
= *minar-i pesh-i darya-i khurram*

Brahmi letters

Glutteral			Palatal			Celebral			Dental			Labial		
𑀓	क	ka	𑀘	च	ca	𑀝	ट	Ta	𑀢	त	ta	𑀧	प	pa
𑀔	ख	kha	𑀙	छ	cha	𑀞	ठ	Tha	𑀣	थ	tha	𑀨	फ	pha
𑀕	ग	ga	𑀚	ज	ja	𑀟	ड	Da	𑀤	द	da	𑀩	ब	ba
𑀖	घ	gha	𑀛	झ	jha	𑀠	ढ	Dha	𑀥	ध	dha	𑀪	भ	bha
𑀗	ङ	nga	𑀜	ञ	nya	𑀡	ण	Na	𑀦	न	na	𑀫	म	ma
			𑀬	य	ya	𑀭	र	ra	𑀮	ल	la	𑀯	व	va
			𑀰	श	sha	𑀱	ष	Sha	𑀲	स	sa			
𑀳	ह	ha												

𑁒	1
𑁓	2
𑁔	3
𑁕	4
𑁖	5
𑁗	6
𑁘	7
𑁙	8
𑁚	9

-	𑀅	a
𑀺	𑀇	i
𑀻		I
𑀼	𑀉	u
𑀽		U
𑁂	𑀏	e
𑁃		ai
𑀑		o

Locations of Khushawar, Bakhshali, Shahbaz Garhi and Takht Bhai/Takht-i Bahi

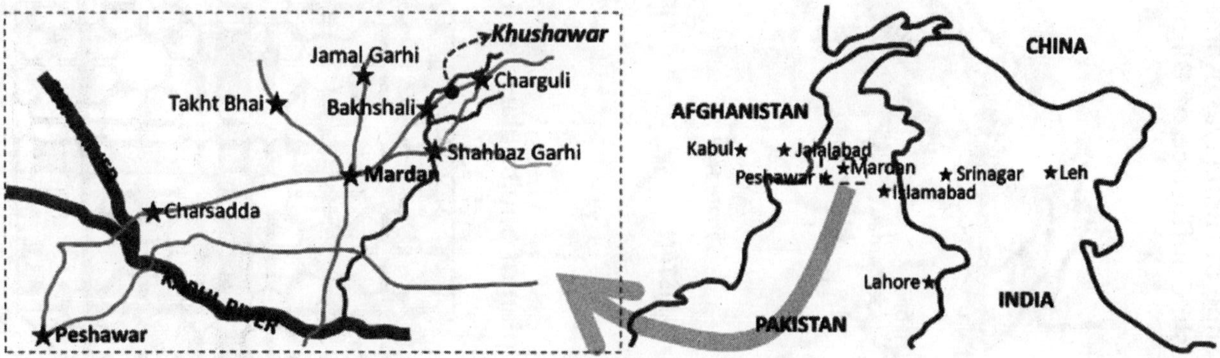

Confluence of Himalayas, Karakoram and Hindukush; Confluence of Gilgit and Indus

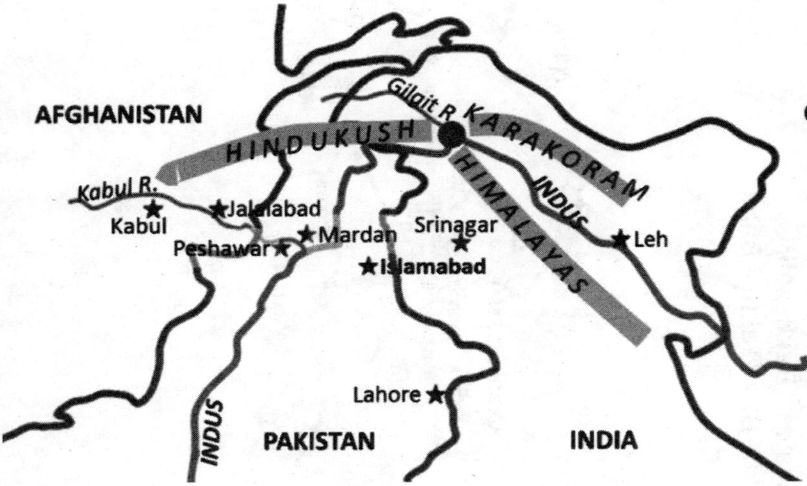

The floor plan of bhulbhulaiya and the 313 rule

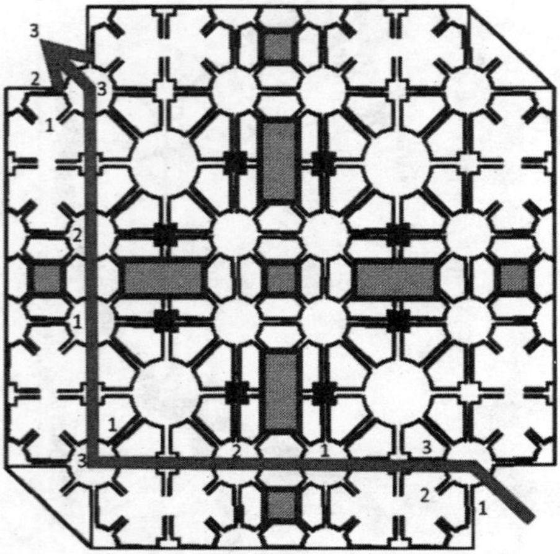

Location of the Final Action

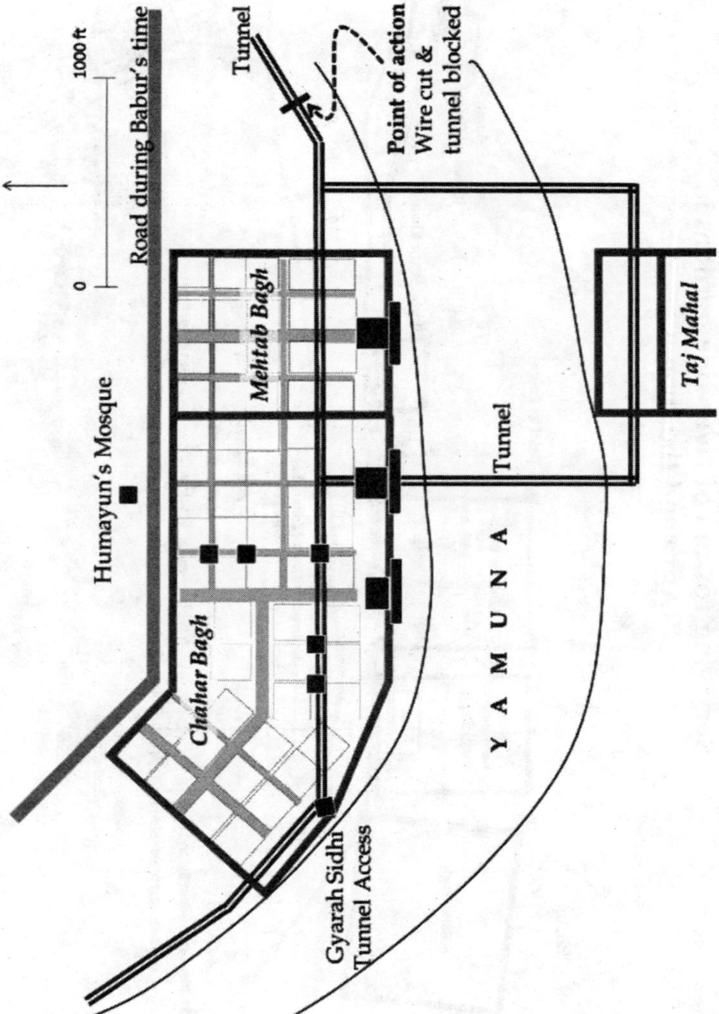

Surviving towers of river-side gardens in Agra and the tunnel

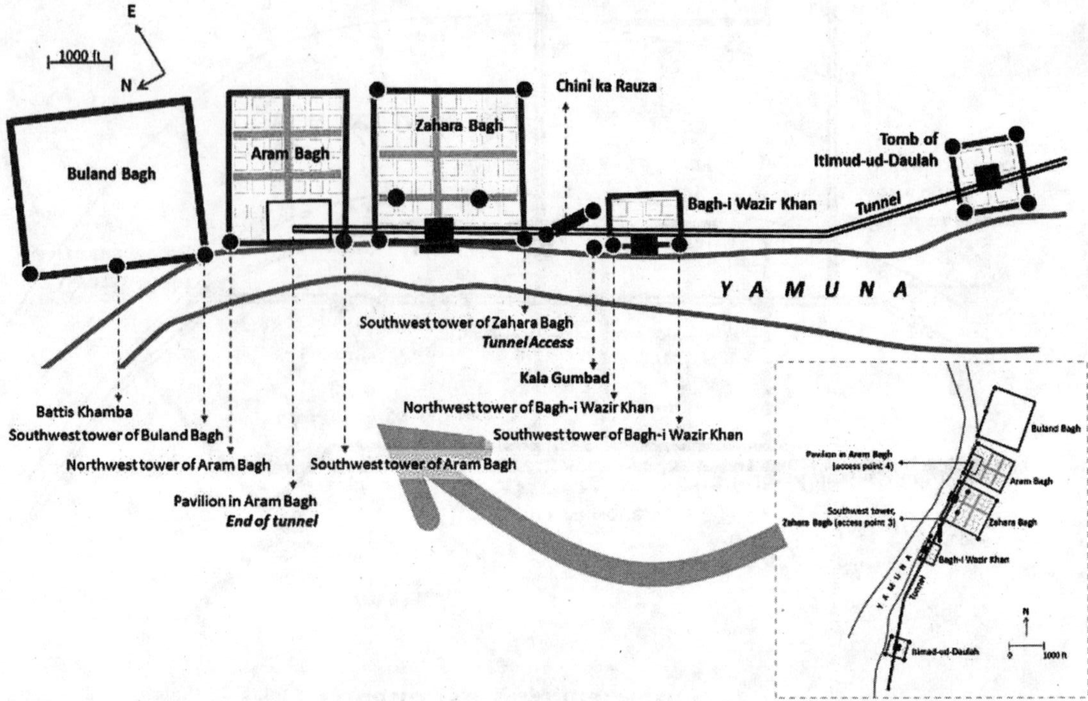

Acknowledgements

The seed idea of this book came from an article written by Thomas Cole, a private dealer who specializes in the art-historical and ethnographic significance of the tribal weavings and textiles from Central Asia (http://www.tcoletribalrugs.com/zarticles.html).

That the apparently simple but beautiful patterns in the Persian or Turkmen rugs could hide behind them such treasure trove of art and history was a revelation to me. The initial fascination and adoration for the topic soon turned into a full-fledged enquiry, which finally resulted into the present book.

The novel wouldn't have been possible without the innumerable academic papers, articles and news items in print and online media and books I've referred to. A selected list of the same is available at the end. Had it not been for the unfathomable amount of resource and energy spent by Google (https://books.google.com) in painstakingly scanning more than 25 million books (out of perhaps the 130 million distinct titles in the world) and making them readily available at the ease of a click, I would have never dared to be an author. Without Google, it would have been practically impossible for me to put my hands on the 150-year-old articles in the *Journal of the Royal Asiatic Society of Great Britain and Ireland* and even older reports by the Archaeological Survey of India (ASI), the seminal works of the likes of Alexander Cunningham, James Fergusson, Vincent Smith, the original Sanskrit works of Aryabhata and Kalidasa and an unending list of books, without which I wouldn't have managed to get even a fraction of the facts and figures I've used so liberally all throughout.

Equally significant are the repositories of https://archive.org, The Digital South Asia Library programme of the University of Chicago (http://dsal.uchicago.edu) and the Center for Research Libraries (http://www.crl.edu), https://www.scribd.com, to mention a few.

I've tried to the best of my abilities to present all the facts and figures as authentically as possible. Any aberration, if not a poetic license, is unintentional and no doubt, my lack of wisdom. For the controversial topics related to the origin of languages and peoples, I've stuck to one of the many schools of thought known to us. And in doing so, I've taken the liberty to choose the ones which suited my narrative, not necessarily the ones which are perhaps the most widely accepted. The general model of the development and spread of the various languages and their peoples in India has been derived mainly from the works of Professor Michael Witzel, an acclaimed philologist, Wales Professor of Sanskrit at the Harvard University and the editor of the *Harvard Oriental Series*, and Professor Asko Parpola, a Finnish Indologist and Sindhologist, a professor emeritus of Indology and South Asian Studies at the University of Helsinki and an authority on the Indus script.

The interpretations and translations of the verses from the Quran are primarily from the online site http://corpus.quran.com/wordbyword.jsp. The references to the misuse of the Quranic verses by the ISIS derive from various news-items available online, and published by the likes of *The Guardian*, *The New York Times*, *Independent*, *The Atlantic*, *The Huffington Post*, *The Times of India*, *The Hindu*, etc.

Samrat Som, a childhood friend who's also an acclaimed fashionista and one of my go-to guys for information on a very diverse range of topics, from beetles to the Beatles, explained me in detail the basics of weaving technology, a cursory knowledge of which helped me immensely in writing this book. Several hours of discussions with him, over phone calls and cups and glasses and puffs of various forms of solids and fluids, enriched my thoughts in many ways, perhaps unseeingly.

Azizul Akbar, a partner in several *crimes* together since my engineering days in Kharagpur, has been always an integral part of innumerable Bengali *addas*, which are much more than just intellectual exchange of ideas. Catalyzed by the creative effervescence of certain psychoactive constituents, the interactions with him always open new paradigms in thoughts and wisdom. Notable among many such sessions with him was one during a leisurely stroll on the bustling Dhakuria bridge in Calcutta on an otherwise busy day, during one of his recent trips to India. Crystals of thoughts, coalesced from those addas, are conspicuous in this book. Being himself very well read, Azi's comments and suggestions during the writing of the book have been very useful.

Aparajita Dutta, co-author of one of my books, Sumana Basu, my niece, and Aniruddha Bagchi, my friend for more than 30 years, were the first to have read an early draft of the manuscript. It was very kind of them to send me very detailed and truthful critiques, without which I wouldn't have arrived at the present publishable form.

Tanmoy Bhattcharya, my senior from IIT Kharagpur and presently a faculty at the Santa Fe Institute, has been very helpful whenever I needed some information I didn't have any idea where to find from. His vast knowledge on linguistics and the history of Bengal and the Bengali language has been handy many a time.

Minakshi Sharma, a co-worker and presently a partner at Insilico, a venture we both co-founded with three others, has turned out to be one of my fiercest critics. Her ruthlessly truthful and nothing-barred comments have started giving me goose bumps, whenever she reads anything written by me. It's not that I always accept her counter views about my thought process and general understanding of many things, but still, I've realized, while writing this book, that I've many a time re-worked entire paragraphs, dreading how she would vivisect those later. Takeaways from several unfinished, or rather forcefully finished discussions with her crept into the book, unknowingly.

Somanjana Chatterjee, a good friend of mine and a Community Outreach Coordinator of the Hindu American Foundation, HAF, has been among the early readers of the manuscript in progress. Herself being an alumnus of the Jawaharlal Nehru University, she has been helpful in authenticating many tidbits and anecdotes about JNU.

I'm thankful to KB for her critique and the radically different views about some of the basic themes of the book. She prompted me to go back and spend a significant amount of time, researching on the facts and figures and revalidating several points I've made in the book.

I'm also grateful to…

Jug Suraiya, a senior columnist with *The Times of India* and one of the most revered journalists of our country, for his encouragement.

Pooja Prabhan (*Deccan Chronicle*), Sravasti Dutta (*The Hindu*), Shevlin Sebastian (*The New Indian Express*), Sooraj Rajmohan (*The Hindu*), Chandreyee Ghose (*The Telegraph*) and Ayesha Tabassum for their kind support.

Kamalika Dutta, for some of the sketches.

The cab driver in Agra, for painstakingly staying put with me while I went into a discovery spree, trying to locate many forgotten monuments of the Mughal era which have been reduced to unidentifiable debris on the left bank of the Yamuna river.

Trisha Niyogi, Bikask Niyogi and Tultul Niyogi, for their love, indulgence and affection.

Manali Das, for editing the final draft of the manuscript.

The entire team at Niyogi Books.

Selected References

Balfour, Edward (ed.) (1873). *Cyclopædia of India and of Eastern and Southern Asia, Commercial, Industrial and Scientific,* Volume 4. Madras: Scottish, and Lawrence Presses.

Basu, Prasun and Gaurinath Sastri (1978). *Sanskrita SahityaSambhar*, Vol II (Bengali). Calcutta: New Age Printers.

Brahmachari, Dr Radhasyam. 'The Distorted History of Taj Mahal'. Available at http://www.stephen-knapp.com. (Accessed in January 2015).

Brown, Stephen (2014). 'Young people "attracted to ISIS by its brutality", says German security chief', *Independent*, 31 August. Available at http://www.independent.co.uk/news/world/europe/young-people-attracted-to-isis-by-its-brutality-says-german-security-chief-9702661.html. (Accessed in January 2015).

Butt, Yousaf (2015). 'How Saudi Wahhabism is the Fountainhead of Islamist Terrorism', *The Huffington Post*, US Edition, 22 March.

Callimachi, Rukmini (2015). 'ISIS Enshrines a Theology of Rape', *The New York Times,* Qadiya, Iraq, 13 August.

CarpetVista. https://www.carpetvista.com (Accessed in January 2015).

Chaulia, Sreeram Sundar (2015). 'ISIS Caliphate's First Birthday—it now inspires lone wolf terrorism across continents', *The Times of India*, *TOI* Edit Page, 30 June.

Chulov, Martin (2014). 'ISIS: The Inside Story', *The Guardian*, International Edition, 11 December.

Clark, Walter Eugene (1930). *The Aryabhatiya of Aryabhata, An Ancient Indian Work on Mathematics and Astronomy.* Chicago, Illinois: University of Chicago Press.

Cole, Thomas. 'Antique Rugs and Textiles'. Available at http://www.tcoletribalrugs.com/zarticles.html. (Accessed in January 2015).

Collingwood, Peter (1969). *The Techniques of Rug Weaving*. New York: Watson-Guptill Publications.

Cunningham, Alexander and E. Hultzsch (1925). *Corpus Inscriptionum Indcarum,* Volume I, Inscriptions of Asoka. Calcutta: Office of the Superintendent of Government Printing.

Cunningham, Alexander, J.D. Beglar and A.C.L. Carlleyle (1874). *Report for the Year 1871–72, Delhi, Agra*, Volume IV. Calcutta: Office of the Superintendent of Government Printing.

Dâjî, Bhâu (1865). 'Brief Notes on the Age and Authenticity of the Works of Âryabhaṭa, Varâhamihira, Brahmagupta, Bhaṭṭotpala, and Bhâskarâchârya', *Journal of the Royal Asiatic Society of Great Britain and Ireland*, New Series, 1 (1/2): 392–418.

Das, Sudipto (2014). *Myths & Truths Behind the Ekkos Clan.* Published by Sudipto Das.

--------. (2015). 'Significance of Palaeography and Linguistic Palaeontology as Important Tools to Decipher Ancient Past', *Sandhi, A Journal of Science and Heritage Initiatives*, 1(1): 51–60.

Dev, Aditya and Arvind Chauhan (2015). 'Court Admits Plea Claiming Taj a Temple', *The Times of India*, Agra, 9 April.

DuTemple, Lesley A. (2003). *The Taj Mahal*. Minneapolis: Lerner Publishing Co.

Elliot, H.M. and John Dowson (1877). *The History of India, As Told by Its Own Historians*. London: Trübner & Co.

Fergusson, James (1868). *Tree and Serpent Worship: From the Sculptures of the Buddhist Topes at Sanchi and Amaravati.* New Delhi: Asian Educational Services.

--------. (1910). *History of Indian and Eastern Architecture.* London: John Murray.

Fiqh – Jurisprudence. Available at http://www.sunnah.org/fiqh. (Accessed in January 2015).

Ganguly, Subhajit (2012). 'Relation between Harappan and Brahmi Scripts', *The General Science Journal.* Available at https://gsjournal.net/Science-Journals/Research%20Papers-Neurosciences/Download/4748. (Accessed in January 2015).

Geiger, Wilhelm and Mabel Haynes Bode (1912). *The Mahavamsa or The Great Chronicle of Ceylon*. Published for The Pali Text Society. London: Oxford University Press.

Geiger, Wilhelm and N.C. Panda (2010). *Mahavamsa, Text with English Translation.* New Delhi: Bharatiya Kala Prakashan.

Habibi, Abdul Hai (1967). *The Two Thousand Years Old Language of Afghanistan or The Mother of Dari Language (An Analysis of the Baghlan Inscription)*. A publication of the Historical Society of Afghanistan. Afghanistan: Government Printing Press.

Hadith. Available at http://hadith.islamicevents.sg/muslim. (Accessed in January 2015).

Havell, E.B. (1904). *A handbook to Agra and the Taj, Sikandra, Fatehpur-Sikri and the Neighborhood.* London, New York and Bombay: Longmans, Green and Co.

Hodgson, J.A. (1843). 'Memoir on the Length of the Illahee Guz, or Imperial Land Measure of Hindostan', *Journal of the Royal Asiatic Society of Great Britain and Ireland*, 7(1): 42–63.

Hoernle, R. (1887). *On The Bakhshali Manuscript.* Vienna: A. Holder.

Huber, Christoph. 'Old Motifs: The Bactria-Margiana Archaeological Complex as a Possible Source'. Available at http://www.turkotek.com/salon_00040/salon.html. (Accessed in January 2015).

Hunter, W.W. (1881). *The Imperial Gazetteer*, Volume II. London: Trüber & Co.

Kanakasabhai, V. (1989). *The Tamils Eighteen Hundred Years Ago*. New Delhi: Asian Educational Services.

Kapoor, Subodh (ed.) (2002). *Encyclopaedia of Ancient Indian Geography*, Volume 2. New Delhi: Cosmo Publications.

Kern, H. (1863). 'On Some Fragments of Áryabhaṭṭa', *Journal of the Royal Asiatic Society of Great Britain and Ireland*, Vol. 20: 371–87.

--------. (1874). *The Aryabhatiya, a manual of astronomy, with the Commentary Bhatadipika of Paramadievara*. Los Angeles: The Library, University of California.

Koch, Ebba (2006). *The Complete Taj Mahal and the Riverfront Gardens of Agra.* New York: Thames and Hudson.

Malalasekera, G.P. (ed.) (1937). *Asoka and the Missions (from Extended Mahāvaṁsa V, XII–XV, XVIII–XX).* Translated by Ānandajoti Bhikkhu. Colombo: Pali Text Society.

Marshall, John (ed.) (1931). *Mohenjo-daro and the Indus Civilization.* London: Arthur Probsthain.

Mazumdar, Bijaychandra (1920). 'The History of the Bengali Language'. Lectures in the Department of Comparative Philology, Anthropology and Indian Vernaculars, Calcutta University.

Mosendz, Polly (2014). 'The Teenage Fans of ISIS', *The Atlantic*, 22 October. Available at https://www.theatlantic.com/international/archive/2014/10/the-teenage-fans-of-isis/381736/ (Accessed in January 2015).

Nath, R. and Ajay Nath (2010). *The Taj Mahal (History and Architecture)*. Jaipur: The Historical Research Documentation Programme.

Oak, P.N. (1965). *Taj Mahal: The True Story.* India: A. Ghosh Publisher.

Parpola, Asko (2005). 'Study of the Indus Script', paper presented at the 50th International Conference of Eastern Studies (ICES), Tokyo, 19 May.

--------. (2008). '"Hind Leg" + "Fish": Towards Further Understanding of the Indus Script', paper presented at the Hunmin jeongeum Society's 'Scripta 2008' conference, Seoul, 9–10 October.

--------. (2010). 'A Dravidian solution to the Indus script problem', paper presented at the World Classical Tamil Conference, Central Institute of Classical Tamil, Coimbatore, 25 June.

Peck, Lucy (2011). *Agra: The Architectural Heritage.* New Delhi: Roli Books Private Limited.

PTI (2000). 'Plea to Rewrite Taj History Dismissed', *The Hindu*, New Delhi, 14 July.

Quran, Word by Word. Available at http://corpus.quran.com/wordbyword.jsp. (Accessed in January 2015).

Rao, A.V. Narasimha and C. Venkatramaiah (2000). *Geotechnical Engineering.* Universities Press.

Rao, Rajesh P.N. (2010). 'Probabilistic Analysis of an Ancient Undeciphered Script'. Available at https://homes.cs.washington.edu/~rao/ieeeIndus.pdf. (Accessed in January 2015).

Sarma, K.V. (2001). 'Aryabhata: His Name, Time and Provenance', *Indian Journal of History of Science*, 36 (3-4): 105–15.

Seṭha, Haragovindadāsa Trikamacanda (1928). *Paia-Sadda-Mahannavo* (The Great Ocean of Prakrit Words), A Comprehensive Prakrit-Hindi Dictioinary. New Delhi: Motilal Banarsidass Publishers Pvt. Ltd.

Smith, Vincent A. (1911). *A History of Fine Art in India and Ceylon, From the Earliest Times to the Present Day.* Oxford: Clarendon Press.

Taj Mahal Conservation Collaborative (2001). Briefing Document for Expert Meeting Conservation of the Taj Mahal, 25–28 September 2001.

Taylor, Isaac (1883). *The Alphabet, An Account of the Origin and Development of Letters*, Volume II, Aryan Alphabets. London: Kegan Paul, Trench; & Co.

Withnall, Adam (2014). 'ISIS Releases "Abhorrent" Sex Slaves Pamphlet with 27 Tips for Militants on Taking, Punishing and Raping Female Captives', *Independent*, 10 December.

Woolner, Alfred Cooper (1917). *Introduction to Prakrit.* Calcutta: Baptist Mission Press.

Yadav, Nisha, M.N. Vahia, Iravatham Mahadevan and H. Joglekar (2010). *A Statistical Approach for Pattern Search in Indus Writing, Segmentation of Indus Texts*. TIFR Bombay, The Indus Research Centre Madras, Oracle Hyderabad.

Praises for *The Ekkos Clan*

'A promising debut in the growing realm of modern Indian fiction'

—Jug Suraiya, *The Times of India*

'An Indian thriller inspired by Dan Brown & Harrison Ford! Fast-paced thriller, replete with murder and miraculous escapes'

—*The Telegraph*

'If you are a history buff and a thriller aficionado, then [it] might just be the book for you'

—*The Hindu*

'A tale of the Indian civilization and culture … takes you on a roller coaster ride'

—*The New Indian Express*

'An interesting read for an afternoon. One feisty woman's partition story'

—*Bangalore Mirror*

'Should be read for its sheer aspiration and the intelligent handling of historical material'

—*The Sunday Guardian*

'Is essentially a mystery novel, but is grounded in a substantial base of research and exploration into our past'

—newsyaps.com

'Bindas writer, a multi-talented personality'

—*Deccan Chronicle*